Dark Mists of Ansalar
Forging the Bond

I0608132

T. R. Chowdhury & T. M. Crim

TRIMOON ECLIPSE

Winter Wolf PUBLICATIONS \Cincinnati, OH

Copyright © 2017, T.R. Chowdhury & T.M. Crim
First edition: 2013 Loconeal Publishing

Cover Art © 2017, by Fantasio
Interior Image Art © 2017, by Kayla Woodside
Edited by Barbara Taft Verducci
Interior Design by James O. Barnes

Published by TriMoon Eclipse,
An imprint of of Winter Wolf Publications, LLC

ISBN 978-0-945039-16-4 (Paperback)

TABLE OF CONTENTS

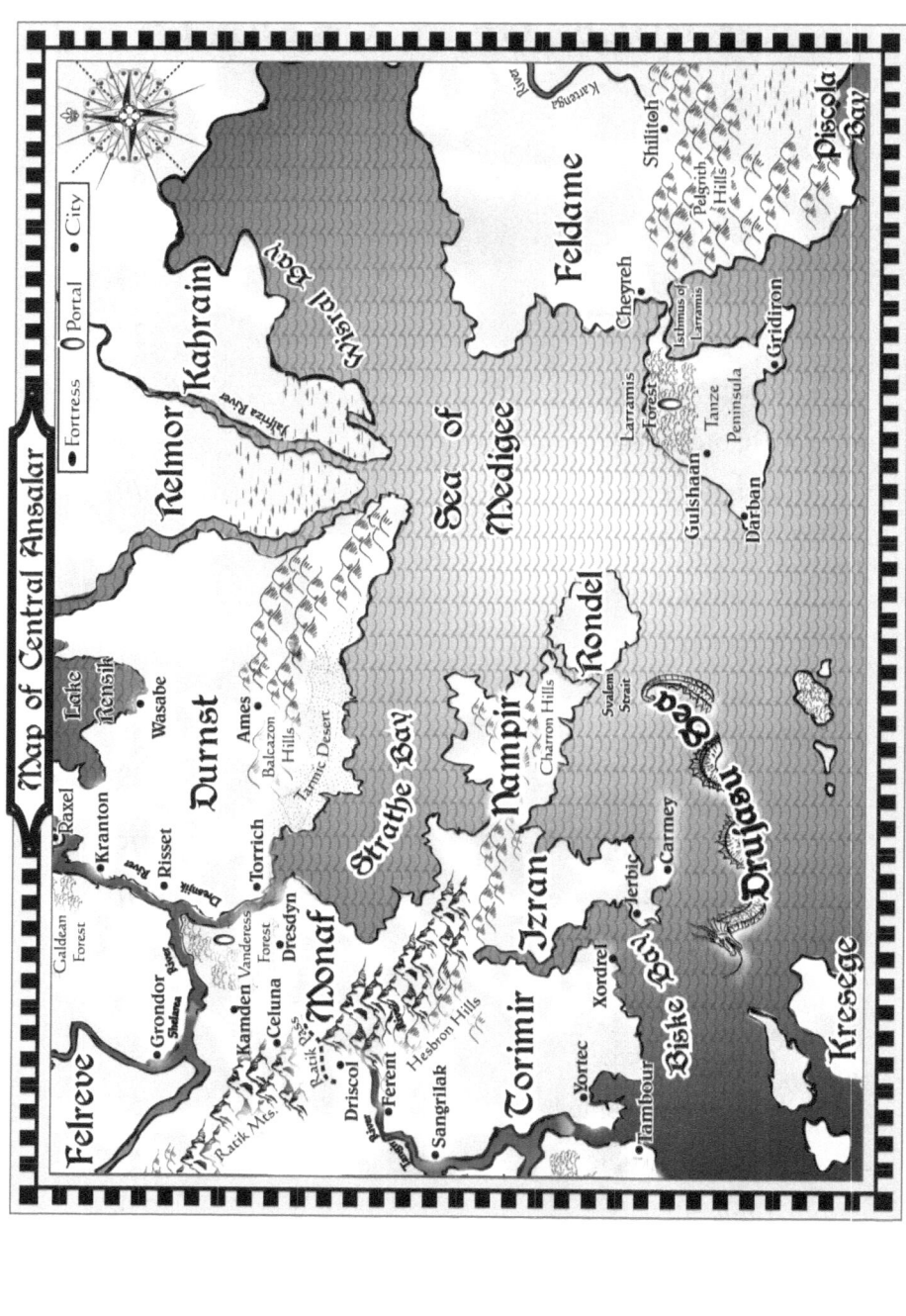

Map of Central Ansalar

Legend: ● Fortress ◊ Portal • City

Grondor River · Shalanni

Felreve

Galdean Forest

Raxel
Kranton
Risset

Dranil River

Lake Rensik

Wasabe

Durnst

Torrich

Ames

Balcazon Hills

Tarmic Desert

Kamden · Vanderess Forest
Celuna
Dresdyn

Monaf

Ratik Pass
Ratik Mts.
Driscol
Ferent

Sangrilak

Hesbron Hills

Torimir

Yortec

Xordrel

Izran

Nampir

Charron Hills

Strathe Bay

Sea of Medigee

Rondel

Svalemi Strait

Carmey

Jerbic

Tambour

Biske Bay

Drujasu Sea

Kresege

Relmor

Kahrain

Yalfriza River

Whistal Bay

Feldame

Cheyreh

Larramis Forest

Gulshaan

Isthmus of Larramis

Tanze Peninsula

Darban

River Karranga

Shiliteh

Pelgrith Hills

Gridiron

Piscola Bay

Forging the Bond

Prologue

With narrowed eyes, Tallachienan watched from across the vast chamber as the dark-skinned, silver-haired drenna flirted with Trebexal. Ma-tia was beautiful to behold, just as exotic in her faelin form as she was in her dragon one. It seemed she had discovered some of the benefits of the faelin form; a sense as simple as that of touch was much more acute. The thick, scaley hide of a dragon simply didn't perceive the minute touches the thinner, more delicate faelin skin could sense. Not to mention, the texture was so much softer, and the lovemaking . . . well that depended upon one's partner.

Of course TC knew none of this first-hand, for he was not a dragon. Instead he had been Trebexal's trustworthy confidant for many years. His friend had explained the preference that many dragons had for their faelin forms during sexual contact, for the experience could be felt ten-fold. The only exception was during a pairing flight. During that auspicious time, a dragon doubtlessly wanted to keep his true form, and it was said that such a flight was one of the most intense unions that anyone could achieve.

TC's fingers clenched at the book he was holding when the sound of tinkling laughter floated through the air to reach his ears. Damnation, why couldn't Trebexal see what was so blatantly obvious? The drenna was just using him. To what end however, TC was uncertain. He could only imagine what it might be. Ma-tia was powerful, unpleasantly so. TC had witnessed her talent first-hand when he met her across the sparring arena a few fortnights ago. They had decided to call it a bligh; no one won or lost and they were considered equals in battle. Ever since then, TC had ramped up his efforts, hoping to out-maneuver her in any contest in which they might participate in the future.

With most of his opponents, he harbored a much better attitude and could forge relationships born of mutual respect. Unfortunately he hated Ma-tia too much to bother with that.

Tolerating her proximity in silence, Tallachienan patiently waited. The two continued to speak for a while before Ma-tia turned to leave. The cloying scent of her perfume filled the air as she approached his location on her way out of the chamber. Without looking up from his book, he sensed the dark drenna slowing to a stop before reaching him. A soft chuckle emanated from her throat, barely hinting at the malevolency she radiated. She spoke so quietly it made him wonder if Trebexal could hear.

"So, not only are you the devoted companion, but the loyal eavesdropper."

TC slowly looked up with an expression of disgust. "Definitely no worse than the brainless whore you make yourself out to be, my lady."

Ma-tia struggled to maintain her calm, but the signature flush over her face gave away her anger. "You had best tread lightly with me, Master Chroalthone. I am not someone you will want to meet on the opposing side one day."

TC raised a brow. "Really? I like to think I would love to see you at the receiving end of my most destructive spell." He cocked his head. "I know what you are doing. Trebexal is no fool; it's only a matter of time before he figures it out."

Ma-tia regarded him intently for a moment before turning her lips up into a smile, a wicked sparkle in her eyes. She lowered her voice even more, and he strained to hear what she said next. "By then it will be too late."

TC silently watched Ma-tia continue out of the chamber, her silvery-white hair trailing behind. He just sat there, the discarded book lying on the table beside the chair. Damnation, with just a handful of words she'd verified what he'd suspected all along. Trebexal was simply a pawn in whatever game she played, a tool she could use and then discard.

TC turned when he heard someone approaching from behind. Trebexal must have seen the residual expression of disgust on TC's face, and the dragon frowned. "You look as though you have seen an abomination."

TC nodded. "Yes, and she just left here several moments ago."

Trebexal pursed his lips. "What is it with you, Tallachienan? What is so wrong with my attempt to find someone with whom I can share my life?" he said defensively.

TC sighed. "I don't think it is sharing she wants, my friend."

"What are you trying to say?" Trebexal demanded.

"Ma-tia is not who you think she is."

Trebexal frowned. "How would you know that?"

"Unlike you, I have had the opportunity to simply watch. I have witnessed how she speaks with the other dragons, manipulating the truth in order to sway them to her nefarious causes. She has ill intent towards human-kind, and she is rallying her army right now. She will pluck your supporters right from beneath your nose if you are not careful."

Trebexal stared at him for several moments. Then, "You are jealous."

TC drew his brows together into a frown. "What?"

"You are envious of my partnership with Ma-tia. You want so much to have someone for yourself that you can't think beyond to have a bit of happiness for me. I am so disappointed in you, Tallachienan."

TC felt his eyes widen as Trebexal proceeded to turn away from him, an indication that the conversation was over. TC swiftly reached out and caught Trebexal's wrist. "My friend, you can't seriously believe that."

"I do," he replied. "Our union would be momentous—her arcane strength combined with my political power could change the world!"

TC angrily rejected the wrist in his hand. "But for what goal?"

"Not what you are thinking!" Trebexal roared. "Humans are a nuisance, a pestilence almost, but never would I wish to eradicate them! Neither does Ma-tia. She simply dislikes them a bit more than the average dragon. But Hells, man! It doesn't mean she is shifting the loyalty of my dragons! Those drakes and drennas have faith in me and believe that I will lead them to a life in which daemon-kind has very little influence."

TC's gaze only hardened. "And I happen to know that Ma-tia has no interest in those goals. She cares naught for the battles between daemon and dragon. She cares only about the foothold that humans have developed within Shandahar, and she wants them gone! You are a fool, Trebexal, and I refuse to stand still for this."

TC rose from the chair, his mind roiling with perceived betrayal. He couldn't believe that Trebexal could allow it to happen. For the second time in his life, a woman was coming between him and a good friend. He felt a pang in his chest with the memory of Shire. The man was long gone a few hundred years ago, but Shire's memory remained. Now Trebexal was walking that same destructive path.

TC turned on his heel and left the cavern without looking back.

CHAPTER ONE

The climate had cooled considerably with their northerly flight, and Aeris struggled to keep warm in spite of the fur wrapped around her. She regarded Jaxom intently from across the fire. Dark hair hung, unbound, alongside his face, and a thick swatch occluded her view of his eyes. His complexion was pale, and his figure very slender. He crouched there before the flames, and seemed to be deep in thought. She wondered what he was thinking.

The history between her and Jaxom consisted mostly of him keeping his distance from her, even after the experience they had shared together after Cervantes' ship had been marooned on an uncharted island. Many moon cycles later, after her rescue from Tholana's fortress, Aeris hadn't cared enough to notice anything that might be different about him. Now she couldn't help wondering what had changed to make him want to desert the rest of the group. Why would he want to take her along with him? She honestly didn't understand, and Jaxom had become an enigma.

However, she remembered the love she'd felt from him that evening on the cliffs when she climbed on his back. He'd offered to take her away so that she could leave all her suffering behind. *He'd told her that they belonged together.*

Since then, at the end of every day, the silver dragon shifted back into faelin form to become the young man she had come to know over the past several moon cycles. After clothing himself in a pair of leather trousers and a tunic, Jaxom aided her in setting up their small encampment. She ate from provisions acquired from the towns they passed, and every couple evenings, Jaxom would briefly leave her alone so he could hunt down a meal for himself.

They hardly spoke, and only about things that were of importance.

Aeris shifted position within the confines of the fur. She winced with the discomfort the action brought, and ran a hand along one inner thigh. Jaxom's scales were smaller where she sat at the curve of his neck and shoulders. When rubbed one way, they were smooth, but rubbed in the opposite direction, the edges could be sharp. Within the first couple days of travel, the scales had cut into the fabric of her trousers, and her legs started to develop sores. With some padded leather they purchased at the last town, they constructed a barrier to be laid across Jaxom's withers in hopes of minimizing the abrasion she felt from riding for so long and so far.

Forging the Bond

It was a great idea, and the construct did just what they wanted. Unfortunately, the damage had already been done. The sores oozed a yellowish fluid and the flesh surrounding them was an angry red. She'd managed to purchase some medicinal salve from the apothecary in the same town and applied it to the sores at the beginning and end of every day. She didn't mention it to Jaxom, and hid her discomfort the best she could. The wounds didn't seem to be getting any better, but they weren't worsening either. She didn't want to say something about it and mayhap trouble him needlessly. Of course, that would assume he would worry.

"You are cold." His voice startled her and Aeris momentarily fought to calm her rapidly beating heart. She gazed at him without making a reply. Hells, she wasn't certain he even expected one.

Aeris watched as Jaxom rose from his place and went to the pile of dry material they had found lying nearby as they set camp. He gathered it into his arms and made his way back. He then fed the fire, the flames eagerly licking about the new source of fuel. The fire grew, and she basked in the heat it emitted. Meanwhile, she watched as Jaxom settled himself back down across from her. She supposed he cared after all, that indeed he might worry if he knew about her wounds.

Once again she wondered why he had brought her with him.

"Where are we going?" She spoke the words with the thought that he might not give a response.

He brought his gaze up to meet hers, and she was caught in their silvery depths. "We are going to Shayamalan," he replied simply.

"Where is that?"

"It is a place located across the Sanmar Ocean."

She cocked her head to the side. "I have heard that nothing resides beyond the Sanmar."

Jaxom remained solemn. "Then you have heard wrong."

She was quiet for a moment. Then, "Well, aren't you going to tell me about it?"

He seemed taken aback for a moment before finally offering a tentative grin. "What do you want to know?"

She returned the smile. "Anything you might want to tell me."

Jaxom became contemplative for a few moments. "The place where I came from is very mountainous. The dragons build their homes in sheer cliffs that overlook a series of canyons. The place is called Thelindaerun, or 'land of the valleys'. It is where I lived after coming to live on Shandahar when the Pact was broken."

"Where did you live before that?"

"On Haldorr, of course."

Aeris nodded. "Yes, of course." In spite of all her dimensionalist training, she had never been there. Before leaving Elvandahar to journey south in search of Mateo, it had been next on Master Dinim's list, and she had been looking forward to the *travel*. Hearing about Haldorr now only reminded her of that and made her yearn for home.

Jaxom must have noticed her forlorn expression, for he continued to speak. "I will take you there someday. It is a wonderful place."

Aeris nodded. "I know. My mother told me about it a time or two."

Jaxom nodded. "Ah, yes. Your mother was a student to Master Tallachienan."

She regarded him intently for a moment. "You knew him?"

Jaxom shook his head. "No, only *about* him. I'd never even seen the man before I met you."

Aeris only nodded and looked away. She disliked the turn their conversation had taken, and now all she wanted to do was lie down and go to sleep. Jaxom seemed to sense this, and was focused on smoothing out his bedding for the night. She did the same, and it wasn't long before she was enveloped by a cocoon of furs, staring at the flames.

Aeris lay there for quite some time, her mind ruminating over the last subject of their talk. Just the mention of Tallachienan's name made her stomach roil. She hated that he affected her so much, and he wasn't even present. She'd come to despise the man, even before her rescue from Tholana's stronghold, and her loathing had only increased before she flew away from him on the back of her silvery companion.

But TC wasn't the only thing she had grown to abhor over the past several moon cycles. It was the entire cimmerean race. They were a shadow over Shandahar, a scourge she hoped would be expunged one day. Her hatred of them was all encompassing, and it was unfortunate her own master was one of these people. A small part of her couldn't help hating Dinim as well, that unrational part of her that threw him in with the rest of his revolting race. Aeris knew such hatred was bad for her soul, that it could one day consume her. At this moment, she didn't care. *And she embraced it.*

8 Enaren CY634

Aeris could feel an intense fatigue emanating from her dragon companion. For over three days they had flown without stopping, and she didn't know how much longer Jaxom would be able to endure it. Their last stop had been a remote island on the southern boundary of the Sanmar Ocean. There they had rested for a full two days, giving them time to develop a better flight harness from some of the materials they'd acquired during their stay at the last town. They had also stocked up on food supplies and other necessary equipment. The waterskins were most important, and those were fixed equally on both sides of a wide leather strap that was laid across his withers.

Once Jaxom had rested and he felt ready for the journey, they took flight over the vast ocean. It was the only course to Shayamalan. He had warned her of the protracted airtime, and that after a while he would begin to tire. Yet, he had made the crossing once before, and he was certain he could do it again. Aeris kept that in her mind as zacrol after zacrol of endless blue passed below. Her body stank from days without washing, and the insides of her legs were sore from constant chafing. In spite of the thick strip of leather that separated her thighs from Jaxom's scaley hide, the continued rubbing kept the sores from healing in spite of the salves she used. She suffered in silence, and when she couldn't handle the pain anymore, she put a few pinches of talsam in her waterskins. Every time she took a drink, she imbibed the pain reducing extract. Unfortunately, it had the added effect of making her lethargic, and she struggled to remain wakeful for Jaxom's sake. She knew how tired he was, and that all he wanted to do was rest. How could she sleep when her companion was in so much more need?

Aeris blinked her eyes, struggling to focus. Damn, she'd put a pinch too much talsam in the last waterskin, and now she was hard pressed to stay awake. More than ever she prayed for some indication that they were getting close to their destination. During the long flight, Aeris slumped over Jaxom's withers and groaned inwardly from the confines of the crude harness they had constructed for her. Damnation, the sores on her legs were so much more painful now, and she was running out of salve. The wounds had increased in size, and were warm to the touch. In spite of the potions she'd imbibed, she knew that she couldn't keep her bodily functions at bay for much longer, and now hoped for an expedient arrival.

When they were suddenly met with open hostility, Aeris found herself re-evaluating those prayers.

A silver dragon swept towards them from northern skies, calling out with a strident voice in a language she couldn't even begin to comprehend. Jaxom immediately responded, quickly shifting into mental alertness. He faltered in mid-air, and she felt her heart stop in her chest for a moment when he was forced to make a leftward turning dip to recapture the air-current. <Damn, I forgot about the sentinels.>

She sensed a mixture of emotions from him, the most prominent being that of relief. He had been uncertain of his ability to fly much farther without rest, and worried about his precious cargo. Yet, she also sensed an increasing anxiety, for when he shifted in order to recapture the current, the other dragon began to consider him a potential intruder. The rezwithrys approached them at top speed, and Aeris closed her eyes tightly shut as his voice thundered through their link yet again.

This time Jaxom answered; even though she couldn't hear his reply, she could sense it through their link

Aeris saw the other dragon slow his flight as he came to the realization that Jaxom had no intention of escaping. That, and he was responding to whatever Jaxom had told him.

<I gave him my identity,> said Jaxom in response to her unspoken question. <My signature coincided with it. We have met before, so Zarjandrahl was able to match it himself without having to call another sentinel.>

The other dragon stopped several farlo away from Jaxom. Immediately taking note of Aeris, the silver spoke his next words in common. <Jaxomdrehl, you have been away for quite some while. Your father is angry.>

Jaxom gave a mental nod. <I know. But I have returned.> He paused and then continued. <I've brought someone with me.>

The other dragon returned the nod. <She may be the only thing that will keep you from suffering the full extent of his wrath.>

Jaxom made no response. Zarjan snorted, wisps of smoke rising from his nostrils. <Come. I shall escort you into the mainland. However, I think you should know that I have orders to bring you to your father right away.>

<I would expect nothing less,> he replied.

Aeris remained quiet as they flew the last zacrol to the coastline. Once there, she saw the high cliffs upon which the surf thundered mercilessly, cliffs that reminded her of the ones she had left behind at the Isthmus of Larramis. Aeris thought of the rest of the group, in particular, her brother. She hated thinking what Alasdair might be feeling . . . hurt, confusion, and maybe no small amount of betrayal. She couldn't blame him, for he was her closest comrade, and she was his. Left in his situation, she would feel the same.

They continued to follow the silver Zarjan, flying first over rugged foothills and then open grasslands. Upon the plains grazed vast herds of strangely humped hexaped beasts she had never seen before. She looked down at the animals as they passed, and when the creatures ran at the sight of the dragons overhead, the reason was not lost upon her.

Glancing back in front of her, Aeris noticed that they were approaching more foothills in the distance. It was then she began to realize the bigger picture. The plain was almost entirely surrounded, and beyond lay the cloud-topped mountain range upon which they had set their course. She settled herself low over Jaxom's back as they completed the last zacrol of their journey. She could sense his unease and made an attempt to send soothing vibrations through the link they shared. Within moments she knew she had been successful, for she sensed his appreciation. Then, for the first time since taking her away from the group, Jaxom opened up just enough for her to sense something else.

It was love.

The dragon Jaxomdrehl loved her, but not as a simple friend or a sensual lover. It was much different from that. It was the way a dragon loves his bondmate—the one other with whom he shares the most intimate of mental connections for the rest of his life. To him, she had become what her mother was to Xebrinarth and what Tallachienan was to Pylarith.

However, just as suddenly as it was revealed, the feeling was gone, hidden once more beneath the wary exterior of the dragon who had left this place to escape a destiny such as the one to which he was now shackled. Aeris threw up her own barriers, protection she had learned from both her mother and Master Dinim. In spite of whatever connection she shared with Jaxom, she was able to keep many things to herself. She knew that the dragon never really wanted her, for he had repelled this destiny for so long. She could only imagine how different her life might be had he not been so resistant of his suresh, *the unconscious pull a dragon feels for the one who is meant be his bondmate.*

Aeris closed her eyes, couldn't help envisioning what might have been. Mayhap she would never have been taken by Tholana. She wouldn't have become a whore to the most of the cimmerean population residing within the goddess' stronghold, and even more, personal slave to the dark mage Ranaghar. Perhaps she would never have become pregnant with Ranaghar's children.

Aeris lay her cheek against the smooth scales of Jaxom's shoulder. She was relatively certain the dragon had no idea that she knew so much of his past emotions. Truth be told, she wished she didn't know either. Yet, she had somehow divined them, and now she was able to keep the knowledge from him in spite of other things he'd been able to perceive from her whether she intended it or not.

Perhaps the reason was simple—as of yet they had not become fully *bonded.* As separate entities, they still had the capacity to keep more from one another than they would once the ordained *bonding* ritual was complete. Meanwhile, the suresh was so powerful-the call often awakening her from deep slumber. It would remain as such until their entwined destinies had joined to become one.

As a young girl, Aeris remembered spending time with her mother's bondmate. She would seat herself in the place Xebrin would create within the curve of his forelegs where he lay in the spot he had chosen to sun himself that day. She would giggle as she situated herself, and then she would look up into his beautiful golden face. <Please Xebrinarth, tell me again the story of how you met Ama.>

Xebrin was always happy to oblige, and after telling her how special she was and how much he loved her, the dragon would tell Aeris how his suresh had led him to the one who was meant to be his bondmate. And once he found Adrianna, he never felt loneliness again.

Aeris loved this abridged version of the tale. However, it wasn't until many years later that she heard the story in its entirety—that Adrianna had been forced to return forward to her own Time in order to rejoin the Wildrunners and defeat Aasarak. Xebrin had waited for over a century to feel her presence in the universe again. The torment had been almost unbearable, but he never let go of the promise Adria had made to return.

Because of her conversations with Xebrinarth, Aeris already knew the concepts of suresh and *bonding*. Because she was 'special', she had been able to communicate with her dragon friends via mind-speak, learning all she could about her large companions. She knew about the world of Haldorr, the dragon Elders, and the ritual one must complete in order to become fully *bound* to one's bondmate. Moreover, when she finally recognized Jaxom for what he was, it was simple for her to make certain conclusions. And somehow, she was able to discover more about him than she otherwise would have.

And now, just as Jaxom had done, Aeris found herself resisting this fate. Who really wanted to be *bound* to someone who would rather live his life alone because his intended was of another race? Just like with Tallachienan, she could see herself becoming merely a token, a thing that was good to have only when it suited the owner. Of course, Jaxom would never intend for it to be that way, for he was not a bad sort. But it would end that way.

Hells, who was she to protest? At least she knew *this* love was real.

It was more than what she had before.

Aeris opened her eyes and saw the rugged foothills below. Before them loomed the mountains. Somehow, Jaxom remained ignorant of her internal struggles, most likely due to his impending encounter with his father. She didn't blame him this anxiety. If it were she who had left home without a word for so long, she would be equally disquieted, for Sirion would have her hide for the infraction.

Zarjan banked to the left and Jaxom followed suit, continuing towards the entrance to a cavern deeply nestled within the rocky foliage. The dragons landed on the debris laden ground, and Aeris felt when Jaxom cut his foot on some sharp protruding rock. He hissed inwardly but said nothing as he followed Zarjan past the vines into the large cave. They made their way among the stalagmites rising like spires from the ground and their stalactite comrades who dropped from the ceiling. It wasn't but a few moments longer before they entered the main chamber, and waiting there was the largest creature Aeris had ever seen.

Jaxom stopped at the sight of the massive dragon. Silvery scales shimmered brilliantly within the light cast by flaming pools behind and alongside him, and his eyes shone with a wisdom that bespoke his age. This dragon had lived longer than anyone might know . . . and he was Jaxom's father. *Eeegads.*

Zarjan lowered his head as he spoke to his superior. <My Lord Trebexal, I present to you your son.>

Aeris almost jumped out of her skin as the older dragon nodded his head in acknowledgment, and she immediately pressed herself back down on Jaxom's back. No, it couldn't be. This dragon was boon companion to none other than the man she wished to forget, Tallachienan Chroalthone. She felt her shoulders slump in dejection. She should have known there would never be an escape, not for her. Hells, it was too much to ask for.

Trebexal's voice boomed through her mind. <Jaxomdrehl, I was wondering when I would finally see you again. Sooner than I expected, I must say.>

Aeris kept herself as low as possible on Jaxom's back, pressing firmly against his shoulders and neck in spite of the chafing pain scorching the insides of her thighs.

<Indeed, Father. I realize I should not have left so precipitously.>

<It took you this long to figure that out?> Trebexal said sternly.

Jaxom gave a slow nod. <You have always known me to be the sluggish one, the son who was always last to realize things for what they were. I have not changed.>

Trebexal shook his head. <But you are wrong. You have changed very much; I can sense it.> The dragon paused and then continued. <Yet, the fact remains that you, my own son, deserted me. I specifically chose you to be a participant in my program. You dishonored me when you left without any declaration of your intention, and now I must devise a punishment for you. Do you not realize the situation in which you have placed me?>

Jaxom swallowed heavily. <Father, you don't understand. I was compelled to leave. At first I didn't know why, but when I met her, I began to understand. I fought against it for as long as I could, but in the end, I came to

the realization that I have found my destiny.>

Trebexal narrowed his eyes. <So where is she then? Where is this 'destiny' about whom you speak?>

Jaxom turned towards his back. <She is right here, Father.>

Aeris felt Jaxom narrow his speech band before he spoke, making sure she would be the only one hearing what he had to say. <Come, my father wishes to meet you.> She breathed deeply inward, and then exhaled as she extricated herself from Jaxom's back. The burns on her legs were quickly forgotten as she raised her head to meet the old one's gaze. She saw the instant recognition within Trebexal's eyes, and his expression hardened as he then addressed his son.

<Jaxomdrehl, I wish to speak to the young woman alone for a moment or two. Please allow her to step down, and await us at the entrance to the cavern.>

She sensed Jaxom's thoughts swirling with apprehension as he lowered himself and presented his foreleg. Aeris slipped down from his back onto the proffered limb, a skill she had learned during the first portion of their journey towards Shayamalan. She jumped down to the ground and then looked up at her friend. He brought his head close. <Aeris, my father wishes to speak with you alone. You have nothing to fear. I will be waiting for you at the entrance to the cavern.>

She gave a mental nod, wondering why he was telling her what had already been spoken by Trebexal. She brought her gaze back to the massive dragon looming over her, Trebexal's silver eyes boring into her. They both waited for Jaxom and Zarjan to leave the chamber before he began to speak. Just like Jaxom, he narrowed his speech-band before he started, wanting their words to remain theirs, and theirs alone.

Trebexal spoke in a monotone voice. <You can hear me in your mind without the arcane measures I customarily employ with other faelin.>

It was a statement, not a question. Inasmuch, she didn't bother with a reply. However, the statement gave her insight in regards to Jaxom's behavior; *he didn't realize that she could speak with other dragons.*

<And you know who I am.>

Once again she made no response.

Trebexal regarded her speculatively. <Tallachienan must be searching for you.>

Aeris continued to remain silent.

Trebexal was also quiet for a moment before he continued. <It's interesting that you are the one Jaxom has chosen to bring before me.> He lowered his head to bring himself to her level. She couldn't help noting the beauty of his eyes as they shimmered before her. She felt his hesitation to elaborate on his last statement, loath to say something about which she might have little or no knowledge.

<I know more than you think.> Aeris could feel that he was taken slightly aback. He waited for her to elaborate. <I am very aware of my heritage. I know that my mother was Tallachienan's consort whilst she was his apprentice.>

Trebexal narrowed his eyes. <And how would you know that?>

<Tholana told me,> she replied in a factual tone.

Trebexal snorted, raising his head high. Despite his agitation she continued. <She captured me and brought me to her stronghold. Tholana did things to me, terrible things, and then gave me to her chief mage. When TC finally came for me, I was already pregnant . . .>

<Stop!> His voice interrupted, ringing through their communication link.

Aeris trembled with suppressed emotion. <But isn't this what you wanted to know? Wasn't this the reason why you wanted to speak to me without the presence of Jaxom nearby? Wasn't it your intention to break me down, if even just a little, so that you could be certain I was a good enough bondmate for your son before the ordained ritual?>

Trebexal snorted again, thick smoke rising from his nostrils. He was silently pensive, regarding her with a cold stare. She returned his emotionless gaze, wondering what he was thinking. Mayhap he would have charred her right there on the spot if she wasn't his son's choice for a bondmate.

<So where is this child now? I don't sense another presence here,> he said gruffly.

Aeris swallowed heavily and looked away, placing the palm of her hand against her flat belly. The loss still weighed on her in spite of the passage of time. <I was wounded and I lost them.>

Once again Trebexal was quiet for a moment. Then, in a subdued voice, <I am sorry for your loss.>

Aeris looked up at him once more, noting the regret in his gaze. <Why? Why are you sorry for me? I am nothing to you but Tallachienan's new whore. Hells, you are just afraid he will come here searching for me. You don't wish to face him because you never shared with him what you are doing here. Am I not correct?>

Trebexal's gaze narrowed on her yet again. Then, <I am sorry because lives have been lost, innocent lives that never had the chance to know the beauty of the world. And I am sorry for you as well, for you no longer see that beauty yourself, Damaeris.>

Aeris felt her breath catch in her throat. She felt the tears pool in her eyes and then tried to blink them away before they were noticed.

Trebexal's gaze softened a bit as he brought his head back down to her level. <However, you are right about one thing. I *am* wary of TC looking for you here. I didn't share my activities with him because I feared he wouldn't be in acceptance of my efforts. He is quite opinionated, you know.>

Aeris wiped the tears from her eyes and found herself nodding. <Indeed, my Lord Trebexal, I am very aware of it.>

Trebexal shook his head. <For you, it is just simply Trebexal. The rest makes me feel so terribly *old.*>

Aeris found herself beginning to relax at the newfound tone in the dragon's voice. <Of course; it shall be just Trebexal then.>

She could feel his smile through their link. Then, <You will be a good bondmate for my son. You will bring him the balance he has always needed in his life.>

Aeris shook her head. <He doesn't really want me. I divined it from his thoughts during our travel here.>

Trebexal exhaled softly and wispy smoke drifted up from his nostrils. <I happen to know that he *does* want you.>

<How do you know?>

She felt the smile widen. <A father *always* knows.>

✕ ✕ ✕ ✕ ✕

Aeris slowly turned in place as she looked about the large, dimly lit chamber. The place was empty except for the bedpallets situated neatly throughout, with metal trimmed wooden storage chests at the foot of each. Along the periphery of the cavern walls were several desks. Atop each one were stylus and ink, a few leaves of parchment, and a stack of books. She slowly made her way over to the closest desk, hissing under her breath with the chafing of her trousers against her inner thighs. Ignoring the pain, she picked up the top-most volume and she read the spine, *Dragon Anatomy and Physiology*. Grunting softly to herself, she opened the volume and began to flip through the pages. She stopped at a page depicting a sketch of a mature dragon with arrows pointing to various external body parts and the names for those parts. A few pages later, the dragon's hide and muscle had been removed to reveal the organs within. She grunted again when she saw many organs that were similar to those existing within a humanoid. However, it was the ones that were different that caught her eye.

"I see you have wasted no time in getting acquainted with the lesson books."

Aeris swiftly turned at the sound of a feminine voice at the entrance to the cavern. She'd been so absorbed by the contents of the book she failed to realize that anyone approached. The woman was of savanlean descent, her short blond hair arrayed haphazardly about her head. The style reminded her of Asgenar, her brother's hair always defying the comb to stick out in every direction. She felt a momentary shaft of homesickness before she squelched it.

"Yes, well I didn't know where I should put my things so I decided to have a look around," she replied with a diffident tone.

The young woman regarded her speculatively for a moment, then pointed towards a pallet to her right. "There's a place right over there."

Aeris glanced to the place she indicated. All of the pallets looked the same, each sporting a brown blanket neatly folded in the center accompanied by a pillow at the head. All but one. That one was situated above a chest which had been left open.

Aeris nodded and made her way over to the pallet. The other woman watched as she then set her travel pack inside the chest and closed it. "My name is Faleema."

Aeris glanced back up at her. The woman's countenance had softened although she stood with a hand at either hip. Aeris could easily see that Faleema was a bit rough around the edges but friendly enough if not provoked. "I'm Aeris," she relied shortly.

Faleema's lips slowly pulled up into a grin. "You are bondmate to Lord Trebexal's son. So, how did *that* happen? I mean, he was so against having a 'mate when he left. It must have been difficult to bring him in."

Aeris simply stared at Faleema for a moment or two. This woman acted like she knew Jaxom, but she couldn't have been there long enough to have met the dragon before he left. And then, she assumed that Aeris had used some strategy to lure Jaxom to her, as though he were a fish on her line. Damnation, Aeris hated the thought that everyone would have similar preconceived notions. Hells, she didn't *ask* for this. It simply *happened.*

Aeris looked away from the other woman. "Uh, I have to go. I am certain they are waiting for me." She walked briskly across the room, brushing by Faleema as she passed. She could sense the other woman's discomfiture as she left the chamber, but she didn't find it within her to care. Once outside the cavern, she walked along the rock strewn path. Not far to her right was the mountain precipice. It was quite disconcerting to know that, without the wings of her bondmate, she would be trapped there on the mountain unless she was to find a way to climb down. That, or use magic to find escape.

Of course, to be technical, Aeris actually had no bondmate. She and Jaxom had not yet undergone the *bonding* ritual. And she wasn't even certain she wanted to. Hells, for the longest time Jaxom hadn't wanted a bondmate . . . and it seemed that everyone knew that. Damn, what a let-down.

It wasn't long before Aeris arrived at the entrance to another cavern.

Glancing inside, she saw only a tunnel that wound to the left. Without much hesitation, she entered and followed the tunnel into a chamber similar to the one she had just left behind. It was filled with bedpallets, chests, and book-lined desks. However, seated at one of those desks was a bronze-skinned faelin man. He looked up at her with a startled expression as she entered.

Aeris shook her head. "I'm sorry. I didn't mean to intrude."

She turned to leave when he called out in response. "No, you aren't intruding. You just surprised me." She turned back around and the young man smiled in greeting and gestured for her to remain. "You must be one of the newest recruits. My name is Thulnar."

Aeris returned the smile. "I'm Aeris."

He placed a hand to his chin thoughtfully. "Hmm. I've never heard that name before. It's nice."

Aeris felt her smile widen with the compliment. "Thank you. But actually it's a short name for Damaeris. That is my given name."

Thulnar's smile also widened. "I like that even more. Where are you from?"

Aeris found herself hesitating for a moment. Didn't he know? She had assumed everyone would. But apparently that wasn't the case. However, if he heard *Jaxom's* name . . . "I'm from Elvandahar," she replied.

Thulnar nodded slowly. "My people know it as the largest forest kingdom in all of Ansalar."

"So, how about you? Where are you from?" Aeris asked in an attempt to divert the focus away from her.

"Oh, here and there," he said. "My family is originally from the southwestern outskirts of the city of Rotham located near the Kierev Forest in northern Bekbor. When I was a younger man, we moved into the realm of Farragut along the northern side of the same forest. It suited us much better there." Thulnar paused and then continued. "My bondmate is Sordranth. Who is yours?"

Aeris regarded the young man solemnly. Here it was, the moment of truth. "Actually, we aren't *bound* yet. His name is Jaxomdrehl."

Thulnar nodded almost offhandedly. "I thought as much."

Aeris narrowed her eyes. "What do you mean?"

Thulnar shrugged. "They said you were pretty." He paused for a moment and then continued. "They were right. Not to mention, you are different from the others. I could only expect as much from the one who is to be *bound* to one such as Jaxom."

Aeris felt a flush creeping over her face, yet she made no response to his comment in regards to her physical appearance. "One such as Jaxom?"

Thulnar nodded. "As the son to Lord Trebexal, it must be difficult for him."

Aeris shook her head as he continued. "Just imagine being the son of a god—what the pressure must be like."

Aeris was suddenly thrust into understanding. Hells, just like Tallachienan, Trebexal was a god. How could she have missed it? And Jaxom, how must he feel about that?

"I'm sorry. I thought you knew."

Aeris glanced up at her new friend and saw the expression of apology reflected on his face. "No, it's not your fault. I should have known something when Faleema . . ."

Thulnar rolled his eyes. "Curses, what did *she* have to say? I can only imagine what it may have been. Listen, don't fret about her. She has a bad social filter. The rest of us strive to remember that, and every once in a while remind her that she is being rude."

Aeris only nodded. Thulnar walked over, stopping about half a farlo from her. "By the way, welcome to Shayamalan."

Aeris chuckled. "What, now are you going to tell me how much I'm going to like it here? It would be a good sales profile for a bazaar merchant."

Thulnar shook his head. "No. The place can speak for itself once you give it a chance. If you want, I can give you somewhat of a guided tour. I am sure Jaxom wouldn't mind if you took a ride on Sordranth."

Aeris nodded. "All right, that would be nice."

Thulnar smiled, gesturing as he began walking through the tunnel leading to the entrance. "Come on; Sordra is this way. She loves to rest in the sun on a ledge nearby."

Once outside the cavern, Aeris followed Thulnar along the path she'd been taking before she was diverted. It led to a fork, and Thulnar took the trail that wound upward. It wasn't long before it ended at the ledge about which he'd spoken. It was rather large, spacious enough for two dragons to rest comfortably. Just as he said she would be, Sordra lay there soaking up the warmth offered by the sun's rays.

Aeris stopped when she saw the dragon. Sordra must have heard their approach, for she was already awake. Her golden head rose from her forelegs, and she regarded Aeris from gentle eyes. Aeris sensed her communicate with Thulnar along the private band that every dragon had with his or her bondmate. Then, a moment later, she felt a delicate probing at her mind. It was much akin to the way a guest might knock at the door to the home of his host. It was a new experience for Aeris. Since early childhood, Xebrinarth, Saranath and Mordrexith always had access to her mind, and Jaxom had never asked permission to enter.

Aeris opened her mind. The moment Sordra's conscious touched hers, Aeris recognized that the experience was equally as new to the dragon. <You can hear me?> Sordra cocked her head as she asked the question.

Aeris gave a mental nod. <Yes, I can hear you.>

<How can this be? We are not *bound*.>

Aeris shrugged. <I don't know, but I have always been this way. I can't recall a time when I did not hear the voice of my mother's bondmate in my mind.> Aeris frowned. <Well, not until distance separated us. Since I have been so far away from home, I can no longer hear him.>

Sordra didn't seem to hear Aeris' last words as she rose from her place and slowly brought her head closer. Twin tendrils of smoke drifted up from her nostrils, and her eyes were wide with wonder. <Who are you? What makes you so special?>

Aeris gave a deep breath. <I am Damaeris Timberlyn. And I'm not really all that special.>

Sordra cocked her head and chuckled, the sound of it rumbling in the space between them. <I beg to differ. I have never met another faelin like you before.>

Aeris hesitated for a moment before speaking again. <Is that a good thing?>

Once more the rumble could be heard and Sordra's gaze became piercing. <I like to think so.>

Again, Aeris sensed the communication taking place between Thulnar and his bondmate. She glanced at him and noticed that he seemed concerned about the attention Sordra had been paying her. A moment later he turned back to face her, his expression incredulous. "Sordra says that she can mind-speak with you."

Aeris swallowed anxiously and nodded.

Thulnar's face broke into a wide smile. "By the gods, I've never heard of anything like this before!"

Aeris relaxed when she noticed his amenable demeanor.

"She likes you already! Sordra usually takes a little longer to accept new people."

Aeris shrugged. "I opened myself up to her. She has seen most everything there is to see about me."

Thulnar nodded in understanding. "Yes, that would be it. She doesn't need to take her time with you because she already knows you are a good person."

Aeris gave him a hesitant smile. "She said that I'm a good person?"

Thulnar's smile widened. "She doesn't have to. I can tell because she wants to fly you wherever you want to go. Sordra is someone who likes to please, and she wants to make you happy on your first day here."

Thulnar took the liberty of grasping her hand. Aeris felt her chest swell with happiness and allowed him to lift her onto Sordranth's back. Aeris ignored the pain in her legs as she settled herself, and a brief moment later, she felt Thulnar follow up behind her. He wrapped an arm securely around her waist as Sordra moved to perch herself upon the sheer rock precipice.

For a brief moment, Aeris felt a thrum of pleasure infiltrate her thoughts. It was Thulnar's bondmate telling her that she would be safe in her care, for she was elirya. *She was sister . . . .*

CHAPTER TWO

Tigerius raked his gaze across the encampment. Everyone was making final preparations to begin the last part of their journey to the den of the vampyr. Jezibel and the halfen brothers had prepared a meal to break their fast, while Mateo and Levander prepared the horses. Cedric, Tiger, Alasdair, Magnus and Talemar broke down the encampment and, when they were ready, everyone participated in loading up the horses. Everyone that is, except for Cervantes.

Tiger stopped packing and looked again, this time more closely. No, Cervantes definitely wasn't there, and neither were his belongings. *Damn, this is an interesting turn of events.* He ceased his activity and walked over to Alasdair. The man was busy with his own preparations, making certain the placement of his belongings in the travel packs were both efficient and accessible.

"It seems we might have a problem," Tiger said in a monotone.

Alasdair looked up from his task and frowned. "What are you talking about?"

"Cervantes is no longer with us."

Alasdair shook his head in denial. "No, don't tell me this. Are you certain?"

Tiger put a hand on Alasdair's shoulder. "I wouldn't be saying it if I wasn't absolutely positive, my friend."

Alasdair took a swift glance around the vicinity before slapping a hand against his thigh. "Effin calotebas! I should have been more vigilant." He bit at his lower lip for a moment. "Go tell everyone to cease preparations while I try to find the direction he might have taken."

Tigerius nodded. "You might want to consider the path we are already planning to travel today. Cervantes was quite upset over TC's revelation about Cortes. He may have simply gone ahead before us."

Alasdair frowned and shook his head. "More likely, he has gone ahead *without* us."

Tiger nodded in agreement, watching as Alasdair strode away to begin his search. He then looked over to where everyone was gathered near the horses and made his way there. It was disturbing that no one had noticed Cervantes' absence, testimony of how fractured the group had become since Aeris and

Talemar's abduction. It gave an indication of how Cervantes must feel on a daily basis—*as though he had no one*. From the corner of his eye he saw Alasdair disappear into the trees not far away. Hopefully the ranger would find something.

Tiger stood there for a moment before taking the liberty of sharing his knowledge. He was surprised by his own callousness, not realizing he could be so mean spirited. "Cervantes Conradi could be dead right now and no one would be the wiser," he said with a deadpan expression.

Much to her credit, Jezibel was the first to look up from her task. "What?"

Tiger pinned her with a malevolent glare. "You heard me."

Jezzie glanced around the area while the rest of the group stared at him with varying levels of hostility. Finally Lev moved to stand beside her. "What's going on Tigerius?"

It was then that Jezzie realized what he was talking about and her eyes widened. "Tiger, where is he?"

He shrugged. "I don't know, just thought it was interesting that no one noticed his absence before me."

Jezzie swallowed convulsively. The rest of the group just stood there quietly, no one having any profound words to offer the conversation, not even the all-knowing Tallachienan. Lev moved away in the direction that Alasdair had taken, and Cedric followed. Tiger made no move to stop them; after all, it would be good for Alasdair to have someone watching his back.

Tigerius went back over to his pack and sat down. It wasn't long before he was joined by Vikhail and Vardec. The brothers each lit a pipe and offered one to him. Instead of turning it down like he usually did, he nodded and accepted the vessel. Vikhail gave him a wide toothy grin while Vardec stuffed a heaping measure of their 'special blend' inside. The pipe was then lit and Tiger took a deep drag. It wasn't often that he smoked, but he'd done it on enough occasions to avoid coughing like an amateur. The flavor was good, much better than others he'd experienced. He had to admit that the halfen were very adept with some things; armed combat, food preparation and pipe smoking were three of them.

Within the hour Alasdair returned. He immediately walked over to him and the other two men. "I began my search in the direction we will take towards the vampyr lair. It didn't take me long to see where someone had passed through the vegetation. I followed the trail for a while, and once convinced it belonged to Cervantes, I doubled back and met up with Lev and Cedric before reaching the encampment."

"While you were gone, I made everyone aware of the situation," said Tiger.

Alasdair nodded. "All right, let's head out."

Tiger watched as everyone made last-moment preparations. Jezzie was obviously upset, and Lev pinned him with a stern glare before he looked away. Once ready, the group fell in behind Alasdair and Cedric. The ranger moved in the direction that Cervantes had taken, and just as TC foretold it the day before, they reached the daemon lair within only a quarter-day.

Tigerius regarded the castle on the hill. The dilapidated structure had once been home to a wealthy lord, his family, and servants. Even at this distance he could see that many of the stone walls were crumbling, and the surrounding grounds were overrun with thorny bushes and prickly weeds. The place had an ominous feeling about it, one that made Tiger feel edgy. He attributed it to the fact that it was now residence to some of the most despicable of beings. In his mind, daemon-kind was a scourge that needed to be eradicated. Unfortunately he happened to fit the same category, *at least in part.*

In spite of Tiger's better judgement, the group moved slowly forward. If left up to him, he would divide the group into parts and approach the lair from different directions. He supposed it was the part of him that had begun to develop a sense for some things that he didn't quite understand yet. After a while they passed through a garden, one that had once been very beautiful. The statues that remained standing were some of the finest he'd ever seen, and there were several places where he imagined there may have been a fountain. So deep in his thoughts, Tiger didn't realize they had stopped. Too late, he saw the large, wemic-like wrothe slink out from among the shadows cast by the statues, hackles raised and teeth bared. Glancing quickly around the area, he counted twice the number of wrothe versus people. A moment later they attacked.

Lev was the first to respond, his flying stars finding their marks rather easily. They were closely followed with fiery spells cast by Talemar and Tallachienan. When the spell-induced smoke rolled away, Tiger, Cedric and the halfen brothers swept in to complete what was started. In his estimation it was nothing short of slaughter, for it wasn't long before the battle was over. He watched Vardec deliver the final blow to the last wrothe, hitting its head with his hammer to crush the skull. In the meantime, the halfen held a hand over the injury to his thigh, a bite wound causing enough blood-loss to saturate the entire length of the leg of his trousers.

Tiger began to move towards Vardec when, all of a sudden at the periphery of his vision, he saw TC abruptly slump to the ground. He turned and rushed over, reaching TC's side at the same time as Alasdair.

"What is it? Are you all right?" Alasdair asked, kneeling beside him.

TC shook his head and smirked. "Just because I am a god doesn't mean

I'm infallible. I didn't realize how weak I've become since casting those scrying spells. They took more out of me than I thought."

Alasdair nodded. "You should just rest now. The rest of us will see to the rescue of our comrades."

Tiger frowned, crossing his arms over his chest. He felt some measure of irritation, believing that the skirmish could have been avoided. "They knew we were coming!" he said. With a rising voice he added, "How else did they know to send the wrothe again? We are fools to move together towards the lair. We need to be secretive and make the enemy believe we have been more seriously wounded than we really are!"

Alasdair grimaced, placing a hand over his blood soaked sleeve. "We *are* wounded Tiger, very wounded. We need to stay together."

Tiger shook his head. "No, our physical weakness is more a reason for only two or three of us to proceed. They are obviously watching us somehow, and if three of us leave the group inconspicuously we might have a chance."

Alasdair's expression shifted to frustration. "They would notice the difference, Tiger. It will be easy to count that there are eleven of us now and only eight of us tomorrow morning."

"I'm not convinced that whatever is watching us has the capacity to understand that," Tiger said, refuting Alasdair's opinion.

"He's right," interjected TC. "They may not realize that there are some of us missing. Most likely, whatever is watching us is not intelligent enough to know the difference if only two or three of us leave. Remember, the vampyr are masters over animal familiars. These servants may take the form of a winter bat, blood raven or mange rat. And we have already met the wrothe."

Alasdair pressed his lips into a thin line. It was obvious he disliked the turn the discussion had taken, especially since it was Tigerius who perpetuated it. But in this case, Tiger knew he was right. With this type of enemy they had to move stealthily; otherwise, the daemons would continue to beset them with their animal minions.

"Fine, do it then. The three strongest of us should go," Alasdair said in a gruff voice.

Tigerius stood there for a moment and thoughtfully considered his options. He hadn't suffered any damage in the attack, and even though he was tired, neither had Tallachienan. Tiger didn't relish the other man's presence with him on the mission but recognized he might benefit from TC's *talent*. The sorcerer's knowledge about the enemy they faced would be an added bonus. Both Alasdair and Cedric had been wounded in the fight, and Jezibel and Mateo weren't ones who should be taken into a small fortress full of daemons. Lev had been wounded in his efforts to keep those two out of harm's way, and

Vardec was similarly damaged. That left Talemar and Vikhail.

Tiger allowed his gaze to rest on the halfen. He felt the benefit would be better with a warrior within his ranks. He lifted his voice so the other man would clearly hear. "So, what do you say, Vikhail. Are you with us?"

From where he stood listening to the conversation beside his brother, Vikhail gave a brief nod. "Ya shud know I am," he replied in a bold tone.

Tiger turned back to Alasdair. He didn't bother asking TC if he would be in accompaniment, somehow knowing the man would agree. "Tallachienan, Vikhail and I will leave the encampment one at a time during the course of the evening. If you don't see us back within three days, you will know something has happened."

Alasdair gave a bland stare. "You know I don't like this," he groused.

Tigerius lay a conciliatory hand on his friend's shoulder. "I know. But I truly feel it is the best strategy to access Jonesy." He paused before continuing. "I believe that Cervantes is somewhere in there too."

Alasdair finally nodded. "I suppose we'll just have to stay here and nurse our wounds whilst you are away." He then allowed a grin to pass over his stoic face.

Tigerius chucked. "Yes, you do that, my friend. And when the daemons come following behind us when we leave their den in the company of both Cervantes and Jonesy, you had best be ready."

Alasdair nodded. "Indeed, brother. We shall be ready."

Tiger was suddenly still for a moment. In all of their years together, Alasdair had never called him 'brother'. Like never before, he felt the bond between them, a bond that began with their fathers long ago. He felt a smile of his own emerge and Tiger gripped the other man's shoulder tightly before turning away. Alasdair had honored him by naming him his brother, but it also expressed to Tigerius that the ranger was afraid for him. *Tiger would be a fool to not feel the same sentiment.*

Aeris stood in the center of the immense bowl, rays from the afternoon sun shining down on her. Being surrounded by massive mountain cliffs, the valley was almost just as deep as it was wide, making it the perfect place for gatherings. The cliffs were littered with multitudes of ledges, natural perches for the influx of dragons to this place for a very special occasion—her *bonding* to Jaxomdrehl, the son that swore he would never be *bound*. Damn, how was it that she had walked out of one disastrous commitment just to enter another?

It was early evening, and she had just returned from her mounted tour with Thulnar and Sordra. The moment Aeris entered her home cavern, she'd been accosted by several people who seemed to function as isterian. At first she was nervous, but when she saw the bath that had been brought, she couldn't help but smile. She had forgone such luxury for far too long. She was quick to throw off her travel-stained tunic and trousers to step into the heated water, hissing when it touched the sores on her legs. She then took her immersion more slowly, noting that the waters had been incensed with some unfamiliar perfumed oils. She found she rather liked the scent, and she told herself to remember to ask someone about it sometime.

After the bath, the servants had presented Aeris with a white gown. She frowned when she saw it, for she had it in her mind to wear her own clothing, which resided within the travel pack she had stored inside the chest at the foot of her bed-pallet not too long ago. Much to her dismay, the isterian refused to allow her access to it, insisting that she wear the gown since it was the one required for the 'ceremony'. Of course, she had no idea what they were talking about, and as she became increasingly irate with the servants, Aeris began to shout. Damnation, she was so tired she could fall over and had yet to eat anything since arriving there.

It was then that Jaxom had arrived on the scene.

Aeris watched as the wide-eyed isterian mumbled something to him and gave a brief bow before quickly leaving. Jaxom had come in faelin form, for the entrance wasn't wide enough to accommodate a fully matured dragon. Aeris calmed under the soothing vibes he sent through their link, adjusting the loose towel more snugly around herself.

She regarded him suspiciously from narrowed eyes. "Why is everyone so nervous around you?"

Jaxom shrugged nonchalantly. "I suppose they think I might take them to task for some perceived wrongdoing," he replied.

Aeris narrowed her eyes. "Is that the way it has been with you in the past?"

He averted his eyes from hers in mild discomfort. "Perhaps."

Aeris nodded as she pursed her lips. Feelings of unease welled up inside her, and Jaxom sensed them immediately. His gaze locked back onto hers, his silver eyes piercing. She could then feel him in her mind, searching for the answers he required. Once having them, his shoulders seemed to slump with dejection.

"Why did you not tell me you felt this way?"

It was Aeris' turn to shrug her shoulders. "You never asked me."

Jaxom sighed heavily and closed the distance between them. "Did I not tell you that we are meant for one another?"

Aeris nodded.

"Don't you believe me?"

Aeris felt her throat begin to ache and she swallowed heavily. "I want to."

Jaxom raised a hand and held it before her, palm outward. "Then put your faith in me. I won't let you down this time. I promise."

Aeris shook her head. "But what about all the things I've been hearing? Jaxom, I know you don't want me . . ."

"That's not true!" he said in a resolute voice. "I do want you; I just didn't realize it at first." He paused and then continued. "Who do you think it was that helped you and Tallachienan escape Tholana's citadel?"

Aeris felt her eyes widen.

Jaxom nodded. "I fought the denizens of the catacombs so that you would have a path to freedom. When I finally realized what the cimmerean bastards did to you, a part of me died inside." His eyes were beseeching. "I have failed you already, but please let me make it up to you. Please."

"But what about . . ."

Jaxom shook his head. "Pay no attention to these people. They know nothing about me and the life I have led since I left here. And they don't know you, and what you could possibly mean to me." His gaze became intense. "All you need to think about now is how much I love you, and how much you might love me in return."

With tear-filled eyes, Aeris regarded the hand still held before her. He was so different from the individual with whom she'd journeyed these past weeks. She heard him whisper in her mind, <Trust me>.

Aeris raised her hand to meet his. The moment they touched, an explosion of sensation swept over her. She could feel Jaxom coursing through her like a wild river, finding all of her most hidden places. She gasped with the intrusion, yet allowed it access. Within mere moments, he knew her more intimately than any other. In spite of it all, his love for her remained.

<What have you done?> she asked incredulously.

Jaxom smiled and curved his fingers around hers. <You are my bondmate, my companion in life. Wherever you go, I will be with you. I will always be your protector, your brother, and your friend.>

And now, with those words in her mind, Aeris stood there within the bowl. She breathed deeply, blinking away the tears threatening at the corners of her eyes. She would be strong, for she had promised Jaxom that she would place her faith in him. And to be quite truthful, she already loved the dragon with all her heart.

The dragon elders arrived all at once, their scales shimmering iridescently in the scanty sunlight remaining to them. They were magnificent to behold, resplendent in their pale glory. They landed at the same time, and the impact of twenty-four pairs of massive dragon feet made the ground shake beneath her. They were huge, for the elders were the oldest and wisest of all those living on Shayamalan. Three of them had golden eyes, and the other three silver. Trebexal was one of them.

Aeris suddenly found herself overwhelmed as she blinked up at the massive dragons. By the gods, she was nothing compared to these beings. Her heart began to thunder in her chest, and her palms began to sweat. She felt herself running out of breath as she rubbed her hands nervously over the sides of her gown.

It was then that she saw Trebexal wink at her. It was hardly discernible, for he did it on the sly. But she knew it was intentional and made just for her because, at the same moment, she felt a slight breeze sweep through her mind. She could suddenly breathe again, and her heart ceased its race. She realized that everything was going to be all right, and it was at that moment that Jaxomdrehl arrived.

Almost immediately Aeris began to hear a chanting in her mind. The voices of the six elders entwined in a soothing melody, spoken in a language she couldn't understand. Yet, she could *feel* the meaning of the words as they swept through her, enveloping her within a rhapsody of tone and nuance. Time seemed to melt away, and all she could see, hear, and feel was the chanting of the elders and the presence of Jaxomdrehl there beside her.

✕ ✕ ✕ ✕ ✕

The dragons and their riders gathered at the center of the valley. As Aeris understood, it was one of several valleys comprising the vast area which Lord Trebexal had claimed a portion for his use in a program he had designed to counter the existence of the foul combination of human and degethozak that currently ran amok throughout western Ansalar. *Dragonriders.* In Aeris' mind, she and the others who trained here would be the same, riders who bore the purpose of using a dragon's capabilities to benefit themselves—only without the foul intent.

Aeris took in the group within which she and Jaxom now seemed to be a part. She was surprised to see Thulnar there with the golden Sordranth, and even more surprised to see Faleema standing there beside her own golden bondmate. In all, there were five pairs, including herself and Jaxom. She wondered what this was about, for she had been awakened within these early morning hours from some much-needed sleep. She hoped it was important.

It wasn't much longer before she noticed the approach of another dragon in the near distance. As it flew closer, she realized it was another helzethryn, and upon his back there was a rider. The pair swiftly landed among them, and before the dragon had stopped, a halfen man was hopping down from the dragon's back.

"Many of you already know me, but if you don't, my name is Rogerus. This is Hadrimaxith." The halfen pointed towards his dragon. "As of right now, you are in the midst of a test and are to have absolutely NO communication with your bondmates, telepathically or otherwise. Don't even consider attempting to cheat, for your dragons once having given a pledge of loyalty towards this program, will not violate its conditions or rules." Rogerus lowered his voice and drew his thick dark brows together into a frown. "'Cause let's face it, people, they are much more noble beings than we could ever strive to be."

Aeris swallowed nervously. What the Hells was going on? How could they be going through a test when she and Jaxom had yet to receive instruction? She swung her gaze over to her bondmate, and he shook his head almost imperceptibly. It was a warning for her to concur with the testing conditions. However, his eyes spoke more, telling her all would be well. He would take action should the need arise. He had asked her to place her faith in him. She would adhere to her commitment.

Aeris breathed deeply of the warm air as the instructor began to speak once more. "By this point in your relationship, a bond of trust should exist between you. This test shall determine the extent of that trust. Each pair of you shall situate yourselves at a location distant from your comrades. The other instructors will arrive soon and each pair of you will be assigned to one. I will explain nothing more about the test, for to do so would potentially cloud the truth of the test results. Inasmuch, everyone shall be testing at the same time in order to divert the same consequence." Rogerus took a moment to glance at the sky. "And here they come."

The area became suddenly filled with another four dragons and their riders. Luckily, the valley was large, able to sustain ten *bonded* pairs. They all spread themselves out, and it wasn't long before Aeris and Jaxom found themselves being joined by the instructor who would be presiding over their individual test.

The man was savanlean, his silver hair just touching the tops of his shoulders. His blue-green eyes regarded Aeris intently as he approached; he was followed by the only other rezwithrys dragon she had seen so far besides her own bondmate. "My name is Kordrian," he said. "But you should call me Kord. This is my bondmate Riloriandrix."

Aeris only nodded mutely. She was still upset over the fact she was being subject to testing after having been upon Shayamalan less than a single day-cycle. Damn, she hadn't even been given the luxury of a full night's rest after several days of air-travel astride a dragon that was most definitely even more tired than she. Her heart went out to Jaxom, for he must be feeling the strain much more acutely.

Noticing the sudden presence of a shadow, Aeris disengaged from her thoughts to find the instructor standing directly before her. "What's wrong? You feel doubtful of the outcome of this test? Well, you should have considered that before coming to train here," he said with a harsh tone. "This is a rigorous program designed for the strongest pairs. Come, let's get on with it."

Aeris pushed her initial retort away. Now was not the time to start an argument, especially with someone who was obviously her senior and the one who would be overseeing her testing. She went to stand in the place the instructor indicated, and once Jaxom was standing above her, they began to receive their instruction.

Jaxom heard what the instructor said to Aeris, and was surprised when she made no rejoinder. He felt bad, for she had been considering his welfare when she hesitated. Already he could sense an energy about Kordrian, and knew that he might be a bit difficult to work with.

Jaxom was surprised again when he received communication from the silver Riloriandrix. <Jaxomdrehl, this is more a test for your bondmate than it is for you. Our companions often come to us with trust deficits, and it is our responsibility to take note of those persons and provide them additional training if necessary. In this program, there can be no question of trust, for in battle, split-second decisions must be made continually. It is imperative that our riders have absolute faith in our abilities, and that we have the same belief in theirs. One day, this test will be in the reverse.>

Jaxom could feel her smile through the communication link. <Kord will blindfold you and then instruct Aeris to move forward. You will also step forward. He will instruct her to walk beneath your feet as you move. All of us but Aeris know that your perception of where she is in space is far superior. We are certain that no harm could even potentially come to her. However, Aeris has to place her utmost faith in you.>

Jaxom gave a mental nod and lowered his head so that Kord could place a cloth over his eyes. He then stood there for a moment, waiting for Aeris to move. And the moment she did so, he could feel the tiny vibration given by her feet as they trod the ground. In spite of his inability to see her, Jaxom knew where she was and he easily stepped around her. And what made it easier was that she walked in a relatively straight line.

After a few moments, Jaxom heard Kord's voice. "All right, Aeris continue walking, but place yourself in the way of your dragon's feet."

Through their link, Jaxom could feel Aeris balk at the command. He didn't fault her, for who would knowingly place themselves at risk? Although, unbeknownst to her, it was no risk at all, for it was an inborn ability he happened to possess. As ordained by the rules explained to him by Rilo, he said nothing to her, hoping beyond hope that she would figure it out for herself. *That all it took was that bit of faith that she already promised she would give him.*

Aeris began by increasing her pace, and within moments she was weaving in and out between his legs. He focused on her movements and moved his own body accordingly, being sure to step in a place where he calculated in his mind that she would never go. Of course, it was still easy, for there were no external influences to interfere . . . *such as the presence of an enemy.*

Jaxom found himself becoming flustered. He knew this was part of the test, but he wasn't entirely certain he understood it. This was a controlled setting, unrealistic for what they would be up against in a combat scenario. In such a situation another factor would be forced into play. But then he was forgetting the aim of this test. It was a moment of truth. Did Aeris really believe in him?

It was only a moment later he had his answer.

While Jaxom fought to control his burst of negative emotion, Aeris had begun to smile. She skipped this way and that, playing beneath the potential threat looming overhead. Yet, she seemed to know that he would not harm her, and like he had hoped, placed her faith in him. He couldn't help but give into the game, and they played for a while. It wasn't much longer before the instructor suddenly commanded them to stop, and just at that moment, Aeris stood beneath one of his massive feet.

Kord nodded, his eyes reflecting how much they impressed him. "Very good, I am pleased with your accomplishment. Now is the *real* test," he said. Jaxom then thought he heard, through the open communion he still shared with Rilo, the instructor's voice in his mind. <Fall down beside her . . . NOW!>

Aeris had closed her eyes when the instructor bade them stop. She took in his words of praise, but knew there was something more. For what seemed like almost an eternity, she silently waited within the shadow of Jaxom's majesty. All of a sudden the ground shook all around and beneath her. The air surrounding her shifted with the impact, making the loose strands of her hair perform a crazy dance for a moment before it subsided. Meanwhile, Aeris never moved a muscle, her mind convinced that Jaxom would never allow physical harm to come to her.

Aeris slowly opened her eyes to find herself confronted with the silver gaze of her bondmate. Aeris grinned without hesitation, and Jaxom was pleased to reciprocate. <I was concerned about you for a moment,> he said.

Aeris nodded. <Me too. But then I remembered what my father taught me when I was younger. The lesson reminded me so much of what I needed to accomplish here today. While working to rehabilitate some injured animals we had found in our domain, my father showed me that I could always master the situation. Some creatures are naturally more fearful than others. This can often be difficult, but when I kept my composure, I was able to maintain control. The animals healed swiftly, and were allowed to return to their homes. With this in mind, I thought to bring some frivolity to our test today, add a bit of fun to the pervading seriousness. My aura of calm made you relax a bit more, and in the end, made you think less about any consequences.>

Through the link they shared, Aeris could sense that Jaxom was pleased. He felt lucky to have her, for not only was she intelligent, but she was intuitive. He'd known that all it would take for her to pass the test was her faith in him. However, she had made his task much easier with her capacity to bring levity to the somewhat stressful situation. For what seemed like the hundredth time, he thanked the gods he had found her, and that she was his.

Later that eve, Aeris awoke to the sounds of the other dragonriders as they returned to the barracks after a long day of training. Slowly seating herself upright, she watched the growing bustle of young people who prepared themselves for the evening. None seemed to mind the presence of the opposite gender among them, for both men and women disrobed seemingly without second thought. After donning fresh attire and seeing to other bodily needs, they left the barracks in search of whatever activity beckoned them.

Feeling a rumbling in her gut, Aeris placed a hand to her belly. She suddenly felt voracious to the point of feeling sick. She rose from the bed, and when a young woman nearby gave her an inquiring glance, Aeris took the opportunity to ask how she might procure a meal. Hells, she couldn't even recall when last she had eaten something. The woman described the location of the place where she could go, a cavern located along the mountain trail past the second barracks cave. She referred to it as the central fire-pits, or simply, 'the Pits'.

Among the deepening shadows that heralded evening, Aeris slowly made her way down the path, taking care not to allow the insides of her legs to rub together. The pain was so much worse now, and she wondered what it was all about, for she had ridden astride Jaxom only to and from the barracks since their arrival. The air was chilled in spite of the warm day, and she rubbed her hands along her upper arms. She regretted not bringing her cloak, which lay in a crumpled heap on the bed-pallet she recently left behind. She considered returning for it but decided against the idea, for the thought of waiting even that much longer for sustenance was terrible to contemplate.

Aeris stumbled as she passed the second barracks. She cursed under her breath, stopping to hold her ankle in her hands. With her luck she would be crippled on the morrow, and gods only knew what activity in which these people would require her participation . . . *of course without previous instruction. Damn fools.*

"Are you all right?"

Aeris turned at the sound of Thulnar's voice. He walked up behind her and then stopped when he was beside her. "Do you want me to take a look?"

Aeris shook her head. "No, I'm sure it's fine. I just twisted it, that's all."

Thulnar knelt before her and proceeded to take off her boot anyway. He felt around on the ankle, stopping when he heard her hiss with discomfort. "We should keep atop of it. Should it worsen, we will go to Barthaltak. He will know how to fix it."

Aeris only nodded silently.

"So, I assume you are heading to the Pits," he said, placing her foot back into the boot.

Aeris nodded once again.

"Good. Now I will have someone to sit with me as I eat." Thulnar smiled and stood, locking his gaze onto hers.

Aeris returned the smile and decided to give him a bit of a hard time. "Who said I wanted you with me?"

Thulnar's grin widened and he huffed. "Who wouldn't?" he replied. "I happen to be the best thing here."

Aeris' grin widened, but she didn't make a reply. Together they slowly walked the rest of the way to the Pits, with Aeris slightly favoring a disgruntled ankle in addition to her previous ailment. Inside the warm cavern was situated a plethora of long tables, each with the capacity to seat at least twelve. Following behind her friend, she approached the fires. Seated before them were those isterian responsible for them. Both she and Thulnar were handed a plate consisting of some unfamiliar fruits, nuts, and freshly baked bread. As they sat at one of the tables, each chose a wedge of cheese and then poured themselves some water from the available flask.

For several moments they ate in relative silence. There were others present, but they sat at other tables and conversed with their own comrades. However, it wasn't long before Aeris looked up as someone sat next to her. It was disconcerting to find that it was the woman Faleema whom she had met the day before.

"Hello Aeris . . . Thulnar." Faleema nodded to them both and seated herself. "I see you have become acquainted already."

Aeris silently regarded Thulnar across the table. "Yes, I had the pleasure of meeting her yesterday," he replied.

Faleema nodded as she took a bite of her bread. "I suppose Sordra has met her as well?"

For a moment Aeris thought she sensed something from the other woman, an ambiance she couldn't quite place. Was it jealousy?

Thulnar nodded in the affirmative. "We took Aeris on an aerial tour of the place before she was beckoned for her *bonding* ceremony."

Faleema turned to her then, all indications of any negative emotions wiped away. "Wasn't it wonderful?" She didn't stop for a response. "It was a rare privilege to see your *bonding*, for many of the 'mates are already *bound* before they arrive here. Thank you."

Aeris found herself taken slightly aback by the sincerity she heard in Faleema's voice. It was unexpected. "You are welcome."

Faleema gave her a tentative smile before she turned back to her meal. Aeris glanced across the table once more to find Thulnar watching her. She nodded almost imperceptibly and gave him a slight grin. He returned the gesture and then turned his attention to his own food.

Several moments passed before anyone spoke. Aeris was content to simply eat her meal without further interruption, and as her stomach reached satiety, she sat back in her seat. Thulnar soon did the same. "So, it seems that they are going to make you catch up with the rest of us as quickly as possible," he said.

Aeris frowned. "Why do you say that?"

He shrugged. "I was surprised to see you at the test today. The rest of us have been here for at least a fortnight, with ample opportunity to have the chance of getting to know our bondmates on another level. But you . . . at the time you tested, you hadn't even been here a full day-cycle."

Aeris regarded him from wide eyes.

"Tomorrow you should come with us to the flight class," said Faleema. "We awaken just after sunrise to get to the practice field on time."

Thulnar nodded in agreement. "Forigard is the instructor. Don't worry; he will have you caught up with the rest of us in no time."

"But that's what I am afraid of," she said plaintively.

Thulnar and Faleema simply glanced at one another and then back at Aeris, their expressions commiserating. "We will help all we can," said Thulnar stoically.

Aeris simply sat there. *What had Jaxom gotten her into?*

CHAPTER THREE

Between the two barracks, there were a total of thirty-two dragonriders of varying skill levels. The most accomplished wore a crimson headband, telling others of their higher status, and Aeris had learned that these students were often called upon by the instructors to help during training. They were referred to as 'redbands', and one such individual was present at the practice arena as Aeris and her comrades arrived. Like Thulnar, he appeared to be of terralean descent. He turned as they approached, his dark gaze settling on her momentarily as she dismounted. He offered no gesture of greeting and Aeris frowned inwardly with the prospect of an unfriendly teacher.

Behind the threesome followed two more dragons and their riders. Aeris recognized them as those she saw just the morning before at the testing arena. It was then she made the realization that these were a group of students of the same rank, a class who would remain together for much of their training. She had now become their peer.

Within but a few moments, another rider approached. It was the third rezwithrys dragon she had seen in the program, for all the others were helzethryn. The silver landed among them, and the rider dismounted effortlessly without the use of the dragon's foreleg. Aeris mused at the maneuver, instantly feeling the desire to master it herself.

"You must be Damaeris Timberlyn," he said as he made his way to her.

She nodded.

"My name is Forigard, but you can call me Fo. This is my bondmate, Seldonraxis." The savanlean paused and then continued. "I will be your riding instructor, and Falon your quarter master." Fo gestured towards the young terralean with the red headband. "You are late in starting, but my goal is to catch you up with the rest of your class whilst at the same time continuing their instruction. What do you think?"

Aeris nodded in affirmative. "Your plan sounds viable. I shall try my best to accommodate you." She cringed inside as she spoke, knowing she was signing her life away until she was on par with her peers. Yet, she knew it was what Fo wanted to hear. She would give him that in spite of her fears.

Fo grinned, his brown eyes sparkling merrily as he then slapped his hands together. "All right everyone—up to the cliffs."

Aeris stood there and watched as everyone mounted their dragons and leaped into the air. They flew towards the top of the closest mountainside, a sheer face of sleek, gray rock. With Jaxom's gentle urging, she mounted his back, holding back the cry that threatened. The pain was worse than it had ever been before in spite of the salve she used. Upon awakening that morning, she'd regarded the angry, red abrasions. The sores had broken open to ooze their sticky fluid all over her nightgown while she slept. She gently cleansed the areas before she undertook any other task, dried them, and then donned her thickest trousers. Jaxom had become aware of her discomfort, urging her to seek the advice of a fellow peer or an instructor. She resisted. Hells, she'd just arrived there! All they needed was a wimpy woman who couldn't withstand a little skin irritation. Jaxom ceased his urging, yet remained alert towards her circumstance. Aeris could feel his attention, and it bothered her and soothed her at the same time.

When they finally arrived at the cavern dug high into the mountainside, Aeris found herself stunned by the complex harness and saddle being buckled onto each dragon. The thing sported so many straps and other accouterments she had no idea where she would even possibly begin. Fo stepped up to her as she stood there beside Jaxom, watching the others with the complicated contraption. He pointed towards the wall of the cavern where another of the contrivances lay. "The one you should use is over there. It's new, never been worn by another dragonrider pair."

Aeris nodded and stepped over to the saddle-harness. She picked the main part of it up from the ground. It was heavy, and she wondered how the Hells she was expected to know what the thing was and how it was to be worn. She squelched down sudden feelings of anxiety, and as she did so, Jaxom sent soothing vibrations through their link. He then brought his head close, eyeing the leather speculatively. <Don't worry,> he said. <We will figure it out together.>

"You know, it's not going to jump up and place itself on your dragon by itself."

Aeris startled and placed a hand to her chest as she turned back to Fo. He regarded her intently and then said, "You look confused. Did you fall asleep during orientation or something? They covered the particulars of this equipment for at least a quarter day."

Aeris frowned. By the gods, what was the man talking about?

"You *have* been through orientation, right?"

Aeris' frown deepened, and then she finally spoke her mind. "What the Hells are you talking about? What is this 'orientation'? And I am very aware this thing won't place itself on Jaxom's back without some bit of help from me!"

Jaxom's draconic laughter rumbled throughout the cavern as Fo held up his hands. "Peace! I'm sorry, I just didn't realize that you have absolutely no idea what is going on, including what type of equipment you will be using." He became silently pensive for a moment and then continued. "You don't even know what your instruction times are, do you?"

Aeris shrugged. "Only what my comrades have told me." She then gestured towards Faleema and Thulnar.

Fo nodded with an air of resignation. He stepped up to her and took the heavy equipment from her arms. Jaxom lowered himself to the ground and Fo proceeded to place the strange saddle just in front of the dragon's withers. As she watched, he tightened the straps to fit her bondmate around his chest and underneath his forelegs. The instructor, or demeter, as she'd heard him called, asked Jaxom if he was comfortable. When the dragon gave an affirmative vocal response, Fo then asked Aeris to climb aboard. Once astride, she remained patient as the demeter adjusted another set of straps to fit around her hips and across her sore thighs. When he was finished, Fo rubbed Jaxom's neck just in front of the saddle for a moment. "This is the most important piece of equipment you shall acquire."

Aeris cocked her head to the side questioningly.

Demeter Fo regarded her with piercing eyes. "It is the one thing that will keep you astride your dragon during combat."

Aeris nodded as he swung around to face the rest of the class. "Everyone, today is our day to focus on our comrade. Fardles, we can chalk up one lost day of riding instruction for the sake of a friend, can't we?"

Aeris watched as the rest of the class cheered, pleased with the respite they would be receiving. She found herself swallowing heavily, wondering exactly how physically intensive this was going to be. Hells, she was a magic-user. Sure, her father and brothers had taught her some things, but most likely it was nothing even close to what she feared may be required of her now.

Fo pointed to the nearest dragon and his rider. "Saliel, I want you and Borgestrix to show our friends the fundamentals of proper paired flight." He turned back to her. "Aeris, rider positioning is our main concern right now, especially in regards to launch, both from the ground and from a lofty position such as this one." Fo indicated the cliff entrance. "If too much strain is placed on the dragon, he will be compelled to compensate. He will be forced to tap into energy reserves he need not use until battle. However, if he has a rider who knows how to sit him without the expenditure of such energies, he has an advantage over his enemies."

Aeris and Jaxom approached the entrance and stood beside Saliel and Borgestrix. Her mind was a maelstrom of thoughts. Could it possibly be that during their entire flight to Shayamalan she had been inadvertently acting as a resistance to her bondmate? It meant that she would have been a primary contributor to his fatigue and . . . .

<Damaeris, please don't fault yourself. You didn't know,> Jaxom interrupted her thoughts.

Aeris swallowed heavily and watched as Saliel and Borgestrix fell away from the cliff face. She felt her eyes widen when the dragon didn't open his wings right away, but when he did, the updraft caused the pair to rise back towards them for a moment. Then, once finding the current, they began to glide.

"All right, now it is your turn." Aeris looked down to find Demeter Fo standing beside them, and she nodded her understanding. Recalling that Saliel had pressed himself close to his dragon as they fell, Aeris placed herself in the same position. It was actually an instinctual response, for she vaguely remembered doing the same when she and Jaxom fell from the cliffs of the Larramis Peninsula, and again when they flew away from the Ansalarian mainland to come to Shayamalan.

Jaxom didn't hesitate as he leaped from the cliff. She held her breath until they reached the updraft, and only when they were stable did she chance breathing out. Aeris struggled to endure the pain between her legs. She could feel the cracked, sore-ridden skin separating under the pressure, and she felt tears squeeze from tightly closed eyelids. Yet she fought against her weakness, refocusing on the task at hand. <How did I do?> she brought herself to ask.

Jaxom rumbled in reply, his equivalent of a laugh. <I suppose we need to work on it.>

Aeris slumped dejectedly.

Sensing her disquiet, Jaxom quickly responded. <Aeris, you can't expect to get everything perfectly the first time. We are here to learn, so let's do it.>

Aeris took a deep breath. <I know. But I had rather hoped I wasn't *that* bad.>

Jaxom smiled through their link and continued his glide. <You aren't all 'that bad'. You are just inexperienced. We will learn this together, all right?>

Aeris finally nodded. <Fine. I suppose we should return to the class now.>

Jaxom hesitated. <You think we should?>

Aeris frowned at his facetiousness. <Of course.>

<But wouldn't you prefer to fly away from here, leave without a second thought to duty?>

Aeris frowned. <Of course I would. But you brought me here, Jaxom. There must have been a reason.>

Through their link, she could sense his pensiveness. <Indeed.>

✡ ✡ ✡ ✡ ✡

Jonesy slowly walked down the length of the corridor, one hand splayed upon the cold stone of the nearest wall. In the other hand she carried a small lantern whose light shuddered as she moved. She concentrated on placing one pale, bare foot in front of the other, struggling to maintain the strength to stay upright. It was the third time she had ventured forth from her chamber, and this time she hoped she would get a bit farther in her wanderings before Seth recovered her. The first two times he had found her, he admonished her gently for leaving her sanctuary and then carried her back to the chamber. Once there, he followed her down as he lay her on the bed, bringing her to ecstasy before leaving her to slumber. Even now she could feel his hands on her body, his lips on hers, and then the sensation of pain as she was swept away in a wave of rapture.

And after each encounter, she could feel herself becoming weaker.

Jonesy stopped as she approached another chamber. The door was slightly ajar. With a tentative hand, she pushed it inward and entered the chamber. Just like everything else she had seen in the place, it was old and very poorly maintained. However, what drew her was the looking glass that dominated the center of the room. She slowly walked to it, and once close, she circled around to its front.

The image that met her eyes was astonishing. Her face had become woefully gaunt, and her flesh was so pale she looked like she could be dead. The area around her green eyes appeared bruised and the rims of her eyelids were red. She was attired in a long, black gown with a neckline that plunged between her breasts to end just above her navel. Around her waist was a tightly tucked silvery sash that glittered within whatever light was given off by the lantern she carried.

Jonesy stepped closer to the looking glass. The image within was frightening. *What has happened to make me this way, so thin and pale I can barely recognize myself?* In spite of their unusual brightness, only the color of her eyes revealed the truth of her identity, and perhaps the auburn color of her hair, which cascaded over one shoulder. It was then she saw it, a blemish on her neck almost hidden by her hair. She stepped closer to the glass and pulled the hair aside to reveal two round sores separated by approximately half a finger's length. They were rimmed with red and oozed a blood-tinged clear fluid. She raised a hand and softly touched the wounds with her fingertips. She vaguely remembered discovering them the first time she awakened, however long ago that may have been. *Why haven't these wounds been tended?*

Jonesy frowned. Seth had said that her friends were safe somewhere in the castle. Why hadn't she been taken to them, or they to her? She had met several of the castle's other inhabitants, men and women who all possessed an unusual beauty that penetrated the soul. However, her chamber seemed to be situated in an area far removed from theirs. Why did Seth wish for her to remain so isolated, taking her meals alone, or only within his presence? Regardless, she'd barely taken any sustenance at all since coming to the castle, and it was comprised only of undercooked red meat followed by a goblet of wine.

"What are you doing here?"

Jumping at the sound of the deep voice, Jonesy swung around to face the entryway. Yet, when she raised her lantern and saw Cortes standing there within the dim wavering light, she couldn't help but feel relief. Finally she would be able to see her comrades.

"Oh, Cortes, I am so glad to see you!" Jonesy smiled happily and stepped away from the glass. "Where is everyone? I was beginning to wonder if you all were really here."

Cortes remained impassive. "Jonesy, does Seth know you are here?"

Jonesy frowned slightly and shook her head. "Cortes, what's wrong? Where is Cervantes? Is everyone all right? What happened after the attack?"

Cortes regarded her intently from eyes devoid of emotion for a moment before he replied. "You shouldn't be here."

Jonesy shook her head, a familiar sensation of weakness stealing over her. "Cortes, wha . . . what's going on? Where is everyone?"

"My dear? My dear Joneselia?"

She heard his voice before he appeared around the corner. Seth swept into the chamber and took her by the elbow. "My dear, I have been worried. I insisted you mustn't stray far from your chamber. You simply aren't well enough!"

Jonesy put a hand to her forehead when she felt the room begin to spin, and her knees suddenly buckled. She collapsed into Seth's arms and he effortlessly picked her up. Wrapping her arms around his neck, she struggled to recall what she had been thinking about before Seth found her. Oh yes, her companions. Were they really there somewhere with her in the castle?

Before she realized it, they were back in her chamber. Her awareness had dimmed, and she vaguely felt herself being placed on the bed. Then she was aware of Seth hovering above her, his eyes raking over her lustily. She thought of her companions again and how much she missed them despite their shortcomings. As Seth hungrily brought his mouth to cover hers, she once more experienced the ecstasy only he could bring. She felt weak, ever so weak, and Jonesy realized she was dying.

As always, Jonesy succumbed to the sensation his lips brought, and her mind spiraled away. Yet the thought remained . . . *it's only a matter of time before all life leaves my body and I will be nothing but an empty shell.*

Cervantes awoke with pain at his neck. He grimaced as he sat upright, holding a hand over the affected area. He groaned when a spinning sensation overtook him, but he breathed through it. When it finally ceased, he opened his eyes to find himself in a shadowed chamber. He immediately felt an overwhelming weakness, but wondered about it only for a moment before swinging his legs over the side of the raised bedpallet and taking a look around the room.

The area was lit only by the light of torches set within two sconces, one on the wall at the entry and the other along the opposite wall. The coarse, gray stone seemed to absorb much of the light, and it took a while for his eyes to adjust to the darkness. Beneath his bare feet he could feel the thick weave of a floor rug, and he wondered where his boots might be. Glancing down at himself, Cervantes realized he wore only his trousers. His tunic and vest had been removed, along with his belt, stockings, and outer footwear. And then there was this sore on his neck, one that oozed something sticky he assumed might be blood.

Cervantes rose from the pallet. He remembered leaving the group behind, angry that they were moving too slowly. He also vaguely remembered approaching a castle. He could only assume he was behind those walls. His mind had a difficult time recalling the rest, for he had no memory of how he arrived within the chamber. However, if he was truly in the castle, he must have somehow been taken by the enemy. And of course he could never forget the reasons why he had chosen to break away from the others and proceed alone . . . *Cortes and Jonesy.*

Cervantes wavered on his feet for a moment before they carried him across the room. He shivered involuntarily a few moments later when his feet stepped onto cold stone. Coupled with the cool air on his bare chest, Cervantes became chilled and he abruptly found himself on a mission to find his clothing. It didn't take him long to find a chest at the far side of the room. Covered by shadows, he hesitated to open it, leery of what might lie inside. Unfastening the latch, Cervantes slowly lifted the top. He was relieved to find only some old clothing inside. He rummaged through it hoping to find something he might be able to wear, and he came across a black padded silk vest. It smelled a little stale, but he donned it anyway. The smell of mustiness was better than the chill he felt. He then took the time to look through the remaining items and found a pair of black leather trousers. At first they seemed a bit slim, but he thought they just might fit, albeit tightly. Cervantes quickly slipped out of his old trousers and donned the new. Much to his surprise, they hung loosely about his waist and he realized he must have lost some weight over the past few weeks. He donned his belt and grieved over the loss of the weapons and other accessories that customarily garnished it. He supposed he would simply have to find others. And then there was the issue of adequate footwear.

Cervantes knelt to shut the chest and decided to lean on it for a moment. He didn't understand why, but he felt strangely fatigued. He suspected that something must have been done to him; he just didn't know what it was. Shaking his head determinedly, he rose from the chest and made his way to the thick wooden door at the front of the room. Once reaching it, Cervantes placed his ear against it. A few moments later, after hearing nothing, he slowly pushed the door open.

Cervantes found himself in a dark empty hallway. He looked it up and down before making the decision to turn right. In his mind he began a mental map, and if the passageways didn't become too terribly complex, he would be able to find his way back to the chamber. As he walked, he passed a few torches set within wall brackets like the ones in the chamber. They were old and tarnished, with years of dust and spiderwebs adorning them. Other than the torches, the walls were rather stark. There were no tapestries or paintings, and the floors were similarly bare of rugs or other coverings. Cervantes glanced into the rooms he passed on his way down the corridor and found them all empty. He counted several before he came to the end of the hallway. There was a large set of doors to his left, and just like before, he placed an ear to the wood.

Cervantes strained to hear anything that might lie beyond. Not for the first time, he envied the faelin, halfen and oroc races of their enhanced auditory capability with the ability to perceive things that any human could not. Hearing nothing, Cervantes slowly pushed at the heavy door. The squealing sound of rusting hinges pierced the silence and he cringed. *Damn! I should have known that would happen. This place is old and has fallen into disrepair. It's obvious the inhabitants have little care for the area in which they have made their residence. That is, of course, if this is truly the lair of the vampyr TC spoke so certainly about.*

Cervantes slipped hesitantly into the corridor beyond the door. He looked around and saw that it led into a large chamber. Pressing himself close to the wall, he walked slowly the length of the passage. Then, once reaching the arched entry, he peered within.

Contrary to what he had seen of the castle thus far, this chamber was well maintained. Even though both walls and floor remained unembellished, the hearth contained a happy fire. There were three lounge tables that dominated the room, and situated around them were several sofas. Also scattered about were floor braziers, a couple of which also contained fires. However, the chamber was empty of any humanoid inhabitants.

Cervantes strode quickly through the room towards another set of doors located at the opposite wall. Once reaching them, he saw that one was slightly ajar, and beyond it he could hear the sound of someone speaking. He stopped at the doors and leaned towards the narrow opening. Much to his excitement, they were speaking in common. In spite of the strange accent they used he could understand everything being said.

"Seth, please remember that we await the arrival of Chorlak. He wishes for the girl to remain pure so that he may bring her before Razlul. I know that you want her, but he will kill you if you take her innocence."

The speaker was a woman and her voice was pleading. It was easy for him to determine that it was Jonesy who was the focus of their conversation.

"Yes, but you know it is difficult for me to restrain myself. You know how much I want her."

Cervantes frowned. By the gods, this daemon thought to take Jonesy against her will, for he could see no possibility that she would accede to any union with him. Daemons were horrific beings, ugly beyond most peoples' worst nightmares. Only dopplegangers were tolerable, for they tended to take the form of any human, faelin, or halfen they chose. He chanced a peek into the room, and when he saw the two individuals within, he recanted his earlier musing. It would be easy for Jonesy to give in. Both the man and the woman were beautiful to behold, with light blond hair and flawless pale complexions. The man wore black leather trousers and a vest, while the woman wore a long form-fitting black gown that trailed along the floor behind her. *And she seemed so familiar.*

The woman put a hand on the man's arm, responding in a soothing tone. "I know, I know. But there will be others."

The man shook his head. "No, Tarianska! Not like her!" he responded emphatically. "There is something about her that stirs me. I don't know if it is her lineage, the taste of her blood, or the fact that someone as powerful as Razlul wishes her in his possession." He paused and then continued in a deepening voice. "All I know is that I *want* her!"

Cervantes could hear the inflection in the man's voice and see the intensity in his cerulean eyes even from his position at the door. Damn, this daemon might just give in to his temptation, despite the probability of death. He had to find Jonesy, and fast. But then there was Cortes. Where could his brother possibly be?

Cervantes shook his head and silently pulled away from the opening. He turned to make his way back through the chamber, only to find himself face to face with the man about whom he'd just been thinking.

His eyes widened with joy. "By the gods, Cortes! I am so glad you are well!" Cervantes whispered exuberantly. "Where have they been keeping you? Have you seen Jonesy?" Cervantes stepped up to the man and put his arms around him in a hearty embrace. Cortes remained stiff in his arms, and when Cervantes finally stepped back, the man simply regarded him without emotion. Cervantes frowned slightly and suddenly recalled what TC told him—that Cortes was gone, and had been for a while. Back then, Cervantes didn't want to believe it, and had even called TC a fraud.

Cervantes slowly shook his head. No, this couldn't be happening.

Noticing the shift in his demeanor, the imposter chose that moment to move. With a closed fist, the daemon struck Cervantes across his face. He reeled back with the impact, his body hitting the door at which he'd been eavesdropping only moments before. He shook his head, hoping to get himself to see straight again. Cortes had quickly cocked his fist back again and was about to strike, when a beautiful woman appeared behind him. With a gentle touch she stilled the daemon's hand, and with barely a nod, he stepped away, melting back into the shadows. Cervantes didn't move, captivated by her cerulean eyes.

✷ ✷ ✷ ✷ ✷

Aeris was sore when she returned to the barracks later that day. She knew she was supposed to attend another lesson after the riding instruction, but she just couldn't bring herself to do it. She was so terribly tired, and she wondered how much of that fatigue was transmitted to her from Jaxom. However, she didn't really care. Hells, she'd barely recovered from the loss of her pregnancy before their trek to Shayamalan. She deserved some rest, even if it was a bit short lived. Choosing to remain nearby, Jaxom settled himself atop the farthest portion of the ridge, giving other dragons just enough space to land and drop off their 'mates. Aeris was touched by his loyalty, and as she drifted off to sleep, she maintained a tight mental link.

Even so, Aeris easily awakened when early evening arrived. Jaxom vacated the ledge as more and more dragons approached, bidding her farewell as he left. Aeris slowly rose from her pallet and was overcome with nausea. She could barely lower her trousers and hissed to herself when she saw the damage to her legs. Indeed, the skin had broken during their training, and while she slept the wounds oozed, making the fabric of her trousers adhere to the angry flesh. She was surprised that Jaxom hadn't noticed the depth of her discomfort, but she was certain it was a reflection of precisely how exhausted he was.

Aeris gently eased the trousers back up. She knew she needed to tend the wounds, but now wasn't the time. She felt somewhat chilled and her skin was damp. She attested it to lack of sustenance, for she'd foregone the mid-day meal when she accompanied Jaxom back to the barracks for some much needed rest. She just needed to find the endurance needed to eat a meal and then take care of other matters.

Aeris didn't realize Faleema's approach until the savanlean was standing before her. The woman nodded a stoic greeting as she seated herself at the side of the bed-pallet. Aeris regarded her for a moment before following suit, wincing slightly at the movement. She picked up a nearby comb and took it through her hair. Yet, when Faleema didn't speak right away, Aeris ceased the activity and gave Faleema her undivided attention.

"Demeter Kordrian noticed your absence today," she stated.

Aeris sat there for a moment, her face impassive, waiting for Faleema to elaborate.

The other woman regarded her with a worried expression. "He was quite perturbed, making the comment that you had attended the riding session, but didn't bother with the dragon anatomy and physiology instruction that went with it. He said you had already earned your score in his evaluation book."

Aeris continued to sit there, digesting this bit of information. *Kordrian.* Yes, he was the very same master who oversaw her testing barely two days before. He had seemed a bit hard on her then, and now, after hearing what Faleema had to say, it seemed that those thoughts were well grounded. *Damn. It's so hard to believe I already have an instructor who dislikes me.*

Aeris shrugged and shook her head. "I was much too tired to attend. I have yet to find the opportunity to rest since I've been here. Jaxom is even more exhausted. I know the class is mine to attend, but I just couldn't do it. Jaxom's fatigue weighed on me just as much as my own. I haven't come far enough to know how to control the intricacies of our *bond*, how to keep his feelings and emotions separate from mine."

Faleema reached out a hand and placed it on Aeris' knee. She jumped slightly with the contact, but Faleema didn't seem to notice. "I know. But I just wanted you to be aware of what you're up against."

Aeris placed her hand atop that of her new friend. "Thank you."

Faleema stood. "Give me a chance to get some clean clothes on and I will accompany you to the Pits."

Aeris gave her a small smile. "I'll be here."

Faleema's pale brows drew together into a frown. "Are you all right? You look a bit pale."

Aeris widened her smile and nodded. Faleema hesitantly returned the gesture and walked away. Aeris turned back to her comb and stared at it vaguely for a moment. Damnation, she felt so tired even though she'd just rested. She put the back of her hand to her forehead and closed her eyes. She felt as though she could collapse at any moment, and her stomach churned. She really didn't feel hungry, and the thought of food made her feel sick. Yet, she was convinced it was the root of her problems. Through their link, Aeris could sense that her bondmate slept. It was a good thing, for she had begun to wonder if he would be able to maintain the strain of such fatigue. Of course, he would try to down-play it with her. But she always knew, much as he seemed to know certain things about her.

Aeris found the energy to finish combing her wild hair. By the time she was finished, Faleema had made her way back over. Aeris took in her friend's hastily dressed person, but before she could comment, Faleema spoke. "I would have spent more time, but I am so hungry I could eat Miramanth."

The statement was meant to be a joke, and Aeris took it as such. Thulnar had explained to her that Faleema sometimes tended to say the wrong things without meaning to, making people feel the need to stay away. Aeris simply accepted this foible about her new comrade, and kept it in mind whenever Faleema happened to say something off-color.

Aeris chuckled. "I am sure that Mira appreciates your sentiment."

Faleema was quiet for a moment, lowering her eyes to the ground. "Oh, I did it again. I said something to which someone could take offense."

Aeris smiled. "Yes, but it doesn't really matter what those people think . . . only what Mira thinks."

Faleema grinned in return. "Oh, she doesn't mind. She knows what I meant." Her gaze became suddenly intent. "And I appreciate you taking the time to understand me too."

Aeris shook her head. "It was Thulnar's doing. He explained you to me."

"Yes, but you chose to stick around after his explanation," she pointed out.

Aeris nodded. "Indeed, I did. But I have found that is my pleasure."

Faleema narrowed her eyes. "How can you know that after having only met me three days ago?"

Aeris shrugged. "I just know."

Faleema's lips pulled up into a smile and her eyes seemed to sparkle. "Jaxom was right to choose you. You are something special."

Aeris shook her head. "I'm not quite so sure about that."

Faleema pointed at her. "You had best believe what I say. I will accept nothing less," she said with mock ferocity.

Aeris nodded solemnly. "All right, I believe you."

Faleema suddenly reached out and took her hand. "Come on. Let's get something to eat."

Aeris chuckled and slowly rose from the pallet. She was about to follow obediently behind when a sensation of weakness suddenly overcame her. The chamber spun and her legs fell out from under her. She heard Faleema call out in a distressed voice as she hit the floor. Everything shifted to darkness.

Ranaghar rose from between her legs, swiftly pulling his robes back into place. Her vision swam, and she groaned when she tried to lift her head from the floor. She'd hit it pretty hard when he threw her down. At least the rape didn't hurt the way it did at the beginning. Not only was she more accustomed to the harsh encounters, but Ranaghar had begun to restrain himself at bit more the past couple weeks. What made the situation difficult to bear this time was the presence of someone else in the chamber. It was even worse that the person happened to be her friend, Talemar Coabra.

Aeris heard Ranaghar speaking, but couldn't quite make out the words in her jumbled mind. She then felt the shift of energy indicative of a spell being cast, followed by the sound of something hitting the wall. She imagined what it might be, and more tears trickled down her temples to join the others that had been shed while Ranaghar violated her. Then he was standing over her, taking a handful of her hair, and pulling her up from the floor. She struggled to rise and felt many of the hairs separate from her scalp. She didn't make a sound, for the pain was small compared to what she had experienced the past several weeks behind the dark walls of Tholana's stronghold.

Ranaghar dragged her to the bed. He followed her down when he cast her onto the pallet, taking her jaw in a viselike grip. "I have decided to make your mage friend suffer a little longer. After the dungeon-keepers are through with him, and after he spends a few days alone in absolute darkness, we will see if he has kept his sanity. I am tempted to kill him myself, but I shall refrain. This will be so much better, and it will prolong your suffering while you hope he will somehow live through the experience." Ranaghar grinned maliciously. "By the expression on his face, I could tell he'd had you before. He hates that you are now mine to control, my whore to take whenever I please. This knowledge will only torment him all the more during the time he rots in the dungeons."

Aeris lay there on the bed after Ranaghar left. She heard activity on the other side of the chamber and knew they had come to take Talemar away. She continued to lie there even longer afterward. She trembled not only with the pervasive chill in the air, but the anger she felt deep inside. Hardly anyone was spared that tumultuous emotion. Of course, first and foremost she hated

Tallachienan. Not only had he hidden the truth of his identity from her, but he had stolen her memories. Next was Cervantes because he was the one who had started the tavern brawl. She hated Alasdair and Talemar for leaving her in the care of the one they called Magnus; then there was Tigerius for not taking her away from the situation at the earliest opportunity, Goldare and the halfen brothers for following their leader so thoughtlessly, and Jaxom for keeping her so far away from him. Finally there was Mateo. Without him, she never would have journeyed to Xordrel. Cortes she hated for his affiliation with Cervantes, and with Jezibel and Dramid it was the same. The only ones exempt were Jonesy, Cedric and Levander.

Aeris placed a hand over her belly. There was a child resting within, and she liked to think that she hated it as well. Talemar had refuted her on that, telling her that it was a part of her, and that she would come to love it.

CHAPTER FOUR

Once again, Cervantes awoke with pain at his neck. His head swam as he sat upright on the bed, and he struggled to recall how he'd gotten there. Oh yes, he had been discovered lurking about the corridors as he searched for Jonesy. Lucky for him, he retained some memory of the map he'd laid out in his mind. However, he knew that it would be short lived. He could feel the weakness of his body, and with it would come memory loss. He knew he had to get the image in his mind down on parchment as quickly as possible. Only, he had no idea where he would obtain either the parchment or the stylus and ink he would need in order to accomplish such an endeavor.

Cervantes held his head in his hands for a few moments. His skull ached abominably, so much that his eyes hurt when he looked around the chamber. He remembered turning away from the conversation he witnessed between a man called Seth and a woman whose name had been very unfamiliar, for he'd never heard the likes of it ever before. It was a conversation that had made him realize how quickly he would need to find Jonesy in order to save her from a terrible fate, either by the hands of Seth, or another daemon they called Chorlak. He'd turned around only to come face to face with the other person about whom he had been thinking—his brother Cortes. *A man who wasn't truly his brother at all.*

Cervantes slowly rose from the bed. He frowned when he suddenly made the realization he was naked. The chilly air made goose-pimples rise over the entirety of his body, and he looked quickly around for his clothes despite the pain pounding in his skull. He found them scattered about on the floor. It appeared that they had been tossed there haphazardly, as though he had no care as to where they fell. He searched through his memories, hoping to find something that would tell him what happened after 'Cortes' found him lurking at the doorway.

Cervantes slowly collected his underpants, trousers, and vest. He then took the clothing back to the bed where he summarily lay down with them, strangely fatigued after his brief activity. He didn't know how long he rested there before the chill in the air stirred him once more. The headache had receded a bit, and he donned his clothing without too much of the pounding he was experiencing before.

He was surprised the daemons had returned him to the confines of the same chamber in which he'd first awakened. He supposed it was because they didn't know the extent of his abilities. Obviously 'Cortes' didn't know either; otherwise, he would have divulged that important piece of information. It told Cervantes that TC had been right all along; his brother was gone. All that remained was the impostor that had taken over the identity of the only family he had left in the world.

Ballocks. He'd thought he lost everything after the theft of the *Sea Maiden*. He'd been wrong. *Now* he had nothing.

Cervantes finished putting on the clothes, wincing with the friction the vest imposed on the myriad scratches that dominated his back. He now recalled what happened after 'Cortes' left, and the emotions the memories evoked were very mixed indeed. It was the woman who'd brought him back to the chamber. And not far behind her there were others.

Cervantes hated to admit it, but he was relatively certain that there were events that took place, events he would never reveal to anyone. Yet, he had never before experienced such sexual intensity, and he knew he never would again. Perhaps it was just as well, for it was not meant for the realm of reality from which he came.

Cervantes stood and made his way across the chamber to the closed door. He was determined to find Jonesy, for she was in grave danger. He hated to think that she had already been taken, that Seth had diminished her by stealing her purity. Cervantes had little care for his own denigration, for his innocence had been lost long ago, seemingly in another life. All that mattered now was the young woman whom he had met aboard his own ship many moon cycles ago.

Despite the weakness of his body, Cervantes sprinted down the corridor. He remembered where to go, quickly bypassing the places he had investigated the time before. He made sure to keep all his senses on the alert, focusing on the task of finding Jonesy and keeping himself safe at the same time. Once reaching the chamber door through which he had passed when he had overheard the conversation between the two vampyr, Cervantes began to slow his pace. For the second time he unhesitatingly opened the door, but this time he was prepared for the loud sound the hinges would make. He could only hope that no one waited within the chamber at the end of the short passage beyond.

Continuing to stay vigilant, Cervantes moved stealthily in the shadows as he approached the chamber. Once reaching the archway, he swept his gaze across the room and seeing no one there, he rushed through it to the door at the other side. This time it was closed as opposed to being partly open when he approached it last. He pulled slowly on the handle, and when it opened without a sound, he breathed a sigh of relief. Glancing inside, he was equally as relieved to find no one there. He quickly moved across the chamber to yet another door situated at the far side. Once again, he opened it without hesitation. He knew he was tempting Fate, but time was no longer on his side. He had to find Jonesy as quickly as possible and then find a way out of the castle.

Hells, that was a lofty goal.

Cervantes once more found himself standing in a dark corridor. Lucky for him, it was empty. He could scarcely believe the good fortune he'd endured so far, and he only hoped it would continue. He passed quickly down the hallway, stopping at each of the chambers he found along the way. All of them were empty until he came to the one near the end—where the passage made a turn to the right and ended at a staircase leading downward.

Just as he had with many of the other chambers, he placed his hand on the door handle and slowly pushed inwards, hoping that a daemon wouldn't be awaiting him on the other side. However, unlike the others, this chamber was occupied. It was dimly lit by fires contained within lanterns hanging on hooks protruding from the far wall. The place was minimally furnished, but there was a bed located at the center of the adjacent wall to the right. Lying there was a woman.

Cervantes felt his eyes widen as he moved into the chamber. She wore a long, sleeveless, black silk gown that accentuated her light skin tone. Long chestnut hair framed her beautiful face where her head lay on a pillow. Her eyes were closed and dark lashes made a smudge below them, enhanced by the paleness of her flesh. Besides her brows and lashes, her rosy lips brought the only other color to her face. A sudden flood of desire rushed through him, for he was looking upon the most beautiful woman on all of Shandahar.

And the reason he knew was because he had seen the heart of the person that lay within Joneselia Mondemer.

Cervantes found himself pausing halfway across the room. He saw how thin she was beneath the gown, and her face was no longer rounded with healthy youthfulness. His desire became suddenly tempered by the realization she had been too long in this place where nourishment was little and far between, and where the inhabitants fed from the blood of their victims.

It was a small detail he happened to recall from his encounter the evening before.

Swallowing the sudden lump in his throat, Cervantes was about to continue his approach when Jonesy slowly blinked open her eyes. His heart almost stilled in his chest. Images of the past several moon cycles swept through his mind: the time when he first met her as she stood next to Aeris above-deck on the *Sea Maiden*, the times he saw her looking over the ship's railing at the sea and noticing how contented she seemed to be, the time he cajoled her into learning the cutlass, and then when he witnessed another man trying to seduce her one evening in the Twisted Tankard Tavern in Gulshaan. He recalled when he spent the night with her at a local festival in the town of Shilitoh, and then a couple fortnights later when he realized she was becoming ever more proficient with the cutlass. The hazel-green eyes stared at him for a moment, and then he saw a smile begin to steal across her lovely face.

Something suddenly slammed into his consciousness, and Cervantes was finally awakened. His walls came crumbling down, and he realized he had already let her in—a risk he had taken long ago when he'd taken pity on the girl who seemed to have everything except a salable skill and decided to teach her how to wield corsair's blade.

Back then he hadn't known any better. But now he knew she would be his saving grace.

Jonesy slowly awoke, opening her eyes to see the image of Cervantes standing across the room. By the gods, he was just as handsome as she remembered! She felt the corners of her mouth pull up into a smile, and when his image proceeded towards her, she felt suddenly overwhelmed. She must still be dreaming, for she had already given up hope that her comrades were there with her in the castle. And to see Cervantes, the only man for whom she ever longed, standing there before her, was something born only of a dreamspun reverie.

But then she felt him touch her.

The gentle caress of Cervantes' fingertips alongside her face bade Jonesy bring herself upright in the bed. She still felt as though she lived in a dream, for Seth had weakened her so profoundly. Yet it felt so real, and she couldn't help but respond.

"Cervantes?" She said his name in barely a whisper.

Saying nothing in reply, he seated himself next to her, his fingertips moving from the side of her face to her lips. She saw his gaze focus there, and she felt a tightening low in her pelvis. Her mind resisted, beginning to disbelieve in the vision and the tactile sensations it evoked.

Jonesy swiftly pulled back. Cervantes' hand fell away as she scrambled to the other side of the bed. Yet, once her feet were on the floor and her legs supporting her upright, she was overwhelmed by her weakness. Jonesy felt her world begin to spin, and just as she was about to fall, she found herself being held in a strong embrace.

Jonesy exhaled, and a moment later, breathed in again. She looked up to find that it was Cervantes who had stopped her fall. The breath caught in her throat. She could see the unveiled desire in his blue eyes, and she felt an answer deep inside. She resisted only a moment before succumbing to it. She allowed herself to melt into him, the length of her body pressing against him. She could feel his chest rise and fall with the breaths he took, accompanied by the beat of his heart against her palm. It was then she thought that he just might be *real*.

"Jonesy, I have come to take you out of here."

KAYLA WOODSIDE

She tentatively placed her fingertips against the side of his face, just to be certain he was really there. He closed his eyes for a moment and then opened them again, reflecting a conflict about which she could only wonder. His face moved ever closer to hers, and she could feel his breath against her cheek. And when she finally allowed her own eyes to close, she felt the gentle pressure of his lips against hers.

Jonesy deepened the kiss, and Cervantes responded in kind. He wrapped his arms around her to encompass her sides, and then ran his hands up the length of her back only to come back down to cup the rounded shape of her buttocks. He swept his mouth down her neck and to her chest where he sucked at the tender skin above her breast, the sensation it evoked making her arch into him. They were about to fall onto the bed, when Cervantes tore his mouth away from her.

"Jonesy, we need to leave now if we want to live," he said breathlessly.

She suddenly became still. In her mind she had not yet resolved the fact that he was a reality. Jonesy struggled with the concept and then spoke in a whispered tone. "Please, I need to know that you are really here."

Cervantes heard the suffering in her voice—her need for affirmation. He pulled her hips against his body, pushing into her so that she would sense the unmistakable feel of him pressed against her. He felt her swift intake of breath, and he might have grinned if the situation had not been so precarious. Instead, he took her face into both his hands and roughly pressed his lips once more onto hers; again proving to Jonesy that he was her reality. He felt her body shudder against him and suddenly felt the wetness of her tears beneath his palms. Cervantes softened his kiss, and he swept a hand gently over her hair. She felt so small and frail within his arms, he was almost afraid she would break. She deserved a good cry, and he would be there to anchor her. He didn't begrudge her the luxury despite their time limitations.

Yet, he knew he would be a fool to allow it to continue for too long. After a few moments, he stepped back and looked into her eyes. "You need to come with me now. You are in grave danger, and I have come all this way to bring you out of here. Please . . ."

Jonesy nodded. Cervantes took her hand within his and as swiftly as possible led her out the door and into the corridor. Of course, Cervantes had no idea where to go, but down seemed like a good idea. They rushed through the remainder of the corridor to the left and then took the staircase to the floor below.

Cervantes' mind reeled with the reality in which he now found himself. He was weaponless, and he had no one there to back him up, for he had left his comrades behind to come after Jonesy and Cortes by himself. He supposed he must have been relying on his brother to be the one to stand by him as they made their way out of the daemon's lair. But Cortes was dead, and Jonesy was more a liability than a help. However, she seemed to have at least been able to pull herself together for the interim, the possibility of escape fueling her efforts to keep up with him as they made their way through another hallway. He berated himself for not having foresight enough to ask TC how the monsters could be killed, so he was at an impasse there as well. In all, Cervantes was as ill prepared as he had ever been. And this was probably the most important heist of his entire life.

Cervantes and Jonesy made a turn to the right, and he immediately slowed their pace when he saw the arched entryway in the distance. He cautiously led them to it, certain that it was the way they needed to take to get out of the castle. There was a familiarity to it he could not describe, and so he could only follow his instincts. He looked back at the woman following close behind him, and he knew that every effort he had made thus far was well worth it. His eyes met hers, and for a moment they locked. He felt a stirring within him once again, and by the expression that flitted across Jonesy's face, he knew she felt it too. Knowing he could do nothing about the yearning, he simply grasped her hand more tightly in his and gave her a slight grin.

They continued towards the archway ahead, and Cervantes placed all of his senses on the alert. Seeing or hearing nothing amiss, he continued forward until they reached it. Once there, they looked through it to find a large atrium. It was easy to see that it was a frequently used common area, for the place seemed to have been revitalized in contrast with much of the remaining castle. It reminded him of the chamber upstairs which also seemed to be a place for persons to congregate. However, this chamber was much larger, sustaining at least three fire-places and several more tables, sofas, and floor braziers. Support pillars rose from the floor to meet the ceiling, and shelves lined much of the adjacent wall to their left. They were filled with multitudes of books and peculiar relics from gods only knew where.

Strangely, the place was empty.

Holding onto Jonesy's hand, Cervantes slowly entered the room. The fires set within the cauldron-like floor braziers cast eerie shadows around the place, and he couldn't help but think how odd it was that no one was there. It was then that the hairs on the back of his neck began to rise, and he suddenly knew they were being watched. Cervantes swiveled around just in time to meet his attacker, pushing Jonesy behind him so that he could take the brunt of the impact. Cervantes realized it was the daemon impersonating Cortes just as he was struck from the side. He stumbled back from the hit, and felt Jonesy fall away from him. Yet, he dared not take his eyes off of the impostor to see to her welfare, for he feared another attack like that one would ground him as well.

When Cortes struck Cervantes, Jonesy imagined she would hit the floor when she fell back. She awaited the impact, but it never came. Instead she felt a pair of arms catch her about the torso, arms that pulled her up and into a cradled position at his chest. Seth carried her away from the ensuing battle, one that she feared Cervantes would not be able to win. Cortes was a big man, and Cervantes had no weapon. How would he persevere against those odds?

However, she hadn't the opportunity to find out, for Seth hurriedly carried her from the atrium into another chamber that branched off it at a doorway that was situated along the adjacent wall to the right from which they initially entered. With growing alarm, her eyes widened when she saw a stone slab over which lay a white laced swath of fabric. Jonesy instinctively began to struggle within Seth's embrace, but he quickly subdued her with the strength of his arms alone. She fearfully wondered at that strength as she was settled onto the shrouded slab. Immediately Jonesy began to tremble as she felt the felt the chill of the stone, and she wished she had a cloak to pull around her.

Jonesy watched in silence as Seth moved around the chamber, first lighting more of the wall torches, followed by the candles situated around her. She sensed some sort of pattern about them, but she couldn't make it out within her current position. Once he was finished, she waited for Seth to speak to her, for she could feel a tension in the air that tended to be a predecessor to such an action.

"Chorlak is almost here. He is on a mission to collect you and then bring you to the one they call Razlul Daemonkeeper." Jonesy felt her heart freeze in her chest as Seth paused for a moment. Then he continued. "My job was to simply hold you here until he arrived, to keep you from those who would only find a means to take you farther away from him. But as it turns out, I would much rather have you to myself."

Jonesy swallowed convulsively past the dryness in her throat. She felt herself becoming faint, and her vision wavered in and out of focus. Where was the rest of the group? Why had Cervantes come for her alone? Effin Hells, Aeris would have come and taken her away from this damnable place by now. Well, at least she liked to think so.

"I have done quite a bit of research, and it seems I might have a chance. You see, the rock atop which you are sitting is an enchanted one, an artifact that grants the person who rests on it the ability to determine the outcome for a single event currently taking place. You, my dear, should find it easy to choose me as an alternative over the mehta of the daemundai, for he wants only to slay you for the same purpose as he did your sister."

Jonesy felt her breath catch in her throat. By the gods, she couldn't believe this was happening to her. Somehow she had been tracked across a vast swath of Ansalar, over mountains and across seas, just so that she could be placed in the same hands of the man who murdered and butchered her sister? It was more than insane.

Her thoughts were bathed in the sarcasm that infused her entire being. *Damn, when did I become so special?*

Seth turned to face her, his eyes gleaming in the flickering light. They were mesmerizing, and so deep that one could become lost within their cerulean depths. Moving faster than anything she had ever seen before, he was suddenly there beside her. He took her face tenderly in his hands and she felt a quickening in her chest that swept downward to settle low in her belly. He always had that effect on her.

"Having chosen me as an alternative to Chorlak, you will use the magic of the stone to alter the course of events to make it so that Chorlak will not take you away while keeping me alive at the same time." Seth then swept an arm to encompass the entirety of the chamber. "And you will have all of them to help you accomplish this feat."

From out of the shadows emerged at least twenty others. All appeared much like Seth, very attractive men and women with light complexions and hair so pale it was almost white. She watched as they congregated at the periphery of the candlelight. Almost immediately she became aware of an expectancy emanating from them, and her senses heightened in response to a feeling of impending danger.

"I have waited so long to have you, Joneselia." Seth lowered his mouth to hers and she was swept away in the power of his passion. It always ended the same—she would climax in a rush of pain and euphoria. Then she would sleep in blissful oblivion until next she awoke.

But not this time.

Seth ended the kiss and looked into her eyes. "I will consummate our union upon the stone, and then I will take you into *transition*. There are not many who are like you . . . rodanthe, those who have the ability to withstand the conversion you will undergo in order for you to become vampyr. It is something in your blood, and I felt it when I tasted you for the very first time. You have been profoundly difficult to resist, my dear."

Jonesy felt her eyes widen with shock. By the gods, he meant to make her into something like him, a daemon who lived off the blood of others.

And he would rape her to do it.

Jonesy surged up from the stone, suddenly desperate to flee. She felt Seth's hands circling her arms, and he pushed her back down. "Hush, don't be afraid. When I take your virginity, the pain will last only a moment . . . and you won't even feel me take you into *transition*. When you awaken, you will see the world from different eyes, and you will experience life as it was meant to be for someone like you."

Jonesy closed her eyes. There was no way she could even begin to stop him. He was much too strong for her, even in her normal state. Now she was even more powerless than usual. Jonesy felt herself slipping into grim acceptance when she suddenly felt it. It was power, a power she could feel emanating from the stone beneath her. She could feel it beckoning her to use it, and then she recalled Seth's words. *"The rock on which you are sitting is an enchanted one, an artifact that grants the person who rests on it the ability to determine the outcome for a single event currently taking place."*

Jonesy's mind reeled with the implication of those words. Seth didn't say it, but it meant that she could use the power of the stone to change other events taking place besides the one that involved Seth and Chorlak. It meant she could divert the *transition* she knew Seth would soon put her through. He must have assumed that she would not have access to the power of the stone until he was ready, perhaps with a particular incantation. And the only reason she knew that much about magical things was courtesy of Aeris, who was good enough to answer the questions of an interested friend.

Jonesy's attention was suddenly diverted from the power of the stone to focus once more on Seth. Once again his lips took hers and a surge of pleasure swept through her. She vaguely felt his hands tearing the lower portion of the gown apart and then moving over the flesh of her thighs. The other daemons surrounded them and watched, their pale blue eyes glittering eerily in the light cast by the candles. She felt herself beginning to succumb to him, just as she always had before. But somewhere in her mind, she knew that it must be different this time, and that she must focus on the power of the stone.

Jonesy struggled to disengage her mind from what was happening to her. It was all taking place so fast that she barely had the time to think about what she was doing. Once more she felt the power of the artifact beneath her, and she allowed herself to become immersed within it. The magic whispered to her of what she needed to do.

And then she remembered Cervantes.

Against terrible odds, the man was fighting against the daemon who had, most likely, murdered his brother. And the reason he was in such dire straits was because he had come there to save Jonesy from her own dreadful fate. Now more than ever she loved him, and she knew she couldn't let him lose his life in her stead. As she focused on her wish, Jonesy could only hope that Cervantes still lived.

Cervantes dodged yet another blow from the daemon that resembled Cortes, and then placed a nearby table between them. Even as children,

Cervantes had never been able to best Cortes at hand-to-hand combat. Already he sported bruises that would be with him for over a fortnight, and his forehead bled from a cut he had sustained from one of his many meetings with the floor. However, as of yet, the daemon had been unable to get a good grip on him, simply because Cervantes was a bit faster. However, he was quickly beginning to tire.

Cervantes grabbed the nearest object at hand and slung it towards his attacker. The candlestick struck the impostor squarely alongside his head, immediately resulting in the rivulet of blood that began to flow from the resulting wound. The daemon growled and then swiftly flung the table out of his way. Cervantes quickly backed away, his mind desperately looking for anything he might be able to use against his opponent.

It was then that he noticed it, a cutlass strung from the impostor's sash. He supposed he hadn't noticed it before simply because he had rarely seen Cortes without the blade. He would have noticed the absence of the weapon before the presence of it. Cervantes grinned inwardly, suddenly revitalized by the thought he might have a chance at victory. He hoped that the theft of identity didn't stop with just physical appearance. *Cortes had never been able to best him with the cutlass.*

Cervantes continued to move backwards, his mind thinking of a way to obtain the weapon. He supposed Tigerius might be more adept at this sort of thing, for the other man was the better thief. He thought it quite interesting that Tiger had come to mind, for the group had become so fractured. Actually, they were no longer a group at all, but simply a bunch of individuals moving along the same path.

His internal deliberations abruptly ended when he felt his back pressed against something, and glancing to the side, he saw that it was a bookcase. Noticing Cervantes' situation, the daemon took advantage and lunged for him. At that moment time seemed to slow down. Cervantes crouched to avoid the large hand going for his throat. Seeing his chance, he then reached out to grip the cutlass dangling from its sheath. He pulled the weapon free only to be caught by the daemon's other hand. Dangling from the fabric of his tunic, he was pulled up until he came face to face with the one that had stolen the face of his beloved brother.

Cervantes watched the dark brown eyes widen with shock when he embedded the blade into his opponent's unprotected abdomen. If he'd had a narrower blade, he may have even given it a savage twist. The hand released his tunic, and Cervantes felt the floor beneath his feet. He thought to pull the cutlass loose, but quickly realized he hadn't the physical space for such a maneuver. Instead, he moved as swiftly as he could to the right, just narrowly missing the hand that once more sought to detain him. Then, circling to the daemon's back, he delivered a side-kick with all of the strength he could muster.

The impostor fell forward against the bookcase. He scrambled desperately for the shelves, grabbing hold of books that subsequently slipped free of their comrades to tumble about his shoulders and back as he descended. As he tumbled to the floor, he voiced an agonized moan as the cutlass continued through his body to come out the center of his back.

The body quivered there for several moments before it was finally still. Cervantes then fell to his knees, suddenly overcome by a rush of exhaustion. By the gods, he couldn't believe he was still alive! His mind shifted to Jonesy. He turned to look around the chamber to find no one else there. His heart skipped a beat, and fear swept through him like a scythe. Cervantes immediately jumped to his feet. He called out, hoping that she might simply be hiding somewhere. When there was no response, his mind began to race. By the gods, where could she be? Or worse yet, who had taken her?

Cervantes swept a hand through his damp hair. He then proceeded to the body of the impostor and turned it over. He pulled the blade free, grimacing with the sickening sound it made, and used the fabric of the daemon's tunic to wipe away the dark blood. Weapon in hand, he then advanced towards the entry from which they arrived.

It was then he heard the scream.

Jonesy cried out when Seth placed a hand at her throat. The onlookers were rushing to the disturbance they heard just outside the far door, a disturbance that bespoke of intruders within the castle. Seth hissed and returned his gaze to her, his eyes shimmering brightly crimson. He had been close, so close. Even now she could feel the weight of his erect organ against her thigh. The disruption had come just in time, sparing her from the transgression she surely would have suffered.

Seth shook his head, his hand remaining to circle her throat. "It doesn't matter, my sweet. I will still have you."

Jonesy closed her eyes and turned her head away. It took some of the pressure off the airway, and she was able to breathe more easily. Tears streamed down the side of her face. There was nothing she could do, nothing *anyone* could do. She could feel Seth hovering above her once again when there came yet another disturbance. This time it was *inside* the room.

Jonesy opened her eyes to see Captain Cervantes standing at the doorway.

As always, he was the epitome of what she perceived as handsome. He was so debonair standing there, clad in black vest, trousers, and boots, cutlass brandished before him. Her heart skipped a beat. He had placed himself at risk to come for her, to rescue her from these monsters.

Cervantes proceeded into the chamber, swinging the cutlass in graceful arcs before him. Seth hissed once again, and before she knew it, he was leaping over her to meet his enemy. Jonesy slowly seated herself upright, suppressing a moan as the scenery began to swim before her eyes. She dropped her head into her hands and stayed there for a moment. She vaguely heard the sounds of the fight behind her, so much wanting to help Cervantes. Then, as some of her strength began to return to her, she rose from the stone. She leaned there for a moment and continued to collect herself, somehow finding the inner strength to recover from her ordeal. With a brief caress, Jonesy finally stepped away, instinctively knowing that without the stone's power, Cervantes wouldn't have survived to be there in the chamber with her now.

She briefly wondered if perhaps it had other powers as well.

Glancing around the room, Jonesy noticed very little that she could use to help Cervantes against an enemy that was too powerful for him to overcome alone. With rising trepidation, she saw Seth throw the captain against the nearest wall. These daemons seemed to have unusual strength, and she could only imagine what some of their other abilities might include. With her awareness returned, Jonesy was certain she had fallen prey to them many times during her tenure within the castle. With a shudder, she cast those thoughts away as she continued to try and find a way to help Cervantes.

It was then she saw it. It was a rock, one situated next to the large stone upon which she had been lying only moments before. Jonesy swiftly picked it up, and without even pausing to consider her next action, she cast it at Seth with all the force she could muster. Eyes widening with disbelief, she watched as it struck him on the head with a resounding thud, and he subsequently fell to the ground. Once again weaponless, Cervantes stood over the man for a moment, breathing heavily from his exertions. He then looked over at Jonesy.

She rushed over as he held out his hand. Without saying a word, they quickly departed the chamber in the direction from whence they had come. She felt a brief surge of sorrow when she saw the body of Cortes as they ran through the atrium to the door located at the opposite wall of the one they originally entered. The pair then found themselves once more within a corridor. Cervantes looked both up and down it before he made his choice. They continued to run for only a short while longer before they reached another chamber. It was wide and spacious, containing six massive pillars that reached high to the vaulted ceiling upon which hung several fancy chandeliers that had become dusty over decades without use. To the left there was a similarly dust-laden grand staircase that led down from the balcony on the second floor. It seemed that the place was more elaborate than Jonesy originally thought, and that it had once been the pride of a wealthy family long gone. At the far end of the room, they could see a pair of doors that looked as though they could be the main entryway into the castle. Cervantes led her towards them, hastening their pace. Then, just as they reached the doors, they heard a distinct howl . . . the song of a wemic on the hunt.

Instinctively she knew the voice belonged to Seth, coming to reclaim her.

Jonesy felt her breath catch in her throat as Cervantes pushed open one of the thick, wooden doors. He pulled her out of the castle and into the chilly air, moving towards the forest trees waiting not far beyond. It was dark, but not overly so, for a full Steralion was beginning her descent while a crescent Hestim was just making her emergence. In spite of the pursuit, Jonesy felt suddenly liberated, and her heart lifted. She was abruptly very aware of her hand held within Cervantes' larger one, and a tingling sensation swept through her.

Without the support of a company he had come for her. Like a lover, he had braved certain peril and then placed his life before hers. If Cervantes hadn't arrived when he did, it would have been much too late.

Within moments they entered the sanctuary of the wood, involuntarily slowing as they were forced to concentrate on the trees that suddenly appeared ahead, as well as the low-lying brush that tended to catch them unawares. Jonesy tripped over some exposed tree roots, and before she could fall, Cervantes caught her about the waist and brought her close to his side. Once again they heard a distinct howl, and Jonesy pressed herself more closely against him. He looked down at her and she could see something reflected in his eyes. She felt an answer stir deep within, and again she felt a tingling sweep through her.

Still without speaking, they began to run. It seemed that verbal communication had become unnecessary for the time being. Tree branches reached out to scrape their bare arms, and the underlying brush hid stones and thorns upon which her naked feet trod. Both of them withheld loathsome epithets that wanted to make themselves heard, instead focusing their energies on the path they made through the wood. There was a tension that had begun to build between them, one that each found exceedingly more difficult to deny.

Just as Jonesy found herself beginning to tire, they were no longer surrounded by only the trees. Slowing their pace, they saw the tall statue of a scantily clad woman ahead. As Cervantes and Jonesy neared it, they noticed that the statue was surrounded by stonework that had once represented a sizable fountain. Glancing around, they also saw other statues hidden here and there among the myriad vines and other shrubbery that had overrun the place. It was then Jonesy realized they stood within a long-forgotten garden, one that must have once been part of the grounds surrounding the castle from which they had just escaped. It was sad to realize the place had fallen into such disrepair, and she began to wonder exactly what had happened to the people who once lived there.

As Jonesy regained her strength, they slowly wound their way around the dilapidated fountain. Cervantes seemed to know that she needed the time to recoup, and she appreciated his efforts. It was so different from the man she remembered aboard the *Sea Maiden*, a man who seemed to care largely only for himself, his ship, and his crew. It was understandable at the time, she supposed, for he had no one to anchor him except perhaps Cortes and Jezibel.

Jezibel. Somehow, the other woman had never been able to tame the captain.

Jonesy felt her belly clench spasmodically when Cervantes glanced back at her and smiled before returning his focus ahead of them. With that look alone, Jonesy suddenly felt her senses explode to life. She didn't understand what was wrong with her, for she had never been so sexually driven before. Perhaps it was simply her joy to see Cervantes, coupled with the tender expression she saw on his handsome face. But then again, maybe it was more than that. Perhaps it had something to do with the conditioning Seth had put her through prior to her escape—conditioning he had used to weaken her and make it easier to subdue her during whatever this *transition* was that he'd been speaking about.

However, it simply didn't matter now. Jonesy felt a rush sweep through her, and she spoke into the pervading silence, her whispered voice sounding strange to her ears. "Captain Cervantes?"

He heard her and turned around once more. She saw the slight frown that crossed his face, for titles had ceased to exist between them long ago. He stopped walking and she closed the short distance that remained between them, keeping her hand enclosed within his.

"How did you find me?"

His eyes met and locked with hers, and she could see the raw emotion that simmered just below their blue depths. "I don't know," he replied in a low voice.

Jonesy blinked and tore her gaze away from his. It wasn't the answer she was expecting. Actually, she didn't know what she'd been expecting, just that this wasn't it. She then heard him continue.

"All I know is that I was somehow drawn to you. Since the moment I became aware of your absence . . ." His voice trailed away.

She took a deep breath and looked back up at him. "Cervantes, there is something that I . . ."

Without hesitating to hear what she might have to say, Cervantes pulled her close. Jonesy's heart stuttered in her chest as he wrapped his arms around her, and before she could form coherent thought, his lips were covering hers. His kiss was more than she ever imagined it would be, full of the same passion she felt deep inside herself. Suddenly it was set free and she returned his ardor without inhibition. They tumbled down onto the cushion offered by the leaves covering the forest floor, surrounded by the ancient echoes of a garden that had witnessed other such unions very long ago.

Tallachienan heard the voices of the wrothe move farther away from the castle. It was easy to tell they were on the hunt, and he imagined they might be in pursuit of escaped captives. He could only hope it was the case as he refocused his attention on the scenario before him. The scorched bodies of several vampyr lay strewn about on the ground. He had made quite an impact on the enemy this time. He had been much too weakened from his spell-casting to really aid the group that much the last time they encountered the despicable wrothe.

Hells, he hated his vulnerability, especially knowing that he had once been so much more.

Yet, TC was very pleased with the current outcome. He raked his gaze across the immediate area. The heads had been severed from the rest of their bodies, the best way he knew to be sure they couldn't rise up again. Just like many other daemons, the vampyr had the capacity to regenerate. Only incineration or decapitation made their demise a surety, so he asked Vikhail to proceed with beheading the fallen enemy.

Tigerius stepped up next to him just as TC heard the voice of the wrothe once again. He turned to the other man, and began to speak before Tiger could open his mouth. "I think that Jonesy has been able to escape the castle."

Tigerius regarded him solemnly. "Why do you think so?"

"The howl we hear is a wrothe on the hunt. It is possible that the beast is simply a vampyr in animal form, and the voice has been moving steadily away from the castle," he said hurriedly. "We need to move now if we are to help Jonesy when it reaches her."

"What about Cervantes?" Tiger asked.

"Let's hope that he is with Jonesy," TC replied shortly.

Tigerius nodded abruptly. "All right, let's go."

The three men quickly began to move in the direction they last heard the howl. They moved swiftly through the trees, the light of the moons saving them from many an impact with tree trunks, whipping branches, thorny shrubbery, exposed roots, and nest holes made by small animal residents. Yet, they would later still be nursing a variety of wounds sustained by their mad dash through an inhospitable wood in the direction they hoped to find their comrades. It was simply inevitable.

Again they heard the song of the wrothe. TC was relieved to note that it sounded closer. He also noticed that the voice had a fevered tone to it—seeming as though it was nearing its target. He increased his pace and the others followed suit as they made the same deduction. He hoped he was right to believe that Jonesy had been able to escape, for if they had left the castle behind and she was still being held within, they would need to devise yet another plan to liberate her.

Unfortunately however, there was much more to the current situation than met the eye. Another threat approached, one TC had begun to feel even before he and his comrades reached the lair. The energy thrown by a greater daemon was unmistakable, an energy signature with which he was quite familiar. He couldn't help but think it had something to do with Jonesy, but he prayed to the gods it didn't. His life could suddenly be much more disagreeable than it was already.

The men slowed when they began to notice a change in the scenery. The appearance of the trees began to thin out, and interspersed among them was a smattering of statues depicting both humans and animals. Moving further into the garden, they saw bowls set on pedestals and stone platforms atop which one could only imagine may have been a surface to rest a support system for overhead shelter. In spite of the diversion, they continued to move swiftly, and it wasn't long before they heard a shout issued from up ahead.

Slipping silently from among the trees, the fog crept nearer. At the periphery stood two wrothe, cerulean eyes boring into them, almost daring them to run. Cervantes felt his heart beat increase its pace, and he could feel Jonesy tremble where she stood beside him, her small hand tucked within his larger one. Cervantes could almost taste the danger in the surrounding air, but he would defiantly stand his ground to the end.

Within the very brief time allotted them, Cervantes and Jonesy had shared a passionate union. It was short and somewhat frenzied, the intensity of it tempered only by his knowledge that it was a novel experience for Jonesy in more ways than one. Yet, she'd matched him in every way, and her discomfort was only momentary. The howls of the wrothe had been very close when they managed to separate. And moments later, when the large beasts were suddenly surrounding them, watching them intently from clear blue eyes, it had been quite disconcerting to say the least.

T.R. Chowdhury & T.M. Crim

The fog paused for a moment near the wrothe, but then it was swiftly upon them. Cervantes could feel the emanating hunger as the fog circled, and he abruptly recalled something TC had said to the group when they first discovered the disappearance of Jonesy and Cortes. *"The most ancient of them are able to shift into a type of fog . . . something that people who have had contact with vampyr call* Crimson Mist. *It is named after the red hue the vampyr fog acquires once the blood of its victims has begun to satiate the nearly unquenchable thirst."*

Cervantes struggled to control his urge to flee. He would rather die under the fangs of the wrothe than to have his body sucked dry of its life's blood. By the gods, at the time, he had been rather perturbed with TC for having disclosed information that would surely serve only to frighten everyone so much they would be a liability in battle. Sometimes ignorance could be an asset. But now, truth be told, he was glad TC had spoken of it.

Abruptly the mist retreated and became still about half a farlo away. It then quickly began to coalesce, and before Cervantes could blink again, the form of a man could be seen within. Moments later, a vampyr was standing there, the one who called himself Seth. With thumb and forefinger cupping his chin, the daemon regarded them almost thoughtfully. Wisps of pale yellow hair blew errantly in the transient breeze, and he slowly began to shake his head. His gaze settled onto Jonesy, and Cervantes felt her press into his side as the daemon moved towards them.

"Tisk, tisk." Seth shook his head. "It hurts me to know that you wish to abandon me so early in our relationship. I would have kept you by my side as my consort . . . my soul-mate. But no, you would rather give yourself to . . . to . . . *this*." Seth disdainfully cast a hand towards Cervantes. He once more schooled his expression into one of thoughtfulness. "However, I will forgive you this time." Seth held out his hand to Jonesy, intensifying his gaze. "Come with me, and you will want for nothing. I will even spare the life of your companion."

Cervantes felt her stir beside him. Tearing his eyes away from the vampyr, he saw Jonesy's gaze locked upon Seth. Hells, he was mesmerizing her—using some type of coercion to lure her into his trap. Cervantes imagined her as the vampyr's mistress, sacrificing her humanity to become something despicable, something vile. Daemon-kind had no redeeming qualities.

Cervantes tightened his hand around Jonesy's, squeezing until she would begin to feel the pain. He hoped it would break her trance and bring her back to him before Seth could take her. He felt her begin to resist before she finally broke away from Seth's hypnotic gaze. His relief was palpable as she brought her green eyes up to his, and he couldn't keep a smile from pulling up one corner of his mouth. As Jonesy came back to herself, Cervantes could see a flash of understanding cross her face, and she returned his smile with one of her own.

Within the blink of an eye, Seth was suddenly standing next to Jonesy. His lips were pulled up into a snarl, exposing his teeth to reveal elongated sharp incisors. "Now you will die," the daemon hissed. Cervantes gave a shout as her hand was torn from his grip. While Seth began to drag her away into the trees, the wrothe lunged towards him.

With a shout from Tallachienan to simply strike and step back, the men surged forward. TC, Tiger, and Vikhail entered the scene just as two wrothe leaped onto Cervantes. Unarmed, the man fell beneath them. The animals tore savagely into him, snarling and snapping at one another. It was almost easy to pick them off their prey, Vikhail swinging his axe into the unprotected side of one as Tiger plunged his sword into the ribs of the other.

Just as TC had requested, both men quickly retreated after their attack. The animals cried out in pain and summarily swung around to face their attackers. Their muzzles were colored bright red with Cervantes' blood, and the long tongue of one even managed to lick at it before he stumbled in place. The other wrothe leaped towards his new foe, but before he could reach Tigerius, he struck an invisible barrier. As the beast hung in mid-air, the silvery strands of what looked like a huge spider's web spanning the immediate area in front of Tiger and Vikhail became more discernible.

The animal began to struggle against the sticky strands, but within moments its fur began to sizzle where it was in contact with the web. Then, just as the scent of burning flesh began to permeate the air, the wrothe began a fiercer attempt to be free, crying out as the strands burned him while still holding him there in place. The other wrothe stood on the other side, staring with wide eyes. Before long, the trapped wrothe shifted into his natural form, and the vampyr screamed in agony as the strands burned through his body. Just like the remaining vampyr wrothe, Tigerius and Vikhail simply stood there and stared, watching with disgusted awe until all that lay before them were parts of the daemon that fell through the strands. When they glanced over near Cervantes, the remaining daemon was already gone.

And so was Tallachienan.

Tiger and Vikhail gave wide berth to TC's unnatural web, rushing to Cervantes' side. The captain had kept himself curled into a protective position, trying to cover as much of his vulnerable places as possible. Terrible lacerations scored across his ribs and upper arms, the sharp claws having easily shredded through the black leather vest he wore. And luckily, Cervantes had been able to keep his throat out of the way of vicious teeth. The torn flesh atop one hand was testimony to his protective efforts. However, another injury gave Tiger a bit of concern, one that bloodied the side of Cervantes' head where it must have struck a rock when he fell.

Cervantes struggled to rise as Tiger and Vikhail knelt before him. With his free hand, he gripped the neckline of Tiger's tunic. "Jonesy. Where is she?"

Tigerius shook his head in sympathy, clasping Cervantes' bloody hand with his own. "I don't know. We didn't see her when we arrived at the scene."

For barely a moment Cervantes stared intensely into his eyes, and then surged upward. Tiger fell back and watched as Cervantes stood, grimacing with the pain the motion caused. Cervantes brought a hand to his head, but when he brought it back covered with blood, he simply stared at it for a moment. Then, holding a hand against the wound closest to his abdomen, the man began to stumble away, most likely in the direction he thought Jonesy to be.

Tigerius quickly rose and laid a detaining hand on his friend's shoulder. Cervantes tried to shrug it away, and when he was unsuccessful, he swung back towards Tiger. "What is wrong with you?" he shouted. "I *have* to go to her!"

Tiger nodded in agreement. "I know, my friend. But please just take the time to listen to what I have to say."

Cervantes shook his head. "Don't you understand? There *is* no time! Every moment she spends with that monster brings her closer to death." He knew it wasn't entirely the truth. Jonesy would still be alive after becoming what Seth wanted her to be. But it wouldn't be the Jonesy he remembered, for the part that made her human would be gone forever.

Tigerius shook his head. "TC was here with us when we first entered the scene. He cast his spell . . ." Tiger pointed to the dismembered vampyr. ". . . and then he left. I am certain he went in search of Jonesy."

Cervantes felt torn. He wanted to believe that TC would bring Jonesy back to him, wanted to put faith in someone he knew harbored so much power. Yet, since the moment TC had boarded the *Sea Maiden* all those fortnights ago, they had always been at odds with one another. Despite all of their struggles, they had never managed to find neutral ground. Cervantes gritted his teeth against a sudden wave of weakness. He could feel warmth making its way down the side of his face, and he knew it was from the skull wound that made him feel as though he might lose the contents of his stomach at any moment—that is, if anything had been there to lose. And then there were injuries to his left side, deep lacerations that came ever so close to the soft flesh of his susceptible abdomen. He had been rather fortunate, for if the vampyr wrothe had spent any more time upon him, they surely would have ripped into his belly or even worse, his neck. In that regard, TC had surely saved his life, for it was his spell that had diverted the daemons.

But for Jonesy there could be no doubts. And the only way he could be certain was for him to go after her himself.

Cervantes shook his head. "I should go after her. She needs me."

Vikhail finally spoke. "Cervantes, yer wounded. Give TC a chance to return to us."

Cervantes continued to shake his head. "No, by then it might be too late." He turned away from his companions, closing his eyes against the pain that swept through his skull. But when he focused his gaze ahead, he saw TC and Jonesy slowly walking towards them from out of the surrounding trees.

Relief swept through him in a wave. It brought Cervantes to his knees, but before he toppled, Tiger and Vikhail were supporting him beneath his arms. He vaguely felt himself being gently laid on the ground, and then saw Jonesy's beautiful face hovering above. She simply smiled, a hand caressing his brow. And he could finally allow the pressing darkness to overcome him.

CHAPTER FIVE

A eris accompanied Thulnar and Faleema through the corridors of the academy. It was a cavern system that was comprised of the halls that sustained classes that were not conducted aboard the backs of their dragons. It was supplemental learning that would educate them about the physical and mental complexities often involved with their bondmates, and to help them understand their dragon friends beyond the *bond*. Today she would meet Demeter Barthaltak as he instructed them about dragon healing. It was a class that went hand in hand with the anatomy and physiology she missed a couple days before, meeting only once every week. She wondered if Kordrian would be there.

Faleema turned to her. "How are you feeling?"

Aeris nodded. "Much better, and I'm so glad you were there. Who knows when someone would have found me?"

Aeris had become quite ill. The wounds on her legs had become septic, the infection sweeping through her body like a wildfire. However, it was caught early enough, and she was given a medicinal regimen that acted quickly. She lost only two days of training, but had orders to keep her physical activity light for at least another three days. Of course Jaxom blamed himself, for if he had been more intuitive, he would have been more insistent that she receive the more specialized treatment she had so obviously required.

Faleema only grinned. "I just can't believe you kept something like that to yourself for so long."

Aeris smiled and gave a shrug. "I had other things on my mind."

Faleema narrowed her eyes and pursed her lips. "Indeed."

"You're just crazy," commented Thulnar. "The wounds were infected. You could have become stricken with sepsis and died."

"But I didn't," Aeris replied. "My body betrayed me in time."

The trio walked swiftly through the amply lit tunnels. They passed several chambers, one of which seemed to be a library. She made a mental note to return there after the class so that she could sift through the literature it might possess. She had every intention of measuring it against that which resided within the Medubrokan Academy back home, the dimensionalist school that her mother founded with the man who was Aeris' Master, Dinim Coabra. Aeris found herself suddenly squelching down feelings of homesickness.

Damnation, she had rather thought she had those under control. Obviously not.

Aeris followed as Faleema and Thulnar turned down another corridor, one that opened into a cavern. The rest of the class awaited them at a wide table: Kahlan, Saliel, and the man that Aeris assumed must be Demeter Barthaltak. Just like Rogerus, the man was halfen, although of thalden descent as opposed to morden. He reminded her of Vikhail and Vardec, and once more she felt a bout of homesickness. It was then she realized that her group of traveling companions had become her 'home' just as much as Elvandahar. Interesting.

"Welcome. You must be Damaeris, Jaxom's bondmate. It is good to meet you," he said.

Aeris smiled with the sincerity she felt from him. "Indeed, it is my pleasure to meet you as well, Demeter Barthaltak."

He shook his head and smiled. "It's just Bart, if you please." He nodded towards the table. "Have a seat and let's get started. I prepared a packet of information for you in regards to the material we have already covered." He handed her a roll of parchments. "You aren't too far behind, just three classes worth. However, I expect you to be caught up with us when next we meet, which will be announced at a later date. Most likely, you will have at least a seven-day to read over the material I have listed there in the packet."

Aeris nodded and seated herself as she flipped through the papers, wondering what awaited her with Demeter Kordrian. And then there was the added pressure of catching up with her comrades in the riding class, for they had a time constraint as to the date they were to begin their combat training. Ah, the rigors of advanced learning.

"Today we will be discussing dragon-fire burn and how we can treat it once we are able after battle. There are a few severities of burn, and each is treated differently. Treatment type is also judged by the location. For example, a burn to the chest would be dealt with differently from one to a wing section."

Bart stepped over to a poster tripod and pulled on the thin rope attached to the rolled parchment situated between the bars at the top. Once pulled down, the parchment revealed the sketch of a mature dragon. "As we already know, a dragon's scales are extremely hardy, sufficient protection for an animal that has such a weak bone structure. Where the dragon is lacking in osseous mass, he is more than adequate in his protective outer shell. Inasmuch, dragon scales are coveted, although there are not many humans, faelin, or even halfen who are willing to seek it out." Bart held out his hands. "Let's face it, the only way a dragon can part with his scales is if he is dead, and such a large foe is considerable for any humanoid. Historically, dragon scales were scavenged from the deceased. They were then passed from generation to generation. But now, since the breaking of the Pact of Bakharas, dragon scales are once more an accessible commodity." Bart paused and then continued. "That is, if one knows how to defeat a dragon.

"However, I am digressing. To get back on track . . . in spite of the great strength offered by dragon scales, they are not entirely immune. They can only withstand so much heat from dragon-fire before they begin to scorch. Such an injury is much more profound if located on one of the wings, for they are the most susceptible of all the body parts. Composed not of scales at all, but only of the under-hide, the wings are very supple. On a sunny day, one can almost see through the membrane-like wings of a dragon if one looks closely enough. The wings are a dragon's most valuable asset, and also his most vulnerable one. It is much easier for dragon-fire to scorch the wings than any other body part, not to mention, offering the most pain. Wounds sustained by the wings are most brutal, prone to ground any dragon, no matter what his size and experience."

Bart stepped sideways to the next tripod and pulled the rope to reveal another image. This time it was a sketch only of a dragon wing. "As you have already learned under the instruction of Demeter Kordrian, there are five sections comprising the wing of a dragon, each separated by a length of bone. The section closest to the body is the most muscular, and as such has slightly more bone and scale protection than any of the other sections. Injuries sustained at the fringes are much more bearable and heal more quickly than those in the centers. Central damage tends to be the most debilitating, and will run a dragon aground rather quickly. Sometimes the fall itself will kill a dragon." Bart turned away from the scroll and regarded the individuals before him. "More often, the fall will kill a rider before it kills his bondmate.

"But that is beside the point," continued Bart. "My job is to teach you all how to tend to a burned dragon, whether the injury be to wing, chest, or tail. Of course we will focus on the wing, and I will even tell you about the time I saved a dragon's wing by taking some hide from his flank and sewing it into the hole that had been left behind after all the burned flesh had been cut away. It has been my crowning achievement since arriving here, and it would be my honor to present my friend to you sometime. Meanwhile, I will go through the procedures on how to treat dragon-fire wounds. First I shall focus on the topical remedies, followed by the ones that must be swallowed so they may work on the inside of the dragon. I will then touch on how a rider should treat the wounds of his bondmate whilst out in the field, away from the support offered by myself and the rest of dragon-kind."

Aeris frowned in consideration. She hated the thought that Jaxom could sustain such massive injury and be away from this place. Of course, it was the most likely scenario, for there were no wars currently being fought upon

Shayamalan. Damn, the information she was about to receive was vital to Jaxom's survival. She could sense the truth of that fact deep within her, and she was suddenly afraid. In so short a time he had become so much to her, courtesy of the *bond*. Once more, she had so much to lose if he was suddenly taken from her. She had set herself up for so much heartbreak.

It was the story of her life.

�֍ ✖ ✖ ✖ ✖

Aeris stared at the message she held in her hand, hissing beneath her breath. It told her she was required to meet with Demeter Kordrian this morning. She had no idea why, for Thulnar had told her that anatomy class didn't convene until the morrow.

Hells and damnation!

Aeris dejectedly removed everything but her small-clothes, and with a towel wrapped around her, she took herself to the bath. Today was her day for the steaming luxury located at the far side of the cavern, and not so long ago she had been looking forward to it.

She wasn't now.

Aeris walked up to one of the four waiting tubs, removed her remaining clothing, and then discarded the towel as she stepped within. After pouring in the scented oils, she simply lay there for several moments. Then she made haste and continued her bath, lathering her hair with the soap provided, and then rinsing it. It took a few moments, for the long mass seemed to hang onto the soap longer than shorter tresses. However, she had given herself more than enough time, so the extra spent on her hair simply put her right on schedule.

Once leaving the bath, she wrapped the towel around herself once more and made her way back to her area. Having laid her clothes out on the bed-pallet prior to bathing, she was able to don them quickly. She then seated herself at the side of the bed to begin the ritual of brushing her hair. When Faleema approached, Aeris glanced stoically up at her friend.

"What is wrong?" Faleema asked.

Aeris sighed with exasperation and lowered the brush. "I have a session with Demeter Kordrian this morning and I have no idea why."

Faleema's eyes became bright with enlightenment. "I know we should already know each other's primary occupations, but it seems we do not."

Aeris frowned. "Yes, I think you are right. But what has it to do with my destination this morning?"

Faleema pursed her lips. "Kordrian is a master of spellcasting. It is every Detarsi that the instructors take those who adhere to their own profession and educate them accordingly. Demeter Fo and Roger are fighters and have taken over the additional training of Thulnar and Kahlan. Part-time, they even train me. However, the other half of the time I report to Demeter Kord, for he is a spellcaster." Faleema paused for a moment. "I suppose you are also a spellcaster."

Aeris nodded slowly. By the gods, she could hardly believe her misfortune. The one master who seemed to despise her so much.

Sensing her disquiet, Faleema took her hand. "I am also reporting to him this morning. We will go together."

Aeris simply shook her head forlornly.

Faleema gave her a consoling look. "Don't think about that. I am sure you will change his opinion of you with time." She then gave a nonchalant shrug. "Besides, you're pretty. Kordrian is a man just like any other."

Aeris regarded Faleema solemnly from widening eyes.

She shook her head in response. "Don't look at me like that. It's the truth."

"Which part?" asked Aeris. "That I am pretty, or that Demeter Kord is like any other man?"

Faleema hesitated for only a fraction of a moment. "Both."

Aeris rolled her eyes. "You're crazy."

Faleema crossed her arms at her chest. "Whatever. I know what I know."

"He may just be like any other man, but I am not all that attractive."

Faleema sniffed. "I beg to differ. You are the new best thing here."

Aeris chortled without meaning to, and then slapped a hand over her mouth to muffle the sound. "Surely you are joshing me."

Faleema regarded her with intense seriousness. "Never."

"Whoever told you so?" she asked.

Faleema shrugged again. "Only everyone."

Aeris shook her head. "No."

At the same time Faleema nodded. "Yes."

Aeris proceeded to brush her hair and then pulled it together into a mass and bound it at the back of her head with a leather tie, for she found she no longer had the time to plait it. "Come. We had best get going. I don't need the man to hold my tardiness against me as well."

Faleema nodded. "Agreed."

Aeris grabbed the shoulder pouch containing her spellbooks, parchment, stylus and ink and then the two women made their way through the long passageway that led from their barracks to the academy. Once there, Faleema briskly led her along a short series of corridors that took them to the chamber where Kordrian held instruction. Once entering, Aeris found that their peers had been awaiting them. Everyone regarded the two intently as they joined the group of four young men and a woman. *Damn.* She supposed the master would have her tardiness on his list after all.

"Ladies, it is good that you have finally decided to join me." Both turned at the sound of Demeter Kordrian's voice. His expression was one of perturbation. "Especially you, Damaeris Timberlyn." Aeris felt a slight crackling in the air as he paused for a moment. Then he continued. "It seems you had no compunction about skipping my instruction session just the other day. So what makes this one so much more worthy of your esteemed presence?" His tone dripped with sarcasm.

Aeris felt her heart almost skip a beat as a result of her nervousness. Did he not know of her illness? She shook her head and replied, "I do not find it to be more worthy at all, Demeter." As Kordrian pulled his pale brows together into a frown, she continued. "It is simply that I was so much more tired that day after Demeter Fo's instruction. I just didn't have the strength to attend. Our journey here was so long and . . ."

"So, you want me to feel sorry for you? Is that it?" Kordrian didn't give her a chance to make a reply. "Like I said at your testing, you should have given more thought about coming here if you are doubtful as to your ability to keep up the pace."

Aeris shook her head. "But I have no doubts, Demeter," she replied solemnly.

"That is not how it appears to *me*," he said.

"I suppose I will simply have to prove it to you."

Kordrian narrowed his eyes. "Indeed."

Aeris retained a stoic demeanor as she stood there beneath his scrutiny. She had no doubt that he wanted to see her crumble, if only for just a moment. However, she refused to give him that satisfaction. Finally, he turned away from her and addressed all the others who were present. "Go ahead and call for your dragons and proceed to the practice field. I won't be there today, but Quartermaster Franchie will help where she can. You should all work on what we were attempting to accomplish last session."

Everyone nodded silently and left the chamber. Faleema cast a woeful glance in her direction before following behind the others. Aeris found herself standing alone in the chamber with Kordrian. It was more than disconcerting, but she wasn't really alone. She had Jaxom with her. And even though he had sworn an oath not to interfere in her training, she knew he would come if the need were great enough.

Aeris remained expressionless as Kord tuned back to her. His eyes were coldly assessing as he began to walk around the periphery of the chamber. "They tell me you are a dimensionalist."

Aeris only nodded slowly in response.

"I suppose your master is Tallachienan Chroalthone."

Aeris shook her head in the negative. "No. However, he was master to my master. You may have heard of him—Dinim Coabra."

Kordrian became thoughtful. "Yes, I may have heard of him long ago, when he was naught but a mere apprentice."

"You may also have heard of my mother, Adrianna Darnesse," she said.

Kordrian suddenly locked his eyes onto hers, his blue eyes penetrating. "Of course. I could never forget." She watched as he raked his gaze over her appraisingly and she wondered if she had made a mistake in divulging her parentage.

"You have met her, then?" She wasn't certain she really cared to know, but she asked the question anyway.

"Indeed, I have," he said. "It is interesting that her daughter should be standing before me now, requiring *my* tutelage."

Aeris cocked her head, still uncertain of how much she wanted to know. "How is that so?"

"Well, you *are* Tallachienan's daughter are you not?"

Aeris recoiled from the statement, both mentally and physically. Of course, she had heard from none other than the goddess Tholana herself that something existed between Tallachienan and her mother. She had even divulged the information to Lord Trebexal. However, in some minuscule corner of her mind, she nursed the possibility that it just might not be true. But now . . .

Aeris tore her gaze from his as she fought to control herself. Yet, she could sense the effect her response had on Kordrian. She hastily cleared her throat. "No, he is not. My father happens to be Adrianna's husband, Sirion Timberlyn, son to the crown of Elvandahar."

Silence reigned for a moment. Then, "My apologies. I hadn't realized . . ."

Aeris interrupted, not wanting to hear anything else he might want to say about either her mother or Tallachienan. "No, its fine . . ." She allowed her voice to trail off.

Kordrian regarded her intently. Once more there was silence. Then, "You are here because you are in need of my instruction, which is to teach you the concentration and discipline needed in order to cast spells whilst astride your dragon during battle. However, I can guide you only so far before you are required to work on the skills I have provided by yourself."

Aeris nodded mutely.

"To begin, I need you to show me the depth of your expertise, just so that I know what I am dealing with. All of my students are of varying *talent* and skill level, and it is important that I stay on track with each."

Once more Aeris nodded. In spite of the sticky mire that seemed to have overcome her mind, she struggled to maintain some semblance of control. She could scarcely keep thoughts of her mother and Tallachienan out of her mind, and she found herself right back at that awful place she'd inhabited when she left TC standing alone on the cliffs of the Larramis Peninsula. For a while, she had actually been on a path of recovery. But now . . .

"Please show me an example of your ability. Choose wisely from your repertoire, for this will not be the first time a master asks you to show him your arcane portfolio."

Aeris solemnly regarded the man before her. Somehow, she knew he hadn't the intention of being malicious when he asked about her parentage in spite of his dislike of her. Yet, he would continue to judge her harshly, for whatever reason he held dear to him. Aeris nodded and began her first spell.

✖ ✖ ✖ ✖ ✖

20 ENAREN CY634

It seemed like a lifetime ago since they had last seen the portal chamber within the Larramis Forest. Jonesy only vaguely remembered it when last they were there, after Aeris and Talemar had been taken by the cimmereans. It was a time she hated to recall, and unfortunately, Aeris still was not there beside her as the bastion of support Jonesy had always hoped the other woman would be. They would take the portal to Krathil-lon; in spite of the extra distance, the group chose to remain in safe lands as they traveled to Elvandahar. The alternative portal route would take them to the portal chamber that lay at the juncture of the Velmist Forest and Bryton Hills, deep within the realm of Karlisle. It would be foolhardy for them to take themselves behind enemy lines, no matter how much closer they would be to their destination.

Jonesy gave a deep inward sigh and swallowed past the lump in her throat. For her Karlisle wasn't supposed to be the enemy. It was home.

Many days had passed since her ordeal with the vampyr. She couldn't even be sure of the precise number, for she had slept away at least two or three days after rejoining the group, and then a large portion of another few days after that. Even now she felt unusually fatigued as dusk approached and she wondered how long it would take her to finally feel normal again.

She imagined that Cervantes must be feeling much the same.

Jonesy's gaze sought him out within the darkness of the underground tunnel leading to the small cave in which the portal was hidden. Just as her thoughts had been on him, it seemed his had also been on her. Their eyes met and locked for a moment. Both then glanced away, but not before Jonesy thought she saw Cervantes wink at her conspiratorially. Inwardly she smiled to herself. To her knowledge, no one was aware of the liaison they had shared in the vampyr garden.

In the company of the horses they chose to bring, the group left the tunnel and congregated within the portal chamber. Understandably it was crowded, but they had been loath to leave all of the animals behind for fear that they would be unable to procure other burden beasts once they passed through the portal. They would have a long journey across the plains of Cortubro, and they didn't want to risk managing it without at least some of the help they would need from their animal companions. Inasmuch, they chose the strongest of the beasts to accompany them, despite any hassle their presence would incur.

Nudging past the backside of the horse in front of her, Jonesy looked around the chamber. Situated at the far side, there were two large brackets standing at least as high as two human men. Ensconced between them was a large oval mirror. About two or three farlo before the construct, there was a section of raised stone upon which resided a pedestal harboring a large tome. TC immediately stepped up to the pedestal and opened the book lying there. It wasn't surprising, especially considering it was he who had constructed the portal system, albeit a very long time ago. Quickly finding the page he was looking for, TC then turned back to the rest of the company.

Jonesy focused her attention on TC. He seemed so regal standing there on the dais. It had been the same when he emerged from out of the trees to confront Seth after the daemon dragged her away from Cervantes' side in the garden. They had barely spoken since Aeris' departure . . . since she'd discovered the truth of his identity. On some level, she recognized that TC was still a man just like any other, but she'd struggled to get past the fact that he was a god.

Jonesy struggled within Seth's bruising grip as he dragged her behind him. He moved swiftly through the trees, and she was forced to run in order to prevent having her arm dislocated from her shoulder. Meanwhile, she clawed ineffectually at his hand, and when that didn't seem to make any difference, she finally lunged for his face. Her nails raked across his cheek, and when he swung back to face her, he hissed. His once cerulean blue eyes blazed a bright red, and his incisors were long and sharp. The frightening visage stalled her completely, causing her to stumble and fall.

Seth stood over her where she lay on the leaf littered ground. "Stupid woman! You think you can escape me now? You think you can leave me in the company of your man friend?" Seth's hand snaked out to grip her by the hair. She cried out when he pulled her up, and the moment she was close, his demeanor shifted. His eyes became piercing as he regarded her, and one corner of his upper lip curved upward. "I can smell him on you."

Jonesy felt her breath catch in her throat. Seth's crimson eyes bore into her and she could sense that she was in danger. "What did your man do?" Seth lifted his nose to the air for a moment before roughly pulling her closer. He put his face in the curve of her neck, and then slowly worked his way down to the space between her breasts. Jonesy trembled when he gripped her waist in his hands and continued down, pausing at her belly and ending at the juncture of her thighs.

Seth lifted his crimson gaze to meet hers, the expression accusatory. He swiftly rose and slapped her across the face with the flat of his hand. "Damn whore! I can smell the reek of his sex on you! He has taken your innocence!" he snarled.

Jonesy held the side of her face. Seth's eyes flashed dangerously and she shook her head, hoping to diffuse his ire. He presumed the gesture as one of denial and once again took her arm in a bruising grip. He pulled her roughly to him and spoke into her ear. "Don't even dare refuting me; my senses never lie." He cocked his head. "But it's not too late! I can still take you for myself."

Fearfully, Jonesy shook her head. No, this couldn't be happening. She abruptly pulled back from Seth, somehow managing to twist herself from his brutal grasp. She was about to turn away when she felt him catching her about the waist. He spun her around to face him, and once seeing the cruel twist of his expression, panic swept through her. Seth raised his hand to her again, and just as he was about to strike her, a deep voice cleaved through the air, speaking in an unfamiliar tongue. She recognized the voice as the one belonging to her good friend Magnus. Or more accurately, the stranger she now knew as Tallachienan.

Jonesy turned and saw TC's handsome face for only a brief moment before the area was plunged into absolute darkness. She could see nothing, but heard the distinct sounds of a struggle taking place close by. She felt herself being knocked to the ground and she simply lay there, only vaguely taking in anything after that. She suddenly realized how very tired she was and all she wanted to do was close her eyes.

It wasn't long before she heard a worried voice speaking close to her ear. "Jonesy, my dear friend, are you all right?" She opened her eyes and found TC kneeling over her. In spite of recent events, she couldn't help giving a wan smile.

"Even though you are a god, you still consider me a friend?"

The expression that passed over his face at that moment was indescribable. She heard his breath catch before he was pulling her up into his embrace and holding her close. "By the gods, yes! You will always be my *friend, Joneselia. Never forget that."*

TC held her there for a moment longer, whispering something undiscernible under his breath before helping her up from the ground. Dried leaves clung valiantly to her clothing and hair, making a crinkling sound as he placed a supporting arm around her back and waist. She leaned against him as they walked; she barely had enough mental power to wonder at the whereabouts of her abductor, much less, to where they were going. But when she began to notice the familiar statues of the garden, she perked up a bit. Then, as the form of Cervantes standing there with blood streaming down his face came into view, nothing else seemed to matter.

"I am going to begin the incantation. Is everyone ready to make the journey through the portal?" Tallachienan looked around at the men and women standing before him. Alasdair, Talemar, Cedric, and Tigerius were unconcerned as they had done it before. Lev and Jonesy seemed similarly unaffected despite having never experienced it. However, Cervantes, Jezibel, Vikhail, Vardec, and Mateo wore expressions of apprehension and doubt. *Teleportation? Hells, what was this guy talking about? He must be crazy*

TC sighed inwardly. He wasn't exactly the most social of beings, and it was in times such as these that he almost wished he had a more empathetic aspect to his personality. He felt a momentary pang as he thought of Aeris. She was one who would be good in this situation, explaining to everyone they had nothing to worry about, that the strange sensations they would feel would last only moments. He supposed he could say those same things. But he somehow knew that coming from him it wouldn't be communicated the same.

When Tigerius stepped forward to convince everyone of their safety, TC felt relieved. In most ways, he supposed he was a good leader. TC didn't hesitate to make split moment decisions, was an excellent strategist, and knew how to tell people what to do. However, he was neither good at discussing things before taking action, nor at taking advice from other people, whether it was good or not. And he definitely wasn't good at talking about his own thoughts or feelings.

TC watched as Tiger talked to the group. Just like Aeris, he knew just what to say in order to ease everyone's fears. Glancing over at Alasdair and Cedric, he could see that they were both a bit surprised to see a side of Tiger they were just now getting a chance to experience. Even without having known him prior to their long journey, TC could see that the young man had matured over the past several moon cycles. And having overheard a conversation or two about Tiger's frivolous past, TC was certain that the maturity was even more than he realized.

It wasn't long before everyone was nodding their affirmation and then preparing themselves for the reaction of the animals that stood within their presence. Already the horses were nervous at being confined within such a crowded space, and they could only imagine how some of the beasts might behave in response to the visual and tactile sensations they would experience once the incantation was started. TC turned back to the book and immediately began to utter the words of magic written on the open page before him. A slight wind began to sweep through the chamber, soon followed by swirls of color that emerged within the center of the mirror. Just as expected, the horses began to react to the strange phenomenon taking place in the crowded chamber. Yet, everyone kept the animals under control as the incantation was completed, the swirling colors of the portal stabilizing into a shimmering wall of blue.

Keeping a good grip on his horse, Alasdair was the first to walk into the portal, followed by Cedric and Talemar with two more of the fractious beasts. Tigerius stood by and ushered the remaining others through, making sure that the last three horses were the first to go. When Jonesy approached the portal as the last of the group to pass, Tigerius gave her a warm smile and took hold of her hand. TC didn't hesitate to step through the portal behind them just as it was beginning to close. He felt a slight wrenching; this was a sensation common for those who entered the portal during the last moments it remained viable. But then he was standing within yet another chamber, one vastly different from the one he had just left behind. It was the portal chamber of Krathil-lon, home to the most influential and proficient druids on all of Ansalar.

It took TC a moment to take in the situation. Despite the crowded nature of the chamber, Alasdair had already informed the guards of the arrival of the remainder of the group. It was obvious the men knew him, for each had relaxed his stance. Cedric and Talemar stood nearby, soothing the agitated horses that strained to be free. Sensing the volatile nature of the situation, the guards swiftly led the horses out of the chamber and into an adjoining corridor. TC could only hope it lead to a place devoid of stone walls, a place where the horses could rid themselves of their anxiety. It had been centuries since he'd been to this location, and he couldn't quite recall the details of the place.

The corridor stretched onward, and then was connected with another. It seemed that they were quite a distance underground. TC cursed to himself as they continued to walk, and the expletives of Cedric, Talemar, Vikhail and Vardec intermingled with the sounds generated by the horses struggling against the men, the confining walls, and each other. The voices of the frightened animals rang stridently throughout the enclosed space, and TC fought to keep himself from covering his ears and running ahead.

TC was more than relieved when they finally made it to the surface. The men stood back and let the six horses run the remaining distance out of the tunnel and into the sunshine that lay beyond. For a moment he became concerned that the beasts would keep running until they were far away, much too far to retrieve. But then he remembered where he was. Hells, these people were druids. They could simply *call* the horses back.

Tallachienan followed his comrades out into the open, ultimately finding himself within a silvery glen; the forest surrounding the area comprised of silver oaks. There was only one other place on Shandahar where such trees grew, and that place was Elvandahar. Majestic mountains comprising the Sartingel range surrounded them high overhead. He could see that much of the rest of the group was similarly awed, for it wasn't every day that one could complete a circle around oneself and see green, cloud topped mountains all around. There was a chill in the air, for they had suddenly arrived at a place that was much further north than they had been in the Larramis, not to mention that they were situated at a much higher elevation.

The druids led the group to the far side of the glen where another building structure was located. Upon walking inside, TC realized it to be quite unique, having an architecture that was closed against the elements, yet giving the feel of being out in the open. The corridor that wrapped around the periphery of the building was only partly enclosed, having large spaces between the pillars of stonework from which one could view the outside scenery with little impediment. Then, once stepping beyond it and going farther into the structure, TC saw that there was yet another corridor that was built much the same way. It was only able to offer more protection simply because the spaces between the stonework were narrower, not to mention that the peripheral corridor surrounding it offered a buffer. The winds swept easily through the inner corridor, but it would be more difficult for anything else to make its way in. Still, it would become wet in a gale, and leaves would blow between the spaces of the stonework, but not many.

Continuing to follow the guards, the group had walked but a few farlo when they saw three men turn a corner in the close distance and begin to walk towards them. It was easy for TC to see that the man in the middle helped himself along with the aid of a staff, and as they drew closer, TC could see that the man's hair was silvered with age. The men all wore plain tunics and trousers, and at their belts they carried no form of weaponry. Only the guards that accompanied the group carried anything of the sort, and then it was merely a simple dagger at one hip.

Alasdair moved forward as they drew nearer the druids that approached. He held out his arms, and as they met, he gave the old man an affectionate embrace. The man returned Alasdair's gesture, a smile of happiness quickly spreading across his wrinkled face. It was obvious the men knew one another and that they were good friends.

"Father Dremathian! It is good to see you," he exclaimed.

The older man nodded. "I didn't expect to see you here, Alasdair. The land is currently fraught with so much fighting. I thought surely you would be at the battle front with your brother."

Alasdair grew quiet. "Father, we have been away for quite some time. I left Elvandahar . . ."

Dremathian's eyes widened and he interrupted. "What? Left Elvandahar? So you know nothing of what has taken place over these past few fortnights?"

Alasdair shook his head and Dremathian's face visibly paled. "You had best come with me, my son. I have much to share with you."

Alasdair solemnly nodded. "Yes, Father. However, I have brought my comrades with me." He gestured behind him towards the rest of the group."

Dremathian's gaze swept over them, eventually coming to rest on Levander. His eyes narrowed for a moment, but then turned back to Alasdair. "They are welcome here within Krathil-lon. Brothers Braeden and Sylas will make certain that accommodations are prepared." Dremathian turned to the men who stood at either side of him and nodded. The brothers then returned the gesture and continued down the corridor in the direction ahead of them.

Dremathian turned back to Alasdair. "Come. Refreshments will be offered to you and your companions while we talk. Everyone needs to hear what I have to say," he said grimly.

✠ ✠ ✠ ✠ ✠

Aeris stared at the immense net stretched across the practice arena. It was a thing that must have been devised from magic, for she knew of nothing that could have been made into the structure before her. Both demeters Forigard and Rogerus were present, as well as quartermaster Falon. She could only imagine what the net was for, and the attendance of additional instructors made her all that much more nervous.

Finally, just as Kahlan and her bondmate arrived, Fo began to speak. "I suppose you are all wondering what all this is about." He swept his hand outwards to indicate the net. "For the next two or three instruction sessions, you will learn how to fall safely from the backs of your dragons. You shall learn not only how to minimize the damage caused by a fall, but also how to trust that your bondmate shall catch you if it is within his or her ability to do so.

"However, before we begin our training, I need *all* of you . . ." Fo gestured towards Aeris and the other riders, ". . . to deliberately fall into the net. The purpose is to prove to your mind that the net will catch you without harm. We have found that, over the course of training many others, such a fear hampered many riders' ability to learn as efficiently as possible. Inasmuch, this activity is the first that we have our students perform." Fo emphatically clapped his hands together. "So, who will be first?"

Silence reigned. Aeris glanced around at her comrades. Hells, she couldn't imagine who would want to volunteer. Rogerus planted his fists at his sides. "Fine, I'll demonstrate," he growled. The halfen proceeded to mount his dragon, and with an upward heave the pair immediately vaulted from the ground. Once they hovered high over the net, Rogerus fell from the back of his bondmate and landed safely within its confines.

"See?" exclaimed Fo. "Demeter Kordrian's net even caught an old umberhulk like Roger." He grinned and Aeris couldn't help but smile in spite of the nervous fear she felt about the net. Damn, he fell from really high up. She was surprised that Jaxom hadn't offered her his own feelings on this, but then realized that he understood that it was a decision she needed to make on her own.

Suddenly, without more thought, Aeris raised her hand. "I . . . I'll go."

Fo turned and waved her towards him with a smile. "There. Now you will all get to see a peer do the same thing and walk away unscathed."

Aeris swallowed heavily as Fo's arm settled about her shoulders. Jaxom sent her soothing vibes through their link, and underlying those she could feel his pride. She hoped she could live up to it. Fo then patted her back. "All right, you're up."

Aeris walked to Jaxom, stepping onto the foreleg he offered at her approach. Once aboard, she felt the familiar pain between her legs. However, it was much muted now as a result of the herbs the priests gave her to drink with her daily tea. She took a deep breath, steeling herself for the rush she would soon feel when Jaxom leaped from the ground. As always, it was invigorating. To be truthful, she was still getting accustomed to it. And now that she was thinking about it . . . this was Demeter Kordrian's net. He disliked her now more than ever. What if . . ."

Aeris felt a rumble of dragon laughter in her mind. <You can be such a silly creature.>

Aeris felt her brows furrow crossly. <It's good to know your feelings, Jaxom. And they are *so* helpful.> She said the last with a sarcastic tone.

Only more laughter resulted. <I spoke only because you are not thinking rationally. Why would Kordrian even *consider* turning the net against you? Do you really think he cares that much?>

Aeris became thoughtful. Jaxom had a good point. Why would Kordrian care? That thought settled her until she saw how high they had flown, and that Jaxom was positioning himself directly over the net.

<There is no chance you can miss.>

Aeris shook her head. Of course Jaxom would place himself in the safest spot. Not only that, but he had made her a promise that he would never allow harm to come to her. It was with that thought that she allowed herself to fall.

All of a sudden Aeris couldn't breathe. She thought to close her eyes and hide from her fear. But then she wouldn't be able to manipulate how she fell into the net. Hellfire, she didn't want to land on her head and break her neck. Her heart began to race in her chest and as the net loomed before her, she twisted herself so as to land on her backside, much as did Rogerus.

The breath left her chest with the impact of her landing. She felt the pressure of the strands of the net close around her backside, felt them stretch to accommodate her. It definitely didn't feel good, but it didn't feel as bad as she thought it might. Then it began to release her. She felt herself swinging back up. The net released her and she was airborne once more. Within barely a moment, the net caught her again, enveloping her within its sturdy embrace, and then she was upward yet again.

After several opportunities to bounce around in the net, Aeris was finally able to make her way to the periphery. There Jaxom awaited her. He placed a foot onto the net, careful not to clip it with a sharp talon. She climbed onto the foot, up his leg, and then onto his back. He carried her to where her peers stood, and once there, they all clapped. Demeter Fo stood at Jaxom's side to help her down. "Very good, my dear! Very good. Your successor is your good friend Faleema. It seems you are a motivation to her."

More than a little surprised, Aeris watched as Miramanth launched herself upward and then began a slow spiral that would take them high over the net. She would never have thought that Faleema would be the one to follow her. Thulnar perhaps.

Aeris took Fo's hand and stepped down from Jaxom's back. Once aground, she moved to stand beside her terralean friend. Thulnar shook his head. "I told her I would go first, but she insisted."

Aeris nodded. "It's not so bad after the initial bounce. You know what to expect after that; not to mention, it winds down relatively quick."

Thulnar only nodded speculatively.

Aeris regarded him from the corner of her eye. "You know I wouldn't lie to you."

Thulnar sighed heavily. "I know. But perhaps my fear happens to be greater than yours."

Aeris frowned. "Why would that be?"

Thulnar brought his gaze to settle heavily on her, his eyes unblinking. "As a young boy I was pushed from a rooftop. I had known only about seven or eight summers. I broke both my legs. The priests considered me *blessed* for they were able to reset my legs. Both healed without mishap, and I was able to walk again within the space of only two fortnights."

Thulnar then lowered his gaze and glanced away. Aeris recoiled slightly with her newfound knowledge, and her heart went out to her comrade. She spoke the words that resided in her heart, hoping they would help. "You know that Sordranth would never allow harm to come to you. Once hovering over the net, she will choose the safest place for you to fall."

Thulnar was silent for a moment. Then, "I know. Thank you for reminding me." He turned back to her, his brown eyes dark with emotion. "You are a good friend."

Aeris reached out and took his hand in hers. "So are you. My friendship with Faleema is proof of that."

Thulnar smiled and squeezed her hand gently. "That is really good to know."

CHAPTER SIX

L evander sat alone within the darkness of the chamber. The flame of his candle had long gone out, and he didn't bother to light a torch when he entered the room after the long talk the group shared with Dremathian. They had learned that the situation in western Ansalar was precarious. And being no fool, Lev knew it would eventually spread to the east. Elvandahar and Karlisle had gone to war, and the surrounding realms were already becoming affected. The emergence of dragonriders had started a trend. Even though they hadn't been seen for a while, lone renegade degethozak had chosen to continue what was started. It resulted in the materialization of dragonslayers, men who were trained to hunt down and kill dragon-kind. It was a sad reality. Gods only knew what would come next.

The moment he felt the weight of Dremathian's gaze, Lev knew that the druid leader was aware of his affiliation. Of course one such as he would know, for the kronshue were the antithesis of everything the druids sought to achieve in the world. And even if Dremathian had never met a member of the brotherhood before, he would have heard of them, for it was quite well known that distance was no barrier to druids, and that information passed easily from one order to the next until it had spread across the continent. But Lev somehow recognized that, at some point in his life, *Dremathian had personally experienced the kronshue.*

Father Dremathian spent quite a bit of time apprising the group of the events that had taken place during the past several moon cycles. Sitting next to Jezibel and Mateo, opposite the rest of the group, Lev saw the shock when Dremathian told them of Karlisle's unwarranted attack on Medea, Elvandahar's northernmost domain. Having learned the ways of the hinterlean faelin over many years of peace and diplomacy, the Karlislians knew to keep the bulk of their focus above-ground, infiltrating the treetops. The fighters ransacked the villages they found, and then burned them when they were through. They then made their militaristic encampments on the ground, adhering to what they were accustomed even if they might have derived a benefit from simply taking over the empty daladins they had chosen to burn.

The group then learned that Elvandahar retaliated. Led by Prince Asgenar, the hinterlean warriors mercilessly reclaimed northwest Medea and then moved into the boundary between Elvandahar and Karlisle. The battlefront currently rested at the tip of the Denegal, where the waterway widened to become more than just a simple steam, growing into a river that would eventually merge into the larger Terrestra. The Terrestra River eventually emptied into the Biske Bay between the port cities of Tambour located in southern Karlisle, and Yortec in the southern-most reaches of the realm of Torimir.

The group listened attentively as the old man continued to speak. "It should be safe for you to move through the realm of Cortubro. They have kept their borders open, showing both Karlisle and Elvandahar that they want no part in their struggle," said Dremathian. "They have everything to lose if they anger either one, for they derive much revenue from the trade they conduct with both realms. Cortubro cannot afford to lose either liaison."

Alasdair's brow was furrowed with worry, "Father, how fares my brother? Have you heard anything?"

Dremathian nodded his head and one corner of his mouth turned up into a small smile. "He is a fine leader and a strong opponent. He serves his people well." It was easy to see that the man felt pride for the young man that was the son of one of his greatest comrades. Yet, it was quite short lived. His bushy brows suddenly swept downward in a frown of concern. "Alasdair, where is Damaeris? Why is your sister not here with you?"

The ranger took a deep breath and then expelled it slowly. "She has left us, Father."

Dremathian's eyes widened. "Bluffing rugwort, where has she gone? Why did you not go after her?"

Alasdair shook his head, bringing a hand over the front of his face in an effort to ease the lines of strain written there. "We couldn't. She left astride the back of a dragon, one who had been disguised amongst us for quite some time." He paused but then continued more softly. "Her leave-taking was voluntary."

Dremathian was quiet for a moment. "She gave you no word before she left?"

Alasdair shook his head once more. "No. She was simply . . . gone."

The old man regarded Alasdair intently, knowing that the young ranger was not divulging the entire story. Yet, he said nothing more about it, instead moving on to another subject. "Well, as it turns out, your grandfather is similarly missing. Sydonnia and his pack still have not returned from their search for Triath and Tianna Solanar."

Lev suddenly saw Cedric and Talemar shift their gaze to Tigerius. He followed suit and saw that the other man's eyes had widened. He stood slowly from where he was seated between the halfen brothers. "Father Dremathian, what are you talking about? I've neither heard of any search, nor the reasons that may have precipitated one. Have my parents been missing?" he asked incredulously.

Dremathian swung his gaze to Alasdair, his blue eyes boring into the younger man. Silence rang throughout the chamber. Alasdair finally had the decency to look abashed. "Did you not tell him?" Dremathian said questioningly.

Once again Alasdair was taking a deep breath. He turned to look at his friend and shook his head. "No. I didn't tell him about it because I didn't want to worry him at a time when he could do nothing to help."

Tigerius swallowed convulsively and the chamber was silent for another moment. "I had a right to know! How could you keep this from me?" His voice resonated, reflecting the bewilderment he felt, laced with grim betrayal.

Alasdair was still where he sat next to Cedric. "I thought I was doing the right thing. We were all the way on the other side of the continent. I knew that you would be distracted. I am truly sorry, Tigerius."

Tiger shook his head. "You thought you were doing the right thing? By the gods, I could have taken the portal back here and gone home had I known! Damnation, what if they had needed me!"

Alasdair's eyes widened with the stark realization of his error. Tiger was right. If Alasdair had divulged the information he carried when he first met up with him in Gulshaan, the other man could have taken the portal back to the western side of Ansalar. He could have been the one to take the message to the druids in Krathil-lon instead of Cedric. He then would have simply stayed there.

"If I hid information from you concerning your family, you would have my head on a pike!" continued Tigerius angrily. "I would never have heard the end of it! Effin calotebas! You have no idea what I've been going through." He stopped abruptly as though not wanting to reveal too much. His face had become ashen, and his body was visibly shaking.

Vikhail and Vardec both rose to stand next to him. "Tiger, yer about ta fall down; rest 'ere fer a moment." Vardec urged Tigerius to seat himself on the stone slab they had all been using. Tiger acquiesced and ran a hand through his light brown hair.

Jonesy was then rising from her own seat and rushing to his side, followed by Cervantes. She took his hand within hers, "Tiger, are you all right? Please talk to me."

Lev's sympathy had gone out to the man. Something was seriously amiss, something that caused Tiger to react so strongly. After collecting himself sufficiently, Tigerius had risen and left the chamber without further comment. It was obvious the talk was over, so the rest of the group began to follow suit. Everyone was led to their own room, a nice change from having to share like they did in the cities and towns they visited.

Lev had been brought to this one.

Drемathian had yet to confront him about his affiliations, his *past* affiliations. Lev would simply wait until he did.

✕✕✕✕✕

Cervantes stealthily moved towards the chamber door he knew belonged to Jonesy. He had paid careful attention when the druids showed them to their respective places, knowing that he would be paying her a visit later. Once being taken to his own chamber, he'd waited, giving the druids ample opportunity to show the others to their rooms. He then waited a little more. Now, as he approached Jonesy's door, he felt a mild sense of apprehension. What if Jonesy didn't feel the same way about him as he did her? What if the thing that manifested between them the night of their escape was a merely a construct born of the conditioning they had received during their stay in the vampyr lair? Cervantes shook his head. Of course that was a silly thought. He'd seen the glances she'd cast him. They couldn't have been imagined.

Cervantes knocked on the door and received an immediate response. "Come in."

He opened it to find Jonesy sitting at the desk across the room. Her eyes reflected surprise as he entered and closed the door behind him. She rose from her chair and gave a tentative smile. "Cervantes, I wasn't expecting you."

For a moment he was confused. Who was she expecting? Then, as he recognized her pleased expression, he wondered something else. *Why wasn't she expecting him?* He then offered a smile of his own. "Why? We finally have a chance to be alone and you thought I wouldn't come? "

Jonesy hesitated and gave a nervous chuckle. "Well, I couldn't help it. That night was fraught with so much adversity, and the future seemed so uncertain."

Cervantes cocked his head and began walking towards her. "So you began to think that our actions were based solely on the hardship we experienced in the lair? You don't recall feeling anything towards me before your abduction?"

Jonesy shook her head. "I didn't say that."

He continued towards her. "Then what are you saying?"

Jonesy took a step back as he got close. "I'm just saying that I wasn't expecting you. If I was, and you didn't come, I would be upset. I don't like to feel upset, especially when it comes to matters such as this."

Cervantes gave a mischievous grin and closed the distance between them. "And what is this 'matter' about which you speak?"

Jonesy stepped back until her backside pressed into the desk. Her gaze became guarded, and she swallowed and turned her face away. Cervantes watched her for a moment, taking in her demeanor. By the gods, she was feeling much the way he was. He didn't hesitate any longer. He pulled her into his arms, picking her up and twirling her around in place to make her giggle with dizziness. Finally he put her down, took her face in his hands, and kissed her tenderly.

Jonesy placed her hands on his shoulders and melted into him, deepening the kiss. His heart thundered in his chest, and he tightened his arms around her. Every night since their escape he'd dreamed of the next time she would be in his embrace, and he never wanted to let her go. It didn't matter that he was many years her senior, or that her life was vastly different from his. She filled a void that he never realized existed until he fell in love with her. At this moment, all that mattered was that they were together. The rest they would tackle when the time came.

Cervantes swung her up into his arms and carried her over to the bed. He followed her down and continued to kiss her, sweeping his hands over the contours of her body. The feel of her beneath him was exhilarating, and his ardor only heightened. Jonesy matched it with her own share of passion, and only when he began untying the laces of her blouse did she hesitate.

Jonesy pulled away and placed a restraining hand over his. "Cervantes, wait," she whispered.

He instantly stopped. "What is it? Is something wrong?"

Jonesy paused. "I . . . ." She took a deep breath and he felt her begin to tremble.

With a frown he pulled back far enough to see her fully as they spoke. The expression on her face was one of yearning, but tempered by another emotion he couldn't determine. He placed a gentle finger to her lips. "Shhh; it's all right. You can tell me."

She blinked and her eyes became glossy with unshed tears. She raised a hand to his face, her fingertips gently brushing his jaw. Her lips quivered. "I want you so much, Cervantes. For all this time I've been waiting for you to come to me, hoping that I would experience you again. But since the morning of that first day, I realized something. I realized that I didn't want to be just another one of your bedpartners." She took another deep breath and continued. "I suppose I can be, if that is all you want from me. But I need to know what I mean to you, only so that I can keep it in my mind. I can't stand the thought of believing something that isn't the truth, of thinking that something exists between us when really there is nothing but the simple act of pleasuring one another."

Cervantes just stared at her for a moment. She honestly thought that all he might want from her was an occasional frolic in the bedfurs. He was awash with guilt; he realized it would be natural for her to think so because of the way he'd always portrayed himself to her. In almost every city or town they had visited during their travels, he'd easily found himself a willing wench. He cursed to himself, hating the thought that she would be willing to give herself to him without any commitment to go with it. She was worth so much more than that. *But she would do it for him.*

Cervantes shook his head. Hells, he didn't deserve her. "Gods Jonesy, I don't want just another bedpartner." His voice broke and he cleared his throat before continuing. "I had rather hoped you'd come to recognize how much I have begun to care about you over these past moon cycles, especially since our escape from the vampyr." He shook his head again. "I . . . I don't really know how to show you."

It was Jonesy's turn to put a finger over his lips. She gave him a tremulous smile before putting a hand at the nape of his neck, pulling him towards her to continue the kiss she'd interrupted. Cervantes became quiet and allowed himself to be swept away by the power of the passion he felt simmering between them, just waiting to be unleashed. A few moments passed and she stopped again, this time pulling herself away and standing up from the bed. Once more he was awash with confusion. Didn't she want to be with him? Jonesy looked down where he continued to lie, her gaze reflecting uncertainty. "I . . . I know that you are accustomed to women who are so much more experienced."

Before Cervantes could issue a response, she was turning and walking away. Frowning, he just sat up and watched her. Damn, he didn't care about those other women. All he'd been thinking about for the past few weeks was the one moving across the room from him. Jonesy looked over her shoulder and continued in a low tone. "How can I possibly compete?" Her customary green eyes had become dark like the sky before a big storm. She slowly turned back around to face him, as her fingers almost finished working at the laces of her blouse. She pulled the garment down over her shoulders to expose creamy pale flesh. "I know you like the wild ones." She was hesitant as she allowed the blouse to fall to her waist. "Show me what to do."

Cervantes slowly rose from the bed and approached, his eyes drinking her in as though she was a fine wine. He had never seen her naked before, and she was more beautiful than he'd imagined. Once standing before her, he reached out to gently caress the side of her face. He traced his fingertips over her jaw and down her neck to where it curved to meet her chest. His voice was husky. "Hells, Jonesy, I don't think you need much showing."

She placed a staying hand over his before it could move lower. "The last time was a bit . . . um . . . rushed," she said softly, reaching her other hand to where his hair lay over his shoulder.

He ached to reach out and pull her to him, to feel the softness of her skin beneath his palms. But he refrained, mesmerized by her sultry gaze. "I remember."

She took a deep breath, taking her gaze from his to focus on his chest. "This time we aren't under the influence of the vampyr."

Cervantes took her hand away from where it lay over his and turned it over to kiss the palm, meanwhile running his fingertips lightly over one breast. He felt her shudder in response to the sensation and he grinned. "No, we aren't under any daemonic influence, but I notice that your response to me hasn't changed."

Jonesy moved closer until her body almost touched his. She placed her other hand under the hemline of his shirt and brushed it lightly over his skin. His loins tightened and he felt the urge to simply grab her and carry her back to the bed. Again he practiced restraint, wondering how much more of her innocent seduction he could endure.

She looked back up, her expression intense. "But it's different this time. I can *feel* you so much more." She took his wandering hand once more in hers, but this time, instead of acting as a restraint, she pressed his palm against her breast.

Cervantes inhaled sharply and he knew he was close to the precipice. He dared not stir as she moved her other hand from under his shirt, over his chest and up to his face. She pressed the full length of her body against him and curved her hand around the back of his neck. "I wonder if you can feel me . . ."

Her words were cut off as he covered her lips with his, kissing her deeply. Only after several moments did he manage to pull away long enough to reply. "My dear, I can *definitely* feel you." He took a ragged inward breath. "This torment is killing me. Please let me take you to bed."

Jonesy made no objection as he picked her up and carried her back to the pallet. He laid her down, and this time, instead of ravaging her the way he wanted to, he kissed her slowly and tenderly.

Cervantes and Jonesy spent that night and the majority of the next day within one another's company. Scattered among passionate interludes, they told stories about their lives. She seemed to enjoy his tales of a boy living in a prosperous port city, with an uncle whose livelihood was earned as a seafarer. Cervantes was equally as intrigued by her anecdotes of a girl who lived behind the walls of a huge castle, with a father who was a great king.

✖ ✖ ✖ ✖ ✖

Tallachienan sat outside the building the druids called the apoptos. It was the one the group first approached after emerging from below ground, the one in which they were being housed for the remainder of their stay in Krathil-lon. The winds were brisk, and TC wrapped his cloak more tightly around him. It was proving to be more difficult than he thought to adjust to the higher altitude. Not only was the temperature much, much cooler, but it was more difficult to catch his breath.

The others had each gone their separate ways after the unfortunate ending to the conversation they shared with Father Dremathian a couple of evenings before. It was difficult for TC to believe that Alasdair had kept pertinent familial information from Tigerius, information that would have led the young man in the direction he was meant to take. His heart went out to Tiger, for if TC could turn back the clock of his own life, he would love to have his sister and mother with him once more. Tigerius had been robbed of his family, and he had every right to want to bring them back. Alasdair had done him a grave disservice.

It wasn't long after TC was in his chamber that the druid leader had arrived. TC wasn't surprised, for he'd noted the glances cast at him throughout the evening since their arrival. The man got to the point of his visit right away. "Master Tallachienan Chroalthone. I can't help but wonder why you are in the company of my young friends."

TC had shrugged. "I suppose Fate has a hand in everyone's lives, including those of fallen gods."

Dremathian had nodded. "I see. Tell me, why do you think that Fate has anything to do with it? I see it differently, more like your desire to remain close to anyone to whom you may have once had an attachment."

TC had regarded Dremathian intently. It was obvious the man knew about his past affiliation with Adrianna. "I suppose I can't fault you for seeing it that way, but you don't know the story."

Dremathian had cocked his head and seated himself on the bedpallet. "Well, tell me about it then. I have plenty of time."

Glancing up from his thoughts, TC saw a herd of leschera interspersed among the silver oak trees in the near distance. They had come to drink at the lake. TC liked to walk around it, for he enjoyed watching the fishes, all beautifully colored with vibrant shades of deep yellow, orange, and red. The largest of them were purple with golden stripes along their sides, and the smallest were little streaks of silver that liked to swim just beneath the water's surface. Tallachienan sighed and ran his fingers through his hair. He had told his story to Dremathian. He liked to believe that the old man comprehended a bit more about him once it was finished. He thought he saw a softening of Dremathian's demeanor when he'd finally left the chamber, mayhap a trace of understanding reflected in his eyes in place of the distrust.

His thoughts suddenly shifted to Aeris. Where had she gone? Was she happy? Did she ever think of him? Even now he continued to harbor deep feelings for her, wanted so much to be the man she needed him to be. One day, he knew he would see her again; he only hoped it would be sooner rather than later, and that he would be able to repair the damage he had inflicted. For the third time that day, TC held his head in his hands, not because of Aeris, but the terrible headache that threatened. Damn, what was wrong with him? It was difficult even to think, and he had even gone so far as to take rathis tea to soothe it. He thought he heard a voice and he shook his head, struggling to clear the cobwebs that seemed to occlude his thoughts. But then he heard it again . . . someone speaking to him as though at the end of a very long tunnel.

<Tallachienan? Please tell me you are out there. I need you to answer me.>

TC shook his head slightly. What was that? Could it really be? But he hadn't heard Pylar for so long . . .

Then in a slightly stronger voice, <Tallachienan, please. You have only to reach out to me.>

His mind was suddenly flooded with sensation. The dragon had finally come close enough to bring their connection back into full force. Through the link, TC could sense how long Pylar had been searching, and he could feel the yearning deep within the dragon. He was struck with feelings of guilt, for he had thought much less of his bondmate than he probably should have. Damn, he had just been so wrapped up in his own losses, he had very little thought for the only one who mattered most to him beside Aeris.

TC hesitantly reached out. He could sense the difficulty, as though something was trying to interrupt the mental connection. But then Pylar was there, a strong entity in his mind. Feelings of joy coursed through the link, coupled with those of intense relief. Pylar altered his flight course to collide with TC's position, and it didn't take long for him to see the ever growing speck of his friend in the mid-day sky.

The herd of leschera vacated the area as the dragon winged closer. A few moments later, TC was standing up as Pylar landed in the clearing situated next to the apoptos. He summarily rushed over to his friend, and as Pylar lowered his head in greeting, TC took it within his hands and rested his cheek over-top the nearest golden eye. The other was covered with deeply scarred tissue, the orb no longer visible. And as he recalled it, the orb may no longer exist, for it had been the victim of acid burn, courtesy of a renegade degethozak. From deep within the dragon, TC could feel a reverberating sigh of contentedness. A part of him felt the same—felt as though he had become more whole than he had been since that morning when he awakened from his restless sleep.

<I am so glad to have finally found you. These past moon cycles have been long without you near.>

TC caressed Pylar's face. <Yes, quite long indeed. If only I knew why our communication has been blocked.>

Pylar nodded. <It has been an enigma to me as well.>

<How did you find me without the power of our *bond* to guide you?>

<I am not certain. Perhaps it has something to do with the history I know about these druids. Their leader was a good friend of the Wildrunners. Somewhere in my mind I must have imagined that Alasdair and Aeris would make their way here and that you might be in accompaniment.>

TC paused for a moment. <I have lost Aeris.>

Pylar was silent. <Yes, I was wondering about her, for I don't sense her presence here.>

<She left the group in the company of her own bondmate a couple fortnights ago. I have no idea where they may have gone.>

Pylar became pensive for several moments before he spoke again. <I have been searching for you for many weeks, and during my travels I met another helzethryn. He was a wanderer, a dragon who had become disengaged from the rest of his race, one much like many others I have in my acquaintance, including myself. He told me of a relatively unknown place, a continent upon which many dragons have made their homes since the Pact of Bakharas was broken. It seems that Trebexal has ramped up his efforts, and he is training dragons and any faelin riders he can find to become an effective aerial combat unit.>

TC was silent as he considered Pylar's words. <You believe that this dragon who has claimed Aeris as his bondmate has taken her to Shayamalan?>

Pylar cocked his head. <Don't you?>

TC was quiet again, contemplating this new reality. Most likely Pylar was right. He stepped back away from his bondmate and regarded the dragon intently, schooling his thoughts into disciplined organization. <You have changed, my friend,> he said.

Pylar snorted derisively at this unexpected comment, twin tendrils of smoke rising from flared nostrils. He was aware that TC made reference to his missing eye. Sensing the frivolity of the remark, Pylar knew that TC cared nothing for the lack; however, it didn't stop him from poking fun. <You have changed as well, my friend. I seem to recall that you had much more at your arcane disposal when last we were in one another's company.>

Tallachienan simply cast him a foul glance. It was then he noticed the approach of the resident druids. Most likely, they wondered about the appearance of a large dragon on their lands. He smiled to himself; it was so good to have Pylar back. *Even though Aeris was no longer by his side, he felt so much more complete.*

✕✕✕✕✕

Tigerius silently stared out the arched aperture from across the small chamber. Light shone in through the opening, yet quickly became swallowed by the pervading darkness. But he preferred it that way, his mental state matching the tone of the shadowed room. It was fitting, he supposed, for someone who deserved it—one who should not achieve redemption, no matter how much he had changed his life.

For he had done his mother the greatest of injustices.

When Tiger was but a boy, he and Tianna shared the most extraordinary rapport. He had thought it was common-place, a relationship every child shared with his or her mother. However, as he grew into adolescence, he began to realize otherwise—that most children couldn't feel, hear or see the things he did. Even now he could see her in his mind's eye, his mother hunkering down before him, her beautiful face always reflecting the love she felt.

"Tigerius, are you my boy?"

He nodded, a grin playing at the corners of his mouth.

"When I am old then, I suppose you shall take care of me."

The phrase was more of a comment than a question. Tiger nodded his assent, still smiling. Mama was silly. He couldn't look past the fact that he was the one who needed her *to take care of* him. *She must surely be joshing him.*

Tianna cupped his small face within both of her hands and brought him close, wrapping him within her warm embrace. "It is settled then," she whispered into his ear. "I am surely blessed to have a son such as you."

Just as much as he could see her, Tiger could feel her arms around him, loving arms he would almost die to feel now. Through the years afterward, he had grown rebellious. The other boys within his acquaintance, sensing his differences, tormented Tiger with unsolicited conjectures about his parents and the history they shared with the hinterlean faelin of Elvandahar . . . more specifically, the Wildrunners. The ridicule drove him away from his father first, the one whom the speculation seemed to center about the most, and later his mother as well. Feelings of resentment grew and the rapport between himself and his mother slowly began to disintegrate. When once he had been able to hear her heart beating, feel the precise warmth of her body, and smell the fragrance of her bath oils even when not in her presence, he eventually lost the ability to sense those things. Much like his father, she became someone Tiger should strive to contradict, for it was easy to see she was in league with Triath, a man who didn't have Tiger's best interests at heart.

Tiger continued to rebel, and eventually reached the point where he no longer cared to disclose his whereabouts, traveling here and there whenever he chose. It was sad, for Triath and Tianna Solanar were the two people who cared the most about him. In turn, Tiger had chosen to show his parents that they were meaningless.

And now they were gone.

Tigerius allowed the anger to overcome him, anger towards Alasdair. By the gods, he had never felt so wronged. What man wouldn't share with his comrade that his parents were nowhere to be found? That they had somehow become missing between this day and the next—no matter how this information might distract him or how far away they might be? What *friend* wouldn't tell his comrade these things? In more ways than one, Tiger felt his heart breaking, not just because his mother and father had become lost to him, but because the one man whom he had called his finest friend was so thoughtless and selfish.

Tigerius lowered his head into his hands. Everything had finally become so clear to him. All of his dreams, all of his visions, and all of those strange *feelings* he had been having for so many fortnights could all be explained now. They were more than just a manifestation of his desire to be home. They were that strange part of him able to perceive those things that most people could not, that same part of him that knew there was something awaiting the group at the entrance to the catacombs leading to Tholana's fortress, that same part of him that was able to erect a shell of energy around himself and Jonesy when they were imperiled by the daemundai.

It was the part of him that had detected that something was terribly wrong, and that his mother, whether she knew it or not, was transmitting to him.

Tigerius felt a tear roll down his cheek. By the gods, she needed him and he wasn't there for her. Where was Triath? How could his father have allowed this to happen? Was he somehow incapacitated? Was he dead? Damnation, Tiger should have never left home all those fortnights ago. How long had it been now? A full year, maybe longer? He couldn't remember.

Tigerius struggled to relax. Perhaps, if he looked deeply enough, he would be able to bring out whatever divine information concerning his mother lingered within his subconscious. Perhaps all those dreams and visions could be taken and elaborated upon despite the feelings of dread they induced. Perhaps he would be able to determine where he should go.

Someone was calling.

Tianna suddenly took a sharp intake of breath, and her eyes snapped open. From where she lay on the stone slab, her gaze darted around the cold dark chamber. The pain she felt was acute, centered low on her belly. She slowly moved a shaking hand to the afflicted area, her fingertips encountering a roughly sewn line of stitching. Tears gathered at the corners of her eyes only to fall across her temples to become lost in her hairline.

I should be dead by now.

The thought was the first Tianna could consciously gather and execute within her mind. She struggled to take yet another breath of the frigid air, and the simple action made the pain excruciating. She knew why Razlul kept her in such a cold place. It was his efforts to slow the growth of infection he knew had begun the moment he opened her. He had worked quickly, for infection would stop for no one, not even the mehta of the daemundai. He had learned all he could before closing her, realizing he needed to find another like her in order to complete his experimentation. That and maybe some help from the dreaded Brotherhood of the Kronshue. Now it was only a matter of time before her body's regenerative abilities would heal her enough so she could be returned to her normal chamber.

It was then she felt it again, the same sensation that had awakened her. It was a caress actually, one that seemed to call out to her. It seemed somehow familiar.

The tears continued to course from her eyes as she clutched at the hideous wound in her abdomen. Indeed, she would be dead by now—if she were human. But since the birth of her son, she was no longer merely that. Triath had done something extraordinary when he put his seed within her, and when the child grew, she changed even more. When Tigerius was finally born, she had almost died. Only with his breath had Triath saved her from death and given Tigerius life. The moment she'd awakened after the birth, she could feel everything the baby felt, and he could feel her too. Their connection was so strong that if one of them perished, the other would surely have followed. It was a bond she never imagined could break. But then Tigerius entered adolescence, and everything had changed.

One day Tiger had come home, and he hated her.

Tianna had been devastated. Triath tried to explain it to her, that puberty oftentimes caused this response in human offspring, and mayhap even more so in daemonic ones. It was an inevitable eventuality. She'd refused to believe her husband, holding fast to that bond that had been forged whilst Tiger was still yet an unborn babe. Yet, as the fortnights passed, that bond withered and fell away. But Tianna never forgot how it was to be loved by someone so unconditionally. And now . . .

As she struggled to take yet another breath, she felt it again. It was the most gentle of touches, a loving mental stroke to her innermost mind. It made her relax enough to inhale in spite of the agony it caused, and it was then she began to recognize the sensation for what it was.

Tigerius had finally become a man, and he was calling out to her just as Triath always promised he would.

Tianna choked on the tears that managed to trickle down the back of her throat. In a million moon cycles, she would never wish for her son to come to this gods'-forsaken place. Razlul would surely kill him if he did. However, if their bond was indeed reestablished, Tiger would easily be able to follow her mental signature to this place.

Tianna slammed up her barriers. She couldn't be certain it would help, but she could at least try. She knew she was no longer entirely sane, for the merzillith had taken bits and pieces of her mind away from her. But beyond any shadow of doubt, she knew this to be true: Tigerius was looking for her, *upholding the promise a small boy had made to his mother a long time ago.*

✖ ✖ ✖ ✖ ✖

Aeris slowly entered the practice arena. Her hand rested on the hilt of the short sword sheathed at her hip, a weapon over which she had told demeters Fo and Roger she claimed some mastery. Of course, she knew she wasn't very good. In spite of her mother's insistence, she hadn't focused enough on developing her skill the way she should have. And now here she was, stuck in a situation that demanded she have some type of previous training. She brought dishonor to both her parents and her master with her lack of skill, and she felt some measure of shame.

Across the arena, quartermaster Falon awaited her, one hand at each hip. His brown hair was held out of his eyes by the red band he wore around his forehead, hair that otherwise liked to lay over his eyes. As always, his expression was impassive, and she wondered if he had any emotion at all for she had yet to see any during the few times she'd seen him. She'd expected to see Demeter Fo; most likely Falon was there to assess her ability on the demeter's behalf, required to report back to him of her strengths, if she had any, and her weaknesses.

Once standing a farlo away from Falon, Aeris stopped. The young terralean man regarded her intently for a moment before speaking. "You seem overly reticent about this meeting."

Aeris simply nodded.

His tone became mildly sarcastic. "I can only imagine why."

She frowned and thought to herself, *What is that supposed to mean?*

Falon shook his head. "And now I am stuck with you. That's just great."

Aeris narrowed her eyes but said nothing. Maybe, on one of her better days, she might have offered some rejoinder. But she was still tired from her unfortunate encounter with septic scale-burn, and she honestly didn't have it in her to argue. *Let the man believe what he wants. Who cares much what he thinks anyway?*

Falon unsheathed his sword and positioned himself in battle-readiness. "Come on, what are you waiting for? Let's get this over with."

Aeris gave an almost indiscernible shake of her head. His arrogance was annoying, but she supposed she could suffer it for a short while. She unsheathed her own blade, a sword she had borrowed from Trebexal's armory. Of course, it couldn't replace the one her mother had given to her, a weapon Adrianna had discovered lying in the bowels of Master Tallachienan's citadel during her training a long time ago. Aeris felt a momentary pang of anguish sweep through her. Damnation, when would she recover from the hurt? She closed her eyes and thought of her father instead. Besides Master Dinim, Sirion had been one of her instructors.

Oh gods, she missed her father so much.

Falon chose that moment to begin his evaluation. He swiftly swept towards her and she barely managed to parry the attack. Aeris followed with an assault of her own, but it was deftly blocked by Falon's blade. She breathed deeply, keeping her father in mind. Sirion would be her focus, her power point.

Falon swept at her again, and this time she skillfully brought her blade up to block the attack. Moments later they circled one another, each looking for the least defensible place on the other. Falon delivered a mock strike, but she refused to fall prey to the bait. She remained focused through a few more attacks that gave Falon pertinent information regarding her expertise, but not without detriment. Her heart ached with continued thoughts of her father, for it had been so long since she'd seen him last. What made it worse was that her mind was naturally drawn to another person in conjunction with Sirion, one whom she had greatly wronged when she flew away on Jaxom's back.

Alasdair.

By the gods, her brother must surely hate her by now.

Aeris faltered beneath Falon's next attack. Ah, she was too weak for this—not just physically, but mentally. She knew that this was important and that it was an integral part of her training. She needed to carry a weapon into battle, one with which she would hone her skill. First she would gain aptitude on ground. Then she would use that proficiency to fortify her whilst in the air. So she would persevere in spite of the challenge provided by her infirmity and the poor attitude of her instructor.

However, Aeris was not above implementing some tactics that many would consider dishonorable. Alasdair always told her that honor and survivorship in battle didn't always coexist, so he gave her the knowledge necessary to keep her alive if her opponent was the better swordsman. It was quite obvious that Falon's prowess was far superior. Aeris faltered and fell, but when he went to follow her, Aeris delivered a swift kick to his unprotected shin.

Falon shouted and fell back. Aeris scrambled backward, and was about to regain her feet when he swept towards her. His blade just narrowly missed hitting her shoulder as she rolled out of the way. His expression was thunderous as he followed, and when he got close again, she executed another well aimed kick. This time it struck him in the other shin.

Falon shouted again, but this time with words. "Damnation, woman! What the Hells is wrong with you? We are here to assess your ability with the sword, not hand-to-hand combat!"

Aeris narrowed her eyes. "Mayhap I would feel more comfortable with the evaluation if your improved your attitude. Tell me, were you instructed to treat me like a pile of lloryk dung to make the assessment that much more difficult? If so, you succeeded. Likewise I hope it has had an impact on you as well." Aeris glanced pointedly at his shins.

Falon regarded her speculatively for a few moments before motioning to her. "Come on; stand up."

Aeris slowly acquiesced, wincing only briefly when the activity caused her discomfort. Once standing, she looked at him with the same intensity he visited on her.

Finally Falon spoke again. "All right, let's start over. This time I will try to remain objective."

Aeris narrowed her eyes. A part of her wanted to know why he needed to try so hard, but the rest of her didn't give a damn. She placed herself at combat readiness. "Fine, I suppose I can oblige."

Falon gave a half smile, and once in position he beckoned her forward. "All right, you start this time."

Aeris shook her head with his about-face but didn't hesitate as she swept in for her attack. Falon parried her blow and followed with a swing that she easily deflected. They continued for a while and at first she thought that he might be holding back on her. However, it wasn't long before he was coming at her with more ferocity. A time or two she thought she saw a look of surprise pass over his face.

Unfortunately, Aeris quickly tired. Falon came at her with a high overhead attack, and she was just barely able to block. She stumbled beneath the strength of it, and Falon followed when she fell onto her back. Her reflexes weren't quick enough make another swing or to roll out from beneath him. Falon pinned her sword arm with one hand while swiftly straddling her hips. He then leaned forward until his face was close to hers. Aeris breathed heavily, a forelock of his brown hair waving between them with each gust.

"You are better than I thought you would be."

She grimaced. "You thought I would be *that* bad?"

Falon cocked his head. "What is your definition of 'that bad'?"

Nonplussed, she didn't bother with an answer and retorted with a question of her own. "What is your definition of 'better than I thought you would be'?"

Falon gave a sigh and released her arm. "I had a preconceived notion of how good you would be with the short-sword, and it affected my behavior when you first walked in here. But you have since demonstrated that I underestimated you." He rose from his position over her and held out a hand. "I'm sorry."

Aeris looked from his hand to face. Seeing the sincerity reflected there, she took the hand and allowed him to pull her up. "So what happens now?"

Falon shrugged. "I'm not sure, but I will give my assessment to the demeters and they will decide if you are skilled enough to begin aerial training with your weapon of choice."

Aeris nodded and turned away. She was so tired; all she wanted to do was lie down in bed for a while. She bent to retrieve her sword where it dropped when Falon pinned her hand. She inspected it for a moment before sheathing it.

"I'm glad I was wrong about you."

Aeris turned when she heard Falon's voice behind her. He was regarding her with a solemn expression, his arm outstretched before him. She didn't hesitate to grasp it in the universal gesture of greeting, one that could also be used as a sign of camaraderie. She nodded and smiled before releasing his arm. "Me, too."

CHAPTER SEVEN

Before the silvery backdrop of Krathil-lon, the group was given an opportunity to rest without worry. They took it, knowing they wouldn't get another—not until the war was over and they were finally home. Meanwhile, the druids prepared the tools, equipment, and beasts they would need on their journey south to the realm of Elvandahar. In addition, they provided food packs for each of them. If used wisely, the packs could last them more than two fortnights.

The group left the sanctuary of Krathil-lon the third morning after their arrival. With the agreeable weather and the six strong lloryk provided by the druids, they made good time as they moved south through the Sartingel Mountains. Once past the foothills, they continued to journey through the eastern steppes bordering the realm of Tusbir, winding their way through the tributaries of the Hodrak River. Continuing ever southward, they then reached unclaimed territory. Neither any villages nor towns existed within that swath of grassland stretching from the tributaries of the Hodrak to the top of the Lordis River where it rushed from out of the Ratik Mountains. And if there were bands of lawless people who established themselves within that area, they were left to their own devices. Inasmuch, the borderlands were known as a rather wild place, where people never knew what they might find. After a few more days traveling south, they would enter the Plain of Antipithanee. Somewhere upon that vast steppe many years ago, a band of helzethryn, rezwithrys and degethozak dragons had come to meet an undead enemy. . . subsequently breaking the Pact of Bakharas and ending life as most people knew it upon Shandahar.

Cervantes looked around the periphery of the encampment. Since his arrival into northwestern Ansalar, he had been quite fascinated by the changes he saw in his environment. The air was much cooler, but that had been expected. It was the plant-life that had caught his attention, and the fact that everything here grew so much smaller. The insects were less abundant, and also seemed to be comprised of much smaller varieties. And the animals were different, much different than those from the southeast. Strangely, as opposed to the plant and insect life, the animals of the north seemed to be of the larger variety. More than once he had been quite taken aback by some momentary appearance, yet he found it all quite fascinating.

After awhile Cervantes focused his attention *inside* the encampment they had made for the night. He had begun to notice that something had changed since they left the druids of Krathil-lon, something that Cervantes had never quite experienced with the group before. It was difficult to grasp exactly what it was, but it almost seemed as though they were more comfortable in one another's company. They had finally reached the point where everyone had made the decision to accept one another for who they were in spite of their foibles.

And perhaps Cervantes had also been a part of that change.

All of the bedrolls had been laid out, and the animals tended. As always, Jonesy was seated before the fire preparing yet another meal. Knowing how much she despised the task, Cervantes felt the corner of his mouth pull up into a grin as he watched her from the spot he had chosen for himself after tending his evening duties. Besides the halfen brothers, she was the only one who knew how to prepare a decent meal. More often than not, she got stuck with the job because Vikhail and Vardec had other duties to perform, one of which happened to be the evening watch. They needed the time to rest after a long day of travel so they would be able to remain wakeful for their turn. It was understandable, so Jonesy never complained. She simply suffered in silence, albeit with Jezibel to keep her company.

However, despite the unity he had begun to see amongst the group as a whole, there was one person who stood out. Cervantes' sympathy went out to him, for he could understand what Tigerius must be feeling. The young man remained distant and withdrawn despite earlier attempts made by Alasdair, Cedric, and Talemar to bring him out of his melancholy. For the most part, Cervantes simply let the man be, stopping only to lay a reassuring hand on his friend's shoulder every once in a while as he chanced by.

But with Jonesy it was different. Many an evening she took the time to bring Tiger a plate of food and then sat with him to share the meal. Cervantes would sometimes watch as she strove to bring Tiger out from behind the thick barriers he had erected around himself. With her light-hearted banter and easy-going manner, she would even get him to smile every once in a while. Not once did Cervantes think the relationship to be anything more than friendly, and he harbored neither discontent nor jealousy. He was secure with the knowledge that the young woman loved him, and that was more than enough.

Cervantes watched Jonesy as she rose from her place at the fires. Her shoulders were slumped, and he realized she was tired. Without a second thought, he rose to his feet to go to her. He paused after several steps to remember that he must remain nonchalant, for they both had agreed that it was best if the true nature of their involvement remain unknown to the rest of the group. Most likely this was quite unwarranted, but it was a mutual decision, one he couldn't explain even if he wanted to.

Jonesy turned just as he stepped up behind her. Startled, she stumbled back and he quickly reached out to grab her arm in order to keep her from falling onto the pot hanging over the nearest fire. She grinned self-consciously as she spoke. "Gods, Cervantes. You need to stop sneaking up on me like that."

Cervantes smiled in return and then shook his head. "No, you simply need to learn to listen to everything around you, even when you are in an encampment with friends. You never know when someone might betray you."

Cervantes felt the smile suddenly leave his face, and Jonesy's gaze fixed piercingly upon his. He could tell she wanted to reach out and comfort him as he dealt with the sudden pain associated with the loss of his brother. He could see the conflict reflected in her green eyes, and then the decision she made to comfort him despite what anyone else might think. She reached up and put her arms around his neck, holding him close as he struggled through the painful memories. And when they finally passed, she released him and took a small step back.

"The evening meal is almost ready. If you sit and keep me company for a while, I just might consider offering you the first portion." She spoke in a light manner, and he felt himself relax instantly. She seemed to have that effect on him recently.

Cervantes sighed with mock inconvenience. "Well, I suppose I can't pass that up," he said.

Jonesy indicated the pile of back pads and leathers that had been removed from the horses and lloryk for the evening. She had situated them conveniently at the fire, and there was just enough space on them for another to sit. Cervantes eyed the pile for a moment before seating himself and he was promptly followed by Jonesy. He could feel the warmth of her side against his, her close proximity immediately placing him at a heightened level of awareness.

Damn, this was harder than he thought it would be.

Sitting there beside her, Cervantes reassessed the reason why they kept the truth of their union from the people who were supposed to be their closest companions. He reached out and put a hand on her thigh, slowly proceeding to massage it. He kept the mischievous smile to himself, for he could only imagine what her response might be. However, he didn't expect her to suddenly stand from her place and deliver a close-fisted blow across his face.

Cervantes fell back from his position on the piled leathers, his backside unceremoniously hitting the ground behind him. He immediately swung his gaze to Jonesy, who stood there looking down at him. Her eyes were wide with surprise, telling him that she hadn't expected herself to respond to his overtures in such a brash manner. Meanwhile, Vikhail passed by with a smug expression on his face. "Serves ya right," he commented. "Ya should'na be taken liberties wit de lady."

Cervantes found himself frowning with the absurdity, for he had already taken Jonesy to his bed on more than one occasion. He glanced back at her, just to see an expression of remorse on her pretty face. He rose from the ground, and once dusting himself off he slowly stepped up to her. With his close proximity she was forced to look up at him.

"Come away from there, my dear," he said. "It seems that the fire makes you more grouchy than usual."

Jonesy struggled to keep her expression under control, yet he could see the smile she fought to contain. She shook her head as she responded. "Our comrade is right. You should not have taken such liberties with me. You deserve what you got."

Cervantes smiled widely. "You know that's not true," he said, lowering his voice. "I happen to know that you want me to touch you that way—just as much as you know I want you to touch me."

Jonesy frowned in mock dismay. Her gaze darted this way and that, looking to be sure no one was paying them much heed. "Well, you're wrong," she hissed. She refused to meet his eyes as she told the lie, for she knew he would be able to see right through her. "Besides, why would I want such a thing? It simply isn't decent," she continued.

Cervantes smiled a smile he meant only for her. "Meet me beyond the northeastern boundaries of the encampment once the first watch has settled," he replied.

"Hey, you two. What's with the hush hush?"

Startled, Cervantes and Jonesy turned as Jezibel flounced up to them with a questioning expression. She turned towards the fire, and seeing the contents of the pot beginning to boil over, she quickly swept up the nearby glove and used it to remove the heavy pot from over the fire. She gave a huff of frustration as she set it on the ground beside her, and then turned back to Jonesy.

Cervantes widened his grin and tugged at Jonesy's sleeve. "Don't forget." With that said, he turned and left her there to suffer Jezzie's obvious ire.

Jezibel regarded Jonesy as she planted both hands at her hips. "I can see you were paying strict attention to the stew-pot," she said sarcastically. "I could have burned myself taking it away from the fire before it scorched."

Jonesy simply shook her head. "I'm sorry. I should have paid more attention. Cervantes, he . . ."

"Oh yes, blame it on Cervantes," Jezzie said with a tone of annoyance.

"It's much easier than accepting the blame yourself. Just go. I'll see to the remainder of the meal preparations."

Jezzie turned away from Jonesy, but not before seeing the hurt expression settle over the other woman's face. She felt a sudden pang of regret, for the harsh words she spoke were begotten only out of jealousy. In spite of her newfound romantic interest in Levander, Jezzie still harbored some residual feelings for Cervantes. She hated to see him pay sustained attention to the wealthy daughter of a king, someone so obviously out of his range of procurement. Or more accurately, *someone who was so much more than Jezzie could ever be.*

Without a word, Jonesy left her to finish the task alone. From the corner of her eye, Jezzie watched as the other woman seated herself on her bedroll, folding her knees up to her chest so as to rest the side of her face against them. Once more Jezibel felt a disquiet, a feeling from deep inside that told her she had treated Jonesy poorly. However, the fact still remained that Jonesy was most often the focus of Cervantes' attention, a status that Jezzie had once held for herself. The experience had been short-lived, for the captain was always back and forth from sea. At first, he would prolong his visits at least two weeks. But after a few years, things changed. Cervantes became interested only in sharing her bed for a night or two before heading back out to the sea, his one true mistress. Now, the possibility of his being enamored with another woman was difficult to bear, especially one that happened to be the youngest heir to the throne of Karlisle. Her bows pulled together into a frown as she idly wondered what Cervantes was talking about when he told Jonesy to 'not forget'.

Jezibel was in ill humor when she ladled out the stew into the bowls that waited, each placed there by each member of the group as he brought it to rest atop the folded blanket beside her. She kept part of her attention on Cervantes and Jonesy, wondering if anything would happen. There was nothing. After a while she joined Lev to eat her own portion of the meal. If he noticed the focus of her distraction, he said nothing. All the while she wondered exactly what it was that had her so miffed. By most outward appearances, there seemed to be nothing but friendship between Cervantes and Jonesy. However, every now and again, she would see the way each would glance at the other with what she perceived to be expressions of vague longing. She supposed she could be wrong about that assumption, except for situations like what she experienced earlier that evening, when they stood closer than usual, speaking in low, dulcet tones with an aura of secrecy.

For what felt like the hundredth time, Jezzie wondered why she cared so much. Certainly she and the captain had shared something in the past, but that time was long gone. In part, she had moved on with her life without him. She'd acquired her own source of income with the jobs she procured, acquired her own lodging, and bedded other men if monetary prospects were good enough. Since her quandary in Darban, and her subsequent tenure with the group, she'd kept her distance from Cervantes. Even though he'd helped her out of a heaping load of trouble, she was immediately aware of the change in him, especially after the theft of the *Sea Maiden*. Things had spiraled swiftly out of control after that with the abduction of Aeris and Talemar in Gulshaan.

Jezzie shook herself free of her thoughts. She watched as the group prepared for sleep. Tigerius and Cedric were set for the first watch, followed by the halfen brothers, and finally Alasdair and TC. The last watch was often the one that shifted the most, for it saw a set of different people every night. Sometimes Lev would be there, or Talemar, Cervantes, or even the dragon Pylar. Sometimes Mateo would help out as well. It gave the men an opportunity to have a night all to themselves with uninterrupted sleep. The women were never expected to participate, and it wasn't encouraged. Jezibel was okay with that, for she prized her sleep—*except this night.*

As the encampment settled and became quiet, she continued to keep her focus on Cervantes and Jonesy. It wasn't too long before Cervantes stirred. He crept from the confines of his bedroll and disappeared into the darkness surrounding the encampment. Moments later, Jonesy was doing the same, leaving in the same direction Cervantes had taken only several moments before.

Jezibel quickly slipped out from the warmth of her own bedroll. She glanced over to see a soundly sleeping Lev, and then stepped out towards the fire to see that neither Tiger nor Cedric were looking in her direction. With the same caution practiced by Cervantes and Jonesy, she slowly circled a portion of the encampment before arriving at the place where she saw them walk into the night. Sensing someone watching, she glanced at Pylar. His golden gaze was settled on her, his wedge-shaped head resting on his front legs. The knowledge that he was aware she was leaving the encampment didn't deter her.

Jezzie quickly walked in the direction she saw Cervantes take. By the gods, it was creepy being out there in the darkness with only the shadows cast by the light of Hestim to light the way. At least it was only the tall grasses she had to navigate, for if it had been anything more, such as forest or hills, she would have been even more disquieted. She was calmed by the fact that a dragon was close by, and that he was an ally.

It wasn't long before she happened upon them. Despite the suspicion that they were clandestine lovers, she never really believed it until now. Beneath the light granted by the distant moons, Cervantes and Jonesy made passionate love. Jezzie couldn't help but watch, entranced by the scene. It was the way Cervantes held Jonesy, as though she was the most precious thing in the world. It was the way he kissed her, slowly and softly. It was the way he looked at her, his eyes reflecting a love Jezzie had never seen from him before. It all made her realize that what they shared was real. And that each of them was deserving of it.

Once returning to the encampment and slipping back into the comfort of her bedroll, Jezibel began to weep. She cried for something she never had, for her inability to oftentimes look beyond herself, and for the hurt she caused the people she'd come to care most about. She knew she needed to accept the reality she'd witnessed, and so she sought sleep. On the morrow, she would be better.

Jezzie turned onto her side, pulling the blanket around her. Damn, it would be hard to finally let go.

Aeris screamed. Jaxom chuckled in her mind, reveling in the torment he inflicted on his bondmate. Down, down, down, he spiraled until they almost reached the ground. Then he quickly swept upward, his massive wings catching the current that would bring them higher into the air. He felt her heart beating rapidly in her chest through their link, and Aeris cursed the day she met him.

However, her curse was his blessing. Before meeting Aeris, Jaxom had lived only half a life. Now he was finally whole. After so long, he had come to see the light. Unfortunately for his bondmate, his 'light' was her duty. He felt her scrambling about within the strange harness contraption that some poor fool, with quite a bit of time to spend, had created. She struggled to place her arms and legs in the positions they needed to be for her to achieve optimal combat readiness during suboptimal flight patterns. It had taken them several practice sessions to get this far, including ones they conducted outside those overseen by Demeter Fo. There were prerequisites they needed to accomplish before they could move on to the actual combat sessions in which their peers were now participating. One of those happened to be the rider's mastery of the harness in every scenario.

Jaxom slowed his wing-strokes and went into a glide. Through their link, he could sense her weariness. She was pushing herself hard, and he wondered if it was beyond her limits. He could sense the soreness of her body and the mental strain of knowing what was expected of her and the fear that she might fail. Damn. Aeris didn't deserve this. He should take her away.

<No!> Her voice thundered through his mind. <I can do this, Jaxom.>

<But at what cost? And for what cause? When I took you away from the group, I didn't promise you this . . . this . . .>

Aeris shook her head. <It doesn't matter what our intentions were *then*, only what is *now*,> she interrupted. <I can do this, Jaxom. You just need to have a little bit more faith in me.>

<Elirya, it's not a matter of faith, it's . . .>

Aeris frowned. <What did you just call me?>

Jaxom paused. <Elirya. It means 'sister' in the common dragon tongue.>

<Yes, I know.> Aeris was pensive. <It is how my mother is often addressed by her bondmate's companions.>

Jaxom gave an affirmative gesture. <Most likely it is because they have such a strong proclivity towards her that they consider her as one of their own.> He paused before continuing. <I have heard many of the other dragons referring to you by this name, and it came naturally to my mind. If you don't like it, I won't use it again.>

Aeris shook her head. <No, it's fine. The name has a nice sound to it.> She paused for a moment. <The other dragons use this name in reference to me?>

Jaxom nodded. <Indeed they do. They consider you 'sister'.>

Aeris continued to be reflective. <Why? What makes my pull so strong?>

Jaxom also became thoughtful and then gave the dragon equivalent of a shrug. <I don't know.>

Aeris suddenly became quiet, sensing a shift in Jaxom's demeanor. He had become aware of her extraordinary ability to speak telepathically with other dragons. He'd heard of no other who could do it. Ordinarily, faelin had only the capacity to speak with his or her own bondmate. The dragon elders were the exception to that rule, able to speak with anyone with whom they chose. It seemed that Aeris was also an exception. Since discovering this unusual quality about his bondmate, Jaxom struggled with surges of jealousy. He wanted her all to himself, but somehow she had a strange connection to every dragon within close enough proximity. In his mind, it made his *bond* to her less special. He was reminded that he never wanted a faelin bondmate to begin with, and now that he had one, he was forced to share her with everyone else. In spite of his love for her, there was a part of himself he still kept locked away. He couldn't help it, for who wanted to share every aspect of himself with someone who was so open to every other dragon on all of Shandahar?

If Aeris had any inkling of what he was thinking, she made no indication. She gave a nod and spoke aloud. "All right. So let's get on with this."

Jaxom tore himself away from his ruminations, shifting his focus back to the task at hand. <Don't you think perhaps we could use a rest? Maybe sun

ourselves on the ledge of your barracks and . . .>

<No, Jaxom! We have work to do. Sunning comes later!>

Jaxom groaned inwardly. He would make her pay for this.

Aeris screamed once more as he swiftly went into a downward dive, catching her off guard. He had to convince himself that she deserved it, if even just a little.

Aeris cut the scream short as the winds took her breath away. With her heart sitting in her throat, she once more struggled to right herself in the battle harness, all the while ignoring the chafing pain she felt on the insides of her thighs. She was still healing from the scale-burn she had acquired during their journey. However, instead of regular trousers, she now wore tight-fitting, dark brown riding leathers, proper attire for sitting astride an ever-moving dragon. There was quite a noticeable difference whilst she rode, and she loved the benefits she could now receive from having leathers such as these. She owed many thanks to the isterian who had them made for her as soon as they realized she had none, courtesy of none other than Faleema, of course.

Much to her encouragement, Aeris was able to situate herself appropriately within the harness. Not to mention, it took less time than it had when Jaxom last made such a dive. She felt her eyeballs plummet down to her chest as the dragon made an upward sweep, yet she was able to maintain optimal position in spite of the sudden shift. Then, as Jaxom leveled out, she began to feel pride. Yes! She had done it. Now she just needed to replicate it.

<You see? I told you I could do it.>

<I never had a doubt,> replied Jaxom in a solemn tone.

<Humpf . . . whatever,> she said haughtily.

<No need to get all high and mighty on me, now. I am your most devout supporter.>

<Sometimes I wonder,> she rejoined.

Jaxom blew out his nostrils, wisps of smoke wafting back to her. For a brief while he remained silent, and Aeris began to wonder if her banter had inadvertently hurt his feelings.

<Sometimes I wonder about you, Elirya, but never do I doubt you.>

Aeris replied in a subdued mindvoice. <All right Jaxom. I believe you.>

<Good, now let's go sun ourselves for a short while before the warmest rays are gone for the day.>

Aeris nodded in agreement. <Yes, I feel we deserve it now. I'm so happy this hurdle is overcome. Although let's face it, this training isn't going to get any easier. Next, we meet the requirements necessary for combat training,> she said grimly.

Jaxom said nothing, simply changing his course for the barracks. She sensed that something weighed on his mind, yet she chose not to press him about it. He would share it with her in his own time. Now all she wanted was rest, for on the morrow the real tests would begin.

⁂ ⁂ ⁂ ⁂ ⁂

Chorlak and his followers quickly made their way through the region of land comprising the western edge of the Selmist Forest and the northeast corner of the Bryton Hills. His temper simmered threateningly just below the surface, and his companions easily sensed it. They remained just far enough away to escape his anger should they do or say anything he might construe as irksome. In short, they made him feel as though he traveled alone when really he did not. Now, *that* was vexing.

Just that morning, Chorlak and his retinue had emerged from a shattered portal system. Stepping through the debris that had once comprised the central mirror and surrounding bronze brackets, he had wondered what fool would destroy such a magnificent arcane device. It had been easy for them to arrive there, but for anyone to leave, well, one would need the expertise of a Dimensionalist, and a skilled one at that. Luckily, Chorlak was not in that situation, and they had been able to walk through the chamber unhampered but for the shards of glass that pierced the soles of their feet.

Chorlak grunted deep within his throat as he snapped yet another overhanging tree branch in his hand. For the tenth time, his thoughts returned to his recent failure, and he still could hardly believe what had transpired. As he and his followers had made their way towards their destination, Chorlak suddenly found his connection with Hospartuek severed. He was immediately on the alert, for the doppleganger had warned him of the increased risk of Seth becoming a deviant, aspiring to take the girl Joneselia through the *Transition.* And he also warned that the brother of the man whom he impersonated had discovered him.

After losing contact with his informant, Chorlak had made considerable haste towards the vampyr lair. However, even though he knew something had gone amiss, he had never really expected the scenario he witnessed upon his arrival.

Even before the castle came into view, the scent of death wafted towards them. Chorlak increased the pace, and only when the dilapidated structure was in view did he slow. Upon the landscape before them lay the decapitated bodies of at least thirty vampyr. The heads stared up at them from sightless cerulean eyes. Chorlak was struck by the magnitude of the slaying, for only someone with significant power could have wrought such destruction to an entire colony of vampyr.

As Chorlak struggled to get his bearings, he ordered his minions to scour the inside of the castle in search of their prey. He knew it was unlikely they would find anything of import, but he would not rest until the search was complete. Meanwhile, he conducted his own search, his senses sifting through the overwhelming stench of wrothe overlain by that of death. He finally picked up a human trail not far from the castle. Just as he set himself to following it, a beautiful woman emerged from the forest ahead of him. Chorlak could immediately sense that she was vampyr, and he wondered how she had managed to be the only survivor.

She spoke in a monotone, her eyes betraying nothing of her emotion. "My name is Tarian. I am the one who has been collaborating with Hospartuek in regards to the human girl."

"Where is she?"

"Gone. Seth was a fool, underestimating the faelin, human, and halfen comrades with whom she made her company. They came for her, just as I thought they might."

Chorlak frowned. "And why did he not believe you?"

Tarian shrugged. "He was too distracted by her to believe me about anything," she said.

"What do you think made her so different from any other human females you have taken before?"

Tarian was silent for a moment. "It is difficult to explain. But even her smell was provocative. The taste of her blood was like the sweetest of wines. Seth felt that he absolutely had to have her, even at the risk of the colony he had created here and even at the risk of his own life." Tarian shook her head as she continued. "I could sense her pull, but it was somehow magnified for him and the other males. Nevertheless, I still feel he should have persevered to overcome her. It was his duty, his responsibility as patriarch." Tarian shook her head. "He was weak."

Chorlak nodded. "He wanted to make her vampyr."

Tarian pursed her lips. "In spite of my warnings, Seth prepared for the transition ceremony."

Chorlak's gaze intensified. "Did he succeed?"

Tarian shook her head. "She escaped with the human man who came for her."

Chorlak was relieved that Seth had failed, yet remained wary of this other man. "I thought you said her entire company came for her."

Tarian nodded. "They did, but not before this man. If I didn't know better,

I would say he was her lover."

Once more Chorlak felt himself placed on edge. Hells, he could only imagine the ramifications of that. But he knew he needed to focus upon the situation at hand. *"Where is Seth now?"* he asked.

A guarded expression swept over Tarian's face. *"He is lying in the garden."*

Chorlak was brought up short. *"He is dead?"*

She simply nodded her response.

"Take me to him," he commanded.

Tarian nodded again, turning away only to disappear into the trees. Chorlak swiftly followed behind, relying on his minions to follow his scent after completing their task within the castle interior. It wasn't long before they reached the body. The vampyr had been burned almost beyond recognition. All that remained was a blackened corpse with a medallion around his neck— the insignia that proclaimed him the patriarch of his family. Tarian knelt before the remains and pulled the medallion away, the skull subsequently rolling away from the rest of the body to rest about a farlo away. She then placed it within the folds of her robe, tucking it securely within.

Chorlak watched her questioningly.

"There are two others besides myself who might have survived the massacre. I will await their return."

Chorlak shook his head. *"And if they do not come back?"*

"Then I will leave this place, search until I find a new colony. Or mayhap, find someone who is not averse to creating his own."

Chorlak became pensive. A few moments later he spoke once more. *"I don't usually speak on behalf of the mehta, but you have been helpful to me here. It is possible that Lord Razlul may offer you a reward, mayhap give you aid as you search for another colony."*

Tarian raised a pale eyebrow. *"Perhaps I shall consider it."*

As Chorlak nodded his response, he became suddenly aware of the approach of his followers. Without care they lumbered through the trees and foliage, making it easy for him to hear them from afar. Of course, such was the way of most of the lesser and medial daemons, stupid creatures who needed another to tell them the precise details of every move they made. Such was the responsibility of baalor and garbatezu.

The gremlins reached him first, for they were able to maneuver the forest floor a bit more quickly than their winged counterparts. The leader was larger than the rest, quickly communicating to Chorlak what had been discovered. Of course, much of it Chorlak knew already, but it was good to obtain information from more than one source. Also, they were able to verify one thing about *which he had heretofore only assumed . . . Hospartuek was dead.*

Chorlak nodded smartly and then ordered everyone to move out. There was nothing he could do for the vampyr community that had been lost. He needed to move on, continue his search for the young woman whom he had been given the lofty duty of bringing before the mehta of the Daemundai. He had finally come to understand the strength of those who had made themselves a part of her company, and he would respect that. He would endeavor to track her via the trail her company would leave behind and simply follow them until the time was right. Only then would he take the girl, and no one would be the wiser.

Tarian stepped up to him. "I have considered your offer, and I have chosen to take you up on it."

Chorlak turned to the vampyr before him. "You have only to accompany us upon our mission to bring Joneselia Mondemer before our mehta."

Tarian simply nodded her assent. Her body began to blur into the form of a wrothe before she was completely turned away from him.

"My Lord Chorlak, I can sense your disturbance. Please speak of it to me so that I might endeavor to help you."

He tore himself away from his thoughts, turning to find Tarian keeping pace beside him. She was no longer in her wrothe form; somehow her gown remained intact between transformations and he guessed that it had some strange arcane property. Out of all the others who comprised his company, she was the first to approach him in regards to his mood. It seemed that, while the others simply accepted his ill-natured temperament without question, this woman felt the desire to understand him on some level. Of course, she would not be able to help him. But her wanting to do so was refreshing.

Chorlak shook his head. "Believe me, I wish you could help, but you cannot." He spoke more brusquely than he intended, but Tarian was not deterred.

"Why don't you confide in me and then allow me to decide for myself?"

Chorlak remained silent for a moment. Hells, he supposed that no harm could come from divulging his latest difficulty. Of course, the entire mission had proven to be much more than what he had thought it would be. Yet, he refused to fail Lord Razlul. He would have the girl, no matter how long it took him to procure her.

Chorlak could only hope she still met the mehta's expectations.

He shook his head. "I was unable to follow directly behind the target like I had wanted when we reached the portal chamber."

Tarian pulled her pale brows into a frown. "Why not?"

"They used the portal to take them into the druid stronghold of Krathillon. Besides dragons, druids are our most committed enemies. Needless to say, daemon-kind has never been welcome to their principal sanctuary. It would have been foolhardy for us to go there. Inasmuch, I was forced to use the portal to take us to a location much farther south. For all I know, they might end up using the portal system to arrive here themselves. But if not, without someone like Hospartuek, I have no idea as to what direction the group plans to take next. I can only guess."

Tarian regarded him for a moment before her thoughts seemed to turn inwards. Silence reigned for quite some time as they continued to walk. It wouldn't be long now before they were out of the forested hills that comprised this particular region and he would order them airborne once more. Within his company, there was one gremlin for every devil, and that left Tarian to fly with him. The thought was not all that unappealing, for he had decided he liked her companionship already.

"My Lord, I was thinking. What about the daemon-bred halfling you were telling me about? Tigerius? Couldn't you attempt to make contact with him?"

Chorlak glanced sidelong at his newest companion. So she had actually been listening to him when he was telling her about the group they were following. The thought intrigued him, as did the realization that she was intelligent—much more so than any of the others who followed him. Yet, he had already considered the possibility of contacting the one she suggested. How could he not? The man was daemon-kind after all, even if just partly.

Chorlak shook his head with a half-hearted grin. "I thought about him, but it won't work. In order to have a connection strong enough for me to get a good angle on his location, I would need to either have been in physical contact with him before, or he would have to possess strong telepathic capabilities."

"Like your doppleganger, Hospartuek."

Chorlak simply nodded his agreement.

"But the illithids also have a powerful sense for telepathy," Tarian pressed. "Didn't you tell me he is sprung from an illithid hybrid?"

Chorlak nodded again. "Indeed, I did. However, the one in question is still but a boy, not yet grown into his abilities. And just as we established already, he is only but a halfling. It is unlikely that he would have even a fraction of the telepathic ability of a full fledged illithid when he reaches full maturity."

Tarian nodded slowly. "Then you are right. I cannot help you."

Once again, Chorlak simply nodded his agreement.

"But let me ask—have you *tried* initiating a contact? Even if the connection isn't as strong as you would like, at least you might have *something* to go on."

Chorlak gave a hearty sigh, an action very akin to that a human would make. Of course, over the years of making his existence so close to theirs, he could not help but adopt many of their gestures. Talking with Tarian, it seemed she had done much the same, albeit perhaps not quite as much as had he. "No, I have not tried."

Tarian suddenly turned to him and placed a staying hand on his bare chest. As he slowed to a stop, she raised an eyebrow. "Why not?"

Not for the first time, Chorlak was aware of her physical presence. In every way, she was the most seductive being he had ever come across. That was saying quite a bit since he had known almost a hundred years. He supposed the vampyr race was much more unknown to him than he had realized. Chorlak shrugged. "Before, I didn't see the point. I was quite certain of my assessment of the situation, and I felt I had a firm grip on it."

"And now?" she pressed.

Chorlak shrugged. "Mayhap you have a point. It might behoove me to make an attempt at contact no matter how small the chance I might have at achieving something that might be helpful."

The corner of her lips twitched as she fought the smile that threatened. He turned away and began walking once more, allowing her the chance to allow it to slip forth without the possibility of it raising his ire. Of course, he thought it to be quite amusing. Obviously, she was not so different from the rest that she would not be somewhat reticent to experience his anger. And somehow he didn't mind keeping it that way.

Besides, her allure was much more enticing when she tried so hard not to displease him.

CHAPTER EIGHT

Tallachienan looked around the dark encampment. The rest of the group had settled for the night, and the fire was banked. Only the shadowed forms of Alasdair and Cedric sat there hunkered over the mugs of hot chag that would see them through their watch. For the merest moment, TC felt the brush of Pylar's mind against his in an affirmation of their *bond*. He welcomed those light touches, and hadn't realized how much he missed Pylar until the dragon was with him once more—not just as a mental presence, but a physical one as well.

In the darkness just beyond the immediate vicinity of the encampment, he could make out the large form of his beloved comrade in the faint light cast by moons that were obscured by clouds. It would soon begin to rain, and a storm would ensue. Pylar would spread his massive wings and TC would seek refuge. He would invite the rest of the group to join him, and the close proximity of so many would keep everyone wakeful throughout the night. Yet, at least they would remain dry.

However, TC wasn't certain he and Pylar would still be there to offer the cover, for he had it in his mind to leave this place. He hated to abandon the group, but in light of the information Pylar had imparted about what was happening on Shayamalan, he knew he had to go there. He hated having no knowledge of what was going on, for he was certain his good friend, Trebexal, was behind it. For one who was accustomed to knowing a bit of something about everything, TC felt quite out of sorts. Not only that, he agreed with Pylar's suspicion that it was the place where Aeris had been taken. It was just another compelling reason to go there. In spite of Aeris' dislike of him, she needed him whether she knew it or not. Whatever she and her young dragon bondmate were doing on that continent, he would stay there until she was ready to leave. Of course, he would facilitate her departure to the best of his ability. And he would have some words with Trebexal as well.

Taking a deep breath, TC glanced down at the velvety pouch he held in his hand. He had taken it from Aeris' travel-pack, for she had abandoned it when she left him on the back of her dragon bondmate. Inside rested the crystals that he and Aeris had been studying before her abduction by the cimmereans. If he recalled correctly, the first crystal she had received as a gift from Adrianna a couple years ago before she took her tests in Andahye. The second she had obtained from the daemundai when they attacked the group in the port city of Yortec, and the third was given to her by Captain Cervantes during their ill-fated voyage to escape said daemundai.

Each ensconced within its own kerchief, the crystals glowed vibrantly within such close proximity to one another, and he remembered the day he and Aeris had brought the three crystals together. The result had been momentous, giving Aeris a vision he himself never saw. Most likely it had much to do with her propensity for dragons as opposed to her use of any *talent* at that particular time and place. Regardless, it made him wonder about her and about the familial heritage of which she knew very little. The union of the crystals gave her a terrible vision of their creation. She had been horrified by what she saw, the images imprinted within her mind forever.

Not only would he go to Shayamalan to search for Aeris, but to bring the crystals before Trebexal.

TC suddenly stood from his bedding and subsequently began to roll it up. Noticing the activity, Alasdair looked in his direction, yet said nothing. After a few moments of packing his things, TC walked over to where both he and Cedric sat before the crackling embers of the reduced fire. Alasdair looked up at him with a questioning expression. TC hunkered down to achieve eye level and he spoke in a low voice. "I think I know where Aeris and Jaxom went when they left."

Alasdair's eyes widened. "I suppose Pylar told you?"

TC nodded.

"Why didn't you communicate this to me earlier?" The man paused, but then continued less than a moment later. "Well, where are they?"

TC cleared his throat. "This might be hard for you to believe, but there is another continent on Shandahar, one unknown by all except a very few. To most of those few, it is known as the Dragon Continent, but its true name is Shayamalan.

"Before the Pact of Bakharas was made, dragons made their homes on this continent, hence it's more well-known name. However, they were forced to vacate once the truce was made, and they returned to the place from where they originally came." TC paused in his recitation, choosing not to elaborate. He knew that Alasdair might not understand, for he hadn't been schooled the way Aeris and other magic users were, especially dimensionalists. In light of their closeness, Aeris may have shared some things with her brother, including that other worlds existed beyond Shandahar. But he couldn't assume that.

TC continued, "However, since the Pact was broken, dragons have returned to Shandahar along with daemon-kind. Most of them choose to populate Shayamalan. Very few make their homes elsewhere. For some reason

Jaxom decided to up and leave. Once making it to Ansalar he took his faelin form. He decided to make seafaring his first venture and joined Cervantes as a crew hand aboard his ship. Finally he met Aeris."

Alasdair thought about what TC said for a moment and then frowned. "But how does all this make you believe he took her back to Shayamalan?"

"For two reasons . . . the first being that he probably originated from there," began TC. "Secondly, there is some type of training going on . . . where faelin bondmates learn to ride astride their dragon counterparts. It was unprecedented before the emergence of the degethozak raiders and their riders. But now it seems that the dragon elders have given their permission to allow the practice in order to combat the threat."

Alasdair nodded. "So how do we get there? We should probably get as early a start as possible."

TC's gaze was piercing as he regarded the ranger. "Shayamalan can only be reached by ship, and obviously by dragon flight."

Alasdair was silent as he struggled to accept that he was still no closer to reaching his sister. However, he was quick to make a connection. "But *you* have a dragon."

TC slowly nodded. It was one of the things that had taken him so long to finally reach the decision to make the journey to the Dragon Continent. Within all of the *cycles* he had shared with his bondmate, he had never before ridden astride Pylar unless it was out of pure necessity. Never.

"It is the reason why you see me preparing for travel. I have decided that I should go to Shayamalan and attempt to bring Aeris back." TC paused for a moment and then continued. "I know that she hates me, but perhaps she will see reason and return. It is well worth the effort."

Alasdair simply sat there for a moment, regarding TC intently. His expression remained stoic and he couldn't tell what the other man was thinking. It was quite disconcerting. However, Alasdair finally put a hand on TC's shoulder. "Good luck, my friend, and may the sun shine upon you."

TC simply nodded and stood. Glancing over at Cedric, he saw that the blade-singer had heard all that transpired between him and Alasdair, for his expression was a knowing one. Cedric gave a nod of agreement and TC returned the gesture before going back to his travel preparations. Pylar's golden eyes were bright as he made his way over after completing his packing, waiting patiently while TC loaded everything onto his back. Meanwhile, he thought about Jonesy. He had decided on this course of action the evening before, and they had already spoken their goodbyes. A part of him wanted to go to where she slept, maybe offer her one more silent farewell. But he decided against it, not wanting to take the chance of awakening her.

When TC was finally ready, Pylar offered the leg that would enable him to settle onto the dragon's back. It took a moment for him to find a comfortable position and wondered if Pylar had a preference. Right away he realized the silliness of that thought; how could Pylar have a preference if the situation had never arisen before? Pylar gave the dragon equivalent of a chuckle as he rose from his place. Neither one spoke, each knowing what the other was thinking as they walked away from the encampment. Yet, when Pylar suddenly leaped skyward and TC felt the power beneath him for the first time in many years, he was awed. When the air compressed against him, making him feel as though he couldn't breathe, he was even more awed.

It was an experience he would never forget.

Asgenar stood on the hill overlooking the expansive hinterlean bivouac. To some it might appear as any other regular encampment: the various dongoes, the clothes fluttering out on lines strewn between poles set in the ground, the fires over which hung pots for cooking, and the corubis roaming here and there. But to his practiced eye, it was obviously a war-camp. The clothing on the line was of the most utilitarian design, there were only a very small number of women, and the place was devoid of the presence of children. Most importantly, it was unusually quiet for just any encampment.

Asgenar pursed his lips thoughtfully. He could tell that everyone was getting restless. Distanced from their familiar arboreal environment, the hinterleans were beginning to feel the strain of remaining on the ground in a place where there were few, if any, trees. Moreover, they missed their daladins and their families. The stalemate with Karlisle remained, no one moving against the other for yet another fortnight. Fully aware of the preparations the humans were making, Asgenar felt disheartened, and wished for a miracle he knew could never happen. The hinterlean fu-ulcrym might be more advanced than the Karlislian army, but the enemy's numbers far outweighed that benefit.

Sensing someone's approach, Asgenar turned to see Caedrus making his way up the hill. The older man acknowledged the intrusion with a raised hand and a nod, and once standing beside him, he took a moment to survey the encampment below. Asgenar was patient, for he knew Caedrus had intentionally sought him out in order to communicate something to him. The man was the most trusted of all his advisors and had served his grandfather for many years. He had the utmost respect for Caedrus and would take the time to wait until the other man was ready to speak.

"My lord, I know you are wondering why I have sought your company," he said finally.

Asgenar turned back to his chief advisor. "Indeed, why have you come?"

Caedrus looked him directly in the eyes as he spoke. "You are concerned about the Karlislians, how they have the means to increase their numbers while we do not."

Asgenar simply nodded.

"I have come to offer you news of something new and unexpected. For quite some while now, as chief advisor for your grandfather, I have been given the liberty of pursuing many of my own endeavors as long as they do not interfere with my duties." He paused and then continued. "Well, in my opinion, those endeavors have reached a point where I feel they can finally be of service to the people to whom I have dedicated every aspect of my life."

Asgenar regarded Caedrus solemnly. He knew the man had no mate and no known offspring. As a youngster he had wondered about it, but once reaching manhood he realized that not every man desired a wife and family. It seemed that Caedrus had been keeping himself busy in other ways, and Asgenar was about to discover the capacity in which he had done so.

"Since King Thalios gave me such freedom, I have been researching and training a potential new type of warrior, one who can fight from the air," he said.

Asgenar shook his head, wondering if he heard the other man correctly. Making attacks from the air? In what capacity?

Caedrus continued. "As you know, I am a ranger much like many of those that make up the fu-ulcrym spread below." He indicated the bivouac with a sweep of his hand. "However, my forte lies not in the forests, but in the mountains, for I am not wholly of hinterlean descent."

Asgenar nodded then, knowing that Caedrus' mother was hinterlean and his father savanlean—those pale skinned faelin who made their homes in the heights of the Ratik and Sartingel Mountains. Even now, looking upon the individual before him, he could see the racial differences that encompassed more than just skin coloration: golden hair as opposed to the customary hinterlean reddish-brown, and blue eyes in place of brown.

"Inasmuch, during one of my many forays into the Ratik Mountains, I came across a relatively unknown avian species. The savanleans call them 'roc', but I call them something different . . . 'chyvian', meaning 'awesome' in the savanlean tongue. Like a thief I took some of their eggs, and when they eventually hatched, the younglings impressed themselves upon those faelin who were present during the occasion. Once seeing the connection that existed between man and bird, I devised the idea of training the creatures to carry a rider. When the endeavor was successful, I expanded and developed the training to encompass aerial combative techniques."

Asgenar was thoughtful for several moments. Then, "What you have told me is quite a feat, my lord. I applaud you upon your efforts. But I don't see how these 'few' chyvians are going to be of any substantive aid to us in our ongoing fight against Karlisle."

Caedrus grinned. "But my Lord Asgenar, there are many more of us now than there were at the beginning."

Asgenar cocked his head to the side. "How many are there?"

"We are over forty strong," Caedrus replied.

Asgenar felt his eyes widen incredulously. By the gods, could this truly be happening? The smiling face of his advisor told him that he wasn't dreaming. He may have just been Elvandahar's saving grace. "Where are these battle-ready chyvian, might I ask?"

Caedrus' grin lengthened. "Why, they are en route, my lord."

"You say they are currently on their way? Now, as we speak?"

"I called for them as soon as I realized the odds against us, my lord."

Asgenar reached out and gripped Caedrus' lower arm. "Now I know why you have always been my grandfather's most trusted advisor."

Caedrus returned the grip and then bowed before him. "Do not forget I am yours also, my lord."

Asgenar shook his head. "No, I shall never forget."

10 Decaren CY634

The moment Aeris awoke she felt a tension in the air. She slowly rose from the bed-pallet, and took in the goings-on in the chamber. To the outward eye, it appeared as though nothing was amiss, but she could feel it—something simmering just below the surface of her consciousness.

Faleema stepped up and seated herself beside Aeris on the pallet. "I feel it too. There is a drenna nearing the height of her estrus, and I am almost completely certain who it is."

Aeris slowly digested this information, then frowned and turned to her friend. "Is this what it is always like?"

Faleema nodded her head. "At first, but after a while it will gain intensity."

"What do you mean?" Aeris was intrigued. By the gods, she had never felt this type of tense expectancy before.

"I am certain it is Zestrimath, Kahlan's bondmate. Right now, whatever we are feeling, Kahlan is feeling it ten-fold. Sometime either tomorrow or the day after, Zestri will rise for her pairing flight. Most of the helzethryn males in the area will rise with her. They will then compete for the right to have her. Most times the competition consists only of the flight itself, determining which male is fastest and has the most endurance. Rarely does it include any physical fighting among them. Whoever catches Zestri will be the father of her next clutch."

Aeris nodded thoughtfully. "All right, I understand then why Kahlan should be feeling this tension, as well as Saliel. Oh, and maybe even demeters Fo and Roger. But why you? Your bondmate is female. And why me? My bondmate is a male, but of another race."

"The desire to mate is so powerful that it affects everyone. Oftentimes it can even be so strong that the sexual desire generated by one female, no matter what her race, can accelerate the breeding cycles of others within her immediate vicinity."

Aeris regarded Faleema intently, took in the worried frown on her face. "You are afraid that Zestri's condition will bring Mira into estrus," she stated abruptly.

Faleema nodded. "This has happened once before. Mira was younger, so she was able to make it through unaffected. However, that was several moon cycles ago. Mira is still young, but there is a chance she will be influenced. I know it's not the worst that can happen, but we both have decided we would like to continue to focus on our training. If she were to become pregnant . . ." Faleema was silent for a moment before continuing. "Sometimes the best intentions become lost."

Aeris laid a hand on Faleema's arm. "You need to trust in your bondmate. I think she would tell you if she were close enough to be affected."

Faleema nodded and straightened her shoulders. "You are probably right. Yet, I can't help but wonder."

Aeris once more looked around the chamber. She noticed how much quieter it was than usual. She caught both Jerlas and Thrades staring at her before she glanced in their direction. Both had male helzethryn bondmates, and they most likely felt the tension more strongly. She suddenly wondered about the physical manifestation of the suppressed tension she felt now, and asked Faleema about it.

"When the female rises, everyone knows. Like I said before, all will be affected, only at varying levels. Those who are *bonded* to helzethryn males will feel it most after Kahlan, then the rezwithrys males. Last will come the other females of either helzethryn or rezwithrys origin. Sometimes, the males of the other race will also rise in response. Historically, there have been very few who have managed to catch the female. Regardless, until Zestri has risen, and the pairing flight completed, everyone will be distracted."

Aeris nodded as Faleema rose from the bed and walked away. She reached out to Jaxom only to find him waiting for her. <Yes, I feel it too,> he said. <But don't worry. I have no proclivity towards Zestrimath. I do not feel the need to follow her when she rises.>

<Yes, but the tension will only continue to rise as her flight approaches,> Aeris stated.

<You are right, but only vaguely do I feel a sexual pull. It serves only as a simple reminder that I have my own destiny to fulfill one day in the future.>

Aeris sent a nod of understanding through their link and rose to prepare for the day. She immediately sensed that she was being watched, and she could only assume it might be the riders of some of the other male dragons. She decided against disrobing in public as she ordinarily would. Donning an over-sized cloak to hide her activity, she chose to practice modesty, and when she was finished getting ready, she vacated the barracks to meet her bondmate.

Once reaching the practice field, Aeris was surprised to see not only demeters Roger and Fo, but Kordrian as well. Also present were quarter-masters Falon and Franchiera. Aeris was beginning to wonder what was going on until she sensed an increase in the general pervading tension. Looking skyward, she saw another dragon and rider approaching. And since everyone else was already present, she could only deduct that it was Kahlan and Zestrimath.

Aeris instantly saw the change in Zestri as the pair landed nearby. The helzethryn female was practically glowing with health, her golden hide shimmering in the rays of the newly risen sun. Kahlan promptly dismounted her dragon and approached the group, her expression stoic. She was the focus of everyone's attention, yet she refused to meet anyone's gaze. Aeris could see that she was uncomfortable and her heart went out to the terralean girl.

Demeter Fo cleared his throat and addressed the group. "We are all gathered here today because we are about to embark on a very dangerous aspect of our training. It involves an element over which we may not always have control. Fire. As part of their combat repertoire, dragons employ fire more than any other weapon. Inasmuch, dragons must learn to take into account the positioning of their riders whenever they choose to breathe it. Meanwhile, they must focus on the enemy at hand and subsequently deal them a forceful blow.

"While you riders have been learning dragon physiology and building on your weaponry skills, your dragons have been learning ways to focus the trajectories of their flames once they are emitted. Under varying environmental conditions, the dragons have been learning how to streamline the trajectory of their flames so that not only does it minimize potential injury to their riders but also maximizes damage to their opponents. Each pair of you shall be assigned to one of us," said Fo, gesturing around at the masters and quarter-masters. "Your dragons will now practice their methods in 'real time' under our guidance. As long as caution is observed and appropriate battle gear worn, training may be accomplished without any problems."

It was then that Forigard gestured to Seldonraxis. The silver dragon moved aside to reveal five sets of armor lying on the ground. "These suits have been produced with the aid of our halfen friends here on Shayamalan. Made of the hardiest material known on Shandahar, these braxen suits will protect you whilst in battle. Each one was produced with the wearer in mind, so they have all been made a bit differently." Fo waved them towards the armor. "Please, try them on."

With Thulnar and Faleema on either side of her, Aeris stepped towards the suits. Once close enough, she could see the differences in the makes. It was obvious which ones belonged to Thulnar and Saliel, for they were slightly more bulky than those made for Aeris, Faleema, and Kahlan. It was easy for Aeris to determine which one was hers out of the remaining three, for the ones made for Kahlan and Faleema included gauntlets. Magic users such as Aeris had no use for them, and while Faleema had some *talent* as well, it was not her focus.

Aeris felt a rush of anxiety sweep through her. Hells, she had just become skilled enough with her riding techniques that she could keep optimal positioning whilst in flight. Meanwhile, Demeter Kord had begun instructing her in the creation of what he called tomahora, a rod-like vessel which she could imbue with her power. Using the spell of her choice, Aeris could direct the energy into the rod, and it would remain stored there until discharged by the user with a power word that she would create solely for that purpose. Additionally, she would soon begin learning how to maneuver herself in hand-to-hand combat whilst astride. It was all quite daunting, and she wondered if she would be able to keep up the pace.

Aeris stooped to retrieve the glistening braxen armor. It was enhanced with dragon scales. Neither silver nor gold, the suit shimmered with radiance, and it had obviously been crafted by those with utmost skill. The suit was a work of art just as much as it was a piece of equipment to be used to protect her from harm. She took a moment to offer silent thanks to those who donated to its cause, and then more to the ones who crafted it. She only hoped she would be able to bring honor to the armor. Through their link, she could feel the approval of her bondmate, and knowing the time was right, she slowly began to don the suit.

Aeris slid the pliable vest over her shoulders, the spaulders settling at just the right place on her shoulders. Just like her tunic, the vest was long and reached almost to her knees. It had slits extending from the lower hem to reach up to her crotch so that it would accommodate her when she sat astride. She placed the artfully designed belt at her waist, and then positioned the matching pieces that slid over her forearms. Then she donned the boots, each one rising just high enough to reach her knees. Finally she placed the decorative helm over her head. It felt strange, for she had never worn such a thing before. Yet, she understood how she could need it in battle astride a dragon. She supposed she would become accustomed to it. Meanwhile, her hands would remain unhampered so that she could cast her spells. If needed, she would have her long-knife tucked within her boot, and another as backup sheathed nearby at her saddle-harness. Fully armored, she turned towards her bondmate, and Jaxom rumbled his approval.

<Elirya, it looks as though you were made for it,> he said, <not just that it was made for you.>

Aeris nodded thoughtfully. <Perhaps.>

Jaxom was quiet for a moment. Then, <What is wrong?>

Aeris smiled and shook her head. <I was just thinking. For so long I have thought of myself only as a sorceress. But now I have somehow become a warrior. I wear armor like one, and I bear physical weaponry into battle. I ask you how all of this came about.>

Jaxom gave her a mental shrug. <You met *me*. It is your destiny.>

Aeris nodded. <Indeed, I suppose it is.>

<Come. They are awaiting us.>

Aeris climbed aboard Jaxom's back. The weight of the armor wasn't as much as she thought it might be, yet it was definitely something she would need to get used to. Jaxom made over to the rest of the group just as Demeter Fo began to speak. "Thulnar, you have been assigned to Rogerus, and Saliel you are with Falon. Kahlan, you go with Franchiera, and Aeris with Kordrian. Faleema, you shall be with me."

Aeris shut her eyes when Fo named her instructor. Damn, she had rather hoped to be paired with someone else. It wasn't so much that she disliked the man; it was that *he* seemed to dislike *her*. And now he knew so much about her—too much. Until her first arcane training session with Demeter Kord, she had disregarded the words of a goddess whose sole intent was to cause her bodily harm and mental discontent. A part of her never really believed that her mother had once been consort to Tallachienan. But that had changed. She would be a fool not to recognize the truth and to come to terms with it as best she could.

Of course, she didn't have to like it. And certainly she felt some measure of anger and resentment, both towards her mother and Tallachienan. Unfortunately, Demeter Kordrian was knowledgeable of such history, and that fact made it more difficult for Aeris. She slowly opened her eyes and was surprised to find quartermaster Franchie regarding her speculatively. The other woman narrowed her cerulean eyes with open hostility and then swiftly turned away. Taken aback, Aeris watched as the beautiful savanlean rose into the air aboard her dragon and could only guess as to the reason for her enmity.

"Damaeris, I hope you have the capacity to maintain some amount of focus needed to keep you alive today."

Aeris swung her gaze towards the man beside her. Astride the silver Riloriandrix, Demeter Kord regarded her intently. He was handsome, more so than the other men whom she had met thus far upon Shayamalan. Perhaps it was just another aspect about him that bothered her so much, for she disliked the attraction, wanting instead to keep him as far from her as possible. Unfortunately, she could not entirely resist his pull.

"Master Kordrian, I will endeavor to . . ."

He shook his head. "It's *Demeter* Kordrian, my dear. You should really try better to remember where you are."

Aeris nodded, feeling her face flush with the embarrassment of his rebuke. Damn, it was hard not to think of him as yet another master. Yet, the term demeter meant nearly the same. What was his problem? Was it simply that he enjoyed keeping her in place?

Once following them into the air, Aeris took note of Jaxom's silence. It had become commonplace during her interactions with other faelin outside of their training. Never did he make any comment, nor did he offer any advice. It was almost as though he wasn't there. Almost.

<It is only because your life should be your own,> said Jaxom. <Even though we are bondmates, you still have a faelin life to live, much as I have a dragon one. One day, I know you will take a mate. He will be in direct competition with me for your attention. However, I am learning how to accept that eventuality from the instruction of my seniors, much as *you* are learning about *me* from yours.>

Aeris only nodded. <Yes, but I still value your advice.>

<Then you have only to ask me for it,> he replied.

Aeris nodded. <But what if I have my own advice to offer?>

<Then, by all means give it,> he said.

Aeris paused for a moment. <Her bondmate does not like me, but Rilo seems to feel quite the opposite towards you.>

Jaxom gave the dragon equivalent of a laugh. He narrowed their speech-band as he replied, making certain that no one could hear his reply but Aeris. <What makes you think so?>

Aeris shrugged. <Only by the way she looks at you. And . . .> Aeris' voice trailed off.

Jaxom shook his head in the negative. <And what? Listen, I don't think . . .>

<It's a feeling I get whenever she is near,> she interrupted.

<All right, what if Seldon is nearby, or Zarjan?>

Aeris only shrugged. <Well, I don't pay as much attention to them, but I seem to recall feeling an ample amount of competitiveness.>

For several moments Aeris felt nothing but silence. Then, <I have my own 'advice' to offer,> he said.

Aeris steeled herself for a blow. <Fine, what is it?>

<Kordrian does not dislike you the way you perceive he does.>

Aeris found herself taken quite aback. What the Hells was Jaxom thinking? It was blatantly obvious how the demeter felt towards her. <You are only saying that to tease me for what I said about Rilo,> she said petulantly.

Jaxom suddenly snorted. <I should have known I would get this type of response.>

Aeris frowned. <What is that supposed to mean?>

Jaxom remained silent. Aeris gave a heavy sigh as Rilo and Kordrian both turned to face them, the silver drenna back-winging so that she could remain in place. Jaxom was irritated, and it was bad timing. Damn. She would be feeling the backhand of Demeter Kord again soon enough, and she hated being at odds with her bondmate. Yet, she supposed she would make the best of a crummy situation. She spoke as Jaxom positioned himself similarly in mid-air. <She *is* beautiful, is she not?> Aeris could sense a stirring in his mind. She then continued before he could formulate a reply. <See how the sunlight plays off the scales of her neck and jaw?>

Jaxom snorted again, this time resulting in smoke. <You are incorrigible.>

Aeris relaxed when she felt some of his tension melt away, smiling to herself as a chuckle rumbled through his body. It was then Rilo and Kord were abruptly sweeping towards them.

Aeris grappled with her harness straps as Jaxom was forced to tumble sharply out of the way of Rilo's sharp talons. Aeris suddenly found herself upside down, the weight of her body immediately attempting to slip out of the confines of the combat equipment. Her heart thundered in her chest as she fought to keep herself astride, cursing her ineptitude. Using the skills she recently mastered under the tutelage of Demeter Fo, she was able to do just that as Jaxom swept into a downward spiral dive, just narrowly missing another swipe of Rilo's wickedly sharp talons.

Aeris couldn't help but hold her breath. She could sense the tumult within her bondmate's mind. Jaxom's usually stoic demeanor was shaken and she realized that he was just as new to this as was she. She glanced behind them as Jaxom flew out of his spiral. Quickly gaining upon them were Rilo and Kordrian, and this time it was Aeris' turn to dodge.

<Jaxom, swing left!> Aeris shouted through their link as she pressed herself to Jaxom's neck, praying that the *Magic Missle* would miss them. Just as she commanded, Jaxomdrehl veered sharply left, and this time Aeris was ready for the abrupt movement. She was able to adjust her own position accordingly, reducing the drag he would suffer should she remain as she was. And just as she predicted, the spell swept just over her and to the right, directly through their precise location just a moment before.

Aeris struggled to regain her concentration. Hells, they had to do something, for it seemed that her master and his dragon had turned against them. Damn, she hated being right about the fact that Kordrian hated her. Aeris swiftly shook her head. That didn't matter right now. All she needed to think about was how to preserve both her hide and that of her bondmate. The only offensive spell she could think of was *Flamesphere,* and she was uncertain of her ability to pull it off under these conditions in spite of its simplicity.

Once more Aeris chanced a look behind them. Riloriandrix screamed a battle cry and a chill swept through her. In desperation, Aeris wracked her mind for some means of evasion. Sensing the intensity of her emotion, Jaxom suggested the lake below them. Aeris immediately concurred.

Again Jaxom went into a dive, this time a straight one. Aeris steeled herself just before they hit the surface of the water, once more pressing herself as close to his back as possible. Holding her breath, she remained within the saddle as Jaxom swept through the water. Aeris was suddenly reminded of the monstrous threat they had been able to escape whilst on an uncharted island upon which they'd become shipwrecked. While Cervantes and the rest of the group repaired the ship, she and Jaxom had discovered a black orb around the neck of a skeleton man they found aboard a strange metal bird. Putting a hand to her chest, she remembered it wasn't there, for she had left it and most of her other possessions behind when she climbed aboard Jaxom's back that night at the Larramis Cliffs.

Just as she thought she would be forced to breathe in the water, Jaxom broke the lake's surface. Aeris took a deep breath of the air, not once or twice, but three times. Only then did she begin to calm. Yet, it was rather short lived, for Rilo and Kordrian landed just as Jaxom was wading out from the lake. Aeris felt herself becoming irate. What the Hells was going on? Was this some kind of test? If so, they should have known what they were walking into before their arrival.

It was then they heard the scream.

Aeris slammed her hands over her ears. Yet, it mattered little, for the cry she heard was just as much mental as it was physical. In her mind, Aeris could hear the agonized voice of a dragon overcome with burning pain. She could feel the sensation of falling, and looking skyward, Aeris could see the object of her mental disturbance. It was Zestrimath, *and the first section of her left wing had been scorched by dragon-fire.*

Oh gods!

Aeris lowered herself over Jaxom's back as he leaped into the sky. The air sweeping over her wet body chilled her to the bone, but Aeris ignored it as they flew unerringly towards the foundering dragon and her rider. Once reaching Kahlan and Zestri, Jaxom offered the wing-support necessary to soften their inevitable landing. In spite of the added assistance of Sidranth and Franchiera on Zestrimath's other side, Jaxom soon faltered beneath the weight.

Aeris felt her breath catch in her throat as a rush of fear swept through her. Confined by the very harness straps that had been constructed to keep her safe, Aeris suddenly found herself within close proximity to Zestri's flailing wings. She struggled to extricate herself, swiftly working her fingers over the buckles, and then attempting to maneuver herself from the straps. Jaxom realized the futility of her situation only a few brief moments before he hit the ground. Aeris' body shuddered with the impact, and she barely caught her breath before she felt something hit the side of her head.

Her world shifted to black.

Jonesy disconsolately rode astride one of the lloryk, vaguely watching as the landscape passed by her. The Plain of Antipithanee was a dull place, having only zacrol upon zacrol of waving himrony, pfelzipat, and tugrassis. The lloryk enjoyed all three varieties of plant-life, but the horses preferred only the golden himrony. Only when none was available would the strictly vegetarian horses bring themselves to partake of the bluish pfelzipat, and the deep purple tugrassis they mostly left untouched. She thought it rather silly how choosy the horses were, and she wondered how they had become that way.

All of a sudden, Jonesy felt a chill sweep through her. It was a warm day, so there should have been no cause for it. But Jonesy knew better; it was the call of home beckoning to her, urging her to return.

Not for the first time, Jonesy looked over her shoulder. Like always, all she saw was the waving grasses through which they had just passed. Each step of the lloryk took her farther away from Krathil-lon and the portal that resided there. She knew it was the faster way for her to make her return to Karlisle, for she had only to take it to the portal that resided within the juncture of the Bryton Hills and the Selmist Forest.

With a deep sigh she returned her gaze to the withers of the beast she rode. In truth, she really didn't know why she still continued to stay with the others. Their objective was simply to find safety in Elvandahar. Once reaching the northern boundary they would achieve their goal. However, she could only imagine what Elvandahar might think of her in their presence. Hells, they were at war with Karlisle, *and she was the daughter of King Zerxes.*

Jonesy picked at the lloryk's spiky mane. She had been running away from her life for quite some while. It was about time that she got back to it, in spite of the peril offered by her brother.

But then there was Cervantes.

Continuing to feel chilled, Jonesy pulled her light cloak more tightly around her. She so much wanted to share everything with Cervantes, but if she did, she knew he would choose to accompany her to Karlisle, whether she wanted him or not. Truthfully, she didn't want his death on her conscience. Rigel would kill Cervantes at his earliest convenience and she would never forgive herself. If she left him behind, even though he would feel betrayed by her desertion, Cervantes would still have his life. That was all that truly mattered.

Feeling a familiar discomfort beginning to creep over her, Jonesy shifted her weight on the back of the lloryk. Her thoughts went to TC and she couldn't keep her gaze from seeking him out even though she knew he wasn't there. He had left a few nights before on the back of his dragon, but not before coming to see her. He had explained to her his decision to leave the group in order to find Aeris and bring her back. She felt heartened by this, for if TC couldn't find Aeris, no one could. She was also pleased that he had thought to seek her out. It meant that he still considered her his friend. She was somewhat surprised to realize that even gods have friendships, and that he valued hers.

Jonesy regarded the man seated beside her. She could sense his sadness and the anguish that accompanied his loss. Over the weeks since Aeris' leavetaking, Jonesy had come to realize the scope of Tallachienan's suffering. His face was more angular than she remembered it to be, and his tunic and trousers seemed to fit a bit more loosely. His eyes were no longer a vibrant lavender, but a dull purple. The losses others had suffered appeared to weigh more heavily on him as well, in particular, those of Cervantes. Somehow, TC had come to realize how bereft the captain had become, and in spite of the animosity that existed between them, he felt sincere empathy.

Jonesy continued to stare until TC turned to face her. He met her unwavering gaze with a raised eyebrow. "Why are you doing it? Why are you seeking her out like this?" she asked.

TC just continued to stare for a moment before he replied. "She is mine. How can I not go after her? Isn't that what lovers do?"

Jonesy looked at him intently as she considered this response. She supposed she should have expected something like it, for TC's behavior regarding Aeris had always been of the possessive type. It put a sour taste in her mouth, for she disliked the thought that a woman might belong to a man as though she no longer had control over her own person. She understood that many times it was like this when a woman married, especially in noble houses. She wondered if it would have been that way for Elinora.

Jonesy's attention shifted back to TC when she heard him give a deep sigh. She saw a pained expression before he turned away, sweeping a hand over his face to settle over his mouth. His voice was muffled a little when he spoke, but Jonesy understood every word. "You and the rest of the group think you have me figured out. I am a self-serving bastard with little care as to the wants and needs of others, a god who has more power than he knows what to do with. You might think it serves me right to have fallen because maybe now I can understand the travails of mortality."

Tallachienan abruptly turned back, pinning her with the intensity of his gaze. "But you don't really know me. You have no understanding what my life has been like. For centuries I watched people live and die. Then, at the turn of each cycle, I watched it happen all over again. You have no idea what that does to a man and what he ultimately decides is the best way to keep his sanity." TC's intensity deepened and he leaned in close. "After a while you begin to shut people out."

Jonesy swallowed convulsively and looked away. TC was right; she never bothered to imagine what it might be like to live cycle after cycle: to see battles fought, to see realms rise and fall, to watch the people you love the most live and die over and over again. Oh gods.

TC suddenly reached out and placed his hand over hers where it rested on the ground between them. "But the Curse of Odion was broken, and I let Aeris in. Hells Jonesy, I love her so much. Without her I am so terribly lonely. I don't want to think what the rest of my life might be like."

TC's voice trailed away and Jonesy felt a tear slip down her cheek. Several moments passed before she collected herself enough to speak. "Y . . . you're right. I didn't know. I am so sorry."

TC squeezed her hand tightly, the brief pain making her look back up at him again. "I don't want your pity Jonesy, only your understanding."

She nodded. "I do understand, but with that understanding comes *sympathy." Jonesy placed her other hand over his where it still rested atop hers. "I can't help but feel sorrow for what you have endured in your life."*

Tallachienan's gaze softened and his hand relaxed. "All right, I can accept that." A moment later found him looking away again, lowering his eyes to his lap. He shook his head. "I let her down. I wasn't the man she needed me to be and now, now I . . ."

Sensing his struggle, Jonesy placed a finger to his lips. "Shhh. You are a good man Tallachienan. I know she will come to you."

He shook his head again. "No, you are wrong Jonesy. You don't know my history or the things I've done."

She cocked her head to the side. "The past isn't important right now, my friend. All that currently matters is what you have become."

"And what is that?"

"I already said." She smiled. "You are a good man, TC. You are so much more than you would like to believe. I have experienced your generosity, your strength, your honor, and your leadership. Most important, I have experienced your friendship. Aeris will recognize these things and she will come to you."

Tallachienan chuckled humorlessly. "You think very highly of me despite knowing my faults."

Jonesy continued to smile. She sat back on her bedroll and it wasn't much longer before she began to sing. The men had told her that they enjoyed hearing her voice, and it made it that much easier to give in to her muse whenever she felt moved to do so. Tallachienan had brought it out in her this time, and she sang a song she hadn't heard in many moon cycles. She only remembered it because something TC said reminded her of the words. With all her heart she sang for her friend. In the end, she was met with the silence that had overtaken the encampment, followed by the applause of her comrades. TC regarded her solemnly and then gave her the slightest nod, making her a promise that he would remember the words of her song.

And that he would find Aeris and bring her back.

Once more Jonesy readjusted herself on the lloryk in an attempt to rid herself of the queasiness. She couldn't seem to find a comfortable position, and she felt herself begin to sweat. She was definitely more sickly than usual this day, and she struggled to find a position that would bring her some iota of relief. It came in a way she didn't expect. Feeling the sudden urge to vomit, she leaped off the back of the patient lloryk and rushed less than a farlo away to heave into the tall grasses. Once finished, Jonesy held a staying hand to her stomach and turned back to find the rest of the group had stopped. All were regarding her with varying degrees of sympathy and disgust. She offered no explanation, but simply walked back to her lloryk and mounted him unassisted, hoping to give everyone the impression that the sudden expulsion did her a bit of good. In a way it had, but she had simply to only wait until the next mealtime when she would feel the unusual sickness all over again.

Jonesy turned when Cervantes rode up next to her. His expression was one of concern, and she was reminded of how fortunate she was to finally have the chance to share herself with him. She gave him a half-hearted smile—one she hoped would convey that she was well. His gaze was intense for a moment before he seemed to relax. He then rode ahead, and she took the hint and followed behind, but not before the periphery of her vision caught the look of speculation upon Jezibel's face. It was she that had borne the expression of disgust when Jonesy got sick in the grass, and for the tenth time Jonesy wondered what had happened to make Jezzie so disgruntled towards her. Since the evening that Jonesy had almost allowed the stew-pot to boil over, the woman had treated her indifferently, mayhap even with dislike. It was strange because they had started to share camaraderie, albeit a tenuous one.

Jonesy strove to ignore Jezzie, instead focusing on Cervantes' back. She could see the shape of him through the tunic he wore, a shape that had become so familiar to her. Even now she could feel the smooth texture of his skin beneath her palms, the width of his shoulders, and the coarse hairs of his chest. Hells, she would miss him so much if she were to . . .

She shook her head to herself. No, how could she leave like that? How could she be alone? But it was almost as though her deep, innermost self had made the decision already, and that she simply had to accept the inevitable.

Jonesy struggled to inhale as her airway spasmed. She could feel her heart breaking and her chest ached so much she could barely breathe. It was rivaled by the constricting pain in her throat, usually experienced when keeping her sadness to herself for so long, caused by the large lump that formed when she suppressed the urge to cry like a child. Her belly clenched in response, and she curved her arm around herself and slumped slightly forward. She didn't need this; she had already gotten sick enough times that she would make a fool of herself.

However, she couldn't help but grieve for Cervantes as though she had already gone. Regardless of the agony it caused her, she knew she could never tell him. *Never.*

CHAPTER NINE

*A*eris lay huddled in the middle of the bed. She watched Ranaghar as he walked across the chamber to the place where he'd discarded his robe, his long black hair an ebony river down the middle of his pale back. If he were to turn just a little, she would still see the silhouette of his erect manhood. After every encounter it always took a few moments for it to subside. She imagined it to be a manifestation of the pleasure he continued to feel in response to the pain he always caused her.

Through slitted eyes she continued to regard Ranaghar intently as he donned his crimson-lined black robes. Her hatred of him had grown over the past few moon cycles, and she dreamed of the day that she would finally have access to her talent. She would paralyze him with her highest level spells and then sheathe his own dagger into his wicked heart. She would smile and watch him struggle to take his last breaths. Once he was dead, she would tear away the shimmering threads she wore on a common day and clothe herself in tunic and trousers. Then she would find a way to escape Tholana's despicable fortress.

Ranaghar didn't bother looking back as he left the room. Once he was gone she allowed herself the luxury of tears. She curved around her distended abdomen, felt the movements of her children deep inside. Instinct told her it wouldn't be much longer before they were born. She would mother them for as long as it took her to kill their father, but then she would be forced to abandon them. There was no possible way she could escape the stronghold with one small child, much less two. And even though a part of her had learned to care about them whilst they grew within her belly, she valued her freedom so much more. That, and a life without pain.

Aeris suddenly awakened. The chamber was dimly lit, and at first she couldn't tell where she was. She put a hand over her belly, and her heartbeat increased when she didn't feel firm roundness beneath her palm. She struggled to sit upright, but an arm across her torso held her down.

<Elirya, I am here.>

Aeris took a few deep breaths before turning towards her bondmate. Once seeing him there beside her, she gave a wan smile. Her voice was unsteady as she spoke. <Jaxom, I'm so glad to see you! I was so afraid . . .>

<Shhh. It was just a dream and it is over now.> His tone was soothing, and she instantly began to calm, allowing the last vestiges of the disturbing images to fall away.

<Where am I? And what are you doing in faelin form?> Jaxom wore tunic and trousers, both colored a deep blue. The sleeveless tunic was trimmed in gray accented with a runic pattern. It brought out the silver of his hair and eyes, and she realized how handsome he was, although it was no match for the breathtaking beauty of his natural form.

He caressed the side of her face with his fingertips. <You are in the infirmary. I couldn't fit inside the chamber, so I had to shift. Demeter Barthaltak has been seeing to your injuries. He says you should be up and about in hardly any time at all.>

Damaeris' breath caught in her throat. <How long have I been here?>

Jaxom shook his head. <Only two days. Don't worry. You haven't missed much.>

Aeris closed her eyes, struggling to recall what happened. It suddenly flooded back to her—Demeter Kord's ambush, their desperate escape, and Zestrimath's terrible burns as a result of a fire-breathing exercise gone terribly awry. She began to tremble again, an involuntary response to the influx of memories. <Kahlan and Zestri, where are they?>

Jaxom leaned into her, folding her within his embrace. <Hush, my friend. They are fine. Both will recover with time.>

<You are certain?>

<Do you really think I would ever lie to you?>

Aeris was quiet for a moment, her mind shifting to another question lurking in her mind. <Jaxom, why am I here?>

It was his turn to practice silence. Then, <You were wounded when we helped bring Zestri and Khalan to the ground.>

<What happened to me?>

<You don't remember?> he countered.

She only shook her head.

Jaxom lowered his gaze, almost as though he was ashamed. <The tip of Zestrimath's wing struck you. The harness straps somehow unlatched and you fell from my back. You were lucky, for if you remained in position, the wing may have battered you to death. Only the grace of the Fates kept you alive.>

Aeris took a moment to think back, struggled to recall what had happened. She vaguely remembered trying to unfasten the harness straps, mayhap to escape the very thing that was ultimately her undoing. <So, what's wrong with me? Why is it difficult to move?> she asked.

<Some of your ribs were broken. With the help of some healing magic,

Demeter Bart has been working hard to mend them swiftly. However, your sleep was very deep; Bart says you were in a coma. Your head must have struck the ground rather hard when you fell.>

Aeris nodded thoughtfully. Then, <Are you all right, my friend?>

Jaxom's gaze became piercing. <Now that you have awakened, I am doing just fine.>

Aeris was quiet for several moments. She then drew her brows into a frown. <What aren't you telling me? You told me to have faith in you, but you aren't making that task very easy when you hide things.>

Jaxom didn't speak at first; she could sense him ruminating over his thoughts. Then, <I made a promise that I would always protect you. I failed to keep that promise. You could have been maimed, or even killed during that fall. I should have shielded you better.> Jaxom paused and then continued. <I have failed you and I am sorry.>

Aeris slowly reached out and placed her hand alongside Jaxom's down-turned face. <Perhaps what you say is true. Maybe you could have shielded me better. But now you know what to do next time. You are not all-knowing or all-powerful. You are a young dragon who was doing his best in a very unforgiving situation. I have moved on. Please allow yourself to do the same. Nothing has changed. I will continue to place my life in your care whenever we are together.>

Jaxom closed his eyes and his hand rose to cover hers. For a moment they remained that way, but then Aeris was making another attempt to rise from the bed. With a frown, Jaxom held her back down. <Where do you think you are going?>

Aeris winced with the discomfort her activity brought. <We have our work to do. You know we can't get too far behind.>

Jaxom shook his head. <No, Demeter Bart insisted you stay here. Any activity will jeopardize his efforts to hasten your recovery. Besides, it doesn't matter if we get a little behind, just as long as you are going to be all right.>

Aeris thrust her lower lip into a pout. <You actually believe him?>

Jaxom waggled his forefinger at her. <I do, and nothing you say will change my mind.>

Aeris gave a mock growl and grabbed at the offending finger. Jaxom was too quick for her and snatched it out of harm's way just as they heard a voice at the chamber entry. "Aeris, are you awake?" Jaxom rose from his chair as Thulnar stepped into the room. "By the gods, you don't know how glad I am to see you awake! Faleema and I have been so worried about you!"

<I will give you and your friend some time together,> said Jaxom. <But don't worry; I shall return soon.>

Aeris didn't realize she had become so tense until she relaxed with those last words. Jaxom bent to kiss her on the forehead, and then turned to clasp Thulnar's hand as he passed the other man on his way out of the room.

"You know, he has been sitting here since the moment they brought you. He refused to leave your side," said Thulnar.

Aeris felt a lump form in her throat. "Really?"

Thulnar nodded and seated himself in the chair recently occupied by Jaxom. "He insisted that he should be here to offer his protection even though you were safe in the hands of Demeter Bart."

Aeris swallowed the lump and a tear fell into her hairline. Then, getting a grip on her emotions, she asked him the questions that weighed most. "How are Kahlan and Zestri? Are they all right? What happened?"

Thulnar shook his head sadly. "No one saw what happened. Speculation has it that Zestrimath unintentionally swerved into Sidranth's flame. Kahlan was lucky to walk away relatively unharmed. Between you and Zestri, Barthaltak has been a very busy man."

"Does he think the dragon will recover?"

Thulnar nodded. "He has high hopes for Zestri." He then paused and addressed her unspoken question. "She will not be rising for her pairing flight."

Aeris was unsurprised by his statement. Nevertheless, she could still feel the unusual tension, heightened mayhap by the nearness of the apex of Zestri's fertility. She supposed it would dissipate after another day or so. Her heart went out to the ailing dragon and her bondmate, and Aeris was glad that she and Jaxom had been able to help them.

She could only hope that someone might one day think to do the same for her.

⚒ ⚒ ⚒ ⚒ ⚒

From his place at the other side of the fire, Tigerius watched as Jonesy loaded her gear onto the dappled gray lloryk, situating everything until it was balanced on either side of the back leathers. The watch was asleep, as was the rest of the group. She had slipped something into the evening chag. The popular drink was once more available to them as they traveled the western side of Ansalar, and everyone had begun to anticipate it after the rigors of the day. However, this night Tiger just happened to notice Jonesy adding an extra packet of powder to the brew. Consequently, he chose not to partake of the drink. It was a good thing, for whatever she had placed within it caused the encampment to fall into drug-induced sleep. He had no idea as to the reason for her misdeed, deliberately remaining awake so that he could discover it. Now he was figuring it out—Jonesy was leaving, and she didn't want the rest of the group knowing she was gone until well into the morning, when she would be far enough away that they mightn't find her. If she had been smart, she would have made the drink concentrated enough so that the group would sleep late, and then be groggy once they awakened.

Tiger imagined that was exactly how it would play out.

Jonesy completed her preparations. She then glanced forlornly about the encampment. It was then Tiger realized she didn't really want to leave, and he pulled his brows into a frown. If she didn't want to go, then why was she doing this? He watched as she then slipped over to Cervantes where he slept on his bedroll. She knelt over him and then kissed him gently on the cheek. Tiger couldn't see it from this distance, but he imagined that she might be crying. It didn't surprise him that she singled Cervantes out from the rest, for he had determined the romantic aspect of their relationship soon after rescuing her from the lair of the vampyr. Cervantes' intense determination to go after her so quickly was explained, as well as the glances he had seen them cast one another every once in a while prior to her captivity. Such glances only increased after her rescue, as well as the occasional touch here and there. Something had happened between them within the daemon stronghold, and they chose to keep it a secret. He didn't really know why they made that decision, but he respected their privacy and said nothing of it.

Tigerius continued to watch as Jonesy finally left Cervantes' side. She made her way to the packed lloryk, and then taking one last look around the encampment, she mounted the animal with a quick, upward surge. She swung her leg easily over the back as she settled herself onto the padded leathers. She then turned the animal into the darkness and rode away.

For several moments Tigerius stared into the shadows of the vicinity where Jonesy had left. His mind raced with uncertainty, but before he knew it, he was swiftly rising from his bedding, rolling it up, and then loading it onto the lloryk he liked the most. He knew he was taking a valuable commodity from the group, but he knew he would need such a sturdy animal to take him where he needed to go. Nothing had seemed right with him for so long, and it was time he figured out what had happened to make him so defunct. If his mother had been taken by the daemundai, he needed to find her. And now, more than ever, he felt himself drawing closer. Like a beacon of light, she drew him nearer and nearer.

Once finished, Tigerius took a quick look at his cousins. They slept ever so soundly, and he could only hope they wouldn't meet misfortune as a result of Jonesy's actions. A part of him was loath to leave his comrades in potential peril, but his desire to follow his own path won out. Just as swiftly as Jonesy had done, Tiger mounted his lloryk and then entered the darkness where he remembered her disappearing not long before.

Tigerius rode through the remainder of the night, striving to keep to the vague path Jonesy had set. Tiger was no tracker, and the darkness made it difficult for him to follow. Yet, once morning arrived and he saw the small outline of someone moving through the tall grasses ahead, his flagging spirits become rejuvenated. Somehow he had been able to follow her and even closed some distance that may have once existed between them. However, he wouldn't hold his breath for the next available opportunity for her to slip out of his sight. Heeling his lloryk into motion, Tiger hurried to catch up to her.

Jonesy's heart thundered in her chest as she heard the approaching sound of lloryk or larian behind her. She knew it wasn't horse, for their feet made a different sound on the turf. She swiftly turned her lloryk to meet the oncoming rider, drawing her cutlass from out of the scabbard that hung at her left side. She had never fought astride, but how hard could it be? She was well-trained in her ability to ride; it was one thing she had always done proficiently, even as a young girl. She supposed it was because it was the least feminine of any of the activities offered to her, and thus more exciting.

Jonesy brandished the cutlass before her as the rider made his way closer. The tall grasses brushed against her legs as they waved in the wind. Damn, she knew she would be at risk traveling alone, but she didn't think she would be attacked so soon after leaving the group. She couldn't believe her misfortune, and she swallowed heavily with the realization that she would probably die at the hand of some unknown rogue. Yet, she was determined to persevere, for her kingdom needed her, whether it knew it or not.

As the rider approached, Jonesy began to notice that the lloryk he rode seemed familiar. Then looking intently at the man on the animal's back, Jonesy realized he seemed familiar as well. A rush of recognition swept through her, followed by one of intense relief. By the gods, she'd been so very frightened, almost as scared as the time she'd watched Rigel and his men stab a girl to near death within a dark alleyway.

The poor girl had lived—but only because Jonesy had been there.

Tigerius rode up just as Jonesy re-sheathed the cutlass. He sat hard on the back leathers to signal the lloryk to a stop. He offered her a grin and then gestured towards her weapon. "I'm sorry I startled you. But I knew I needed to catch up for fear of losing sight of you."

Jonesy frowned. "Tigerius, why are you here?"

He shrugged as he made his reply. "I want to travel with you as long as I can before we must part ways. So far, you are moving in my direction."

Jonesy narrowed her eyes. "How did you overcome the effects of the effresdyn powder I put in the chag this past evening?"

Tiger's smile widened. "I noticed you putting something in the drink. I chose not to partake of it. I am glad I didn't."

Jonesy cast her eyes downward. "You must think me a terrible person to drug my comrades so easily."

Tiger shrugged again. "I don't think the decision came easily. I think it was something you considered for several days before the execution."

Jonesy was silent for a moment. "So, where are you going?"

"To be quite honest, I'm not sure," he replied. "All I know is that I need to go back." Tiger gestured to the north. It wasn't entirely the truth, but he couldn't help expressing the desire to travel in the same direction he thought she might be going. "Where are you headed?"

"Back to Krathil-lon," she replied shortly.

Tigerius frowned. "Why?"

"Because the portal located there can take me closer to where I wish to be."

Tiger nodded in understanding, suddenly realizing where she wanted to go. Jonesy's destination was Karlisle. He couldn't really blame her, for Elvandahar would simply make her their prisoner as soon as they discovered her identity. They would eventually choose to use her as a bartering tool, but not before they wore her down with the seemingly endless interrogation that would accompany lack of food, drink, sleep, or all three.

However, taking the portal to the Bryton-Selmist juncture was not without its dangers. It was a place located near the hotbed of dissension between Elvandahar and Karlisle. Without knowledge of even the general location of the battle-front, Jonesy could find herself in the midst of something that could easily get her killed.

"It will be good for us to travel together," he continued. "You are vulnerable out here alone, but with me beside you, the Lawless will think twice about approaching us."

"The Lawless?"

Tiger nodded. "They are the people who make their homes here in this unclaimed territory. They have no ruler, and as such, no laws. They also have no one to protect them should they come under attack. They live for no one but themselves, pay no taxes, and have a tendency to prey upon those who are foolish enough to travel alone."

Tiger's voice trailed away as he took in her expression. He then shook his head. "It would be much better if we traveled in the company of a caravan."

Jonesy frowned. "If you think you can lull me into complacency, and then take me back to the group, you are very mistaken." Her green eyes glittered with the strength of her conviction.

Tiger shook his head slowly. "I am not here to take you back to the group. I just want a companion with whom to travel as long as I may. Then . . . then I will be forced to travel alone. The companionship will be good while it lasts."

The lies came more easily to him than he imagined they would. Certainly, there was a part of him that felt compelled to accompany Jonesy. However, even greater instincts bade him travel west into the realm of Tusbir. Krathillon would take him far out of his way.

Jonesy allowed her guard to relax and she offered him a tremulous smile. "All right, it will be good to have you by my side for a while."

Aeris stood silently in the center of the chamber. Before her were the men who had actively participated in her training since arriving to Shayamalan: Demeters Forigard, Rogerus, Kordrian, and Barthaltak. Just that morning, the halfen priest had announced that she was mended enough to return to training. Of course, if left to heal naturally, the broken ribs would have taken much, much longer to repair. The same could be said for her skull fracture. But with the arcane remedies Bart had stored in his tiny little bottles, and the spectacular skill he wielded at his behest, she recovered ten times as quickly as she ordinarily would—only a few days as opposed to a few *sevendays*.

"You are probably wondering why you are here," Demeter Fo began. "The reason is quite simple, actually. It has come to our collective attention that you have performed exceptionally well in the three tests you have taken: that of trust, that of falling, and that of keeping your seat in an ambush." Forigard paused for a moment. Then, "Of course no one could have foreseen the unfortunate circumstances surrounding Kahlan and her bondmate." The man's clear blue eyes fastened onto hers. "And once again your actions spoke louder than any words."

Surprised, Aeris was silent for a moment before shaking her head. "No. That was all Jaxom. He was the one that rushed to Zestrimath's aid," she said in a formal tone.

Fo cocked his head to the side, his eyes narrowing speculatively. "Well, no one told me of any objections on your part. Besides, a dragon knows the heart of his bondmate and will often act according to what he or she would do in circumstances that arise."

Aeris was thoughtful before shaking her head again. "Regardless, the praise should go to him. It took me a moment longer to realize what was happening."

Fo crossed his arms at his chest. The other demeters simply stood there, saying nothing. "You are a rare individual, Damaeris Timberlyn."

She gave a nod. "I have been told so before."

Fo raised an eyebrow. "What would you say if I told you that your bondmate was deficient in a mineral he needed to keep his flame strong . . . that the only way for him to have it would be to leave the world of Shandahar to travel to another one?"

Aeris felt her eyes widen, yet she remained calm. She had left Shandahar a few times before in the past under the tutelage of Master Dinim. It was an aspect of her training as a dimensionalist, for she took much of her power from places that were not a part of the world upon which she lived.

Aeris shrugged. "What has it to do with the testing you mentioned?"

Forigard smiled. "Everything. You see, Jaxom will need to remain upon Haldorr for quite some time in order for the mineral to build up in his body. Your exceptional tests have shown that you may continue your training upon Haldorr whilst Jaxom receives his fill of the mineral he needs. This advanced training will require the presence of Demeter Kord, of course, for he is a specialist in all things arcane."

Aeris shook her head. "But what about my comrades? I shall need someone with me where I am going."

Fo cocked his head once more, and a sly grin spread across his face. "Are you thinking to strike a bargain with me?"

Aeris only regarded him innocently. "Demeter, why would I even consider such a thing? It is simply that I feel the need for a faelin companion to accompany me to such a faraway place."

Aeris heard what sounded like a muffled cough emanating from the vicinity of the other three demeters standing on Fo's left side. She momentarily shifted her gaze to find that Rogerus wore a hand across his mouth. His eyes spoke volumes, sparkling with amusement as he regarded her. However, she kept her expression solemn as she returned her focus to Demeter Fo.

"I see," he said slowly. "So who is this comrade you would like to accompany you upon your journey?"

Aeris feigned thoughtfulness. Then, "It would definitely have to be Faleema Sanagard and Thulnar Raredon."

Demeter Fo furrowed his brows. "You mentioned bringing one companion, yet now you give me the names of two persons."

Aeris shrugged noncommittally in spite of the ire she felt radiating from Fo. "One is not complete without the other. Damnation, if I had just one accompany me, I would have only half a comrade." She widened her eyes with emphasis and planted her hands at her hips. Once again she heard a muffled cough from one of the other demeters.

"And if I told you it would simply not be possible to bring such companions with you . . ." Fo let his voice trail off, yet the intended question hung between them.

Aeris shook her head. "I simply don't think I could function without them near. Hells, it was Faleema who saw to my scale-burn when I first arrived here. Without her, it probably would have become infected and overcome me. And without Thulnar I still might not know where to get a decent meal." Aeris then placed her fingertips to her lips. "Hmm, Faleema might not know either."

Forigard held up his hand, palm outward. "Stop. I assure you that your arguments are quite amusing, but you must think me a fool to believe them."

Aeris interrupted, her eyes widening with feigned seriousness. "Never, Demeter. I would never consider you a fool, merely a benefactor." Aeris said the last with a small smile, one that she hoped wasn't too presumptuous.

Demeter Fo sighed, shook his head once more, and stepped towards her. "You know that these decisions are left up to the dragon elders to decide," he said in a subdued tone.

"Aeris nodded. "I figured as much. Yet, it is best if I have someone to speak for me, is it not?"

Fo rewarded her with a slight chuckle. "Indeed, I suppose you are right."

Aeris smiled, for once allowing a bit of her facetiousness to show through. "Thank-you," she said quietly.

"For what?"

Aeris shrugged. "For always being there to offer your strength and encouragement."

"You know that Lord Trebexal is going to think me a fool."

Aeris shook her head. "No, he will have me in mind and may be open to my requirements for traveling to Haldorr."

"You are so certain of his agreement, then?"

"No, just hopeful to a fault," she replied. At that moment, she considered asking Fo if he would take the place of Kord as her primary instructor when she journeyed to Haldorr, yet abstained. She knew that he was needed too much here. Damnation, it was quite unfortunate.

It was then that Fo raised his voice once more and stepped back into his place alongside the other demeters. "Your tentative leave date shall be three mornings from now. It gives you ample time to prepare."

Aeris simply nodded, turned, and left. The moment she was out of the demeters' presence, she was opening her mind to her waiting bondmate. Within moments she was suffused with his excitement. <Eliyra, this is wonderful! I will contact Sordranth and Miramanth right away!>

Aeris chuckled as she felt his mind retreat from hers. She was taken slightly aback, for she had never felt such emotion from him before. Certainly she had felt his happiness, especially during the times they flew together and accomplished the goals set before them. But this was different. He was actually *excited* about something, and the sensation was new to her.

By the time Aeris made it back to the barracks, her friends were already there. Thulnar and Faleema both rushed over to her, but it was Thulnar who shook his head and spoke. "What the Hells have you done?" he asked incredulously.

Aeris placed a hand on his arm. "Please, I would really like for you to be there with me."

"Are you certain we will be allowed to come?" Faleema asked.

Aeris turned to her and nodded. "Don't worry; Lord Trebexal will give the permission."

Thulnar held out his hand. "How do you know?"

Aeris only smiled. "I just do."

Thulnar then pursed his lips. "You know, I don't want to get excited about this for nothing. Not to mention Sordra. She would absolutely love the chance to go home."

Faleema rolled her eyes. "And, of course, don't bother to mention that we have never been off world before."

Thulnar swung to her with narrowed eyes, his expression one of exasperation. "I didn't want to state the obvious, Faleema," he countered with a note of irritation.

Faleema only shrugged her shoulders dismissively.

Aeris sighed and placed her hands at her hips. "Come on, you two. Stop fighting. Besides, I did enough of that to get Demeter Fo to agree to ask the elders to have you with me."

Faleema's eyes widened. "You *fought* with him?

Aeris shook her head with a grin. "No, not in the physical sense."

It was Thulnar's turn to roll his eyes. Aeris whacked him playfully on the shoulder with a swipe of her hand. He cringed away in mock fear and she whacked him again for good measure. "You had both better begin your preparations if your intention is to come with me."

Thulnar straightened and nodded. "So, what about Demeter Kord? What does he think about all this?" he asked.

Aeris shook her head slowly. "I really don't know. He didn't say anything at the meeting today."

Faleema sighed. "It's quite unfortunate that he will be in accompaniment. His presence shall dull the experience for us all," she said.

Thulnar scoffed. "Why the Hells do you say that?"

Faleema narrowed her eyes. "You don't know him as Aeris and I do."

Aeris nodded in agreement. "He does tend to take the joy out of things."

Thulnar allowed himself to be swayed by their opinions. "All right, I hear you. But . . ." He was suddenly interrupted when Saliel burst into the chamber. His brown eyes were bright with excitement, his face flushed in spite of its bronzed tone.

"Have you heard?" He didn't pause for a response. "We are all to be going to Haldorr! By the gods, can you believe it?"

Aeris felt her eyes widen with astonishment and a moment later both Thulnar and Faleema were turning to her in surprise.

"The announcement was just made," continued Saliel. "It was something about our dragons needing replenishment of some kind of mineral." He shook his head. "I don't know; it had some weird name. All of the demeters will be going, as well as you three, Kahlan and I, and Falon and Franchiera." He shrugged. "And maybe a few other people; I don't remember who they are. Anyways, I'm off to tell Kahlan now. She will be thrilled about this!" With that said, Saliel was rushing through the chamber and into the tunnels that led to the academy where the infirmary was located.

The three stared after him. For a few moments there was nothing but silence. Then, "You didn't say *everyone* would be coming with us," said Thulnar in a monotone.

Aeris raised an eyebrow. "You didn't ask."

Faleema gave her a sideways glance. "You didn't know."

Aeris nodded. "True."

"I guess we had best prepare for our trip," Thulnar said.

Aeris continued to nod and gave him a piercing look. "I recall stating that already."

Thulnar narrowed his eyes. He gave a low growl in his throat and curved his fingers in a beastly mock threat. "Curses woman, you think you're so smart. I'm gonna come over there and . . ."

He stopped speaking and lunged for her. Aeris shrieked and leaped out of the way. She laughed as Thulnar gave chase while Faleema tried to jump in to try and save her. Aeris darted among the bedpallets but wasn't fast enough. She screamed again as Thulnar caught her about the waist and swung her around before tossing her down on the nearest one. He loomed over her with his curved fingers and proceeded to lay siege to her vulnerable belly.

Aeris laughed until her sides ached, and her bondmate chuckled in her mind in response to the silliness taking place. And for the first time in very long, she was able to *forget*.

CHAPTER TEN

Alasdair looked out across the sea of tall grass surrounding him. Squinting in response to the late day sunlight, he momentarily put a hand to his forehead, his mind continuing to harbor the muzzy sensation he had been experiencing since awakening not very long ago. The feeling was reminiscent of having been ill for a couple days and then trying to return to normal life—mild disorientation coupled with mental vagueness and overall fatigue. Not to mention, his head ached abominably. Yet, he didn't recall having been ill recently, and the rest of the group seemed to be suffering the same affliction.

With quite some bit of thought, it was finally Talemar who came to the conclusion that they had been drugged, and at about the same time, Cervantes noticed that Jonesy was missing. Not long after, they discovered Tigerius was also no longer in their company. When the halfen brothers made the realization that two of their lloryk were also gone, they all suddenly came to the understanding that their comrades had left them sometime in the middle of the night.

Most likely, Tiger and Jonesy had been the culprits of their drug-induced sleep.

Now here he was, standing out in the middle of the savanna. Alasdair had already lost their trail. His tracking proficiency was specialized to the forest, for he knew just what to look for in that type of environment. In terrain such as this, he was only mediocre, and at this time of the year the grasses were unusually tall. If he tried really hard, Alasdair had a chance of success. But truthfully, he didn't want to bother. He was too angry. Besides, the abhorrent act of poisoning ones comrades communicated a desire to be left alone, and Alasdair was more than willing to oblige.

Alasdair cursed to himself, hating the thought of heading back to the group. The environment back at the encampment was strained, for they had slowly lost almost half of their number since leaving the catacombs surrounding Tholana's stronghold. Aeris and Jaxom had been the first to depart, followed by TC, and now Jonesy and Tigerius. He didn't even know why any of them had decided to part with the main company except for Tallachienan, who had the decency to approach him with his intent to part ways in order to bring Aeris back from the dragon continent.

It came as such a surprise to realize that Jonesy had abandoned them, for Alasdair had come to think of her as a good person. She was more than just the sister of the woman who was once destined to become the wife of his brother, and more than just the youngest daughter to the king of a realm who had declared war upon Elvandahar. She was a friend. Certainly, he hadn't known her as well as many of the other group members, but he'd thought he knew enough to recognize an honorable individual.

He was wrong.

Alasdair liked to think that she wouldn't have made such a serious transgression against them if not for a cause that was very important to her. Unfortunately, he didn't believe that. He had little faith in people recently, and he supposed he had Aeris to blame for that. He could only imagine what Cervantes was feeling right now. Alasdair grudgingly turned back in the direction of the encampment. Cedric silently followed, he having been asked to be in accompaniment in case Alasdair should need some backup. He understood the reasoning, but hated to be in the company of another when he really preferred to be alone. It was simply his way. Most likely Cedric felt the same.

It took them a bit longer than he expected to reach camp, not realizing he had gone so far afield in his search. Unfortunately, there was little usable daylight left within which to travel. As they walked, Alasdair had already accepted the possibility they would be camping in the same place for another night. The realization was a bit irritating but something over which he had no control. He wasn't surprised that Cervantes was the first to notice their return. He supposed he couldn't really blame the man for his desire to have the trail found. Cervantes and Jonesy had thought they were successful at keeping their relationship secret, but most of the group was well aware of something transpiring between them. Alasdair had only to shake his head in order to communicate his failure to the other man. He watched the wave of disappointment wash over the captain's face, and he felt a tinge of regret. In spite of his feeling that they should not continue any pursuit of their comrades, he felt bad that Cervantes would not be able to find surcease. He watched the man turn and walk into the nearby grasses, most likely to simply be alone with his thoughts for a while.

Alasdair made his way to his travel pack and equipment. Nearby was his disheveled bedroll. He had left it that way when he hastily made some attempt at tracking Jonesy and Tigerius. On his way over, he noticed Jezibel at the fire, a place where he recalled Jonesy spending much of her time. Jezzie was looking in the direction Cervantes had disappeared into the grasses, and he shook his head. She had begun to pay the captain quite a bit of attention in spite of the attraction she'd begun to share with Levander.

Jezibel couldn't help but watch the place where Cervantes had made his disappearance. She could sense his agony over Jonesy's abandonment, and instead of feeling good that her competition was no longer present, she was saddened by the hurt she knew Cervantes was feeling. Yet, he didn't even know the half of it, for Jonesy had not been very forthright with him about many things, one of which obviously happened to be her intent to leave the group. *The other was the state of her physical condition when she left.*

Jezibel shook her head. She had begun to dislike Jonesy even more the moment she realized what had happened. Hells, most likely Jonesy didn't even know the truth for herself, for she probably had none of her own experiences against which to make any reference. Jezzie chose to say nothing, struggling to accept the reality that another woman would have something she had always wanted for herself. She didn't bother helping when Jonesy became overwrought with the sickness that tended to overcome women in this condition, and instead chose to regard her with cold disdain.

Now Jonesy was gone.

Jezibel was suddenly confronted with the possibility of having Cervantes for herself. The thought was intriguing; however something had changed. Cervantes still yearned for Jonesy. But even more, Jezzie had also seen another path, and it didn't include Captain Conradi. *Jezibel had begun to realize she was in love with another man.*

She swallowed the hard lump that suddenly formed in her throat. By the gods, she knew next to nothing about Levander, not even his last name. That realization alone scared her, not to mention that she was deviating from all that she knew into unfamiliar territory. Lev was from another place, one with its own culture and beliefs. She'd heard a little about the Brotherhood of the Kronshue, and that he was one of them. She needed to know more about him, much more, and she wanted him to be the one to tell her. If he chose to keep everything about himself away from her, Jezzie would never know the real man. And she so much wanted to know and needed to know. *Oh gods.*

Jezibel stood from her spot next to the fire and walked in the direction where she last saw Cervantes. It had been much too long since they'd shared any real conversation. Since their meeting in Darban, she had shut him away, leaving the splendid friendship they had once shared somewhere along the dusty trail left behind in the wake of their hardships. Now she would endeavor to reinstate it, and hope it wasn't too late. She saw Lev watching her as she passed by, and she offered him a small smile. His stoic expression immediately softened, and he returned the gesture. Jezibel was glad she finally knew what she wanted. Now all she had to do was pick up the pieces of the mess she had left behind during the process of her discovery.

Jezzie walked more deeply into the swaying grasses. Despite the light offered by the setting sun, she was reminded of the last time she had followed Cervantes. Yet, she realized she didn't feel the same way about it now as she did then. She had finally come to terms with the course of events that conspired to make the present. Loving and losing Cervantes had been part of that path. Now, whether it was good for her or not, she had Lev. She'd been holding herself back, but now that she was free of her past, perhaps she would freely open herself to him. And perhaps he would decide to share more of himself with her in reciprocation.

Jezibel found Cervantes not far away from the encampment. He simply stood there, staring out over the seemingly endless waving savanna. She could tell that he was aware of her presence the moment she stepped up behind him, and she remained silent until he spoke.

"I began to think you had forgotten me," he said in a low tone.

Jezibel shook her head. "Cervantes, I could never forget you." She paused and then continued. "Besides, we have shared far too much together."

Cervantes gave a soft chuckle. "You are definitely right about that."

She smiled. "I will never forget how you saved me from those men from Gridiron. I owe you so much."

Cervantes simply shook his head. "No Jezzie, you owe me nothing. I would have done the same for any of my friends."

Jezibel shook her own head. "No, you wouldn't have. I know you, Cervantes. You would only have done it for *me*." She was silent for a moment as she fought to collect herself. "And I am so glad." She stopped at that, as she felt her voice begin to break. She could only hope that he hadn't heard.

Cervantes swept his intense gaze over her. He was silent for a few moments before he spoke again. "Jezzie, what are you doing away from the encampment?"

She remained quiet, her eyes cast to the ground. She should have expected such a response, for she had indeed left Cervantes to his own devices for quite some time. "Hoping to be your friend again," she said finally.

Cervantes simply regarded her. "But why now?" he asked.

"Perhaps because you might have need of one, now more than ever."

It was Cervantes' turn to maintain the silence. Then he slowly shook his head. "I can't believe she is gone."

Jezibel reeled with surprise for only a moment before swiftly collecting herself. It was heartening to see that he felt he could confide in her despite the distance she had placed between them. She stepped forward and put a comforting hand on his arm. "I am sure that her decision to go was not a hastily made one."

Cervantes furrowed his brows. "You mean to say that you think she had been considering this for quite some time?"

Jezibel immediately heard the shift in his demeanor. With only a few words she had offered him aggravation instead of the calm she had hoped to impose. "No, that's not what I meant," she said quickly. "I only meant that she did not make the decision lightly, for I am certain it was difficult for her to leave her comrades."

Cervantes nodded and then began to settle. He was thoughtful for a moment and then, "You were her friend. Did she say anything to you?"

Jezzie found herself taken quite aback. She'd never really considered herself Jonesy's friend, for surely Jezzie hadn't treated her as such. But for some reason, Cervantes perceived their relationship differently, either because of something Jonesy said to him, or because he had noticed something that she never realized.

Jezibel shook her head. "No, she said nothing." She paused for a moment and then continued. "It's just another reason to believe that her leave-taking wasn't something she had been planning all along."

Cervantes shook his head, sucking at his lower lip. "I don't know. She seemed somehow different these past few days. It was almost as though she was waiting for something."

As Cervantes' voice trailed away, Jonesy's condition came to Jezzie's mind. She couldn't be entirely sure, but it could account for the difference he noticed during the days leading up to Jonesy's departure. Yet, she didn't know if she could say anything of it to Cervantes in spite of the fact that he deserved to know. And it was only because, as of yet, he still hadn't told Jezzie that anything existed between them. She only knew because she was a spy, and a bad one at that.

Jezibel decided to play ignorance. She didn't really know what else to do, and it seemed the appropriate way to go. She proceeded to shake her head and then splayed her hands before her. "Cervantes, I know she was your friend, but why does this matter so much to you?"

His gaze swung over to meet hers and their eyes met and locked. The intensity of his stare bore into her and she realized he knew that she knew.

He blinked once and then solemnly responded. "It is the reason why you have distanced yourself even more from me this past fortnight. Don't play dumb with me, Jezzie."

She tore her gaze away and cast it to the ground. Hells, he was more astute than she thought. But then it would also mean that he probably knew how much he had always meant to her.

Jezibel steeled her eyes as she looked back up at him. She nodded as she replied. "You are right. I know about the relationship that you and Jonesy share. And now I also know that all this time you didn't bother to help me address my own feelings for you. Why?"

Cervantes was silent for a moment, digesting her words. It was then his turn to look abashed and he shook his head in a gesture of helplessness. "I didn't know how." He paused for a moment, and then spoke again. "I'm so sorry Jezzie."

She only shook her own head and sighed. "Don't be. I needed to work though it myself anyways."

Cervantes regarded her intently. "And all is well?"

Jezzie nodded. "I think so."

Cervantes continued to look at her. "I have always cared about your happiness; you must know that."

She couldn't help smiling. "I know."

"What is going on between you and Lev?"

She shook her head, feigning ignorance. She thought no one had noticed the scope of their rapport, but she should have known better. Of course Cervantes would notice. "What are you talking about?"

Cervantes gave a low chuckle. "Again you think to play dumb with me. After so many years, you should know that is impossible." He cocked his head. "You like him very much, and I can see he likes you."

Jezzie only nodded, but in her mind she felt a surge of delight. Someone else had seen that Lev bore some romantic inclination towards her. It was good to know because sometimes he seemed so aloof, so withdrawn, that she wondered what he might be thinking about her.

"I just want you to be careful. Certainly, Lev is a good man. I have determined that fact over the time we have spent in one another's company. But he was once a member of the kronshue, and I don't know how connected he is with the brotherhood."

She nodded again. "I know. I have thought about that already."

Cervantes was quiet for a moment. Then, "I suppose I should tell you to take some care with his heart. I am thinking he hasn't encountered women the way many men in your experience have done."

She smiled again, for the Cervantes she had known several fortnights ago would never have bothered to say something like this. Loving Jonesy had changed him, and it was definitely for the better. She only wished it could remain so easy. Gods, he deserved to know the truth! There was a woman out there who was probably carrying his child. How could she keep that knowledge from him?

"Cervantes, there is something that I need to tell you. Jonesy probably doesn't even know of it herself, and I feel badly that I never discussed it with her."

Cervantes frowned with immediate concern. "What is it?"

Jezibel paused, wondering if she was doing the right thing. What if divulging this information made Cervantes more upset than what he was already, bringing him even more turmoil? Or what if Jonesy wasn't pregnant at all and Jezzie was making Cervantes suffer needlessly? But now he was regarding her expectantly.

"I think that Jonesy is pregnant."

Cervantes became suddenly still and his expression conflicted. "How do you know?" he asked finally.

Jezzie shrugged. "It's a feeling I have based on what I have seen."

His gaze became agonized. "Why didn't she tell me?"

Jezibel shook her head. "Like I said, I don't think she has yet realized it. She couldn't tell you something she knew nothing about."

Cervantes ran a hand across his face. "You are certain of this?"

She shook her head again. "No, not completely. But certain enough to say something to you."

Cervantes was silent for several moments. "I have to go after her."

"But you don't know where she has gone," she objected with a frown.

"The only place where I can think she may have gone is to her home, the Kingdom of Karlisle."

Jezzie's eyes widened with alarm. "Cervantes, Karlisle is at war. We can't go there!"

Cervantes shook his head. "I know *we* can't, but *I* can." He swept past her as he made his way back to the encampment. She stared after him for a moment, her mind reeling with the implication of his words. By the gods, he sincerely meant to go to war-infested Karlisle!

Jezzie rushed after him. "Cervantes, no! You don't know what you are saying! If you are caught, they will kill you!"

The man before her said nothing, simply continuing until he reached the rest of the group. He made towards his supplies and equipment, and then began to pack everything away. Jezibel rushed over to him, placing a staying hand on his arm. "Cervantes, please listen to me. You can't help Jonesy if you are dead!"

Cervantes turned to her then, his blue eyes bright with the intensity of his determination. "I can't help her by staying here, either."

Her voice became broken. "Cervantes, please . . ."

"What's going on here?"

Both turned in the direction of Alasdair's voice. The ranger stepped up to them, his eyes regarding the partially packed travel sack sitting before Cervantes questioningly.

"I am going after Jonesy. I know where she is headed."

Alasdair frowned. "Cervantes, not all that long ago that woman poisoned the evening brew that left us vulnerable all night and well into the morning. She obviously doesn't want us with her, wherever she is going. And I am not one for imposing my presence on anyone." He shook his head. "We just need to let her go."

Cervantes returned the frown with one of his own. "You seem to forget that Jonesy is not the only one who left the encampment last night. As I recall it, she is in the company of your good friend. What, are you just going to let him go too? Is that what friends do—just let one another go in spite of the danger they might face?" Cervantes' voice became more gruff. "Well, that isn't friendship if you ask me. I suppose I have a different definition for the term."

Cervantes once more went about preparing for travel, rolling up his bedroll and tying the ropes at either end to keep it secure. Jezzie gathered up his mug and bowl, placing them within his pack, and then took up his blanket and began to fold it. Meanwhile, Alasdair just stood by and watched with a thoughtful expression. It didn't take Jezzie and Cervantes long to complete the preparations, and only then did Cervantes stop. He regarded Alasdair for a moment before speaking.

"I am going to need one of the horses. I am hoping you are willing to part with one."

Alasdair simply stood there and said nothing, his expression still one of pensiveness. Cervantes waited patiently for a moment or two, but when the other man didn't honor him with a response, he only shook his head and swept abruptly past Alasdair. It was then the ranger shot out a staying hand, grabbing the upper fringe of Cervantes' vest. The captain stopped to face Alasdair, his blue eyes reflecting the anger he felt.

Alasdair tightened his jaw almost imperceptibly. "You are right. Friends don't let friends go, especially with no explanation." Alasdair then paused and cast his gaze to the ground. "I feel ashamed for not understanding what you realized right from the start. I hope you can forgive me."

Cervantes immediately relaxed his stance, shook his head, and laid a hand atop Alasdair's. "There is nothing to forgive."

Alasdair took a deep breath and then exhaled. "If you don't mind waiting, I would like to accompany you in your efforts to catch up with our comrades."

Cervantes grinned. "I don't mind at all."

It didn't take long for the remainder of the encampment to prepare for travel. Everyone agreed to follow their companions in the direction that Cervantes felt Jonesy wanted to go. They didn't have much daylight left within which to travel, so they would attempt to make the best of it and travel swiftly until nightfall, upon which time they would construct an impromptu camp that would be easily packed away early the next morning. Led by Cervantes and Alasdair, the group followed in the footsteps of their friends, not in the direction of the protection they hoped to have within Elvandahar, but back in the direction from which they had come.

They retraced their steps to the portal located within Krathil-lon, the place Cervantes knew Jonesy would go to return to Karlisle.

Aeris screamed in exhilaration as they flew the Haldorrian skies. Wispy white clouds floated nonchalantly within a pale purple sky, and the sun shone brightly overhead. Jaxom added his own voice to the outcry, and within moments, Aeris heard the voices of three more dragons and their riders around her. For the first time in her life, she felt freedom. She realized she was no longer bound by the confines of hinterlean society, her profession, or the expectations of those she left behind. The recent experiences in her life that had submerged her so completely no longer fully defined her. Her *bonding* with Jaxom had given her a new lease on life, and at that moment she felt as though she was being reborn.

Jaxom trumpeted his joy, feeling her revelation through their link. He increased his speed and she raised her arms into the air, pumping her fists in the universal signal of victory. With her dragon by her side, she felt as though she could conquer any adversity. An answering trumpet to her right revealed Thulnar and Sordranth, and on her other side flew Faleema and Miramanth closely followed by Saliel and Borgestrix.

Aeris laughed gleefully as Jaxom swept into a dive. Taking him up on the challenge, the other dragons followed suit. Below them stretched the vast Haldorrian jungle, a place that was just as much dangerous as it was beautiful. Aeris had heard that the plant-life could be just as voracious as the myriad of animal creatures that lived there. Xebrinarth had told her about the giant pods that would snap shut over their unsuspecting victims after luring them with the scent of freshly killed meat. The prey would slowly digest over a period of several days, and she had always wondered what that might feel like. But those stories had been told so long ago, and seemed to have been heard by another person altogether.

For quite a while the dragons and their riders cavorted within the sky.

They took pleasure in the good weather, the exemption from duty, and the company of comrades. And when they finally tired and became hungry, they returned to the place where they had originally been brought, a mountainside fortress so large Aeris was certain she would see no other like it ever again. The corridors were wide and the ceilings vaulted, ample space to suit a passing dragon. The walls were inlaid with a treasure trove of gems, all firmly ensconced within the dark rock. The gold-veined floors were covered by elaborately woven rugs depicting colorful patterns. Even the wall sconces were artfully designed, made by the most talented of artisans.

The friends made their way to the chambers that would house them for the duration of their stay on Haldorr. Aeris, Faleema, and Franchie would reside in one room while Saliel, Thulnar, and Falon shared accommodations in one of the two adjacent chambers. It had been decided that Kahlan and Zestrimath couldn't accompany them, the dragon's injuries too severe for them to partake in the rigorous training regimen Forigard had planned. The friends had been sad to leave their comrades behind, and it put a damper on their departure. However, excitement had taken over the moment they saw the rift.

Of the four rifts on the entirety of Shandahar, Roxalayas was the one situated over the dragon continent. Aeris had sensed it a full half-day before they reached it, for the aura it exuded was so incredibly potent. Demeter Kordrian had felt it as well, glancing back in order to assess her reaction. To him, it was a tool to measure her sensitivity. Saliel didn't notice it for a while longer; she could tell only by the shift in his demeanor. Not to mention, he sought her out in the group and caught her gaze. She'd nodded in response, telling him she felt it too.

And when they were upon it, Aeris could only stare at the rift incredulously. It was one of the most beautiful things she had ever seen. Darkness had fallen, making it easy for one to view the swath of soft green light trailing across the sky. It shifted and wavered, almost as though it danced. By the glow offered by Roxalayas, Aeris could see the entrancement of her comrades. It was magic in its rarest and most basic form, something to be held in highest regard. As such, it was very heavily guarded.

From out of the space all around, several dragons suddenly appeared without warning. Everyone winged to a halt as Forigard and Kordrian relayed their permission to pass. Moments later the silver and gold sentinels dissipated and returned to their posts. Both demeters then turned and pointed everyone towards the rift. When the soft light from the rift had surrounded them, Aeris found herself transported to another world—the *world of Haldorr*.

Aeris now followed behind as they made their way across the first chamber and into the short passage that took them to the adjoining one. Thulnar gestured everyone to the bedpallet on which he had previously set his travel packs and opened the largest one. He dug around inside it for a moment, and then his hand re-emerged with a corked bottle about the size of his forearm.

"Do you know what this is?" He didn't pause long enough for anyone to answer. "This is only one of the four bottles of wine Saliel and I discovered in one of the chambers of the academy in Shayamalan before we left." He raised his eyebrows and grinned with glee. "When we have reached our greatest accomplishment, we shall drink to our success!"

Faleema folded her arms, her expression one of complete seriousness. "How do you know it's wine? Besides, four bottles won't slosh all of us."

Thulnar's expression became slightly mischievous and Saliel chuckled. "I happen to know firsthand that the liquid contained within this bottle is strong wine, and that it is powerful enough to slosh all of us should we so choose. Saliel and I drank the fifth one the evening we discovered we were coming here. That one bottle had us both mumbling incoherently. And you know that really pretty girl I mentioned to you a couple weeks ago? Well, her name is . . ."

Faleema suddenly became irate. "Shut it, Thulnar. I don't need to hear about your latest bedpartner."

It was Thulnar's turn to frown. "You make it sound like I have so many. There have only been the two . . ."

Faleema showed him the palm of her hand. "Like I said, I don't need to know."

Thulnar suddenly dropped the bottle on the bed and threw his own hands up in the air in agitation. Aeris covered her mouth so no one would see her smile. She caught Saliel looking at her and she gave a small shrug. By the knowing expression on his face, he had come to the same deduction she had; Faleema had feelings for Thulnar. The only reason Thulnar even cared to explain any of his activities to Faleema was because he cared about her too.

He just didn't realize it yet.

Saliel finally spoke up, imposing his voice over that of their comrades. "Hey, let's keep it down." He then lowered his voice conspiratorially. "We don't want our good 'friends', Falon and Franchiera, knowing anything is amiss, now do we?"

Once more Faleema placed her folded arms across her belly. Thulnar only pursed his lips and turned away from her.

"Come now, Faleema. Let's make this the best experience it can be." Aeris put a comforting hand on the other woman's shoulder. "Besides, we have only a limited amount of time to be here. Let's make the most of it and have the bickering wait until we are back on Shandahar."

Hesitantly, Faleema nodded. Out of the corner of her eye, she could see Thulnar finally begin to relax. Aeris then glanced back to Saliel, and once receiving her nod, the hinterlean gestured towards Thulnar's pack. "Two more bottles currently reside at the bottom of my own travel pack. Should we keep them there, or find a place to hide them?" he said in a quiet voice.

Thulnar gave a heavy sigh as he recovered from his bout with Faleema. "I think we should keep them as close to us as possible. No one will go through our travel packs. Let's keep them there." He picked up the bottle and stuffed it back inside his travel pack just as a fully armored quartermaster Falon entered the chamber. The man frowned when he saw them and planted his hands at his hips. "Where the Hells have you all been? I've been looking for you since we arrived here. The demeters want us battle-ready right now!"

Aeris gave parting glances to both Thulnar and Saliel as she and Faleema rushed back to their own chamber. They hastily donned their armored gear and when they were ready, stepped out of the cavern and onto the ledge to meet their awaiting dragons.

<Why didn't you let me know we were to have training?> Aeris asked almost breathlessly.

Jaxom huffed with discontent. <I didn't know myself until Rilo contacted me. By then, you all were in the midst of something, and I didn't wish to interrupt. It seemed important.>

Aeris gave her own huff. <It wasn't all that important. Next time you should just tell me.>

Jaxom gave his equivalent of a nod. <Agreed.>

The dragons and their riders followed Falon and Jeriandrith to an immense bowl. From out of the pervading jungle it had been cut, and from where she viewed it, the trees encroached as closely as they could, almost as though in hopes of regaining what was lost. In the center of the arena awaited Demeters Fo and Kord. Both wore expressions of disgruntlement.

"Do any of you pay attention to your itinerary?" said Kord when everyone had gathered. His voice became more irate as he continued. "It wasn't prepared simply for the sake of giving Demeter Fo something to do on top of the multitudes of other duties he needed to perform before coming here. Damnation, people! We are here for a specific purpose, and even though the passage of time will not be the same back on our world, it still will pass. We must take advantage of the luxury we have in being here, yet not take it for granted!"

Aeris nodded her agreement. Demeter Kord was right; they had a duty to their training. This wasn't intended to be a pleasure visit. Yet, didn't they deserve at least some little bit of time to enjoy Haldorr?

"The first thing we must do is begin the task that brought us here in the first place," began Demeter Fo. "Your dragons require the ingestion of a certain mineral that is in abundance here on Haldorr. Of course, it is present on Shandahar as well, but it's a rare commodity, and most likely guarded by Lord Razlul's degethozak and their riders. Since we have the ability, we chose to come here instead. Very few know of the rift that we passed through on our way here, so secrecy is of the utmost importance.

"The mineral your dragons require is called ignissium. Without it, they can produce no flame. To most dragons, the mineral is rather tasteful, easily ingested by eating a variety of plant life. However, a plant by the name of zarefessia roots in geologic areas containing the highest levels of ignissium. It is for these plants that we are here on Haldorr."

Aeris felt Jaxom's disquiet for barely a moment before he was speaking. He broadened his speech-width so that both she and other dragons could hear what he had to say. <What about the animals that eat of the zarefessia? Can we not obtain the same nutrient through their flesh?>

From atop Seldonraxis, Demeter Fo developed the faraway expression that often characterized those who were communicating with their bondmates. After a few moments, he regarded Jaxom steadily while Seldonraxis responded with Fo's reply. <No. It is not the same. The concentration is lower within these animals, and one would have to eat twice the number of these as opposed to simply eating the plants themselves.>

Jaxom remained resolute. <I had no problems producing a spectacular flame when I lived here as a youth. I rarely ate the plants, for they are distasteful to me. But the rock-hoppers that lived nearby were quite delicious.>

Once receiving Jaxom's words, Fo rewarded him with a raised eyebrow and Seldon's voice was heard again. <If you think about what you just said, you were a youth, then. Now you are an adult, producing a much larger flame and needing that much more ignissium. Animal flesh is no longer enough for you, and although I am sympathetic towards your distaste for the zarefessia, I encourage you to partake of it. One day, your flame may be the only thing that will save your life and mayhap even the life of your rider.>

Aeris could sense Jaxom's inner displeasure. He was definitely not happy with what Fo had said. She sent soothing vibes through their link, but he refused to be quieted by them. She sighed and wondered exactly what she had gotten herself into this time.

CHAPTER ELEVEN

Tallachienan lay flat across Pylar's withers. Through their link, he could feel the dragon's fatigue lying over him like a sodden winter cloak. For the hundredth time, he wished he had the priestly ability to imbue another with the energy and stamina required for a trek such as this one. He closed his eyes and concentrated on giving Pylar all he could of himself—simple mental remedies he had learned during their lifetimes together as bondmates. They drained his body just as much as they did his mind, and he once more cursed the frailty of his mortal being. If given access to the power he once had at his beck and call, he would have been able to give his friend so much more. Ah, but that now seemed so long ago, and so much had transpired since then, it almost felt like his past belonged to another.

After leaving the group, the pair flew back to the druid community nestled within the Sartingel Mountains. It was the location of the closest portal that TC could use to reach his destination. Much to his dismay, riding astride had its drawbacks, and the most painful one was the abrasion he suffered as a result of Pylar's scales rubbing against the inside of his thighs. The scales were smaller than those that encompassed much of the rest of his body, for the neck was a flexible thing, much like the tail and the joints of the legs and wings. As such, they were more numerous and caused more damage than the larger scales may have done.

Thus, once reaching Krathil-lon, TC sought the aid of their healers. Against his desire to jump into the portal system to reach his next destination, TC rested for the duration it took for scabs to form over the widespread burns on his legs. It didn't take long, for the druids had poultices they used to hasten the healing process. Father Dremathian was quite hospitable, giving him the use of the chamber he inhabited when last he visited. The druids also made Pylar comfortable, just as they had when the dragon first arrived there not much more than a fortnight before.

Once the poultices served their purpose, they were removed. TC was then instructed in the use of the ointments he needed in order to continue the healing process. The druids presented him with a pair of padded trousers, and these he accepted with gusto. He thanked the druids profusely for their aid, and then, with Pylar at his side in faelin form, they stepped through the portal.

They arrived at a place TC only vaguely remembered, a cave located somewhere along the juncture of the Hills of Shiadem and the Stonefist Mountains. It was just east of a realm ruled by a theocracy, the Theocracy of Nenth to be precise, merely a fracture of the Brotherhood of the Kronshue. Of course, he wouldn't be there long enough to find trouble.

They left the portal chamber and passed several similar rooms on their way to the outside. Once there, they discovered the reason why they were so cold—a winter storm raged, and there was no way they could leave. Discouraged, they turned back and set up a small camp within one of the chambers they had previously passed. It was there that TC thought to bring the dragon crystals together once more. Just maybe he would have the vision that Aeris experienced. No longer was he merely Magnus, but the powerful Tallachienan Chroalthone. Surely he would see something.

TC took a moment to remember the last time the crystals were unsheathed. He and Aeris had stood across from one another, the pieces beckoning to be joined. Despite their enclosed location, a slight wind teased the loose tendrils of crimson hair that fell across her beautiful face. It was when the third piece had connected with the other two that Aeris received her vision. Her deep brown eyes had become sightless to the world around her, instead focusing on what she saw within. She had later explained that it was unexpectedly intense, the content so much more vibrant than any vision before. She had seen the creation of the dragon crystals: the sacrificial blood of the trapped dragons and the torment it involved. The vision had placed its mark on her, for it was as though she had been right there. And strangely, the crystals had somehow become broken apart once again—mayhap a result of the strain Aeris may have placed on them when she fell back after receiving her vision.

TC brought each of the glowing crystals from their protective cloths. He laid each on the cavern floor beside the light given off by the glowsphere he'd created. With slow deliberation, he joined two of the crystals. They flashed momentarily, and then reverted back to a more bearable intensity, not one as low as it was before the union but definitely more tolerable than the bright gush that occurred during the liaison. Now, just like before, the crystals seemed to call to one another, longing to be one.

TC slowly picked up the third piece and brought the crystal to its comrades. Just like before, there was another bright flash of light. It was accompanied by a mild impact that pushed him backward. He closed his eyes with the slight sense of disorientation he felt, but within only a moment it was gone. He opened his eyes, and before him lay the joined crystals. They pulsated with a deeper shade of the pale yellow hue they possessed while separate. He brought his brows together into a frown and wondered where the Hells his

T.R. Chowdhury & T.M. Crim

vision had gone.

TC pressed his lips into a thin line as he tentatively reached out to touch the glowing object. Upon picking it up, he began to feel the power of it in his mind. He could feel the close presence of a target individual—a dragon. And somehow, he had the ability to determine the amount of power it would take to bring the beast under his control.

TC shook his head smartly. It was easy to determine the identity of the creature that the crystals honed upon, for he had known the dragon for more decades than he could remember. The dragon in reference was Pylarith.

Suddenly TC felt Pylar in his mind. The dragon had been awakened, and the beast wondered what it was that drew him so strongly. Befuddled, the golden eyes glanced about the chamber; they took in the deep crevices that lined the walls, the broken stalactites and stalagmites that now littered the cavern floor, the deep green hue of the various vines and ivy that overhung much of the entrance, and the hunched form of his bondmate seated not far away. In that instant, his gazing intensified, and Pylar wondered what it was that TC was doing over in the most distant corner of the chamber. It was the direction in which he felt the disturbance, and it was quite disconcerting to say the least.

Tallachienan looked up from the crystals to find Pylar's gaze resting heavily on him. The dragon didn't move, but the intensity of his golden gaze was increased twofold. In the heavy silence that followed, TC could hear each breath he took. He continued to clutch the glowing talisman in the palm of his hand, yet made no overtures to the powers he felt lurking around it. He now knew the precise importance of the crystals, and why they were so coveted by the daemundai. The crystals would enable the user to exact control over dragon-kind. Given enough crystals, the user had the potential to control tens, if not hundreds, of such beings.

In order for a sorcerer to have had the power to make constructs such as these, he would have needed blood, a lot of blood. The blood of many dragons.

<Tallachienan, what is it you have over there?>

TC shook his head. <Oh, just some crystals that Aeris didn't take when she left. I've been keeping them safe until her return.>

Thoughtfully, Pylar nodded in the affirmative. <Yes. That is good of you, TC.>

He watched as the golden dragon slowly lowered his head back down to his folded forelegs. Swiftly, TC put the talisman away, not wanting to disturb his comrade any further. That night, TC's sleep was restless, but by early the next day the storm was ending. Before leaving the sanctuary of the cavern, TC donned his long sleeved tunic and wrapped himself in his winter cloak. The

winds were still rather brisk, and he could sense the imminence of another
storm. Nevertheless they close to fly. TC raised his hood, and once climbing
aboard Pylar's back they were swiftly airborne. They flew east towards the
coast, and once reaching it they embarked on the long oceanic journey to
Shayamalan.

TC finally re-opened his eyes. Below him lay the blue ocean, and in the distance before him, an unexpected smudge hovering on the horizon. At first he stared at it in disbelief, and then, once the realization struck him, he shouted into the open air. He felt Pylar rouse from his state of vague alertness, a technique the dragon used to conserve as much of his energy as possible. It had left TC up to the task of remaining vigilant to any weather changes or unwanted attention. But he didn't mind, it was the least he could do for his friend.

<What? What is it? A storm?>

TC shook his head. <Would I be this excited if it were a storm? Look, my friend! Gaze into the horizon before us and tell me what you see.>

With his superior dragon-sight, Pylar was able to see easily what TC strained to view. Of course, had he been human, he would have yet to see anything at all.

TC felt Pylar's excitement burble through the link. It was followed by intense feelings of relief. Pylar's marathon flight was almost over.

It was then they suddenly heard a trumpeting roar in their minds, followed by a darkening speck emerging from the place towards which they were headed. Hells, it was a sentinel, a guardian from the place they approached. It was quite unexpected, and TC struggled to collect his thoughts as Pylar responded in kind.

A few moments later, the voice of the approaching dragon entered their minds. <Your signature is unfamiliar to me. Who are you, and why have you come to Shayamalan?>

<I am Pylarith, and my bondmate is Tallachienan Chroalthone. We have come to see Lord Trebexal.>

TC waited with tense expectancy as the swiftly approaching sentinel absorbed this information. Then, <Not just anyone may seek audience with Lord Trebexal. Only the most . . .>

<Do you not recognize my name and the name of my bondmate, weanling?> thundered Pylar.

TC felt the anger surging through his dragon, and he immediately sent soothing thoughts to him through their link. Pylar was only rarely this upset, and he attributed much of it to simple fatigue. Suddenly they heard another trumpeting coming from the northeast. It was a second sentinel, called as reinforcement to the one who was now entirely visible before them.

<Your names may be familiar to me, but your signatures are not,> said the helzethryn. <By law I am forced to bring you in under the custody of myself and my comrade.>

<So we have become nothing less than your prisoners, then?> said Pylar.

The golden dragon gave a mental nod. <Precisely.>

TC felt Pylar's hackles rise. <No, Pylar! Now isn't the time. We can admonish Trebexal when we see him. Our goal right now is to simply make it to Shayamalan.> TC gave a mental shrug. <And these wonderful dragons are willing to see us there.>

Seeing the reasoning behind TC's words, Pylar quieted. The second sentinel arrived shortly thereafter, and within the custody of the two helzethryn, TC and Pylar pressed forward towards the dragon continent. TC gave a breath of relief. *Finally he would see Aeris again.*

Tallachienan regarded his old friend with a baleful expression. He was disappointed, although the old dragon at least chose to have enough respect to have met him in faelin form. Trebexal gave a sigh of heartfelt weariness, yet TC found it very difficult to commiserate. He felt betrayed by Trebexal's hidden activities, and more than that, hurt.

TC's emotions must have somehow become translated to Trebexal, for the other's demeanor became somewhat softened. "I am sorry to have left you in the dark, my friend, but you were so absorbed by your own endeavors, not to mention that I was loath to argue with you over an enterprise I had already chosen to undertake. I knew you would be against me."

TC inhaled deeply and also gave a sigh. "You didn't know that for certain," he replied.

Trebexal raised a silver eyebrow. "Well, I felt it to be the truth. I acted upon what I was feeling at the time. Then there was the *Fall*. Not long afterwards, I began my project here upon Shayamalan, and the renegade degethozak and their riders increased their destructive efforts. There were a couple of times that I put out a search for you, but each one was fruitless. After that, I simply hoped you would someday emerge from whatever hole in which you had found yourself. And now here you are."

TC only nodded, taking in what his friend said. He knew that Trebexal now awaited an explanation for his prolonged absence without even the simple courtesy of some type of communication. He knew that Trebexal deserved such an explanation, yet he was in no frame of mind to give it. He was equally as aware that he needed to share with the dragon his discovery of the crystals within his possession. Similarly, he was in no state to reveal them. Nevertheless, in spite of his hurt in regards to Trebexal's actions, he knew now was the time to tell his friend the primary reason for coming to Shayamalan. Of course, if he was smart, the dragon would have figured it out already. TC expected nothing less. "Trebexal, I am sure you have deducted the real reason for my visit."

The dragon nodded. "I was wondering when you would mention her."

TC waited for a moment for Trebexal to elaborate, and when he didn't, TC continued, "I have come to bring Damaeris back to Ansalar."

Trebexal cocked his head questioningly to the side. "Are you certain she wishes to return with you?"

TC felt his eyes harden. "Should it matter? I have only come to collect what is mine. I insist that you not interfere."

Once more Trebexal gave a sigh, this time tinged with sadness. "My friend, Damaeris Timberlyn is not here."

TC's mind reeled with the response. Then, "What do you mean, 'she isn't here'?"

"She is on Haldorr, continuing the training we have set before her. You might be surprised to learn that she is a good student, excelling in most trials we have set before her. She will make a good dragonrider."

Tallachienan pursed his lips. "You are right. I am surprised. Aeris is no warrior. Her strength lies in her *talent*."

Trebexal only shrugged. "I am only telling you what her masters have told me."

TC nodded. "All right, on the morrow I shall go to Haldorr, then."

Trebexal frowned. "But what about Pylarith? He will still be fatigued from his trans-oceanic flight."

TC regarded Trebexal solemnly. "I will go without him. Pylar will rest here while I continue my search."

Trebexal suddenly turned away from TC. His long silver hair cascaded down his back, and the length of his white robes dragged along the stone floor of the cavern as he moved. TC could feel the tension emanating from his friend, and he wondered what it was that made Trebexal so resistant of his desire to take Aeris away with him. It wasn't as though he didn't have other students. Besides, how good could she really be?

Trebexal then swung back around to face him. "Please reconsider, Tallachienan. As your good friend, I ask this of you."

TC frowned with consternation. "Why? Why is she so important to you?"

"It isn't just me, Tallachienan. It is Damaeris herself. Can't you see that she needs this? Can't you feel her desire to be a part of something—to *excel*?"

TC diverted his eyes, an attempt to shut Trebexal out. "She does excel—with her magic. And what she really needs is *me*." TC paused for a moment before continuing. "She just doesn't realize it yet."

Trebexal breathed inward, increasing his stature to the best of his ability. "No. You are wrong. She needs herself, and mayhap the one she has chosen as her bondmate."

TC brought his gaze back to Trebexal, narrowing his eyes angrily. "Your son." He almost spat the words.

Trebexal's silver eyes flashed. "Yes, *my son*."

"I am sure you are aware of how he deceived us all and then took Aeris when she was at her most vulnerable. I can't say that he acted with the best of intentions."

"I am certain he did the best he could under the circumstances."

TC pulled his dark brows into a deeper frown. "As I see it, he was trying to escape your little project here. Unfortunately, it happened that he met Aeris en route."

Once more Trebexal's eyes flashed defensively for a moment, and then dulled. He slowly shook his head. "Tallachienan, I do not wish to fight with you. Regardless of my son, I am only imploring you to consider waiting here for the girl to return from Haldorr. It would please me greatly, and perhaps Damaeris will be the happier for it as well."

Silence reigned for several moments as TC considered Trebexal's words. Truthfully, he was tired, and it wouldn't hurt him to rest for a while. Not to mention, he hadn't yet come up with a solid plan of how he would approach Aeris. Besides, he supposed Trebexal's request was reasonable. Finally he spoke. "But what shall I do whilst I wait?" He knew it sounded lame, but he could think of no better response.

Trebexal's face broke out into a gratified smile. "Oh, I think I may be of help."

TC raised an eyebrow. He then listened to what Trebexal had to offer.

✕✕✕✕✕

They traveled north across the savannah, a waving sea of grasses stretching endlessly before them. It was broken here and there by copses of trees most often accompanied by a small body of water. The lakes were great, affording them the opportunity to bathe. However, the fact that they traveled through unclaimed lands was never far from their minds.

Talemar wiped a hand across his forehead, grimacing with the amount of sweat that had gathered just above his eyebrows. The seasons were shifting, and the heat of summer would soon be upon them. This day was uncharacteristically warm for late spring, and he wished he'd chosen not to wear his long-sleeved tunic this morning. Yet, the air was much cooler then. He would never have imagined it would get this hot so fast. Glancing ahead, he noted that his comrades sweltered similarly to himself. Well, at least he wasn't the only one.

Talemar lowered his hand and dried it on the fabric of his trousers. Beneath him, the larian walked with a lowered head, the tall grasses of the savanna brushing against them as they passed. The animals were similarly affected by the heat, for they had yet to shed the rest of the hair that comprised their winter coats. Inasmuch, they suffered all the more. Pity for the poor beast suffused his thoughts and he slowed the animal to a halt. He called out in a deep voice so everyone in front of him could hear, and the rest slowly came to a stop. Talemar dismounted and grabbed the water flask that hung from the side of the saddle. He then took the bowl from his travel pack and poured some of the liquid into it. He closed the lid to his flask and offered the bowl to the larian. The beast drank thirstily and he was once more riddled with guilt.

Once the water was gone, Talemar repacked the bowl and looked around at his comrades. Everyone had taken his lead and offered their animals a share of the water. By the look of the animals, they couldn't go much farther at the grueling pace they were keeping, especially in this heat. He understood the reason for their haste, but when the lloryk, larian, and horses fell beneath them, they would definitely be out of luck. He caught Alasdair's glance, and both men nodded in agreement. The ranger's strident voice rose over the small area in which the group stood. "Let's break early today. The animals have had it."

Everyone nodded in agreement as they spread out and began preparations to erect an encampment. Nearby there happened to be a small copse of trees, a good place to start. Talemar looked towards Cervantes, but even he seemed to admit the inevitable. Of course, the other man wasn't happy about the delay, but he was accepting of it—so much different than the hot-blooded captain who had started a tavern brawl not much more than a couple moon cycles ago. Talemar looked away as he led his larian over to where Mateo had begun to lay out the various tools he would be using to groom the animals that evening. The task was quite a big one, for every one of the beasts was in the process of shedding excess hair. It made Mateo's job that much more laborious, but the boy was rather good at it, compliments of the lady Aeris of course.

Talemar pursed his lips. Thoughts of Aeris tended to upset him, mayhap more than they should. Her abrupt leave-taking had been so wrong on so many levels that he had a difficult time believing that she left of her own accord without coercion by the dragon or force from the man they now knew to be Tallachienan Chroalthone. Of course, Talemar blamed himself for not recognizing the man, for he had met the god on an occasion or two when he was a young apprentice. Damnation, how could such familiarity have eluded him?

Talemar left Mateo to his work, making his way back to the other things that awaited his attention. His thoughts continued to ruminate over Tallachienan. Obviously he hadn't been so familiar. And now, to know that Aeris had shared a relationship with the man was more than vexing. It was beyond reprehensible, and Talemar had no qualms about revealing how he felt with malicious stares, venomous comments, and profound hopes that the man would simply fall into a deep hole and never reappear. It was good that TC had left, although he wished it had been for a different reason.

Talemar shook his head, cursing to himself. He wished he'd never laid eyes on Tallachienan. All of a sudden, something sped past his face. An arrow impaled itself into the ground before him, swiftly followed by another. He looked up into the sky to see others trailing behind their already land-bound comrades. What the *Hells!*

The arrows originated from the nearby trees, and Talemar cursed himself for not thinking. Damn, they had were about to experience their first skirmish with the Lawless. It was about time.

The men swiftly emerged from out of the copse. They were unkempt, rugged individuals. They lived by no authority but their own, choosing a life free of the monetary servitude that comes with protection gained by living within the boundaries of a kingdom. As such, they were vulnerable, open to any threat that might arrive, and they would fight to the bitter end. Each man was very aware that he fought for his family, not some distant, lofty monarch who sat on a padded velvet chair behind the walls of his fortified castle.

They were quite barbaric.

The men stopped several farlo away to form a rough semi-circle around the group. Alasdair held empty hands out before him, palms facing out in a universal gesture that stated that no fight was wanted. There were at least twenty lawless men, all bearing battle-worn swords and bows that were years past their prime. Mayhap it was the only reason Talemar hadn't been hit by one of those arrows, and he cringed inwardly at the thought. He'd rather hoped it was from lack of skill.

Alasdair spoke in common, loud enough for all to hear. "Please, we pass through these lands in peace. We mean no harm to anyone, and we will be gone as soon as dawn tomorrow morning."

The semi-circle of men parted to reveal one who looked much like the rest but for a trio of long scars that ran diagonally across his face. They appeared to have been made from some type of predator, one from which he'd been fortunate enough to escape. His expression was fierce as he regarded Alasdair, and he raised his bow as he spoke. "What will you offer us in return for allowing you passage?"

Taken slightly aback by this response, Alasdair struggled for a moment to come up with an appropriate answer. "Of course we have some coin."

The leader shook his head sharply. "No, money means very little to us. However, your weapons would be quite beneficial. Mayhap your clothing as well. And your beasts, definitely your beasts."

Alasdair gave a half-hearted chuckle. "It seems you have interest in many of the things we might have to offer. Pick one so that we may present it to you as a gift for your willingness to grant us the passage we need."

The leader turned his mouth upward into a cruel smile. "We don't need any presentation, my friend. We will simply be doing the taking." The smile ended abruptly. "Drop all your weapons, now!"

It was only then that Talemar glanced furtively around at his companions. Vikhail and Vardec brandished axe and hammer; Cervantes had drawn his cutlass; and Cedric drew his long-swords. Mateo and Jezzie stood at the center of the protective circle made around them, their eyes wide. Levander simply stood to the side with his hands hidden deep in the folds of his robes, most likely grasping the star-shaped projectiles he'd witnessed once before. Talemar took the leaders' command as indication to begin casting a spell, any spell that would divert the enemy and cause as much damage as possible within a short period of time in a conveyance of strength.

The *Flamesphere* was easy to cast, a spell that seemed to act as the back-up to any magic-user. One had only to have care in the precise direction he wanted it to go. Talemar swiftly spoke the incantation and drew the runes. Heartbeats later the *Flamesphere* swept towards the leader, down through the center of the semi-circle. The enemy was surprised by the attack, for most likely they had never come across someone such as him. Warlock, sorcerer, daemon-spawn . . . there were many names that commoners used in regards to spellcasters. Those with *talent* were rare, and to many they were simply a tale to be used by parents when disciplining their naughty children. Hells, who else but one of evil descent would have the ability to thrust a massive ball of fire at his adversaries?

Indeed.

In spite of the stressful situation, Talemar's thoughts shifted to Mateo. Compared to others in his situation, the boy was privileged. He had been one of the lucky few who had been 'discovered'. If not for the old Sage Paxil, the boy might never have been found, instead forced to lead a life in which he was ostracized by his family. Through the years, he may have been able to quell his *talent*. If not, he would eventually be spurned by others, and mayhap even killed. It wasn't uncommon for undiscovered *talents* to burn at the stake, feared for their strange abilities. However, if fortunate, they were only deemed as peculiarities and rendered outcasts by 'normal' society.

Aeris had saved Mateo from that fate. If she had been any weaker, and bended to the will of her brother all those moon cycles ago in Xordrel, the boy may never have escaped. Based on what Aeris had later told him, Mateo's parents had been all too willing to be rid of their unusual son. It was obvious they would never bother to keep contact with him. The thought made Talemar angry. No matter how strange any son or daughter of his may appear to be, he would never let them go. Ever.

The enemy fled under the fiery onslaught. Five of the men screamed in agony as the leader and the four flanking him on both sides were burned by the sphere. The others scattered as the rest of the group leaped into action, galvanized by the spell. Vikhail and Vardec swept in together as a brutal fighting force. Vikhail swung his battle-axe, trapping the sword of one of the lawless with the head of it and redirecting the swing into the side of another of the enemy. The afflicted man staggered with the impact, yet found himself able to follow through with his own swing. The blade very narrowly missed the arm of the halfen warrior as Vikhail spun away in order to parry the attack of another lawless man.

Meanwhile, Vardec followed immediately behind. After watching the sword of the first lawless slice into the side of his enemy comrade, the halfen proceeded to smash his hammer into the back of the man's leg, taking advantage of the moment of shock the man would feel upon wounding his brethren. Vardec felt the power of his blow shatter the bone, and the man screamed in agony as he fell heavily to the ground. Vardec simply leaped over him, swinging his hammer in an overhead arc that connected with the skull of the lawless that now clutched at his bloody side. Fragments of bone interspersed with bloody tissue flew through the air, spraying the back of Vikhail's tunic, the face of his current opponent, and the tall grasses that surrounded them.

Spinning on his heel, Vikhail blocked another attack from the enemy before him. This one was good, a bit better than the others. Yet, he hadn't a chance. Seeing that his brother was ready to move in, Vikhail made an unexpected maneuver, sweeping behind his blood-spattered opponent in order to begin assault upon the nearest lawless. He swept towards his new foe, severing the enemy's arm at the shoulder. A terrified Mateo simply stood there motionless, a short-sword clutched in one hand, his gray eyes wide with terror.

Vikhail gestured at the boy with a nod of reassurance, and then moved on to engage his next adversary.

Vardec swiftly swept forward as Vikhail moved on. The change flustered the enemy only briefly before he realized what was happening. It was just enough time for the halfen to smash his hammer into the foot of his opponent, easily crushing the bones through the weak leather of the ancient boots he wore. The enemy bellowed in pain, his face contorted with agony. However, he found the motivation to retaliate. He was strong, much more so than Vardec gave him credit. In spite of his pain, the enemy cut a swath before him, hitting Vardec across his upper arm with his sword. The halfen hissed his displeasure, and retaliated with a swing of his hammer. He brought it out and up into the face of his opponent. Unlike before, the hit was solidly centered. The man crumpled into a lifeless heap, a pool of blood immediately forming beneath his head and saturating the ground.

Vardec waited only long enough to realize the man would never rise. He then swept toward his next foe, his shoulder stinging abominably from the wound he sustained. The enemy was missing an arm, courtesy of his brother, and he imagined an easy victory. However, seemingly out of nowhere emerged another adversary. Shield held before him, the enemy struck Vardec. The halfen fell heavily onto his wounded side, and he grimaced with the impact. Less than a moment later, the enemy was standing over him. Battle-axe in hand, he prepared for the killing blow. Thinking quickly, Vardec savagely kicked out, sweeping his foot under those of his enemy. The lawless fell to one knee, giving Vardec just enough time to collect himself and rise to his feet. Once standing, both men began to circle one another, and Vardec had just enough time to wonder if Vikhail had yet realized that he was no longer following behind.

Cervantes swung at yet another opponent. The Lawless were fearless in battle, yet untrained. Of course, they were better than most commoners might be, but poor compared to a seasoned warrior. He slammed his cutlass into the shield of his adversary. The man grunted with the impact and staggered back. Cervantes took the advantage and pressed forward. The enemy fell back. The captain finished him quickly, and then turned to assess the remaining situation. Not for the first time, he found himself staring in awe of the halfen brothers.

The two men had swept through their opponents like a living scythe. The men lying dead on the ground in their wake were testimony to their skill. However, there was also the issue of their weaponry. The axe wielded by Vikhail and the hammer by Vardec were quite possibly the most magnificent specimens of their type he had ever seen. The metal was like none he had ever seen before, colored a strange pale blue. And then there was the issue of size. The weapons definitely seemed much too large for any man to carry, be he halfen, human, or faelin. In fact, they appeared as though they would be wielded by no one smaller than Cortes. Cervantes felt his shoulders slump as the dejection swept through him.

Cortes, his dead brother.

It wasn't much longer before the fight was ended. Cervantes looked out across the area, taking note of the trampled grasses, shorn and splattered with blood. Nearby stood Alasdair, his amber eyes wide with what they had witnessed. It was easy to see that he hated what had transpired and that he wished the circumstances could have been different—that the lawless men had seen reason before it was too late. Once more, death surrounded them. Luckily, this time it was not their own.

A light rain began to fall as the group piled the bodies a short distance away from where they decided to make their encampment. They chose to go ahead and burn them, for the mild precipitation would keep the fire contained. They then began to settle for the night. Lev saw to any wounds than had been sustained in the fight while Jezibel struggled with the evening meal without the help of the halfen brothers. Without Jonesy there to take control of the preparations, Jezzie was feeling the strain of such a responsibility. With an inward sigh, Cervantes rose from his place at his bedpallet and made his way over to her. She glanced up only briefly before continuing her work. "How can I help?" he asked.

Jezibel stopped for a moment and regarded him in surprise. Hells, she had every right to be. Even when it was Jonesy who was rushing about in an attempt to feed the encampment, Cervantes had never offered his aid. Jezzie narrowed her eyes. She could either consider his offer a gracious one and accept the help, or she could take offense to the offer and send him along his way. Regardless, he knew next to nothing about what she was doing, so he would only be in the way. Yet, she wouldn't tell him that.

"Just talk to me for a while. I need the company."

Cervantes nodded in relief and settled himself nearby. He scoured his mind for something to say, and the first thing he could think of was a bit more boorish than his usual. "I do so hate the smell of burning flesh."

Jezibel looked back up at him in surprise.

He raised his hands in defense. "What? Don't you?"

Jezzie pursed her lips and fought back a smile. "Always the scoundrel, you are."

Cervantes sighed heavily. "Yeah, I know. Nonetheless, I can't help but feel glad that we were the victors today."

Jezibel only nodded as she went back to her work. Cervantes watched her for a moment before speaking again. "So, did you notice Vikhail's battle-axe and Vardec's war-hammer? They *must* be made of magic."

Jezibel shook her head with a doubtful expression. "No. They would have told us."

Cervantes chuckled humorlessly. "How do you know?"

She shrugged. "I just do."

Cervantes pursed his lips as he watched her go about her business. It was interesting to see her now, for she was so different from the girl he had first met so many years ago. It was difficult to realize that so much time had passed during their journey up to this point, and that somewhere along the way she had become a woman. He couldn't help but smile at the memory of their first meeting. Even then she had been quite the flirt, and her efforts to procure his coin were memorable to say the least.

Jezibel had been a serving wench, working the tavern closest to the docks in Darban, his home port. It was before he'd purchased the *Sea Maiden*, a dark time in his life when he'd been struggling with the death of his uncle and the powerful temptation to drink away his sorrows. From out of all the other patrons to visit the Hazy Mayzee Tavern that night, Jezzie had chosen Cervantes upon whom to lavish her attention. He remembered thinking her a bit young to be working the tavern, but thought nothing more as he drank himself further into his mugs. However, in spite of his drunken state, he later caught her trying to steal his coin purse. He'd slapped his hand down over hers as it was about to extricate the pouch from his belt, and her blue eyes widened with alarm. He'd grinned widely, but dumbstruck by her pretty face, chose not to make a scene.

"Cervantes, what the Hells are you smiling at?"

He suddenly came back to himself, looking up at the woman standing before him. With a hand at her hip, she regarded him with mild amusement, her eyes bright with suppressed mirth. He shook his head and smiled. "Do you remember the first time we met?"

Jezibel rolled her eyes and gave a gusty sigh. "How could I ever forget?"

"You actually thought you could get away with stealing from me."

Jezibel chuckled beneath her breath and then glanced about furtively to see who might be listening in to the conversation. "I am certain you recall what happened afterward."

Cervantes enjoyed her discomfiture. "Of course."

Jezzie raised an eyebrow and once more pursed her lips. "You were more of a gentleman than I ever would have thought. To this day I still wonder why you chose not to take me to your bed that night. Of course, at the time, all I really wanted was your gold."

Cervantes feigned mild surprise. "Really? In spite of everything else I had to offer?"

Jezzie grinned. "Of course, my sentiment changed after a while."

It was Cervantes' turn to chuckle. Still smiling, she turned back to her tasks. She stirred the contents of the stewpot and then pulled the remaining bread from the nearest travel sack. She broke it up into nine parts, portioning them as equally as possible. She then took the last of the cheese and did the same. Cervantes was surprised that either had lasted this long without acquiring an excess of the fuzzy green substance that seemed to invade such items.

Jezibel then tuned back to him. "So, are you just going to sit back there or are you really going to help me?"

Cervantes held out his hands. "I thought all you needed was someone to talk to you."

She made a sound in her throat. "It's obvious you aren't so good at that."

He frowned. "What do you mean?"

"I haven't heard you speak since I came back over to the fire."

Cervantes acceded to that and rose from his seat. Then, once standing before Jezzie, she instructed him on what he should do. Digging into the nearest travel pack, he took out the bowls and proceeded to set them out. He then placed a piece of bread into each one. Moments later Jonesy ladled the stew, covering the bread in each bowl with the thick mixture. And on top of each she placed the cheese. She then called out across the encampment.

It wasn't long before everyone was coming to claim their bowls. Each member of the party nodded their thanks as they picked up their meal and Jezibel gleamed with the praise. Lev was the last to arrive. He slowly approached where she sat before the fire, offering her a wink as he took his bowl. Jezibel smiled widely and Cervantes looked away. Hells, where was Jonesy? What had possessed her to leave him without any word? He had thought there was more than that between them. And then there was Tigerius. Cervantes wasn't fool enough to think he and Jonesy had been able to keep the truth of their relationship from the man. Cervantes considered Tiger a friend, and he'd thought the feeling was mutual. Inasmuch, how could the man possibly have been party to the crooked undertaking that characterized his and Jonesy's abrupt departure?

"We will find her, Cervantes." He looked up to find Jezibel standing there, holding his bowl out to him. Her eyes reflected the pain she felt on his behalf.

Cervantes shook his head as he accepted the bowl with both hands and brought it to rest in his lap. "Mayhap she doesn't want to be found."

She seated herself beside him, put a hand to his face, and turned it towards her. "Does it matter? Whether she knows it or not, she needs us. Don't second guess yourself for wanting to follow her."

Cervantes continued to shake his head. "But she has Tigerius."

Jezibel pursed her lips in consternation. "Don't be asinine, Cervantes. Tigerius didn't leave with the sole purpose of accompanying Jonesy. He has his own destination in mind."

Cervantes narrowed his eyes. Now that he thought about it, Jezzie was probably right. He recalled the ill-fated meeting within Krathil-lon the first evening the group spent there. Tiger had been devastated to learn that his best friends had withheld vital information pertaining to his family. He was never the same afterward. Cervantes didn't blame him.

Cervantes felt his jaw tighten involuntarily. Tigerius had gone to answer the call of family duty. Thinking once again of his dead brother, Cervantes wished that he had the opportunity to do the same. But that ship had sailed away long ago, and he never even realized it until it was far too late.

Cervantes looked away from Jezzie and down at the bowl in his hands. The stew was simple, made up of the most common edible roots, tubers, and greenery they could find as they traveled. The thick broth was what made it palatable, and just as he spooned the first bite into his mouth, he wondered exactly how much Jezibel had learned from Jonesy before she left.

Cervantes found himself pleasantly surprised to find the meal quite tasty. There was a pleasing blend of herbs and spices that brought out the flavor of the ptarmigan that Alasdair had brought to them the evening before. It was the reason she had cooked it a bit longer than usual, for leftover meat could often be a source of sickness. Of course, Jezzie still had much to learn. Jonesy had become quite good at what she did. He now believed that Jezzie could be just as good.

Meanwhile, he would miss Jonesy *and wish she had never left him.*

CHAPTER TWELVE

Jonesy sat before the fire with her knees drawn up to her chest, her gaze vaguely taking in the dancing flames. Her mind was numb from knowledge concerning a reality she didn't know existed until several moments ago. Of course, all the signs had been there for many days now, but she had failed to recognize them for what they were. She had only herself to blame, for she should have taken more care. But for some reason, the concept had eluded her, and she never thought twice about going to Cervantes' bed, no matter when the fancy suited her.

Jonesy shifted her chin where it rested on one knee, turning her head so that her face lay there instead. She squeezed her arms more tightly around her legs, and she closed her eyes tightly shut. She knew that Tiger would wonder about her after a while, but she didn't care. She didn't have the mental capacity to think of anything beyond her dilemma.

Oh gods, what will I do with a child?

Jonesy gave a deep breath, struggling to keep from being heard. Tears escaped from between her eyelids, and after a brief moment or two she began to feel the urge to sniff. Once doing so, she cringed when the sound came out louder than she imagined it would. She stilled herself, waiting to see if Tiger had noticed.

"Jonesy, are you all right? Are you still feeling sick?"

Ah Hells, of course he'd heard. Tiger's senses were acute, more so than ever before. She never had a chance. "Yeah, maybe a little."

"Here, let me pour you a mug of tea. Maybe it will help."

Jonesy considered not giving a response, but decided that it was out of character, not to mention a bit disrespectful. However, by the time she was about to make a reply, Tiger was already at her side, pressing a mug against her hand. She took another deep breath, and when her body gave a slight shudder, she knew it was over. Tiger set the mug down and planted himself in front of her. "Jonesy, what is wrong?"

She remained quiet for a moment. There was a part of her that wanted to tell him, for she so much needed a confidante. But she wasn't a fool. She knew that Tiger could easily overcome her, tie her to the lloryk, and take her back to the group. As such, the larger part of her insisted she keep her condition secret, not wanting to give Tiger any more reason to do just that.

She finally lifted her head and looked at him. "I'm sorry; I don't mean to make you worry. It's nothing more than what I have been feeling already. It just so happens that today I'm feeling it a bit more than usual, but I will be all right."

Tiger raised a speculative eyebrow, his expression doubtful. "Are you sure?"

She managed to give him a slight grin. "Of course I'm sure. Why would I lie?"

Tiger shrugged. "I don't know, but people do it every day." He then rose from his place before her and took up the mug again. "Here, drink this. I made it with a mixture of herbs that should help soothe your stomach."

Jonesy nodded. "All right, thank you."

Tiger nodded as he moved away to settle himself back across the fire. She felt guilty, for she hated being a liar and the knowledge that she was carrying Cervantes' child made her feel sicklier than ever. She told herself that she was too young for this, but obviously she wasn't. Women her age had children all the time, and she obviously wasn't an exception.

Jonesy drank from the mug, and once realizing how much she enjoyed the flavor of the contents, she drank the rest rather quickly. She took herself to her bedroll and settled down, thinking about when the conception could have taken place. Was it the first time they were together during their escape from the vampyr? Or was it one of the many other times that took place after? Once pondering it long enough, she realized it must have been that first time, for her menses had been conspicuously absent since then. Damn, how far along did that put her?

Jonesy closed her eyes, the effects of fatigue overtaking her more quickly than they did before she left the group. A few heartbeats later and her belly rumbled with hunger. It was then she realized she had yet to take the evening meal. However, she wasn't about to get up. Besides, if she ate, there was the possibility that she would bring it back up later. It simply wasn't worth it.

Jonesy allowed her mind to drift. She thought about Cervantes and the short time they had spent in one another's company. She had sensed a change in him during her final days with the group, and she wondered about that. She also wondered if he thought much about her, if he still loved her in spite of her desertion. Her thoughts branched outward to include the child. Was it a boy or a girl? Would it be more like its mother or its father? What would Cervantes think if he knew about the child? Even more important, what did *she* think? More than anything else Jonesy felt at a disadvantage, *for she was going home to a very dangerous situation.*

Jonesy hoped that Tigerius was either too far away or too tired to hear her quiet sobbing as she allowed the tears to come. More than ever she felt vulnerable. In this current state of being, Rigel would certainly overcome her, and when he was finished with his torment, he would kill her. *Oh gods, I don't need this! I already struggle enough without the added burden of another life to consider. The child makes me sick to my stomach and more tired than I have ever felt before. Indeed, mayhap I should go ahead and return to the group. After all, how can I fight my battles in this condition?*

Tigerius watched Jonesy from across the fire. He could tell that she was crying, her shoulders convulsing beneath the blanket draped over her. There was something wrong, and he knew that it was more than just her feeling sick. He wished she would confide in him, but she still kept him at arm's length in spite of their camaraderie. There was something about her, something special that drew him.

On more than one occasion, Tiger had found himself struck by Jonesy's unusual charisma. Since their foray into the underdark, she had become more and more of a source of distraction for him. Even now, he could honestly say that his attraction for her was not so much sexual as it was instinctual. During their battle with the daemundai, she saw the power he was capable of executing. Her secrecy on his behalf only endeared her to him further. Somehow, she took it all in stride. And in spite of his strangeness, she accepted him.

Damaeris had also accepted him.

Tiger closed his eyes and allowed the terrible sadness to sweep through him, a sorrow he felt every time he thought of her. His throat and chest ached from holding back his emotion. *Oh gods, Damaeris! What I would do to take your pain away! In my dreams I am there to champion you, to fight the cimmereans and keep them from taking you away from me.*

Tiger hardly remembered a time he didn't have some infatuation with Aeris Timberlyn. When they were young, he simply wished to be in her favor. As they grew, it turned into a desire to have her in his bed. Before their journey to Yortec, he had been a thorn in her side, an insatiable boy who had interest only in adventuring and whoring. Only after becoming her guardian on their journey back home had he become more, a man worthy of her affection.

But he had failed her. They had all failed. Aeris had suffered so much at the hands of the cimmereans, more than anyone should have to face in an entire lifetime. He blamed himself, as well as every other man in their company. There was no reason for her to have slipped through their fingers, and it wasn't important who started the tavern brawl. They had all failed to protect what mattered most after the fight started.

Like he did every time he thought of her treatment in Tholana's fortress, Tiger imagined the pain her body had endured, a mind that was subjugated, and a soul that became lost. Aeris wasn't the same after their escape from the underdark. With her wild maelstrom, she had saved himself and Jonesy from certain demise at the hands of the daemundai. But that was all. She'd barely glanced at him since, and they never spoke. The group discovered her pregnancy only when she had lost the baby, except maybe for Lev, who seemed to know something about everyone.

And then she was gone.

Tiger opened his eyes. Across the fire he could see that the blanket covering Jonesy had become still. Her breathing was even, and he could tell that she was sleeping. Just like he had for Aeris, he felt protective of this young woman. He'd wondered a time or two why he felt so strongly, but he could never come up with an answer.

In the end it didn't really matter.

✗ ✗ ✗ ✗ ✗

Aeris was momentarily distracted as Jaxom expressed his discontent through their link. Her heart went out to him, for no one wanted to eat something they hated. He was forced to partake of the zarefessia every day, and each time she was made acutely aware of his displeasure. Other things that bothered Jaxom were often kept to himself until he was ready to share them with her at the end of the work day when she wasn't so busy. But not with the zarefessia.

Out of every seven-day, there were six days dedicated to work. Two of those days were given to physical endurance. For riders, that meant weapons practice and strength training, and for dragons it entailed flight maneuverability. Another two days saw everyone focused on mounted combat. The remaining two days were dedicated to skills associated with everyone's different professions. That meant Aeris and Saliel would refine their spellcasting whilst astride, while Thulnar and Faleema continued with the more physical aspects of mounted combat, in particular, jousting.

The lances were huge. Aeris had never seen anything quite like them. Spanning at least half the length of a dragon, the lances were constructed from the most lightweight metal known, a material called braxen. However, the secret of braxen was known only by the halfen race. Inasmuch, those people held sole propriety over the forging of the lances. It just so happened that a halfen smith by the name of Nampaul made his home upon Haldorr, courtesy of his *bond* with the helzethryn dragon Knorrith. His work was legendary, even on Shandahar.

Aeris sighed heavily over the tome resting next to her on the bedpallet. A braided length of crimson hair wound over her shoulder like a thick rope to touch the top-most page of the book. Within her right hand she held a bronzed braxen rod, a receptacle for the power that was about to be directed towards it. Kordrian had given her the spells needed to infuse the rod, but it was up to her to figure out the intricacies of casting them. Not yet skilled enough to cast the spells without the use of runes, she inscribed the words of magic into the air just as she began her incantation. She then reached into her pouch to extract the component she needed, a bit of unrefined glass created by lightning when it struck sand.

Lightning was the power she wished to harness within the confines of the rod.

Aeris completed the incantation, tossed the glass into the air before her, and then a flare of electrical energy zapped through the chamber. Aeris screamed as the spell misfired, scorching the ends of her plaited hair and the upper right corner of the book before smashing into the far wall. She dropped the rod, and with her hair in one hand and the book in the other, she blew upon both until they smoldered. She then tossed the book back onto the bedpallet, following it down with her own body until she lay next to it, her gaze focusing on the vaulted ceiling above.

Damn, she had forgotten to include the part of the spell that would make the rod vulnerable to the spell infusion.

Aeris sighed heavily. She would have to start again on the morrow, for the spell had drained her. She glanced at the far wall, taking note of the blackened indentation that now adorned it. *Curses, that is where all of my energy went.*

Aeris closed her hands into fists and put them over her eyes. It was her fifth attempt at the infusion. In her favor, each time she failed she was able to figure out what went awry. Only this time was the most destructive. Hells, how would she be able to create the weapon she *really* wanted when she couldn't even perform the spells needed for *this* one? Who wanted to bother with holding onto a silly rod in the midst of battle when one could *wear* their weapon like a glove! She had been doing some research and it seemed that she just might have the capability to perform such a feat. That is, if the braxen-smith would help fashion it for her, and mayhap if Demeter Kord gave her a little bit of guidance. Unfortunately, the latter was unlikely.

Aeris didn't move when she heard someone enter the chamber. The individual stopped for a moment in order to assess the situation and then continued towards her. Aeris knew it was Faleema before the other woman spoke. "Aeris, are you all right?"

Aeris took her hands away from her face and regarded her friend from bleary eyes. "You saw the wall?"

Faleema nodded mutely.

Aeris nodded in return.

Silence reigned for a moment. Then, "I need to get this, Faleema. If I don't prepare the rod soon, I will lose time in activation. This is important."

Faleema nodded. "Just as important as it is for me to master coordination with my lance and for Thulnar to learn precision with his." She paused and then continued. "If it makes you feel any better, Saliel isn't any farther along with his spellcasting."

Aeris nodded. Actually, it *did* make her feel a little bit better.

Faleema sniffed at the air. "Hells, Aeris. It really stinks in here."

Aeris cast an irritated glance and then saw the merriment reflecting in the blue depths of her friend's eyes.

"Yeah, I didn't notice it until you came in," Aeris retorted in a mock, scathing tone.

Faleema narrowed her eyes. "Yes, well, as the black hole in the wall does give a rather distinctive look to the place, I honestly believe it could have been omitted."

Aeris regarded Faleema for as long as she could before bursting out in laughter. She tried to stifle it to no avail. She was finally able to speak. "I wonder what Franchiera will think of it?"

"Humph. I wonder what Demeter Kord will think." Faleema waggled her eyebrows suggestively.

Aeris grabbed the nearest pillow and threw it.

✖✖✖✖✖

Jonesy hesitated, her eyes reflecting surprise. Tigerius chuckled in response, and she frowned in disgruntlement, warily accepting his challenge. Among the tall grasses it was almost impossible to delineate the boundaries of a sparring ring, but who cared? He was tired after so many days of travel without anything to occupy their time except to prepare meals and take care of the animals. He remembered that she had enjoyed sparring with Cervantes, and thought mayhap to replicate it in his own fashion.

Tigerius watched Jonesy retrieve her cutlass. Her stance was tense, and she watched him warily from slightly narrowed eyes as she made her way back over to him. It was obvious that she was nervous and it was only then that he recognized the possibility that she felt something about him—much the way he felt something about her. The thought was intriguing, and he offered her a reassuring smile as he placed himself into position.

In spite of her hesitancy, Jonesy was the first to attack. He parried her swing with a quick deflection with his blade, and was surprised at the strength he felt behind her assault. Hells, he didn't know any woman who could hit that hard except perhaps for Sheridana Darnesse, the sister of Aeris' mother. He took his own turn and swung, only to have Jonesy sidestep his attack. She followed up with another assault of her own, and once more he brought his blade to deflect it. It wasn't long before Tigerius found himself astounded by the level of her skill. If he didn't know better, he would think Jonesy had been under the tutelage of a master and had trained for at least two to three years. But he knew for a fact she had only Cervantes. The captain was good, but definitely not a master. Not only that, but the training had been somewhat sporadic, and took place during the space of only a year, probably a bit less.

The spar progressed. Tiger was glad for the unusual potency of the sensory abilities that he'd developed. Since his foray into the underdark, he could see, hear, and smell much better than ever before. And there was more. His physical strength had also increased, as well as his stamina. He had experienced the change first hand when he fought against the wrothe. Now he experienced it again. Strangely, this girl came close to matching it, and very quickly Jonesy was becoming an enigma.

Tiger took in the expression of grim determination on her face, the ferocity reflected in her green eyes. Much like himself, she was bathed in sweat, and her flesh was flushed from her exertion. He found himself becoming perturbed. Who was this girl? Who was she to be able to withstand the strength and strategy of his attacks with such speed and accuracy? And why the Hells was he so drawn to her that he wanted to grab hold . . .

Tigerius suddenly reached out and grasped her forearm. Jonesy stopped in mid-swing, her eyes widening in response to his intensity. His gaze met and locked with hers and he saw that she felt something very akin to what he was feeling himself. It was a sense of knowing that they were somehow connected without understanding why.

"What are you?" The words blurted out of their own accord, without any forethought.

"I was just thinking the same about you," she responded brokenly.

"I'm not entirely sure," he replied with a frown.

"Me neither."

Tigerius swallowed heavily and released her arm. He knew right away that he had hurt her, for the flesh was already beginning to change color. He sighed and closed his eyes, remaining that way until he heard her voice again.

"Tiger, what's happening to me?" she asked quietly.

He opened his eyes to see the uncertainty reflected in her gaze. He shook his head. "I don't know." Then he paused for a few moments, expressing utmost seriousness as he stated his next response. "I apologize for bruising your arm."

Jonesy only nodded. She said nothing more, keeping her eyes averted. He sensed her confusion, and wished he could help her. He didn't know what it was about her that drew him so strongly. He suddenly wondered if it had anything to do with their newfound abilities.

Jonesy stepped away from Tigerius and walked over to her travel pack. Her hands shook as she returned the cutlass to its sheath. She felt sick to her stomach and decided it would be best to sit down for a few moments to compose herself. She wrapped her arms around her legs and rested her forehead on her knees. She stared at the ground, at the thick grass that lay crushed beneath her, and the small hartebeetles that valiantly fled the immediate vicinity. Her mind picked apart the sparring match, wondering exactly which moment the magic took place. It took her a while to realize that it may not have been just one moment at all, but several moments that had begun before she and Tiger ever left the group. She recalled the last session she had shared with Cervantes, how much easier it had been for her to breach his defenses. She remembered that he'd been a bit out of breath and that he'd been surprised by her skill.

Jonesy continued to ponder her situation. She still hadn't experienced a menses, only verifying what she already knew. She still continued to get sick at the beginning of every day, a sickness that was calmed only when she partook of some of the bland rations in her travel pack. By the gods, in spite of the pregnancy, she was stronger than she'd ever been before. Her endurance had increased, and she was fast, somehow able to evade many of Tiger's attacks. Many times it seemed she had been swinging on instinct, or mayhap that she'd been a master with the cutlass for several years. Of course, the latter was not the case, and the former seemed so implausible. She was about to thank the gods for such a wondrous gift, one that would be invaluable against her brother and any other enemies that awaited her in Karlisle. *But then she remembered that the gods had fallen.*

Jonesy took a deep breath and rose from the grass. She looked around and saw the lloryk standing only a short distance away. Tiger stood between them, running his fingers through the thick, wavy hair that lay along their necks. She took in the scene for a moment, and noted that each beast had its head turned towards Tiger with muzzles pressed gently against his sides. Now that she thought about it, the animals seemed to have developed a liking for Tiger since their leave-taking. It wasn't that they had disliked him before they left the group, only that they had come to know him so much better over the past several days. And now, to see them like this was remarkable.

Tiger looked up as she began walking towards him. His gaze was guarded and she wondered what he'd been thinking. Once close enough, she spoke. "What do you think about staying here for the evening? Maybe we can hone our archery skills and do a bit of hunting. Fresh ptarmigan for the stewpot would be a good change from our dried rations and grain mix."

He regarded her for a moment before offering a smile. "I think it's a great idea. Something a little out of the ordinary would be good for me." His smile widened. "Not to mention, a good change in our dietary intake."

Jonesy returned the smile. "Well, we had best get the lloryk settled quickly. We don't want to lose our daylight."

They swiftly worked on setting up an encampment. As Jonesy made preparations for a fire and laid out their bedrolls, Tiger rubbed down the lloryk, inspected their feet, and gave them each a handful of grain. The beasts would take the remainder of their meal from the surrounding grassland and the hartebeetles that abounded there. With the plentiful food supply, their scaly coats had begun to shine with health. If treated well, the animals would take them as far as they needed to go.

Once ready, they unpacked their slingshots and some stones. The small weapons would be best to hunt the ground-dwelling ptarmigan. The companions slowly moved away from the disruption they'd caused when they prepared the encampment. Because of the abundance of hartebeetles, the multihued squat birds were also very plentiful in these grasslands. In spite of her paltry slingshot skills, she should be able to help Tiger bring down at least four birds: one for each of them, and the others to be given to the lloryk. The animals had traveled far and fast, and they could use the extra meat to continue the rigorous pace.

Jonesy walked beside Tiger within the tall, waving grasses. Once again she thought about their sparring match and marveled at her ability to equal him. She turned to glance in his direction and a moment later he turned and offered a friendly smile.

It was good to know that nothing had changed.

✖ ✖ ✖ ✖ ✖

Farenze and the men under his command slunk through the narrow underground corridor. The rock pressed relentlessly around them, making them perspire from thoughts of never making it to the surface again. They couldn't help it, for it was unnatural for most men to traverse such paths without fear of consequence. It was their belief that normal men were meant to spend their lives with their feet on *top* of the ground, not *beneath* it. That had to mean that halfen weren't normal. Similarly, he supposed the dragonriders weren't either, for they had a tendency to hover at least several zacrol *over* it.

Farenze felt a humor-filled rumbling in his mind, testament of how Sifrozelnik felt about the final element of his ruminations. Of course, the dragon thought it rather silly, for he'd spent much of his own time in the air since learning to fly as a youngling. Farenze frowned. Hells, the dragon simply didn't understand.

"Farenze, the men are getting restless. Are we almost there?"

He felt himself being thrust back into his physical surroundings as he heard the whispered voice. Hells, he wondered the same thing. However, he couldn't say that to Kithanjun and the rest of the men behind him. Instead, the men needed to hear words of encouragement, words that would help propel them forward through the cavern system. As for himself, all he could do was remember what Ma-tia had told him. Farenze often wondered about the awe-inspiring dragon goddess. She bore a strong hatred for human-kind, yet she had saved both him and Kithanjun from certain death at the hands of the kronshue. He was afraid of her, yet he mustered the courage to speak with her whenever she called an audience with him. For some reason she had chosen him above all of the other men to lead her missions.

The missions that were designed to break down any potential opposition.

This time it was a clutch of helzerthryn eggs laid by the mother only a few weeks ago. Like any new mother, the drenna had been overly solicitous at first. Over time she'd allowed herself brief absences so that she could hunt for the meat she needed to sustain her. It was during one of these times that Farenze and the others hoped to infiltrate. The eggs were defenseless and would be easy to dispatch.

Walking a while longer, Farenze hoped for an end to their underground journey just as he felt a rise in ambient temperature. A few moments later, he saw a break in the wall ahead. Making the abrupt gesture for silence to the men behind him, he slowly approached the crevasse. It was the source of the warm air, and the perfect indicator that he had reached his goal. The opening would allow a narrow man to fit through, one much like him. However, he couldn't say the same for many of the other men in his company. *Damnation! Why does everything have to be so difficult?*

Farenze turned away from the crevasse to regard the men. He could see that Kithanjun had arrived at the same conclusion and was sizing up each man to imagine him fitting through the narrow fissure. Hells, it wasn't like any of them was overly large or fat—only that the space was so small. Unfortunately, Farenze had always measured on the puny side; he'd always been the one the other boys picked on in school when his parents demanded he procure some education. *Needless to say, he hadn't bothered with that fruitless endeavor for very long.*

Kithanjun motioned one of the men forward, quickly followed by another. They stepped over to join Farenze, and his heart sank. By the gods, how was he going to accomplish this? He knew that Sifro and the other dragons were acting as sentinels near the main entrance and that they would warn him should the mother return. Likewise, he knew that the remaining men out in the corridor would make certain that no one entered the chamber behind him. It was just that he'd imagined there would be a few more with him to destroy gods only knew how many eggs that lay in the chamber beyond.

Farenze gestured the two men forward. "I will go in first, then signal you to follow when I have determined it is safe." He looked at Kithanjun and gave a brief nod before turning away. He knew that his comrade would keep everyone focused while he was gone. He then proceeded to the large crack, pausing to look through it. He saw nothing that indicated much about the area except some stalactite remains.

Farenze slipped through, the only hindrance being the loose fit of his tunic. It caught on some sharp rock, but he easily pulled it free as he moved further into the chamber. He walked slowly. The air carried a damp smell underscored by something he'd never sensed before. It made him that much more alert and aware of his surroundings, and he proceeded with caution. He paused by the fallen spires. At first all he saw was some debris where there should have been complete structures. There were a couple pools of water, continuously filled by some underground stream, and there were mosses growing on the walls that made them glow eerily green.

It wasn't long before he saw them. Lying in the far corner, the pale round orbs were a contrast to the darker stone surrounding them. There were at least ten, *and they were all alone.*

Farenze glanced back at the fissure and silently gestured for the other men to join him. The first one slipped through, struggling for only the briefest moment—much as he had. But the second man was a little bigger. Farenze heard him issue a soft grunt when he finally made it, releasing the belly muscles he'd sucked in. He rubbed a hand along his chest and Farenze imagined he would have some bruising the following day.

With light steps, Farenze approached, the men following behind. The mother wasn't there, but something told him to exercise caution. For all he knew, there was another dragon nearby. Once there, he walked among the eggs, each one easily the size of a human man. He reached out to touch one and realized the shell wasn't hard like a bird's might be. It was thick and pliable, more like that of a snake or lizard. He smiled, overcome with relief. His mission might be easier than he initially thought.

Farenze drew his sword. He hesitated only a moment before plunging it into the egg he'd just touched. He withdrew the weapon, and when nothing happened in spite of the hole he'd just made on the side, he stabbed the egg again, this time pulling the weapon downward.

The shell was thicker than he thought, but the sword cut through it. The contents spilled out—blood-tinged, yellowish fluid along with the small form that would have become a young dragon. His mind rebelled at the sight, instantly thinking of his companion who awaited him outside the mountain cavern. Much to his surprise, Sifro's mind was instantly in his, sending soothing vibes through their link telling him all would be all right.

Farenze moved to the next egg while the other two men drew their own blades. They made short work of the nest, leaving behind a lake of thick fluid the mother would be forced to walk through in order to reach her deceased offspring.

CHAPTER THIRTEEN

The group continued to move northward across the grassland back to the mountains. For the most part they had avoided the villages and towns, and only when necessary did they frequent a city or two. At the last one, the city of Turbanak, Levander had conducted a bit of reconnaissance. The hope was to find out if their deductions had been correct and if they were on the right path. The news had been good. A man and a woman of both Tiger's and Jonesy's descriptions had passed through not long before.

Much like their predecessors, the group didn't linger long. The desire for rest and relaxation in a decent establishment wasn't part of their agenda. They simply wanted to make better time than their comrades, and if they were not able to catch up with them, they could at least close the distance as much as possible. In the meantime, Alasdair couldn't shake the feeling that something was going to happen, that it was big, and that it involved both Jonesy and Tigerius.

He frowned to himself. Traditionally, Aeris was the one cursed with the gift of foresight. Alasdair always hated it whenever he happened to receive his own paltry premonitions about things. Strangely, this time was different; his feelings were quite strong. Unfortunately, it didn't change anything.

Just that morning, they had left the small city, heartened by the knowledge that Tiger and Jonesy passed through only three days before. Three days was a long time to try and match for distance, but at least they were on the correct route. Not only that, but the animals had been well fed and given a good rest in the sanctuary of a stable. They had restocked their food rations, purchased a few more necessities, and headed out early that morning.

Now it was mid-day, and the sky was overcast. The air pressed heavily, making travel that much more uncomfortable than usual. The animals were also more restless than normal, and he vaguely wondered what they were fed the evening before to make them behave with such orneriness. It was quite miserable, and Alasdair wondered when it would finally be over.

As the day passed into early evening, the air became more stagnant. Meanwhile, the animals were much more fractious. The group stopped and everyone dismounted, hoping to find a way to quiet the beasts and mayhap even discover the source of their unease. Alasdair felt his frustrations rise, and he wondered how much of that had to do with the animals as compared with the uncanny calm that had overtaken the savanna, a place where the tops of the grasses constantly shifted with the winds. Much to his dismay, it was just their luck that they would come across another group of travelers. There were eight of them, all human, each leading his or her similarly restless lloryk. The oddity of yet more recalcitrant beasts struck Alasdair for barely a moment before a predominant feeling of wariness overcame him, for the overall demeanor of the others struck him as unpleasant. As the two groups passed one another within the tall grasses, he noticed their eyes linger overly long, and not one gaze was remotely friendly.

The six men were all well-muscled, each bearing long-swords, battle-axes, or war-hammers. The one that traveled at the forefront gave a brief nod as he passed, his thick dark brows pulled into a frown over his eyes. The two women were also armed to the teeth with cross-bows, short-swords, and a dagger at each hip. Alasdair wasn't surprised when they turned back around once passing them along the road, weapons drawn. Even before he heard the voice of the leader calling out in the common tongue with a menacing tone, Alasdair had it in his mind that nothing short of a conflict would result in this meeting.

Quickly mounting their lloryk, the enemy group rushed towards them.

Alasdair's eyes widened with alarm, for the enemy had easily taken the advantage. Hells, even if they had the time to swing up onto the backs of their own beasts, it wouldn't have mattered. *Most of his comrades had never fought astride.*

Alasdair cursed as he swung up onto his lloryk. He immediately felt the tension in the animal and once more thought of his sister. Damn, she would have already figured out what was wrong with his beast along with all the others. He kicked the animal forward, only barely recognizing that the sky had adopted an eerie, sickly yellow-green color. Behind him, he vaguely noticed his comrades following suit, and less than a moment later heard the slight whir of Lev's flying metal stars as they swept past his head.

Alasdair was just reaching the leader when he heard shouts of pain coming from the enemy. However, the force of his opponent's blade against his made him focus on the task at hand. He grunted with the impact, keeping his wrist steady to thwart the enemy's effort to render him weaponless as they rode past one another. Meanwhile, a light rain began to fall and the winds finally made their return. He didn't think much of it as he quickly swung his mount around to face his adversary once more.

It was Cedric's voice that broke through his haze. "Twister! 'Ware and take cover!"

Alasdair felt his heart skip a beat and he saw his opponent's eyes widen with alarm. It was then he realized the increasing strength of the winds that buffeted them. Glancing furtively about, he caught sight of the deadly storm. The clouds had coalesced into the shape of a dark funnel. In the near distance, it danced swiftly over the grassy landscape, throwing debris wherever it touched.

Ah Hells!

With sickening clarity, Alasdair suddenly knew what it was that had caused the lloryk and horses so much discomfort that day. It wasn't that they were trying to be difficult, merely making an attempt to follow basic instinct. Alasdair now felt like a fool; with his training he should have recognized the conditions favoring such a storm and then paid heed to the natural world around him. Not only had their own beasts given him clues, but so had the other wildlife that made the savanna their home. If his father had been there, Sirion would have picked up on these cues quite some time ago, and he would have directed the group accordingly. Unfortunately, his comrades had only himself to rely on. *Much the shame.*

Now everyone was in danger, for the tornadic winds destroyed whatever lay in their path. He was grateful to his cousin for issuing the warning, but there was no cover to take in open grassland such as this. Their best chance lay in fleeing. Alasdair tore his gaze away from the storm and took in the terrified expressions on the faces of his comrades. Even the stoic Levander gazed at the approaching winds with a look of disbelief. Alasdair's voice bellowed over the ever deepening sound of the twister. "Everyone, run! Run!"

Talemar was the first to respond, followed by Cervantes and Jezibel. Within less than a moment, the group was speeding through the tall grasses. They handed control over to their animals, for better than anyone else they knew where to go. A few farlo away, Alasdair could see their adversaries also attempting to outrun the storm. On a calm day, only the upper backs of the lloryk would have been visible. But now the grasses bent under the power of the winds, and the entire chest and barrel of each beast could be seen.

Alasdair turned to look over his shoulder, his unbound hair whipping about his face. The twister had decreased the distance, and he urged his lloryk to increase her pace. He leaned over the back of the animal until his cheek touched the sweaty neck of the poor beast. Damn, if only he had listened. Instead of allowing his mind to be cluttered with thoughts of his sister and multitudes of other things, he should have focused on his job. He just may have been able to avoid the events that now unfolded.

They continued to run. Somehow, the animals stayed together, another instinctual response. Over the fortnights they had come to know one another, and each beast was part of the herd, whether they were lloryk or horse. It was good, for the desire to remain with one's companions won out. Herd mentality ruled, and there was strength in numbers. It was a good thing, for Alasdair didn't relish the thought of hunting down the location of everyone in his company. Not only would it take a lot of time, but resources as well.

The sound of the winds became almost deafening. Alasdair strained to hear over them as they ran, hoping beyond hope that they would escape. He didn't chance another look over his shoulder, for not only did he fear what he would see, but it would distract him from his path to freedom. The animal beneath him ran her hardest. He could imagine her fear, her heart beating wildly in her mighty chest, and the hard breath she expelled with every hoof-beat. He could feel her muscles relaxing and contracting as she moved swiftly before the path of the hideous thing behind them.

But then she foundered.

Alasdair felt his heart skip a beat as the lloryk stumbled. He felt the unmistakable crack of breaking bone reverberate through her body where he sat on her back. Keeping his wits about him, he readied himself for her fall. He thrust himself clear as the animal went down to her knees. He rolled away and when he came to a stop, Alasdair just lay there within the grasses for a moment. Shaking his head, he forced himself upright. Looking back in the direction of the storm, he saw that it had begun to veer away to the west. He put a hand over his face in relief, for the immediate danger was over.

As the sound of the winds finally began their decline, he started to search the nearby grasses. His lloryk lay hidden somewhere within, and he knew that she needed him. A part of him recognized that he should be spending his efforts on the other members of his company, but at the moment he simply couldn't wrap his mind around the thought of walking away. Any other man would probably have decided to just leave the beast behind, striking her from him as merely a burden animal. But Alasdair wasn't any other man. He was a hinterlean ranger, bound to the animals that served him. The lloryk had most likely saved his life this day. The least he could do was end hers with as much care and speed as possible. He knew that she was beyond repair, and the reality of that fact saddened him.

In her honor, he would kill her with a single thrust of his long-knife.

Alasdair found her lying in the grass not far away. Immediately he could sense her agony. Her left front foreleg was angled in an unnatural position, and his thoughts pertaining to his ability to help her were verified. Within less than a moment he was at her side, caressing her sweat-dampened neck with long sweeps of his sun-bronzed hand. He crooned soothingly to her in hinterlic, telling her all would be well and that her pain would soon be over. He thanked the animal for her service, telling her that she had been good to him. His heart wrenched slightly when he said the last, for he felt that he could have been a much better comrade to her. If he had paid more attention to her, heeding her signals of impending distress, she would not be lying there before him now—about to die.

With tears in his eyes, Alasdair reached to his side and unsecured his long-knife from the sheath. He brought the weapon before him, kissing the blade and murmuring a few words of prayer. He then raised it over his companion, and with all his strength, swiftly brought it down. The blade entered deep into her chest, striking her heart. Beneath the palm of his other hand, he could feel it shudder and then cease beating.

Alasdair then proceeded to lay himself over the body of his friend as she took her last breaths. He knew when she was gone. The light left her eyes, and her body became still. What was most difficult was that she was still warm to the touch. His tears flowed freely, wetting the already damp fur beneath his face. Then he cried, his body shaking with the force of his sobs. Alasdair wasn't able to stand for a while. He looked at the body of his companion and shuddered with the pain of loss. He hoped she was now in a better place, and he hoped also that he had helped make her transition there a less agonizing one. Alasdair finally looked away from her into the damp, swaying grasslands before him. The twister was gone, taking its deafening noise with it. Much to his concern, there wasn't another soul in sight.

2 Finoren CY634

The newborn flames of the campfire danced happily before him, offering the warmth he'd endeavored to acquire in their making. Tigerius closed his eyes and inhaled deeply. Fatigue washed over him like a wave, and he wished so much he would find peace while he slept. Over the past couple days he'd realized it would not come, not until he had reached his destination. A more westerly route had begun to beckon him as they traveled, often giving him a sick feeling in the middle of his gut. Some times were worse than others, but the sensation never went away. Something urged him in that direction, but the details of it only appeared as shadows in his mind, ones that dissipated every time he strove to recognize them.

Truthfully, Tiger had almost traveled as far north as he could. It was only a matter of time before he would be forced to part ways with Jonesy in favor of the more westerly route. He fretted that she would be traveling alone, so he balked at leaving her side. Without her company, he would have taken the risk of traveling through the northern rim of the unfamiliar Sheraxi Forest. Instead he had chosen to remain east of the forest to continue north towards the mountains. He felt it was worth the trouble to have the luxury of traveling with a friend, especially since she would be more vulnerable once they parted.

However, much to Tiger's dismay, the sacrifice lay heavily. His dreams gave him no respite, and his body endured the strain of not following the shortest route to his destination. The nausea was worst, making him so sick that he would vomit in the nearby grass. He wondered a time or two what Jonesy might be thinking, but realized it couldn't be too bad, for she'd suffered a similar malady since before leaving the rest of the group. He wondered only vaguely as to the reason for her illness, but ultimately attributed it to the strain her own mission must be causing.

From the corner of his eye, Tiger watched Jonesy from across the small fire. Many nights they had been forced to sleep without this luxury, for dried wood couldn't always be found out in the grassland. But this night they were fortunate, and the smoke of burning burrwood rose from the flames between them, encompassing them within a sphere of wonderful scent. Within her hands was a mug of steaming chag, and she blew on it a moment before taking her first drink. She then thoughtfully regarded him from over the rim.

Looking at Tigerius from across the flames, Jonesy saw a haggard man. He had become restless the past several days, and sickly. She would catch him looking west every once in a while, and she knew the time for them to part ways was coming close. His sickness seemed to be a physical manifestation of his need to travel his own path, the route he was required to take in order to meet his destiny. Faced with the reality of their parting made her realize how much she had come to value his company and thoughts of his absence were depressing.

Jonesy swallowed past the sudden lump in her throat. Somewhere over the many zacrol they had traveled together, Tiger had become a very good friend.

Once again, Jonesy blew on the hot drink contained within the mug she held between her hands. Of course, Tiger had been a travel companion since she first met him and Aeris in the port city of Yortec. Little by little she got to know him over the many moon cycles, but it was when he saved her from the daemundai after the group escaped Tholana's catacombs that she realized so much more about him. More time had passed, and now he was more than Aeris' guardian, more than the man with strange abilities. *He was the man who tracked her through the darkness of the night so he could have a companion with whom to travel upon a path that she didn't know anything about.*

Jonesy suddenly found that she was interested in Tiger's destination.

Throughout their journey this far, she had never asked him the reason why he'd deserted the group, and he hadn't asked about hers either. She hadn't wanted to be intrusive, and as such, didn't want to divulge very much about herself. But now she thought better of that decision. What if Tiger needed someone in whom to confide, and what if she needed the same? Should they part ways without at least one person knowing their intentions? What if one or the other of them never came back, and neither family nor friends had any idea where they could even think of beginning a search?

Jonesy was thrust away from her ruminations when she became aware of Tiger's gaze focused on her. She broke eye contact, but not before she saw the speculative expression on his face. There was silence for a moment before he spoke. "I know you are wondering about me again."

Jonesy became still and then slowly brought her gaze back up to meet his. For a moment they regarded one another intently before he spoke again. "That's okay. I would wonder about me too if I were in your position." He paused for a moment and then continued. "I am just surprised that you have managed to resist this long."

She waited a moment before she replied. "Perhaps it is because I have too many of my own secrets to keep."

Tiger nodded and then looked back at the fire, prodding it with a slender, green branch taken from one of the nearby bushes. She could see that he was formulating a response, for his expression had become somewhat pensive. Moments later he was looking back up at her. "Aeris is a good friend, someone who keeps the secrets of others to herself," he said. "I respect her for that."

Tigerius then focused his attention back on the dancing flames between them. Jonesy found herself doing the same. He was right. It seemed that, out of all the members of the group, Aeris had known more secrets than anyone else. She had known not only about herself and Tiger, but TC as well. Gods only knew what knowledge she harbored about anyone else. And somehow, she had kept it all to herself. Jonesy could only imagine the strain it might cause. However, it seemed that, in the end, Aeris simply didn't care about much of anything. After she lost the child, nothing was important anymore.

They both glanced back up simultaneously and regarded one another intently. Tiger shook his head. "I honestly don't know where to begin. But perhaps I should start with my most imperative objective." He pressed his lips into a thin line. "I am looking for my mother. I can feel something of her emanating north and west of Elvandahar. At first I was receiving vague impressions, but every day since then it has become clearer as to where I must go."

Jonesy couldn't help but stare at him for a moment. By the gods, he could sense the whereabouts of another person. But how he did this she didn't know. She took the moment to ponder it and made the realization she could do the same. She couldn't understand it, but somehow, she knew when Rigel was near. She nodded with acceptance and gave a deep sigh. "You probably already know that my destination is Karlisle. No matter the danger my brother imposes, it is my duty to return there."

Tigerius' gaze became piercing. "Really? Even if your life is forfeit? It is worth that risk?"

Jonesy nodded solemnly. "My brother is next in line to inherit the crown. As his sister, only I have the power to accuse him and demand that he stand before the council."

"Of what crime are you accusing him?" he asked.

Her throat clenched around her next words. "Rape with the intent to murder."

"How do you propose to make anyone believe you?"

"I was there to save one of the women whom he had left to die," she replied.

Tiger's complexion paled.

"I plan to make her my witness when I make my accusation."

"You are certain she will do it?"

Jonesy nodded. "Yes, I think so." She pulled the medallion free from its place beneath her blouse. "She gave this to me. I like to believe that she may have intended it to be the means for me to find her one day."

Tiger was silent for several moments. Then, "I believe that your brother will kill you before you have the chance to place any accusation."

She shook her head. "But it is worth the risk. The livelihood of my people rests on me." Jonesy looked away, swinging her gaze back to the fire. She didn't want him to see her indecision.

Tiger narrowed his eyes. "There is more that you are not telling me," he stated bluntly. "What is it?"

She hesitated. The knowledge she carried was a burden, and she had come to realize why Aeris tried to keep her own situation concealed. However, Jonesy knew she needed to tell someone. She swallowed heavily. "I am pregnant. I have begun to question my resolve, and I fear the risk might not be worth the life of the child I carry."

Jonesy watched him wrestle for a moment with the newfound knowledge, but his response was nothing like what she was expecting. Tigerius shook his head and the corners of his mouth turned up in a slight grin. "Damn, I had a niggling feeling in my mind that there was the presence of another here with us. I never made the connection." Tiger huffed and then chuckled at his own expense. "How silly of me; I should have known." He paused for a moment. "The father is Cervantes, is it not?"

Jonesy simply sat there for a moment. It was strange that Tigerius could know so much. In a way, it was a little bit creepy. She nodded and then pulled her knees up to her chest, lowering her chin to rest on them.

Tiger's gaze became piercing. "Does he know?"

Jonesy shook her head. "No. I didn't realize it until after we had left the group. I never really suspected until I missed another cycle."

"How long has it been?"

"A few weeks," she responded.

Tiger was silent for a moment. "Jonesy, we should really consider going back. I am certain we will catch up with the group if we move fast enough. In spite of your prowess, your condition might weaken your defenses as it progresses. You are in no state to fight any battles."

She immediately shook her head. "No, I need to go home. My father needs me. My *people* need me. I have left them long enough."

Tigerius regarded his friend intently. He could see the conviction written on her face, the need to set right a wrong. One day, this woman would make a good leader. By the gods, there was a part of him that felt he should accompany her, stand by her side as she went to meet her destiny. But he knew he couldn't do it, physically or mentally. He had his own path to follow.

"Jonesy, please be reasonable. You need a company to back you up in something like this."

Jonesy drew her lips into a thin line. "No, it is much too dangerous and the reason why I left the rest of the group behind without even a farewell— including Cervantes."

Tiger looked her intently in the eyes. By the gods, she was so stubborn. And she was silly, so willing to face whatever danger was awaiting her without the support of her comrades. He leaned towards her from across the fire. "Jonesy, I am serious. The danger is the very reason why you really need at least one person to stand by you."

Jonesy raised an eyebrow. He could tell that she was getting upset. "Oh, and you think that person should be you?" She shook her head. "No. What I must do, I need to do alone. You need to let me go. That was the unspoken agreement between us when you joined me."

Tigerius frowned. "Contrary to your belief, the person I have in mind isn't me. I have my own obstacles to overcome, and now wish I hadn't been so foolish as to leave my comrades behind. My cousins were stupid to hide pertinent information about my family, but I know they would have helped me.

Knowing there is strength in numbers, the rest of the group would most likely have followed behind." He slapped his hands down on his thighs. "So fine, I shall leave you to your own devices. I suppose I will do the same. My mission is for me and me alone because I deserted my friends."

Jonesy nodded and chose to ignore his insinuation that she made the same idiotic mistake. "It is best this way because my brother will surely kill you or anyone else I might bring with me."

Tiger scoffed. "He could just as easily kill you as well."

Jonesy was stoic. "It is unlikely, for there are too many people who would suspect." She stopped but then continued. "One of those persons is you. My trail has thickened over these past fortnights, and it isn't quite so easy to be rid of me anymore."

Tiger narrowed his eyes. "Does Cervantes know any of this?"

Jonesy slowly shook her head and Tiger sighed heavily to himself. Curses, the man deserved to know. Somehow she had kept her dark secrets from the captain. It definitely wasn't right; the crazy woman was carrying his child. He picked up the stick beside him to poke at the embers of their fire. The flames licked about it playfully, barely managing to burn the young branch.

Finally, Tiger looked back up, his expression one of acceptance. "We had best get some rest," he said. "We have another long day on the morrow."

Jonesy simply nodded. He turned to lie down on his bedroll, bringing his worn blanket up to his chin. For several moments he stared into the dying flames of the fire. They hadn't bothered with night-time watches since the first night, keeping their sleep light and relying on the lloryk to warn them of any approaching danger. He dreaded the morning, for it was one step closer to their parting company. And the war within his mind would intensify—the one that was fought out of his silly protective desire to act as an escort for her.

Suddenly he heard her voice from across the fire. "Tiger?"

"Yeah?" he mumbled.

"I am going to miss you when you are gone."

He was silent for a moment. Then, "I will miss you as well."

Once more Jaxom went into a spiral dive in an effort to maintain a safe distance between himself and any others who ventured too close. Aeris cursed her lack of concentration, yet told herself she needed only to become more accustomed to the sensations she felt whilst astride. It would take practice, and no small amount of extra effort to accomplish her goal—to boast the ability to cast at least a handful of offensive spells whilst in flight.

Aeris glanced to her right side. In the near distance she spied Saliel attempting to do the same. Meanwhile, it was Franchiera's duty to harass them whenever she deemed it necessary. Damn, it made it even more difficult to concentrate, for the quartermaster could approach at any moment. Unfortunately, Franchie had a partner in crime; Demeter Kord had decided to perform the same task. It was only a matter of time before Aeris and Jaxom discovered how well they would perform under such duress.

Aeris began to cast her next spell. So far, she had been able to cast the *Flamesphere* five out of ten attempts. At least she could do it right half of the time now. And she'd finally accomplished the arcane task of infusing her power-rod, or tommahora, with lightning. Now she needed only to activate it; this was an endeavor that would take several days of successful spellcasting to accomplish. She wasn't looking forward to it.

Aeris completed the spell and cast it into the space before her. Much to her chagrin, she realized too late that someone was in her way. Aeris' *Flamesphere* swept towards Franchiera, and it took every effort for the quartermaster to evade it. Jaxom immediately urged them to take themselves away, but Aeris couldn't bring herself to leave without first knowing that she was unharmed.

Sidranth hissed her displeasure as Franchie focused her thunderous gaze onto Aeris. She realized too late that Jaxom had been right to suggest they leave as the enraged pair swiftly flew towards them. Aeris pressed herself against Jaxom's neck while he maneuvered to evade the golden drenna and her rider. As they pair passed, Aeris sensed the gravitation of magic indicative of spellcasting. She recognized the incantation at the last moment, warning Jaxom to bank to the right as the *Prismatic Bolt* swept at them. Aeris was certain it was meant for her, so when the spell struck Jaxom, she felt her heart skip a beat.

Hellfire . . .

The strength of Jaxom's reaction washed over her via their link, enveloping her with anxiety and fear. She attempted to calm him, to make him realize that all would be well. He was blinded by the spell, but she could still see. She would be his guide as they flew to a place where he could land.

As Aeris struggled to communicate with her bondmate, Sidranth and Franchie emerged up ahead of them, the drenna back-winging so that both could determine the damage they had wrought. Aeris could see the momentary expression of alarm pass over Franchie's face before she hid it beneath the layer of deep dislike she bore Aeris. Damnation, this was a despicable spell to cast at a pair of novices who had been entrusted to her instruction.

It was absolute craziness.

Aeris tore her gaze away from Franchie. <Jaxom, bear right and begin a

T.R. Chowdhury & T.M. Crim

shallow dive. We are going down.>

He mentally struggled against her command for barely a moment before placing his faith in her and allowing her to navigate him to safety. There were images he could glean from her mind, just as she could see some things from his mind every once in a while. She imagined that the phenomenon might take place more often as they became increasingly accustomed to one another and their bond. Jaxom began his descent, and just as he began to calm, they were once more beset by their 'enemy'.

Aeris felt her eyes widen as the Franchie/Sidranth pair approached. By the gods, were they insane? They had already taken retaliatory action because of Aeris' mistake; what more did they want? When Aeris noticed the tell-tale signs of impending dragon-flame, she ordered Jaxom to deepen his dive. Again she pressed herself close to his neck, attempting to reduce any potential drag she might cause. Meanwhile, Sidranth breathed a wide swath of fire. Aeris closed her eyes as the flames licked overhead, bathing them with intense heat. It quickly dissipated as they continued to drop, and Aeris just managed to crack open her eyes to see the treetops rapidly approaching.

Her eyes instantly widened in alarm. <Jaxom, pull up!> she exclaimed.

The dragon immediately obliged, lengthening his wingspan to catch the air-current. Just below them jutted the tallest of the treetops. Jaxom would have been seriously wounded if he had flown into the midst of such thick vegetation. His wings were particularly vulnerable to the puncturing and tearing he would have endured.

She calmed her rapidly beating heart and took a deep breath. <All right, let's settle a bit higher so I can get a better view for a place to land.>

Jaxom concurred and rose a bit before stabilizing. Aeris scanned the area below them, looking for a good-sized open area, and then beyond into the distance. She strained her eyes for a moment, struggling to see what appeared to be another practice arena. It just might be the perfect place to land.

Aeris was about to communicate her finding to Jaxom when she noticed the abrupt presence of a shadow hovering above. She looked up, and the golden drenna screamed as she descended. Aeris felt Jaxom shudder and a wave of fear swept through her. Franchiera and Sidranth were serious, treating them like they would a true enemy. Hells, Jaxom relied on Aeris to get him to ground. She would be sorely taxed to do it whilst under attack.

<Jaxom, keep as you are. Once at the next arena we shall land.>

She knew he could hear the fear in her mind-voice, yet he said nothing. He simply followed her instruction, hoping that she was making the correct decisions for them both. Aeris' heart thundered in her chest and she strove to contain her emotions. She struggled to find that calm place within, the place where she always went to cast her spells.

Sidranth settled herself alongside Jaxom. Through their link Aeris could feel that he sensed the drenna's presence, yet he made no move to detract from his current path, relying entirely on Aeris. She glanced at Franchiera, and at that moment, the quartermaster leaped from her dragon and onto Jaxom.

Aeris cursed as Franchie curved an arm around her throat, and she brought both hands up in an effort to offer resistance. <Jaxom, keep with your present course. Don't stop!>

Aeris felt his understanding, as well as an increase in his speed. She struggled to grab her dagger while continuing to be the eyes Jaxom needed. She thought how foolish it was for Franchie to have boarded them, for now she was just as much at risk as Aeris. However, it was soon apparent that safety was the last thing on Franchie's mind as the woman tightened her grip over Aeris' throat. With her free hand, Franchie managed to remove Aeris' helm and then proceeded to hiss into her ear. "You little whore! How dare you think you can replace me! *I* am his favorite, and always will be. You are merely a distraction, a pretty face to turn his head for a moment. But think again if you consider keeping him for yourself!"

Aeris felt her eyes widen anew. What the Hells was the woman talking about? Had she gone insane? She continued efforts to acquire her weapon as she maintained her gaze on the 'scape before them, refusing to let Jaxom down. Franchie tightened her grip until the back of Aeris' head lay against the quartermaster's breast-plate. It wasn't long before Aeris was struggling to breathe. Somewhere in her mind, she felt Jaxom's response to this new danger. However, before he could attempt to take action, another dragonrider pair emerged into the airspace beside them. Aeris felt a release from the viselike grip, and slumped limply over Jaxom's withers. She then heard Rilo's voice through their link, <Jaxom, keep moving forward. There is an end to the jungle not far ahead.>

Closing her eyes, Aeris was filled with relief. By the gods, Demeter Kordrian had come to save her from an absolute madwoman. She focused on breathing while the sounds of dragon-battle permeated her auditory field. She could only imagine what was happening as she heard a scream from Rilo followed by another from Sidranth. A concussive force thundered close by, and Aeris felt Franchie's body suddenly spasm behind her. The woman then slipped from Jaxom's back.

Alarmed, Aeris opened her eyes. Below them, she saw Franchie dropping away. Before she could issue a new command to Jaxom, she saw Rilo position herself beneath the quartermaster's body. Kordrian caught the woman in his arms, and then positioned Franchie over Rilo's withers in front of him. Aeris continued to watch until they left her line of vision, and she finally began to calm. Before them stretched the practice arena within which they were to alight. With a fair portion of her wits about her, Aeris guided Jaxom into a safe landing. Ironically, it was then that his vision began to return.

With trembling arms and legs, Aeris somehow managed to dismount. Jaxom breathed gently on her as she stumbled from his foreleg, offering her his head should she need extra support. A brief moment later, Rilo was landing nearby. Franchiera remained unconscious on the silver's back, safely positioned in front of the battle-harness. Aeris didn't bother looking at the man seated behind. Aeris walked about a farlo before sitting down in the middle of the field. She felt like crying like an infant. Hells, she deserved the luxury! But the presence of a master kept her from obliging herself.

Yes, *master.* Why should she care that Kordrian was irritated by a harmless shift in title?

Aeris didn't bother to turn as he stepped up behind her. Indeed, she was grateful for his help, but she'd developed a suspicion about whom Franchiera had been referring when she held Aeris hostage aboard her own dragon.

"Damaeris, what happened up there?" She noticed that his voice was more concerned than authoritative.

Aeris was silent for several moments before making a reply. "I cast a *Flamesphere* spell. I didn't know she was so close. She just narrowly missed it and became angry." Aeris paused and then continued. "In retaliation, Sidranth breathed fire, and Franchie cast a *Prismatic Bolt* spell. I tried to dodge it, but it blinded Jaxom. I take full responsibility for that mistake. I suddenly found myself acting as Jaxom's eyes, and just as I thought the battle was over, Sidranth was attacking us again. Franchie boarded Jaxom and . . ."

Aeris suddenly paused in her recitation. She wasn't about to tell Kordrian what Franchie had said to her. Silence reigned for a short while before anyone spoke again.

"Are you all right?"

Aeris gave a nod. She had never before heard gentleness in his voice, and she was a little surprised. "Although, it seems I am in need of a new helm," she replied. "I seem to have lost mine."

Aeris heard him move closer, but kept her back turned. A moment later, something dropped on the ground beside her. She looked down to find her helm lying there. She finally turned and looked up at the man standing behind her. "It was in the quartermaster's grasp when she fell. Rilo reached out a talon and grabbed it when I caught her."

Taking hold of the helm, Aeris rose to stand before Kordrian in a single fluid motion. She thought it interesting that he chose not to use Franchiera's name. "Thank you for being there to help me." Aeris paused for a moment. "I only wish I knew why she hates me so much." The words came to her lips before she had a chance to really ponder them. Of course she had some idea, but something in her wanted to see his reaction. She wanted verification, and this was the only way she knew how to get it without asking straight out.

She immediately noticed that he was taken slightly aback by her statement. His gaze dropped away from hers and he shook his head. "Yes, well her behavior is unprecedented. Once we return to Shandahar, she will be taken to task for her unusually aggressive tactics in the training field. You will probably be summoned to comment on what happened here today."

Aeris nodded silently and then stepped past him to rejoin Jaxom. Given his behavior, she felt that her suspicions were confirmed. Of course she couldn't be entirely certain, but she had a good feeling that she was right. It was quite disconcerting to know that Demeter Kordrian shared a strong enough relationship with one of his students that said student felt she could claim ownership.

Aeris reached her dragon and mounted him with ease. Keeping her line of thought, Aeris gave full consideration to the place in which she found herself. Intimate relationships were not uncommon, simply because of the added emotions given by their dragon bondmates. For all she knew, Sidranth had risen for a mating flight and Kordrian was one of the men close by. Perhaps an attraction already existed between them, making it that much easier for them to come together. And now it seemed Franchiera had claimed Kordrian for her own.

Unfortunately, Aeris happened to be stuck in the middle.

Focusing his strength into his haunches, Jaxom crouched just before he leaped into the air. The ground fell away, and Aeris watched as the figure of Kordrian became smaller and smaller. Her bondmate had full use of his sight once more, and she could feel the intensity of his relief. He had never been sightless before, and she was sure the experience would haunt his dreams for fortnights to come. She sent soothing vibes through their link, hoping to offset his pessimism. Of course, she was certain she would have her own fair share of bad dreams.

CHAPTER FOURTEEN

Levander considered the group to be immensely fortunate. Not only had each of them managed to keep themselves astride during their perilous dash across the plains, but they had also succeeded in staying together. Once Lev had determined that the sound of the winds was decreasing, he chanced a look behind him to find that the twister had veered away. It proceeded to make a different path for itself, cutting a swath of destruction that did not include him and his comrades. He slowed his horse to a stop, and once the others made the same realization, they did the same. Somehow, Mateo had maintained his hold on the reins of their pack-horse. It was quite a feat, for the situation had been quite extraordinary. And what was even more miraculous was that the animal still carried all they had packed on his back that morning.

The only thing missing was Alasdair.

The group didn't begin their search until they were certain the storm was far enough away that it would not return. Already, the skies had started to clear, and tentative rays from the sun emerged from the prevailing cloud-cover. Levander organized the search, each person less than a farlo from the next as they scoured the nearby grassland for their comrade. It didn't take long for them to find the ranger where he stood next to his fallen lloryk.

Levander slowly dismounted. Instinctively, he gestured for everyone else to remain as they were, sensing the volatility of the man before them. Alasdair was very obviously upset. His red hair was an unkempt mess that stood upright from the crown of his head, and his amber eyes were alight with pure energy. Lev cautiously approached the man. Alasdair nodded as he closed the distance between them. "It is good to see everyone well."

Lev also nodded in response. "Yes, everyone took your lead and outran the storm. Even the pack-horse remains with us."

Alasdair pursed his lips with discontent and his thick dark brows drew together into a frown. "I should have known better," he said. "I was derelict in my duty. Now my faithful lloryk is dead. You are lucky to have escaped the same fate."

Levander shook his head. "You are being too hard on yourself, my friend. I know you feel responsible, but you are only a man. Your thoughts have been elsewhere as of late, and that is to be expected. No one blames you for this. Sometimes these things just happen."

Aladair shook his head. "No. Not to me. I was trained better than this. I have failed not only the people that comprise this group, but the animals as well. They trust me to make the best decisions for all of us. I am unworthy."

It was Lev's turn to frown. "You are only unworthy if you allow one mistake to tilt your world so far down. Granted, you may have failed at this particular task, but no man is perfect. The only way to rectify the wrong that has been done is to be sure it never happens again. In the process you will have learned something and become a better ranger." Lev paused and then continued. "And mayhap even a better man."

Alasdair sighed and ran a hand through the tangled mass of his hair, gripping it almost savagely for a moment before dropping the hand away to slap it against his thigh. Lev suddenly realized why the hair looked as abominable as it did. His heart went out to the man, for he could feel that Alasdair truly felt responsible for the group. He respected the young ranger for that.

Lev slowly closed the distance between them and then placed a comforting hand on Alasdair's shoulder. "Come, my friend. You have given your comrade the honor she deserves. She now resides in a better place."

Alasdair glanced down at the fallen lloryk once more and then nodded. "We had best find a suitable campsite for the night."

Lev smiled and slightly increased the grip on his shoulder for a moment. "Indeed, brother."

A flicker of surprise passed over Alasdair's handsome face before he turned to accept the ropes of the pack horse from Mateo, who had chosen to approach in spite of Lev's gesture for the group to remain distant. Lev was similarly taken aback by his own statement. However, he was able to recognize the truth of it right away. He had begun to think of these people as replacements for the brethren he had lost when he broke away from the Brotherhood of the Kronshue. Inasmuch, his loyalty towards them had grown. In almost every sense of the words, they had become his brothers and sisters.

Only one day he hoped that Jezibel Pyratt would agree to be so much more.

Levander mounted his horse and followed behind the rest of the group. It was his customary position, for he felt he could see so much better at the rear. It allowed him to view all of his charges as they made their way before him, and then to keep near constant vigil behind them. With his innate ability to detect approaching danger, sentry-work was one of his strengths. Of course, the twister was different. His ability only encompassed any danger posed by other humanoid beings. The natural world . . . well, that was best left up to rangers and druids.

It wasn't long before they found a suitable place for setting up an encampment. Once stopped, everyone quickly went about their duties for the evening. While Alasdair and Cedric went to procure some meat for the stew-pot, Vikhail and Vardec set about helping Jezzie make preparations for the evening meal. Cervantes and Talemar busied themselves by setting out everyone's bedrolls, and Mateo shouldered the hearty task of seeing to the burden beasts. This night, Lev would aid the boy in this task, for no one seemed to have been injured during their escape from the storm. He would give each of the animals some extra attention to make certain that they were strong for the next day of travel.

The men were quick to return with a sack of ptarmigan, the flightless birds that took up residence in most of the grasslands that encompassed western Ansalar. Jezzie and the halfen brothers got to work on them right away, thanking the hunters for their efforts. Alasdair and Cedric were jovial, claiming that the creatures had been easy to hunt. Of course, it was because their populations were high this time of year, not to mention that many of them were still nesting. Lev couldn't help but be sucked into their enthusiasm, for there had been too little of that emotion as of late.

As the food underwent preparation, the men settled down to their weapons and armor. Spirits were high, and it wasn't long before a sparring match was initiated. Lev was gratified to see Alasdair and Cervantes take opposing sides of the arena. Things had changed between them since Jonesy and Tiger left, and it was definitely for the better. After so long, the group had finally started to come together. Old differences were set aside, and past transgressions dealt with. The men competed against one another not only to win, but also to make one another *better warriors*. Lev found himself gesturing to Mateo, indicating to the boy that he should join in the camaraderie. Mateo smiled his appreciation and jogged to where the others gathered. Vikhail and Vardec clapped him on the shoulders, already having deserted Jezibel at the stew-pot. Lev glanced over, only to find the woman smiling in his direction. He returned the gesture, and then focused his attention back to the horse before him. He patted the animal soundly on his neck and was rewarded with an answering nicker deep within the animal's throat. Grinning to himself, Lev moved on to the next beast . . .

✖✖✖✖✖

Aeris slowly walked into the warm chamber. She sniffed at the air, the scent of a forge burning nearby. Glancing about, she took note of it at the far end of the room and then the weaponry and armor lining the walls, each piece a fine specimen that would be easily desired by anyone who knew how to wield or wear it. She gripped the strap of her pack, the rod nestled within. She had finally mastered the infusions and activation necessary to make it into a weapon suitable for combat. However, she hoped to create something more from it. It would be something that could be used only by her, having the ability to deflect any other user. And it would fit her perfectly.

Aeris simply called it "Lightening Glove".

"Kin I 'elp you, ma lady?"

Aeris swung around to face the halfen man who emerged from the entry to a side tunnel nearby. He was dressed in plain tunic and trousers. A wide leather belt around his waist held the instruments of his labors: a hammer, chisel, pair of tongs, and mayhap what looked like a bending fork. Below the belt he wore an apron. He wiped his hands on it in an attempt to remove the soot that covered them. However, as the apron itself was covered with soot as well, he wasn't making all that much progress.

"By any chance, are you the braxen-smith Nampaul?" she asked.

The halfen regarded her intently. "Who's askin'?"

"Uh, me. I'm Aeris Timberlyn, one of the students brought here from Shayamalan. Please, if you know where he is, I really need to speak with him."

The halfen ceased his efforts at wiping the soot off his hands and continued to regard her for a moment. Then, "I am Nampaul. What'cha need ta talk ta me fer?"

Aeris gave him a tentative smile. "Well, I have this rod . . ." Aeris swung her shoulder pack before her and pulled out the rod she had infused. Nampaul reached out and took it from her, holding it up close to his eyes for inspection. After a moment he nodded.

"Yes, 'tis my own work," he said as he looked back up at her.

Aeris cast him a questioning look. "How can you tell?"

The halfen smith simply shrugged his broad shoulders. "A smith kin always tell 'is own work from dat of anudder."

Aeris nodded. "Well, I need your help. You see, I have infused this rod with the magic I chose to be discharged from it. However, I don't want to have to hold onto a rod whilst riding astride a dragon in the middle of battle. I would rather wear it like a glove. You see, I can imagine it being more functional in such a capacity, less likelihood of dropping something that I'm actually wearing as opposed to carrying."

The halfen regarded her speculatively as he pondered her request. He then shook his head slowly back and forth. "I dunno. Such a glove may prove ta be a bit cumbersome. Da braxen contained widdin 'is 'ere rod wud need ta be melted down, an' den carefully remade in da shape 'o da glove. I fear 'at da size of it would be more a hindrance dan 'elp."

Aeris became thoughtful, considering the halfen's words. Damn, she had been so excited at the prospect that she had gone and hunted the braxen smith down by herself. She had been so certain he could help her. Holding out her hand, she accepted the rod back into her palm. Then she had an idea. "But what if the braxen could be spread out, perhaps structured into a glove that fit up the length of my arm? Would that help with the bulk a bit?"

Nampaul placed his sooty hand beneath his chin and rubbed at the dark beard growing there. Once gain his expression was pensive. But this time, he nodded. "Yes, may'ap that cud work." He then took her forearm into his hands. "T'would extend up t'about 'ere." He indicated to a place just below her elbow.

With a smile, Aeris only nodded. The pads of his fingers were rough and calloused, and they scraped against her skin as he moved her arm this way and that. They left sooty imprints on her flesh. Finally noticing the marks he'd made, Nampaul mumbled an apology as she attempted to brush it away. "Ma lady, so sorry ta 'ave . . .."

Aeris shook her head and interrupted as she pulled her arm from his grasp. "No. No apology is needed. It is I who should be thanking you. Please, when can we get started?"

Nampaul offered her his first smile, the wrinkles around his eyes deepening with the gesture. "Why, as early as t'morra mornin'. I 'ave nuthin' pressin' ta work on at da moment. Ya chose da perfect time ta come ta me."

Aeris felt the excitement well up within her. "I'll be here just after sunrise."

"I'll be awaitin', ma lady."

Aeris nodded, then turned and left the chamber, restraining herself from the insane desire to jump up and down like a child. She hurried through the passageway back towards the outside where Jaxom patiently awaited her. She began to slow her pace only when she made the realization that she was already scheduled to meet Demeter Kordrian the next morning for a session of personal training.

Aeris almost stopped in the passage. Damn! The excitement of having the opportunity to work with the braxen-smith must have temporarily overridden her senses. And it wasn't like she could go back now. She would look like an idiot. Hells, Demeter Kord would be angry with her if she didn't turn up for their meeting.

Jaxom raised his head from his forelegs as she emerged onto the ledge. <Come, sit with me for a while,> he said.

Aeris gave a heavy sigh and flopped herself against the warm scaliness of his side. She knew he was aware of her situation. She could feel his mind ruminating over it, hoping to offer her some type of advice. Several moments passed before he spoke. <Elirya, I am pleased that the smith is willing to work with you. It is such an honor for one so renowned to accept a project such as yours. It is very kind of him to do you this favor.>

Aeris continued to lean there against her dragon. Jaxom, who was many years her senior, had wisdom far exceeding her own. Inasmuch, he was more apt to place value where value was due. She nodded her head in understanding, recognizing the actions she must take. By the gods, what would she ever do without him?

Sensing that she understood, Jaxom gave a satisfied rumble as he curved his long neck to bring his head closer to hers. Aeris lovingly accommodated him, scratching her fingernails along his jaw and the ridge over his nearest eye. She even cracked a smile when his eyelids closed with contentment. <You know I love you,> she said.

The dragon suddenly paused, his silver eyes opening to bore into her intensely. <It is the first time I have heard you speak those words to me.>

Aeris stepped away from him and planted both hands at her hips. <But you can sense how I feel about you through our link,> she replied.

<It is one thing to feel it through our link, but quite another to hear the words spoken.>

<Then I shall endeavor to say it more often,> she said with a smile.

Jaxom only continued his rumble as Aeris vaulted onto his back. On the morrow, she would send Faleema to Demeter Kordrian to tell him that she would be unable to meet with him until later in the day. Meanwhile, she would assist the smith at his forge, learning all she could about braxen.

Jaxom fell from the ledge to catch the air current not far below. Aeris raised her arm in victory, for within the seven-day she would have the weapon she yearned for.

�֍ ✖ ✖ ✖ ✖

It was almost mid-day when Tigerius and Jonesy slowly brought their lloryk to a halt. Before them rose the Sartingel Mountains. Two days of constant travel would take Jonesy close to where she wanted to be. The druids would surely find her and escort her the remaining distance to Krathil-lon. Tiger remained anxious about leaving her, but the farther north he had traveled, the sicklier he had become. More strongly than ever he was drawn to the west, and he found it increasingly difficult to deny those urges. Never in his entire life had he felt so torn.

Damn, he couldn't help but wonder why he felt so beholden to a girl who had already expressed her disinterest in any help he might be willing to offer.

Tiger dismounted and placed a staying hand on the other lloryk's closest hindquarter as Jonesy did the same. He noticed that she was more careful of her movements as her body gradually accommodated the growing child. They both stood there for a moment, a bit closer than most people might. Their friendship had grown and the closeness felt natural. It made Tiger feel even more indecisive.

He struggled to keep the strain from his voice. "Are you sure you don't want me to stay with you?"

Jonesy nodded. "I am certain."

Tiger's lips pulled tight. "You know this is difficult for me. I can't help but feel that you might need me."

Jonesy nodded. "I know."

He breathed deeply and then let it go as he stepped forward and splayed his hand over her belly. If she wasn't so thin, he wouldn't be able to feel the slight swell indicative of the progressing pregnancy. Of course only he would feel it, for anyone else would simply consider it an aspect of Jonesy's natural shape.

He spoke the pre-requisite farewell, cringing with each word. "May the sun shine upon you and the child as you journey. And may Destiny be your guide as you endeavor to overcome the forces against you."

Jonesy placed her palm on Tiger's cheek. "We will meet again one day."

He nodded brusquely and pulled her close, enveloping her in a fiercely gentle embrace. He forced himself to pull away, placing his hands at her waist. With the barest of effort, he set her astride once more. She looked down at him from green eyes and he swallowed convulsively before turning away to mount his own lloryk. When they were ready, each saluted the other and walked away to begin their separate paths, his to the west and hers to the north.

Jonesy rode deeper into the foothills of the Sartingel range. Only when darkness threatened did she stop. She didn't bother to light a campfire, deciding instead to just light the lantern she kept hanging from her travel pack. It offered just the amount of illumination she needed to tend to the lloryk and then herself before settling down for the night. Of course she hardly slept, for she had never been so alone before, and she found herself second guessing her decision to conduct her endeavors unaided.

Once the barest hint of dawn crested the horizon, Jonesy was riding again. She knew that time was of the essence and that each moment she spent alone placed her more at risk. The path became steeper as she entered the mountains, and she imagined it couldn't be much longer before the druids recognized an intruder on their lands. She was right, and with alacrity they took her to Krathil-lon. Once there she spoke with Father Dremathian. He immediately recognized her need to be home, to try and repair the damage that had been wrought. He didn't question her about the rest of the group; it was almost as though he knew she was there on a clandestine mission. He was sympathetic to her plight, and more than willing to help put a stop to the war that raged between two realms that had once been at peace.

Jonesy rested within the sanctuary of Krathil-lon for one night. The next morning found her at the underground portal system she had arrived through more than a moon cycle ago. Tightly holding the ropes of her lloryk, she vaguely heard the voice of one of the druids where he stood next to Father Dremathian and read the incantation that would open the portal. She watched the swirling colors that ensued, and once they stabilized, she stepped within.

Jonesy walked into darkness. The lloryk beside her snorted and then whinnied in fear. He suddenly reared up and her shoulder nearly dislocated as she struggled to keep hold of the rope. She stumbled back just as he brought his forefeet back to the ground. She considered letting go, for he could easily trample her, but instead she attempted to soothe him in spite of the lack of light. With a soft voice and gentle hand, she was able to quiet the beast long enough for her to grab the lantern.

Luckily for her, the small flame was still there. Opening the shutter, she allowed more air within, and the flame brightened. She opened it more, and once the flame was bright enough, she thrust the lantern before her. It illuminated the walls of a small chamber very similar to the one from whence she had just come. Stepping forward, she felt something crunch beneath her feet. Looking down, she saw that it was pieces of glass. She frowned and glanced all about, wondering what it could be from.

The lloryk snorted again. The shadows the lantern cast made him almost as fearful as the total lack of light they initially experienced. She soothed him once more, and when he was ready, she led him towards the arched doorway. Jonesy found herself in a corridor. The walls were more confining than what the lloryk was accustomed, but he seemed to trust Jonesy and allowed her to comfort him as they walked. Luckily for her, the corridor was short, leading them into another chamber. It was much larger than the one they had just left, and it led her to the outside.

Jonesy walked out of the cavern and into the western edge of the Selmist Forest. To her left lay the Bryton Hills, and to her right was the remainder of the wood. If she traveled north, she would reach the Denegal River within approximately two to three days depending on her haste. Her goal was to locate the battle front. She imagined that the Karlislian encampment must be somewhere along the river; she had only to find it. However, for all she knew, they had procured the river and the encampment was located somewhere on the other side. Regardless, Karlislian scouts would surely be patrolling this side of the Denegal, and after a while she would certainly come into contact with them.

Jonesy proceeded north through the hilly forest, quickly becoming disconcerted by the nearness of her brother. Of course she'd felt the prickling sensation before, back when she was on the run and hiding out in the port city of Yortec. Maybe it was because they shared familial ties, or perhaps it was her knack of perceiving the proximity of danger, but her ability had helped her to avoid Rigel long enough to meet Aeris. Jonesy would remain eternally grateful for the aid she'd received from the Elvandaharian princess, and believed it was what ultimately saved her from Rigel.

That evening Jonesy camped near the outskirts of the forest. Just like before, she lit only the flame of her lantern. In spite of her fatigue, she remained wakeful throughout most of the night. Mostly she thought about Tigerius and wondered how he fared on his own mission. Without him she felt so alone, and the sounds of the forest at night were much more disturbing, even with the lloryk standing sentinel barely an arm-length behind her. Placing a hand over her belly, she also thought of Cervantes and her heart ached. What she wouldn't give to see his handsome face again, to hear his voice whispering in her ear, and to feel his arms around her.

It seemed like forever before the first light of day emerged. Jonesy quickly rose to break her fast and continue her journey. She traveled steadily through much of the morning, the trees becoming sparser as she traveled north. She was shocked when some men stepped out of the surrounding trees. Hells, she never anticipated that the forces of Elvandahar would be situated so far south of the river.

They were rangers, each with an arrow nocked and ready to fly with only the slightest provocation. She felt her heart skip a beat and her breath caught in her throat. The men quickly encircled her, the closest one lowering his bow and taking the rope of her anxious lloryk. One man emerged from among the others, his weapon still looped over one arm to cross his back. His tone was sardonic and he regarded her with the false smile people tended to wear when they imagined the most reprehensible things. "It seems that this isn't going to be your lucky day," he said in heavily accented common.

Fear coursed through her. To these men she was just another human woman, a potential Karlislian enemy, someone to be despised. She could only imagine what they might do before they killed her. Jonesy unconsciously tightened her legs around the lloryk, the customary signal for him to move forward. Sensitive to her surge of emotion and his desire to do her bidding, he suddenly swung his head up. The ranger holding onto the rope cursed in hinterlic and startled the animal. Jonesy instinctively lowered herself over the lloryk's back as he reared, his cloven hooves pawing the air before bringing them back aground. The ranger struggled to maintain his hold on the rope, but cursed again when the lloryk pinned his ears and rushed backward, roughly pulling the rope from the man's hand. The animal then swung around, hindquarters bunching as he placed all of his weight onto his rear legs to execute the maneuver.

For the barest moment, Jonesy imagined they might win themselves free.

Unfortunately it was too late. Three more rangers were already leaping forward to accost the wayward lloryk. A fourth gripped her thigh. Her heart beat a staccato rhythm against her ribs as she instinctively kicked out. The man went soaring through the air, but another was there to take his place as the first one landed at least a farlo away. The second one grabbed her about the waist and roughly pulled her from the lloryk's back. She heard the animal scream stridently at the abuse and she fought a sudden wave of nausea. She placed her hands along the ranger's forearm in a pathetic attempt to loosen his grip about her vulnerable belly, pushing against it as he dragged her over to the leader who had stood silently by to watch the fray.

Jonesy continued to fight the sickness as she slowly looked up at her captor. His brown eyes were cold as they regarded her from an indifferent face that had mayhap seen its own share of hardship. "State your name and your business for being here alone in the middle of nowhere without an escort," he growled.

Jonesy's heart quickened again. She was so afraid, but knew she couldn't show him that. She didn't want to die, but foolishly chose a path that could easily end in that fate. "Who the Hells are you to ask? Take your filthy hands off me!" She followed with a brief struggle to reinforce her statement.

The hinterlean restraining her tightened his grip on her arm. "Right now I am your judge, jury, and executioner," said the leader. "Tell me who the Hells you are, wench."

Jonesy decided to use his preconceived notion to her advantage. "I am nothing more than you think me to be. I recently departed from a caravan to make my way to Karlisle."

The man frowned and narrowed his eyes. "Well, I would think that you would know that Karlisle is at war and has closed the gates to most of her cities and towns located near the borders of Elvandahar."

Jonesy offered her own frown. "Well, I happen to be quite renowned throughout the kingdom. It will be easy for me to gain entry."

The man cocked his head. "Damnation, you must be something special. Tell me then, who are you that you would be someone so renowned to be allowed entry during wartime?"

It was then another man stepped forward, an older one. His eyes were wide. "Hells, this isn't just any woman, Karrik. She is Joneselia Mondemer, the long lost youngest daughter of the King of Karlisle. I would know her anywhere!"

Jonesy felt a rush of alarm and the ranger keeping her restrained tightened his grip. The leader turned to the newcomer. "What? How do you know?"

"She looks just like the late Queen Isadora, especially her eyes."

Karrik swung his gaze back over to her, reaching out to grab her. The other ranger released her as the leader jerked her forward, his fingers biting mercilessly into the soft flesh of her arm. "Is what Mardok says true? Are you the Lady Joneselia Mondemer?"

Jonesy considered lying until she looked deeply into his eyes. They were devoid of emotion. He knew the answer already; believed the words of his comrade. He just wanted to hear her affirmation. Her hesitation was enough for him to take action. Karrik's expression was fierce as he pushed her to the ground. "Mardok, get me some rope."

She recoiled and finally found her voice. She spoke tremulously, a response to the strain her body felt. "Please, all I want is to return home."

The man chuckled mirthlessly and shook his head. "Are you daft woman? There is no way I will let you go. You are my prisoner now."

Jonesy almost choked on her next breath. The leader stepped back as Mardok made his approach. She instinctively reached for her cutlass and crouched into a fighting position. The ranger's eyes widened when he heard the hiss of the weapon leaving the scabbard and danced back as she swept towards him. She vaguely heard the shouts of the other rangers as they rushed to subdue her. She turned to meet them, slashing first at one man, and then another. Suddenly, a searing pain shot through her shoulder. The impact of the arrow sent her stumbling backward, and she was quickly apprehended during her moment of pained confusion.

Jonesy heard the voice of the leader above those of the other rangers. He spoke in hinterlic, imagining mayhap that she wouldn't understand it. "Don't hurt her any more than what she is already. Prince Asgenar will surely want her in decent condition."

She felt the cutlass knocked out of her hand and then her wrists being bound with rope. The pain in her shoulder was excruciating, but she immediately felt the friction of the rope against her skin and knew the area would quickly become raw. At this point she remained passive, her protective efforts now focused on her unborn child. She would not fight, for to do so would definitely cause harm.

Three days passed. Travel was rigorous, for the rangers spared her nothing. They took her out of Karlislian territory and crossed the Denegal River. The men saw to her injuries only once the entire journey, and by the time they reached the hinterlean bivouac she was weak from blood-loss and sleep deprivation. Many times she had almost fallen off her lloryk, and after a while the rangers simply tied her to his back.

However, she was awake enough to be captivated by the scenario through which she finally passed. Hundreds of tents had been pitched, each housing at least five or six fighters. Among them were also several corubis. Their long legs gave them speed, and their beautifully spotted hides helped keep them hidden beneath the shadowed forest canopy. The last time she had seen one of the tall, wemic-like animals was long ago as a child during a visit to Elvandahar with her father. She had learned that the animals were mentally bound to their faelin companions, and the friendship was one that lasted a lifetime.

The rangers wound their way through the center of the bivouac. Jonesy saw the occasional woman or two, those that fought alongside their male counterparts. It was much similar to a human encampment, only here there were much fewer females, and they not being of the more denigrating variety. It was quite pleasant to see a militaristic site without the accompanying whores, and she quickly realized one of the many cultural differences between human and faelin.

The scouts immediately took Jonesy to their leader's tent, or dongo, as they called it. The structure was larger than the rest, and once entering it, she took in the opulence one could somehow achieve within an encampment at wartime. The only reason she noticed was the fact that she'd been somewhat deprived during the past many moons cycles during her travels; almost anything that constituted a shelter overhead was considered elaborate. They passed through the main enclosure before pulling aside another flap that separated it from yet another area. They brought her into the smaller enclosure and she saw a table situated at one side and a bed-pallet at the other.

The men positioned her against the post dominating the center of the enclosure and then bound her ankles under lock and key. They didn't bother with her hands, for the entrance of the dongo would be guarded, not to mention she would be unable to get very far without her legs to carry her. For quite a while Jonesy waited, both hungry and thirsty beyond belief; none of the faelin had offered her anything but the occasional sip of water during their travel. She supposed she couldn't blame them, for she was the daughter of their much hated enemy. Jonesy chose not to say anything, simply endured what she could before succumbing to exhaustion.

She didn't know how much time went by before her eyes snapped open to the sound of someone entering the tent. She heard a man speaking in hinterlic, and it was only a moment later before the flap separating her from the main enclosure was being flung aside. To her immediate dismay, she found herself staring up at an individual she had met only briefly on a few random occasions during her childhood. Jonesy immediately knew who he was; with his moonlight blond hair and dark eyes, she'd always thought him rather handsome.

The man was heir to the throne of Elvandahar, Asgenar Timberlyn.

His gaze settled on her the moment he entered. From her position on the floor, she looked vaguely up at him, only barely recognizing the significance of his presence. She considered rising into a standing position, but her weakness kept her remaining almost motionless. It seemed that all her strength had been used up. She could only stare up into his flawless face, a face her sister should have had the pleasure of seeing for the remainder of her life as his wife.

How she wished Elinora could be there with her now.

Jonesy returned the attentive gaze. Asgenar's eyes were conflicted, yet gave away nothing of the precise nature of the thoughts going on within his mind. Abruptly turning away from her, he shouted in hinterlic to one of the men who stood nearby, gesturing towards her commandingly. The man quickly left to do his master's bidding, and Jonesy was instantly impressed with the magnitude of Asgenar's power over those who served him. She had once desired to command such a response from the servants in her own home. However, she never had the self esteem to impress herself upon others, and there was always someone there to undermine her.

Realistically, she never had a chance.

Asgenar swung his dark eyes back to her, considering her speculatively. He then spoke to her in common, the universal language of the varied races residing throughout Ansalar. Most children learned it alongside their native tongue, hearing it spoken regularly during their daily lives. And if they didn't, they were at a sore disadvantage later in life if they chose a profession which involved traveling from place to place. "My lady, what are you doing here?"

Jonesy frowned and replied in a low voice. "Your men brought me. Why don't *you* tell me the reason I am here, my lord?"

Asgenar's lips pulled into a thin line. "Princess, it is not my desire to force you into submission, but I will do so if the need arises. I repeat, what are you doing here?"

Jonesy swallowed heavily. He expected another answer from her, one that wasn't the truth. By the gods, would she be forced to do what Aeris did all those moon cycles ago and incriminate herself to Magnus and the rest of the group to facilitate her survival?

Jonesy decided to say nothing; she was never good at lying anyway. Even Rigel could testify to that fact. Damnation, all during her journey she had thought only of her confrontation with her brother, not the possibility she could be intercepted by the opposing side. And now she could only assume both he and her father would soon know of her whereabouts.

Hells, she could only imagine the varied outcomes of her situation, and none of them were good.

Asgenar frowned at the young woman sitting on the ground before him. Her green eyes reflected so many things; it was difficult for him to be sure what he was seeing. Foremost there was nobility and strength of spirit. Both were underscored by fear and deep sorrow. He also saw determination and no small amount of doubt. However, even though he could see so much, there was a mysterious quality about her. It was obvious this woman had her secrets, and it wouldn't surprise him should they be of the darker quality.

Asgenar folded his arms before him. Lady Mondemer continued to stare up at him through hallowed eyes. Her complexion was pale, and tendrils of her chestnut hair had escaped the once tight plait that ran down the length of her back. She had been accompanied by a lloryk when they found her, and the animal had been loaded with a blanket and bedroll, a leather pack containing water flasks, food rations, and additional pouches containing chagatha, various teas, and other miscellaneous herbs. Her primary travel pack lay close by, but he could see she had made no efforts to open it. Unless his men had sifted through it, the pack most likely contained another weapon, probably a dagger. Both mug and bowl would also be there, along with small-clothes, fresh tunic and trousers, and a variety of things any woman would need in order to maintain her face, hair, skin, and other body parts.

Yet, the lady had reached for none of those. Instead, she sat there with an arm across her abdomen, too weak to even rise to protect herself should the need arise. The isterian returned. With him was a platter bearing an assortment of fruits, tubers, and legumes-as well as a tall ceramic flask of water and a mug. The servant set everything down on the nearest table. At the sight of the flask, the young woman seemed to brighten a bit. Asgenar hated to think that his men had offered her no water on their journey to the encampment, but he couldn't help but suspect. He bid the isterian to leave them before turning away from the youngest daughter to the King of Karlisle, sister to the one whom was once destined to be his wife.

Asgenar slowly went over to the table and poured some water into the waiting mug. Then he turned and made his way over to his captive. He stopped and knelt before her, but before offering the mug, he repeated his question-this time in a slightly different way. "Joneselia, why are you here? What is a daughter of Karlisle doing behind enemy lines?" He used her name with the hopes of getting an appropriate response, yet he could hardly believe he remembered it for he had heard it only a handful of times throughout his life.

She shook her head. "I didn't know I was behind enemy lines. My purpose is simply to return home," she replied impassively.

Asgenar narrowed his eyes thoughtfully. Hells, this was the girl who had gone missing so soon after her sister's abduction. It wasn't long before they knew she hadn't been taken captive like Elinora, yet she had already thrown the realm into upheaval. He was convinced it played a part in Karlisle's decision to go to war with Elvandahar, albeit an indirect one.

Now, here she was sitting before him, claiming the desire to 'simply return home'. Damnation, where had she been all this time? Did she even realize the uproar she had caused? Did she care?

Asgenar thrust the mug towards her, and once she had taken it, he swiftly returned to his standing position. She seemed so phlegmatic about the situation surrounding her, and he found himself rather irate. Who the Hells did she think she was, gallivanting around with no escort and very little information concerning the war happening within the very place she called home? The childishness of it irked him and he felt his anger escalate.

He turned away as he spoke again. "Where have you been all this time? Didn't you know there were people looking for you?"

There was silence for a moment. "Yes."

Asgenar swung back around. "Doesn't that matter to you?" he said vehemently.

She stared at him from wide eyes. "Yes."

He regarded her with exasperation and then threw up his arms. "So, if you knew they were looking for you, why didn't you make yourself known?"

He watched as she set the empty mug down, her hand trembling before she brought it back to rest at her belly. "I didn't wish to be found," she stated stoically.

Asgenar simply stared at her for a moment. She had her eyes cast to the floor and her complexion had visibly paled. Yet, it didn't entirely diffuse his ire. "Why the Hells not? You had to know what it was doing to your father and to your realm, especially after the loss of your sister . . ." He let his voice trail off and then turned away again. Damn, he couldn't believe she intentionally stayed away even knowing what it was doing to Karlisle.

His statement was met only with more silence. Of course, he hadn't really expected one, given the emotional outburst accompanying it. He rubbed a hand over tired eyes, and then up and back into short blond hair that had a tendency towards randomness-one part sticking out here, and another one there. Yet, it seemed to do him justice enough, for far too many people complimented him on it. But of course he was the future king of Elvandahar; who wouldn't compliment him?

Jonesy regarded Asgenar solemnly. She'd known her last statement wouldn't settle very well with him but she'd said it anyway. She was about to formulate some reply when he was questioning her again.

Asgenar sighed heavily. "So, where have you been hiding?"

She shrugged almost nonchalantly. "I haven't really been hiding. Circumstances made it easy to . . ." She stopped before saying too much. Hells, this man had no idea she had been traveling with his sister, and then a bit later, his brother as well. She had no desire to give a recount of her history, not to mention the turmoil it might cause for him to discover that Aeris was no longer with the group. That is, if he didn't know it already. It would have been Alasdair's decision to inform his brother of such particulars. Of course, she wasn't certain he had done so, especially in light of the fact that Asgenar was probably plotting against Karlisle and might not have the mental capacity to deal with stresses outside that of the strategies he currently planned.

"Easy to what?" he inquired with a gruff tone. Asgenar abruptly swung an arm out behind him and grabbed hold of the nearby chair. He brought it before him and then turned it around. He subsequently seated himself, placing first one arm and then the other over the back.

Jonesy startled with the sudden movement. Asgenar noticed and gave her a moment to settle, his dark brown eyes continuing to regard her intently. There was something about the man before her, something that drew her into him in spite of the interrogation. She didn't quite know what it was. Mayhap it was simply his demeanor; or then again it could be the underlying expression she saw when he looked at her. Perhaps it could be the way he moved, or the warmth of the aura that surrounded him. Damn! She couldn't believe her father had declared war on the very realm with whom they had been on the brink of embracing through Elinora's marriage to this man—a hardened man who might do things to his prisoners that he would never consider doing outside of wartime.

Jonesy swallowed heavily. He awaited her response. "Easy for me to simply disappear until I was ready."

"Ready for what?" he asked shortly.

For a moment Jonesy didn't know what to say, and she felt her heart accelerate in her chest. "Ready to return home, of course."

Asgenar's gaze became hooded with the obscurity of her responses. He had learned very little since entering the dongo, and he was becoming frustrated. Jonesy hated the position in which she now found herself, for she didn't want to tell the enemy that she'd left Karlisle to escape her own brother, and that she had striven to remain undetected to save herself from certain death. She didn't want to tell him that joining Aeris' group was a boon, for it removed her from Rigel's grasp indeterminately when she boarded the *Sea Maiden* and subsequently sailed out to sea.

Eeegads, how ridiculous would that sound?

"So, what made you decide to leave Karlisle to begin with?" he replied. "And what are these 'circumstances' you spoke about that made it easy for you to avoid your duty?" His eyes glittered with unsuppressed disparagement, and she couldn't help but cringe under the criticism.

Instead of answering his question, she replied with one of her own, one to which she so much wished the answer. "Have you informed Karlisle of my appropriation?"

Asgenar's gaze remained impassive. She could see him deciding whether or not to answer, for she hadn't bothered to give any appropriate answers to the questions he'd imposed first. The possibility of an answer was bleak.

Much to her surprise, he offered a response. Perhaps it was because he hoped for one in return, one that was more informative than what she'd provided before. Or perhaps he was soft at heart, for it was probably very easy to see how much the answer meant to her.

Damn, mayhap it was both.

Asgenar shook his head. "No, as of yet, Karlisle has not been informed."

Jonesy breathed in deeply and then exhaled. She tried to stop the sudden trembling that overcame her, but it was to no avail. Seeing this response to his answer, Asgenar was immediately vacating the chair and kneeling beside her. She continued to shake, the strain of the last few days taking its toll. At first he didn't seem to know what to do, but then he was enfolding her in his arms. It was just what she needed. Wrapped in his warm embrace she felt a sense of safety, a feeling she never experienced except in the presence of her companions.

For several moments Jonesy wept in the shelter of his embrace. She couldn't think beyond the immediacy of the moment, and was just focused on the relief she felt knowing that her location was still unknown. It must have been weighing on her more than she realized. When the trembling ceased, Asgenar slowly took his arms from around her and sat back on his heels. He regarded her solemnly and seemed to be waiting for her to say something.

"That is good," she said in a quavering voice. "More than I expected."

Asgenar frowned as he rose from beside her, splaying his hands outward. "Why? Why is it so important that your own father remain unaware you have been taken into my custody?" Asgenar paused and then continued. "And what benefit does it offer me? Our kingdoms are at war. I need to use everything I have at my disposal to get an upper hand." He then leaned towards her. "The lives of my people depend on it."

Jonesy immediately understood the truth of his words. Prince Asgenar had no reason to keep her captivity a secret, for he could easily use her to barter for the lives of those who might be within Karlisle's detention. This realization weighed on her, yet she shuddered with the thought of telling him to reveal her whereabouts.

Jonesy shook her head and swallowed heavily. "I agree; there is no benefit to you to keep me hidden." She paused for a moment, loath to continue. Then with a lowered voice, "I can't tell you why I am hoping you will find it in your heart to keep my secret."

His expression shifted to one of stupefaction, followed by ire. "Woman, do you think me a complete fool? I demand a reason for my silence upon this matter! Not to mention, I still have yet to hear the 'circumstances' behind your being here!" he said caustically.

Jonesy remained silent and watched the turmoil play across his features for several moments before Asgenar rose abruptly from the chair, turned and swept out of the tent. She stared after him for a while, wondering what action he may decide to take as a result of her unwillingness to answer his questions. As a wave of renewed fear washed over her, Jonesy held a hand to her churning stomach. Anxiety combined with water intake without the added benefit of food was making her nauseous. She scrambled as close to the periphery of the tent as she could before vomiting, the much needed liquid slowly soaking the ground until nothing remained but the mild scent of someone having been sick.

Jonesy slowly withdrew from the rancid spot. Her body ached from the rigors of travel since leaving Tigerius and being captured by the hinterleans. She berated herself for the physical weakness, and even more, the mental. She sniffed back the tears that threatened to trickle from her nose, and she struggled to shimmy herself back to the post. She then slumped against it and put her hands to her face. Damn, maybe she could have at least told Prince Asgenar that her brother was a greedy bastard who wanted the crown only for his own malefic purposes. Or perhaps leave Rigel out and instead focus on her father, whom everyone already knew was mentally unbalanced. Both of those things would be sufficient for Elvandahar to realize that Karlisle's knowledge of her whereabouts could be a detriment to her personal welfare.

Not that Elvandahar would care that much.

Once her capture was known, Karlisle would barter for her release. Elvandahar might very well regain all those poor souls who had been taken prisoner during battle. Then, once she was within the clutches of Rigel's army . . .

Jonesy shuddered convulsively. She wrapped her arms around her belly and thought of the tiny being that resided deep within. She hated the possibility of something happening to it, for she loved the child already. It had been conceived of the love she shared with Cervantes, a physical testament to their union. She wondered what thoughts he might be having now, aside from those that focused on her desertion. One day, when they met again, would he still love her? Or would he despise her for having left him without a word?

Sobbing piteously, Jonesy slumped sideways onto the ground. She curled upon herself, bringing both hands and knees to her chin. By the gods, if Elvandahar were to deliver her to Karlisle in her current condition, she would surely meet her demise. She could already imagine what Rigel might do with her. There would be nothing to stop him, for none of her supporters in the city were aware of her return, and he might not care that she had left a trail.

She had no one to back her up. *Somehow, she had left her comrades behind.*

CHAPTER FIFTEEN

As stealthily as possible for a being his size, Jaxom crept through the foliage of the thick jungle. Beneath her helm, Aeris blinked away more sweat that ran into her eyes and cursed to herself. In general, Haldorr was a hot place, and as such, it was sweltering beneath the canopy of the trees. Beneath her armored vest she wore a sleeveless tunic, the only shortcut she could take with her attire, for her padded leather trousers were a must.

Attempting to remain alert, Aeris glanced around them and into the surrounding flora. Topping many of the tall stalks that were so abundant in the area were large vibrantly colored flowers whose heads were so heavy they drooped. One could easily see within, each flower sporting feathery yellow stamens and bright red pistils. There were bushes that had deep green leaves half her size, all streaked with yellow veins. Another plant had roots that grew at the surface of the ground as opposed to deep within, making it difficult for the unwary to trip and fall.

In spite of the alluring scenery, Aeris' attention kept returning to her discomfort. Intensely frustrated, she finally swept the offending helm from off her head. Sensing her ire, Jaxom stopped to glance back. His silver eyes glinted with amusement as she emitted a low growl in her throat. She swept her hand over her forehead and back into her hair. <What the Hells are you smiling about?> she grouched.

<You are such an endearing creature, Elirya. I simply can't help myself.>

Aeris frowned. <Well try harder. And what are we stopping for? We are in the midst of a potential coup.>

Jaxom sighed and continued forward. He then issued a chuckle through their link. <A coup, hunh? Aren't you being a bit presumptuous?>

<No, only determined,> she replied huffily.

It was a game, one suggested by Demeter Fo to torment them. Aeris, Faleema, Fo, and Falon were on one team while Thulnar, Kord, Franchie, and Saliel made up the other. Each team was required to incapacitate the other while attempting to capture a flag that had been carefully hidden by each. The only rule was that the spellcasters were not to use magic. It was a rather universal game, one played by children all across Shandahar every day. Yet, it was also one that would test the mettle of both dragon and rider.

Jaxom continued through the jungle as Aeris fiddled with the helm. Damn, she hated wearing the thing, especially in this heat. She needed to put it back on, but mayhap give her head just a moment longer to cool down.

All of a sudden Jaxom stopped. Aeris looked up just as a dragon barreled from out of the trees ahead. <Elirya, 'ware and sit tight!>

In a silvery blur, Riloriandrix was upon them. Jaxom shuddered with the force of the impact, and Aeris' helm dropped while trying to reposition it over her hair. She cursed her foul luck, immediately looking in the direction of Rilo's rider. By the expression on his face, she divined Kordrian's intent the moment before he took action.

Aeris steeled herself as Kord leaped from Rilo's back to join her on Jaxom. Her thoughts instantly shifted to the last time her dragon was boarded, and a rush of distress swept through her. Jaxom immediately sensed her fear. Aeris lay herself flat across his neck as he reared into the air, shaking himself in an effort to dislodge the threat to his bondmate. Struggling to maintain position, Kordrian insinuated an arm around Aeris' middle and looped his legs around hers. In retaliation, she applied her elbow forcefully into his abdomen and was rewarded with the terrible pain associated with striking a very hard surface. She had conveniently forgotten that Kord was wearing his braxen-link armor, just like she was.

Rilo took the opportunity to push against Jaxom in an attempt to topple him. Meanwhile, Aeris grappled for the dagger that was sheathed in her boot. Feeling her struggle, Kordrian swiftly took her forearms in a vise-like grip. Aeris savagely twisted herself within the restraints of the battle-harness, and was even able to wrest one arm away from her attacker. She knocked the dark helm from off Kordrian's head. Glancing over her shoulder, she noted the expression of surprise cross his handsome face before shifting to anger. Before he could react Aeris twisted around, closed her hand into a fist, and pulled back. Her knuckles struck Kordrian's jaw and his head snapped sideways. Rilo pushed even harder and Jaxom staggered beneath her weight. Through their link, Aeris could sense his fury. He hissed his vexation, and just as he moved to retaliate, Jaxom communicated his intentions to Aeris. He lunged for Rilo, his teeth just narrowly missing the vulnerable area of her neck. He then coiled around, and with his claws extended, raked them over the drenna's shoulder.

Aeris startled as Rilo screamed. Kordrian shook his head to clear it just before his hand snaked out and caught her by the hair. He pulled her head back to his chest and then subdued Aeris within his embrace. He wrapped his arms snugly around her, pressing the side of his face against hers. She felt his ragged breaths as they moved the errant tendrils of her hair, and she vaguely smelled the scent of the bath oils he'd used that morning beneath the pervading odor of sweat. She knew he could feel Rilo's pain, and that he was incensed. She had to remind herself that he was not truly her enemy, and that she should not strive to kill him. She wondered if he was reminding himself of the same.

Aeris renewed her struggled within Kordrian's embrace, hoping to offer a distraction as she maneuvered her hand to unclasp the harness restraining strap. Once free, Aeris abruptly swung her leg around and reversed her position on Jaxom's back. Time seemed to slow as she found herself face-to-face with the man who had become her primary instructor. She could suddenly feel it, an energy between them that had been hinted at briefly once before. His gaze became piercing, and she knew he could feel it too. He regained his grip on her as his eyes swept to her mouth. They then moved down to her chest, where the tops of her breasts swelled slightly above the restrictive armor. Her heart pounded in her chest and she felt her breath catch in her throat . . .

In spite of the pain Jaxom's claws inflicted, Rilo was quick to retaliate. She lashed her tail around in a swift arc, landing it across Jaxom's side like a whip. Aeris took a swift intake of breath, felt her own body tremor in response to Jaxom's pain. She felt Kord's hands tighten on her arms and looking into his eyes she thought she saw a softening in his expression. Jaxom shielded her from the pain as best he could, slamming up his mental barriers as Rilo's tail struck him yet again.

This time Aeris arched her body in response to the vicious lash, closing her eyes tightly shut. It struck Jaxom along the same side, causing previously damaged scales to tear away. She felt Kordrian wrap his arms around her as she slumped forward, Jaxom staggering beneath the onslaught. Then, while Jaxom forced himself into some semblance of recovery, Aeris found her chance. She reached for her dagger, bringing it up just in time to meet Kord's blade where it had begun to approach her vulnerable neck.

Aeris' heart beat double-time as she strained against her mentor. Her arm trembled beneath the pressure Kord placed on the dagger, and it was disconcerting to see his blade waver ever closer. Making it so much more difficult was Jaxom's movement. If only she could find a way to connect to her bondmate on a deeper level. Perhaps they could be so attuned that she would be able to anticipate his next movement. Aeris took a shuddering breath and blinked away the sweat that trickled down her forehead and into her eye. Demeter Kord's customary unforgiving gaze seemed to soften once more for a moment as it focused again on her mouth. She couldn't help but notice that his eyelashes were pale, just like the color of his hair, and that he had a tiny scar alongside his nearest temple. It was then she realized neither of them had yet to utter a single word.

Gathering all her remaining strength, Aeris suddenly swung her legs upward. Maintaining her balance, she dropped back on Jaxom's neck as she kicked Kordrian with all the power she could muster. He fell back as her feet landed solidly on his chest, and he scrambled at the harness to catch himself as he descended from Jaxom's back. Sensing Aeris' victory, Jaxom leaped forward, just narrowly missing another swipe of Rilo's tail. It whipped over Aeris' head, the breeze it created stirring the hair that had become loosened from its customary plait. Then they were away from the enemy, bounding through the jungle with vast strides and no intention of stopping.

That is, until they saw another dragon appearing up ahead. Jaxom hesitantly slowed his headlong rush as they approached Seldonraxis and his rider. Forigard turned and gestured to them excitedly. "It's here. We've found it!"

Sheathing her dagger and glancing nervously back into the trees behind them, Aeris replied. "What? Is it the flag?"

Fo nodded, his blue eyes sparkling with excitement.

"So, why don't you go take it then!" she exclaimed.

Fo's nod turned into a shake of his head. "Damaeris, don't you remember the rules? A demeter cannot be the one to physically capture the flag. It must be a student or quarter-master."

Of course she remembered. She had thought it a stupid rule. If they were a team, everyone should be equal. She shook her own head. "You don't understand; we don't have time. Take the damned flag. Riloriandrix and Kordrian are just behind us."

Forigard's eyes widened. "Aeris, no. I can't . . ."

Aeris glanced again behind her and saw a flash of silver in the trees. "Do it! Take it now!" she shouted.

Seldonraxis rushed towards the flag as Jaxom turned in place to meet the oncoming threat. Rilo crashed through the jungle foliage without care, fueled by her desire to protect the much sought-after object of their attention. Aeris steeled herself for the fight, not realizing what Jaxom was doing until it was too late. Having already stimulated his fire with an intake of air into his third air-sac, Jaxom paused for only a moment before he was breathing out. The trees before them were incinerated within moments, and from within the conflagration Aeris heard a scream.

Damn, Rilo was *angry.*

Just as Aeris began to wonder what was going on with Fo and Seldon, the silver Rilo swiftly emerged from out of the smoldering trees. Jaxom trumpeted his intent, and Aeris could feel the depth of his anger through their link. For him, the game had become serious when Rilo lashed at him so vehemently with her tail, for his claw attack had been nothing in comparison. He now held no qualms about reciprocating, hence the fire. Hells, he was up for a good fight.

In regards to herself, Aeris wasn't quite so certain. From astride his bondmate, Kordrian looked so intimidating, and Aeris couldn't help but think he was angered by the fact she had kicked him off of Jaxom's back. The thought was founded when, capturing her gaze with his own, Kord first held up her helm in one hand, followed with his own helm in the other. He then raised an eyebrow. Curse the man . . .

<We have the flag. We are heading in the direction of home base.> Aeris was heartened to hear Seldon's voice in her mind. Jaxom didn't bother with a

reply as he faced Rilo. She feigned an attempt to rush past him in pursuit of Seldon, but Jaxom blocked her path, hissing his displeasure. Hells, Aeris knew she was up for quite a ride unless she found some way off his back.

Jaxom became still for a moment. <You are right, Elirya, If you wish it, you should dismount now.>

Already free from the restraints offered by the battle-harness, Aeris hastily leaped from Jaxom's back. It was a maneuver she had practiced many times, one she had perfected since beginning her training. Once on the ground, she rolled to a halt, rising with her short sword in hand. She immediately assessed the situation, watched as the two silver dragons both screamed and rushed one another. It was then she realized Rilo was riderless.

Aeris spun in place to find Kordrian behind her, his own blade held before him. Now was the telling moment. Were those weapons practice sessions she had begun to assiduously attend with quartermaster Falon doing her any bit of good? Wearing black armor, he looked just as the enemy should: dark and imposing. Kordrian swept towards her, his blade reflecting the rays of the late-day sun as he arced it first this way and then that. Aeris dodged his first swing and parried his second. She labored beneath the power behind his attack. In spite of her skill, she quickly realized she needed much more training than what she had received already. Of course, she was already tired from their previous encounter.

Pirouette, block, retreat—Aeris quickly began to tire. Sweat dripped down her back beneath the armor she wore, and once again she cursed it. In spite of its light-weight nature, the braxen armor had become a liability, for it sapped her remaining strength by adding weight to her body and warmth to her overheated skin. She dodged Kordrian's next swing, his blade just barely slicing across her bare upper arm. She hissed with the sting it caused, and wasn't surprised when she felt the trickling sensation a moment later. Aeris kept moving, and when she finally rallied the strength, she lunged, sweeping her blade in a broad arc. Kordrian just barely raised his sword to block the blow. On light feet she danced around him, and once in position, she hooked her foot around his ankle.

Kordrian faltered as his leg was swept out from under him, but somehow he was able to regain his balance. Aeris cursed to herself. *Damn, that was my last chance.* She swiftly moved in for another attack, but was easily blocked. Kordrian regained his composure, and then rushed towards her.

Aeris staggered beneath his next attack: hating her weakness. She simply wasn't strong or fast enough to be any match against him. She just barely moved quickly enough to avoid his next swing. Nevertheless, she went down onto one knee, her blade held defensively above her head. And when Kord brought his wrath down on her one last time, she hadn't the strength to oppose him. His sword easily broke through her resistance and struck her. Aeris felt herself falling and she landed heavily on her side. For only the barest moment, Aeris registered the concerned face of her mentor looming overhead before her world shifted to dark.

Tigerius kept a steady path across the Tusbirian steppes. His stops were few and far between, yet he kept his lloryk watered and fed, resting the animal when needed, day or night. His travel was that much quicker, his journey continuing uninterrupted throughout the darkest hours of the night. His senses were more than adequate for such travel, as well as his endurance. He found that he didn't need much sleep, his body somehow didn't require so much anymore. However, the lloryk struggled to keep such a rigorous pace in spite of the extra grain Tiger provided, and the animal became despondent. He imagined he might need to purchase another beast to keep the lloryk company and help carry the burden. Tiger disliked having two lloryk to look after, but he felt he didn't have much choice.

When Tigerius did finally manage to find sleep, he dreamed the terrible nightmares that plagued him since his parting with Jonesy. Many of the images were ones he had viewed before, flashes of scenes that seemed to come from someone else's memory. It was always dark, the stone walls reflecting very little of the paltry torchlight. Sometimes he could even see the wall sconces, but only if it was bright enough. The visions often contained other individuals. Once it was a girl tied to a stone slab, her naked body riddled with bruises and abrasions. She would have been quite beautiful if she had been cleaned up and given a few good meals to put a bit of meat to her bones. Another time it was a hideous daemon, the thick dark tentacles emerging from the lower jaw reaching towards him menacingly. And several other times, there was a man, quite possibly the most beautiful man Tiger had ever seen. He had cerulean blue eyes and flaxen hair. However, the horrid truth lay in his mocking smile and maniacal expression. In the dreams, Tigerius often felt the sensation of cold stone at his back, his hands and feet bound. Always there was the knowledge that the doors were locked, and there were no windows. *There was no escape.*

Tigerius decided to stop in the small town of Keisling. He credited himself for having set aside a fraction of the gold from his heist in Cheyreh, for it would enable him to purchase much needed supplies. At the time, he had hated the small deception to his comrades, but had felt very compelled to stash away a portion of his earnings before presenting it to the others. Now all he could feel was a vast sense of relief. He purchased food rations to last him several days, as well as another bag of grain for the lloryk. Tiger felt that it was only appropriate, for the animal was giving his all during their journey. Inasmuch, he wished to show his appreciation as best he could. Once, Tiger would never have given a second thought to his beast of burden. It was one of the many ways in which he had changed since beginning his journey with Alasdair all those many moon cycles ago.

The days passed, broken only by the occasional copse of trees that infiltrated the swaying savanna grasses. Meanwhile, the sickness worsened. He thought it should have begun to release him from its malicious clutches, for he was closing the distance between himself and his goal with every passing moment. However, it was only developing a new intensity. He kept down even less of his meals, and his body ached as though he'd climbed the highest of mountains. Meanwhile, his lloryk companion was also changing. The once agreeable animal was becoming skittish and easily aggravated. This nervousness had only become worse over the past couple of days, and Tiger could only wonder if his use of the beast was becoming limited. He also wondered if much of the lloryk's anxiety was a manifestation of Tiger's strange, enduring sickness.

Tiger continued in the direction his instincts led, west with a slight southerly bent. His thoughts ceased focusing on his current objective, instead concentrating on those whom he had left behind. In particular, Jonesy came to mind. He struggled with his decision to leave her to her own destiny, somehow convinced that he was meant to be a part of it. He didn't understand this obsession he seemed to have for her, and needless to say he didn't like it. But somehow he knew that something was amiss, and he was nowhere near enough to be of aid.

The thought haunted him as he traveled. After a while, it became occluded by sickness and a new urgency to reach his destination. Tiger could only hope he would make it in time.

✵ ✵ ✵ ✵ ✵

Aeris felt the pain the moment she awakened. Moving a hand to her head, she groaned. Just that simple movement caused more pain, and she groaned again. Oh gods.

"Elirya? Are you awake?" The voice was tinged with hopeful excitement.

Aeris struggled to open her eyes. Damn, the voice sounded like Jaxom, but why was he communicating to her in normal speech?

Hearing her thoughts, the dragon answered her question. "The master healer said it would be better for you this way."

Aeris struggled to rise from the bed and Jaxom's hands pushed her back down. "No, you mustn't get up. You have been unconscious for far too long. We feared you might not awaken at all."

"But why?" she asked shakily.

Jaxom shook his head. "You suffered a skull fracture when we aided Zestrimath in her fall. It acted to your detriment when you fought against Demeter Kordrian in the jungle three days ago. He was forthright, telling us that he struck you on the head during your skirmish, albeit unintentionally. The trauma caused you to go into another coma." Jaxom paused for a moment and then continued. "I was afraid you would never awaken, Elirya."

"Three days?" she asked. "I have been unconscious for three days?" Her pitch rose as she completed her sentence.

Jaxom only regarded her impassively.

"Did we win the game, at least?" she prodded.

Jaxom continued to regard her intently for a moment before he replied. "Yes. Demeter Fo scored us a victory when he claimed that he procured the flag under your direct orders."

Aeris awarded him with a crooked smile and sighed. "Good, now I don't feel as though everything was in vain."

Jaxom regarded her solemnly. "It was that important to you?"

"Hells, yes!" she exclaimed. "It is reward for the three days of training I have lost."

Jaxom grunted beneath his breath.

Aeris narrowed her eyes. "What? What is it?"

"You could have died, Elirya. Yet, you are only concerned about falling behind in your training."

Seeing the hurt in his eyes, Aeris swiftly reached out a hand and grasped his arm. "You know that isn't the truth. It is merely a consolation prize. You know that my heart always thinks of what would befall you should something happen to me."

Jaxom lowered his gaze from hers and made no reply. Aeris wondered what he was thinking, yet remained silent. Then, "Damaeris, if something were to take you from me, I would surely perish."

Aeris shook her head. "No, you would go on without me. It is the way of things."

Jaxom also shook his head. "It is the way of things for faelin-kind, but not dragons. You must always remember that what is right for one person might not be the same for another."

Aeris frowned and cocked her head. "I understand what you are saying, but I do not like it. I would rather think that you would continue to live without me."

Jaxom looked back up at her and gave her a small smile. "You may think what you want, but the truth is that I will die without you. Usually, once a dragon takes a bondmate, it is for life. At the end of that life, the dragon seeks death."

Aeris simply stared at him.

"It is why I am always so concerned with your welfare. It is my duty to protect you, for if I preserve you, I preserve myself."

A wave of realization suddenly swept over her. Now she knew the full reason why he rejected her for so long. It wasn't simply because she was faelin and her lifespan so much shorter than his. It was because of the condition itself. *To have a bondmate meant that one's life, or death, hinged on the activity of the other individual.*

Aeris reached out a hand and touched the side of his face. It was so strange to have him in faelin form, for she was accustomed to the feeling of his smooth scales beneath her palm. Yet, his eyes were always the same, no matter what form he took. They were colored beautifully silver, and shone with all of the love he had to offer her.

And it was so much.

"That means I must always strive to keep my life, even if it is only for you," she finally said.

Jaxom made no reply, simply brought up a hand to cover hers.

✠ ✠ ✠ ✠ ✠

Asgenar paced outside the front of his dongo. He ran a hand through his hair, most likely leaving it sticking out from one side of his head like a lopsided yellow stalk. He really didn't care, had ceased caring long ago when the disarray was inevitable in spite of his every effort to maintain the unruly mass. It was a nuisance he was forced to contend with daily, and he sometimes felt he should simply shave it away and be done with it.

Asgenar felt like such a pile of lloryk dung for not realizing the full extent of the poor physical condition of his young captive. He'd returned to his dongo that evening following his initial questioning with the intention of continuing what he had begun. However, while standing there outside the flap separating his sleeping area from the rest of the enclosure, he'd heard Joneselia crying on the other side. It was a low pitched, heart-wrenching lament that may have remained undetected by a human. It very well should have been, for Asgenar had shaken his head and walked away, unwilling to manage Lady Mondemer's frailties for a second time in the same day.

However, quite a while later when Hestim was at her zenith, Asgenar had returned yet again to the dongo only to find Joneselia lying in a fetal position. He called out to her, but when she didn't respond, he rushed over to discover that she wasn't quite conscious and warm with fever. Cursing sternly to himself, he'd gone to the nearby dongo occupied by Chaysin, one of the two esteemed nivorlan who had chosen to accompany the fu-ulcrym. The master healer followed him back to his dongo, and once Joneselia was carefully picked up and laid out on Asgenar's bedpallet, Chaysin bade him leave the immediate vicinity.

For a while, the nivorlan allowed no one entry and Asgenar had waited impatiently. Only when Joneselia was properly cared for did the man emerge from the sleeping area. With a perplexed frown, Chaysin had told him that Mondemer's young daughter suffered from severe dehydration, and that she probably hadn't eaten in days. Asgenar was disturbed to hear this, for such abysmal treatment of a lady, no matter her identity, was not tolerated under his command. Asgenar had then dealt with his men very harshly, and they were demoted before their peers. He knew he was taking a risk, for he was still an unproven commander, but his principals wouldn't allow the infraction to go unpunished.

It was a moral code he had learned from his father. All of Sirion Timberlyn's children had learned it, as well as any man or woman whom he made an apprentice.

Now, shaking his head, Asgenar entered the dongo. Situated in the center of the main enclosure was a large table upon which there was a series of maps. Sooner than he would like, all of his advisors would be standing around it, each one offering his opinion about how they should proceed next against Karlisle. But now wasn't the time to focus on that meeting. He had set aside this time for the woman who lay beyond the fabric separating this area from the next, a woman who had become quite an enigma to him.

Asgenar stepped up to the flap and pulled it aside. From her half-seated place on his bedding, Joneselia turned to him, her green eyes watching as he slowly made his way over. She must have had a bath, for her skin was absent of the evidence indicative of prolonged travel. She had been given a dress to wear, and her long chestnut hair was plaited. Once there, he seated himself beside the pallet. He struggled to maintain absolute calm. "I hope this day is seeing you well," he said.

She nodded. "Much better than before, my lord."

Asgenar nodded mutely in return, not really knowing what to say next. He had no wish to question her again as of yet, but felt compelled to see how she fared. Her complexion was much improved, and her eyes devoid of the vagueness that had characterized them the day before. Of course, she still retained her aura of nonchalance. However it was somewhat different now, mayhap resulting from a proper meal, water and rest. Asgenar slid his gaze away from hers, unwilling to be taken in. The color of her eyes fascinated him, for he had seen none quite like it before.

He also had no wish for her to decipher any turmoil that might be currently taking place in his mind.

Asgenar swiftly altered the direction of his focus back to her face. "Your clothes have been washed and are drying outside on the line. I hope you don't mind." Asgenar crinkled up his nose. "Although, I am sure you were aware of their dire need of immersion."

He noticed her stoic demeanor soften a bit. It was his intent to facilitate his questioning of her later, and he was glad to see he might be successful in that endeavor. However, Asgenar didn't anticipate the twinkle that came to her eyes.

"You should talk," she replied. "Most who enter I can smell the moment they arrive, despite the separation." She nodded towards the flap. "However, I must accede that with you it is different. What do you use? Perhaps I can introduce it to Karlisle one day."

Asgenar sensed a duality in what she said. She was funning him about his use of aromatic soaps, yet not entirely in a condescending way. She thought it unusual for a man to care enough about his body odor, but also that his choice of soaps would be something she would enjoy for herself.

He remained stoic as he made his response in spite of his desire to laugh out loud. "Lirylac made from young flowering buds extracted at their most aromatic, which is right as they are about to blossom."

Joneselia nodded. "Yes, I can sense that now. I suppose my clothing was in need of something like it." She then closed her eyes and he watched as her nostrils flared briefly. "But I smell other things too, things that initially hide the scent of the lirylac from me."

Asgenar allowed himself to grin for a moment while her eyes were still closed. Once again he sensed there was something about her, something out of the ordinary. It wasn't just any woman that would try to determine the ingredients of his bodywash.

It was then that she opened her eyes. She caught the tail end of his smile before he could take it from his face. Yet she said nothing about it. "So? What are the other ingredients?"

Asgenar shrugged. "I honestly don't know."

There was silence for a moment as they each regarded the other. "It figures," she stated finally. "I suppose it's to be expected."

He shook his head. "What do you mean by that?'"

"As of yet, I haven't met a man who can tell me what he bathes with. One would think it important to know what one is placing upon his own skin." Her expression was all seriousness as she regarded him intently.

Asgenar schooled his own expression into compliance. "You are right. "I should know about this."

She nodded and was about to reply just as one of his isterian entered. The man bowed and Asgenar gestured for him to speak.

"Lord Felzeem is here, Prince Asgenar," he said in hinterlic.

Asgenar frowned and stood from his position next to the bed. "He is a bit early, is he not?"

"Indeed, my lord."

Asgenar then turned towards the woman before him. "I must attend a meeting," he said in common. "You will be situated at a nearby dongo for the duration. Afterwards, I will come and bring you back here."

Joneselia nodded solemnly. He could see that her barriers had been reestablished, and it bothered him more than he thought it should. Asgenar abruptly turned away, and as he did so, he noticed the forgotten tray of fruits, legumes, and tubers that he had bid brought for her the evening before. It continued to lay there untouched on the desk. Even more bothered, he strode quickly from out of the enclosure.

Tallachienan regarded Trebexal through wide eyes. "You are telling me that one of the main reasons you allowed Damaeris and your other dragonriders to go off-world is because of their dragons' ignissium stores?"

The dragon must have noticed the intensity of his demeanor; through faelin eyes he stared at TC, his body still. "Of course," Trebexal replied defensively. "The strength of their flame is of utmost importance to me. Haldorr has a plentiful amount of this resource; we have no fear of depleting it."

TC just stared at his friend for several moments, his guts giving a sickening twist. For over a fortnight now he'd been awaiting Aeris' return. Every day spent without her had become agonizing, and he longed to have her near. It didn't matter that she had abandoned him on the back of her bondmate. All he cared about was to see her beautiful face, to feel her in his arms again, and to hear the whispering in his mind telling me that she was his destiny. He knew that he had hurt her, and he'd vowed to himself that he would make it right. He would promise her the same thing.

But right now, all he could feel was a powerful anger. TC narrowed his eyes and he could sense the surrounding arcane energies gravitating towards him. "You stupid fool!" he shouted. "Long ago I recognized the importance of ignissium. It didn't take long for me to formulate an extract for Pylar to drink every so many moon cycles." TC threw his hands up into the air. "How did you think I managed all these centuries? Did you really think that I would keep Pylar shackled to something so easily replicated within my laboratory? All these years, you never stopped to think that I would have the capacity to devise something to restore my dragon's flame whenever necessary?" He shook his head. "Idiot! I have too many enemies for that; Pylar is a part of my primary defense arsenal!"

TC swept a hand through his hair, his gaze boring into Trebexal. The bitter truth was difficult to swallow and it cut him to the core. The hurt he felt was much more than he had ever felt before, except perhaps back when Trebexal had made the monumental mistake of trusting Ma-tia over him—a mistake that ended in over fifty percent of Trebexal's followers deserting him in favor of the goddess' causes. Thinking back on it now, TC recalled the destruction Ma-tia and her dragon army had wrought by attacking human towns and cities. Meanwhile, Trebexal had continued his work against daemon-kind. War erupted, and in spite of their differences Tallachienan stood by his friend in battle. The death toll had been high on both sides, and a truce was struck. The Pact of Bakharas was born, and both dragon and daemon-kind were required to abandon Shandahar.

Trebexal raised his own hands in supplication. "Now TC, there is more to it than just the ignissium."

TC narrowed his eyes. "Oh yes, I seem to remember the umberhulk dung you fed me a couple weeks ago when I first came here, something about Aeris excelling in your program and being a good dragonrider. You spoke nothing about the ignissium then."

Trebexal nodded. "Yes, that is because those reasons far exceeded the one pertaining to ignissium," he said defensively.

TC began to back away. "I don't believe you. You have become quite the master manipulator, my old friend." He shook his head. "My faith in you has crumbled, and I feel betrayed. You know what Damaeris means to me, yet you keep her away from me with words that evoke guilt."

TC cocked his head to the side, his lips pursed. "Once, a very long time ago, you accused me of not wanting you to find someone with whom you could live your life. Of course you were wrong, and you found out the hard way about Ma-tia. Now I am going to do the same, but in my case I know the accusation is correct."

TC continued to back away, uncaring of the expression of hurt on Trebexal's face. "Even after all my centuries of loneliness, loss and suffering, you don't want me to have a mate. You don't want me to have happiness, and you don't want me to share what life is left to me with anyone."

TC ceased his retreat, and he stopped to stare at Trebexal. "I should have made the realization when I found you leading a mission that you kept hidden from me. You knew that I must have been searching for Damaeris, yet you made no efforts to try and find me and tell me she was here." He swallowed his emotion, determined that Trebexal have no idea how strongly he felt. "You are no friend; you are just another loss among all the others throughout my existence."

TC barely took in the horrified expression on Trebexal's face as he turned on his heel. "Tallachienan, stop! You know that isn't true!"

He stormed out of the bejeweled cavern, and once reaching the cliff-side, he fell onto the back of his dragon. Pylar lifted him high, and when he finally decided to glance down, he saw Trebexal staring up at him. Of course, the man had the capacity to shift into his natural form, follow, and continue their conversation via mind-speak. But Trebexal wouldn't do that, for it would be a show of disrespect.

For a while they flew, TC lying slumped over the neck of his dragon. His fingers skimmed over the surface of the harness, over the straps and buckles that helped him from straining so much to stay astride. Pylar wore it well, uncomplaining even when the loose parts rubbed against his scales to create raw patches. They had trained alongside some of Trebexal's other dragonriders in preparation for battles that had yet to be fought. Of course, being much older than many of the other dragons, Pylar was quick to pick up on many of the maneuverability tactics. And for the same reason, TC was quickly becoming adept with spellcasting whilst in flight. This was something they did to pass time while waiting for Aeris to return to Shandahar.

Now, all TC wanted to do was leave. However, he wasn't about to do that without his primary objective. He didn't know how he was going to do it, but he needed to convince Aeris to go with him. Of course there was her bondmate as well; he would have to persuade the dragon. He would need to make mention of her family, especially the older brother who was leading Elvandahar into war against Karlisle. TC shook his head. He was getting too far ahead of himself. She wasn't even here; she was on the world of Haldorr.

In spite of Trebexal's protestations, maybe he just needed to go there himself.

Chapter Sixteen

A eris stood alone in the center of the practice arena, short-sword in hand. Demeter Fo had instructed she wait there. She watched as her comrades left the chamber, each one of them nodding as they walked by her. They were glad to see her up and about once more, but just like herself, they wondered why she had been separated from the rest. She figured she was about to find out.

Aeris waited for only a few moments longer before she watched a hooded figure walk through the archway leading into the practice chamber. She narrowed her eyes, wondering who it might be. An ivory cloak swished around ankles encased in brown leather boots. The sound of them tapping against the stone floor became louder as he approached. Once standing before her, the man finally lowered his hood.

Her eyes widened when she beheld Demeter Kordrian.

Aeris lowered her sword dejectedly. By the gods, this man was the last person she expected to see. Not once had he bothered to make an appearance whilst she lay in recovery. Hells, it was an injury he had perpetrated during an exercise meant for training purposes, one that could have killed her. She closed her eyes, her mind abruptly overwhelmed with recollection of recent events that began the morning of the day prior to their fateful game.

Aeris had chosen Nampaul's smithy over her training session with Demeter Kordrian in spite of the risk of rousing his ire. The experience was a once in a lifetime opportunity, for how often would she find herself residing upon Haldorr for any length of time again? She had asked Faleema to deliver the message with the hope of allaying at least some of his anger with the courtesy. However, later that evening, her friend accosted Aeris the moment she entered the residence chamber. Faleema's eyes were round and she gripped fiercely at her arm. "Oh Aeris, please tell me you will never do this to me again!"

Aeris frowned and set down her shoulder pack. "Faleema, what are you talking about? What's happened?"

"By the gods, Aeris, he is so angry with you! I tried to explain it to him the way you told me to, but Demeter Kord simply didn't want to listen. He was even more perturbed that you failed to notify him yourself instead of sending

me to speak for you. He then said that I was to pass on the message that he expected to see you in his chamber this evening."

Aeris felt her breath catch in her chest. "What?"

Faleema shook her arm. "You need to hurry!"

But Aeris was already breaking away from Faleema, swiftly heading to the entryway at the other side of the chamber that led to the interior of the mountain keep. She rushed through the interconnecting corridors to the one she knew Kordrian shared with Forigard. A part of her anticipated that the demeter would not be present. She would ink a parchment telling him she had been there, and hopefully prolong the inevitable. But then there was the other part of her that simply wanted to be done with it.

Aeris slowed as she approached the chamber. Demeter Kord was instantly aware of her presence and rose gracefully from his seat in front of a desk situated at the far side of the chamber. She could immediately sense his ire—pale brows furrowed over calculating blue eyes and full lips pressed together with discontent.

"So, it seems you find it rather easy to disregard your training. This is not the first time, Damaeris." He paused for a moment and then continued. "As an entertaining twist, you send your comrade to inform me of your activities."

She remained silent. As this point, she dared not make a response, knowing that he had something more to say.

"It is quite irritating to say the least." Kordrian raised an eyebrow. "You must think you are special somehow."

Aeris shook her head. "I assure you that your deductions are inaccurate. I sent Faleema merely as a courtesy. Of course I wanted to communicate to you my impending absence."

Kordrian continued as though he had not heard her. "You must think that because you are the daughter of Adrianna Darnesse that you merit an easy time here." He became thoughtful for a moment and then he continued in a more strident voice. "You think that because your family is established with Tallachienan Chroalthone that you are more deserving than others."

With a feeling of dread, Aeris shook her head. "No, that isn't the truth. I . . ."

"Then mayhap you consider yourself above the rest of us for other reasons? Is it the fact that you are an indirect heir to the throne of Elvandahar? Or mayhap because you are descended from the legendary Wildrunners?"

Aeris felt herself taken aback by the realization that Kordrian even knew of the group of people who had succeeded in destroying Aasarak. But then again, who didn't know about the Wildrunners? It was more that he knew that her father, Sirion Timberlyn, had been a member. That was what was most surprising.

Kordrian began to shout. "Hells, maybe it is because you have been trained as a dimensionalist . . . and once more we are back to Master Tallachienan. I assume you have met the man on several occasions, for I remember he was quite close with your mother." Kordrian pounded his fist upon the desk beside him. "Tell me, Damaeris, what is it that makes you different from all the rest, able to resist the necessity of attending your required training sessions?"

Aeris simply shook her head. She would have attempted to explain, but the words simply wouldn't come. She blinked her eyes as she suddenly felt a sense of lightness about her, and disjointed thoughts swirled about in her mind. Steadying herself against the wall with an out-thrust hand, the image of Tallachienan was once more thrust before her, an image that was now connected to that of the woman she had once loved more deeply than any other person upon all of Shandahar. As a child, Aeris had loved her mother like none other. As a young woman, Aeris had met Tallachienan and she inadvertently fell in love with the man, unknowing of the history.

Many moon cycles later, Aeris was captured by the goddess Tholana, and the relationship between Adrianna and her mentor was brought into stark relief.

Unfortunately, sometime in the past, Demeter Kordrian had met them both when they were still master and apprentice. Now he made Aeris very aware of that fact.

Aeris didn't bother making a reply to either his questions or his accusations. She blinked her eyes rapidly once more, straining just to focus on the nearest wall. With an awkward turn, she stumbled back through the corridor from which she had come. Strangely, he didn't order her back. She couldn't really be certain of his goal this eve, but if it had been to break her, Kordrian had surely succeeded.

With no small amount of effort, Aeris tore herself away from the memories. Kordrian was regarding her silently, his blue eyes searching hers to find the conflict raging within. Her thoughts shifted to their final skirmish on the game field. She couldn't help it, for she had dreamed of it nightly since awakening from her coma. What confused her most were the recollections of those strange pauses in between, pauses that often signified the space between his actions and hers, space dignified by the expression on his face or the feel of the air surrounding them. And then there was the space between his thoughts and hers, spaces made up only of their heartbeats.

Oh gods, what was happening to her?

Kordrian sighed heavily before he spoke, his expression the epitome of formality. "I must apologize for what happened in the jungle. I sincerely didn't intend to maim you in our encounter." He paused for a moment. Then, "In recompense for my infraction, I have chosen to offer you instruction in the use of the short-sword. I came across this idea whilst you slept. I thought, if you should awaken, I would pledge to bestow my knowledge to the best of my ability." He paused for a moment, pursing his lips slightly. "The question is whether or not you accept my instruction."

Aeris immediately began shaking her head. "No, you don't need to do that. I mean, everything is fine. I have come to realize it was only an accident."

Aeris cleared her throat nervously as she told the falsehood. An accident? Hells, she didn't recall exactly what happened that day in the jungle. At this moment she didn't care. She just wanted say something, *anything* to make him go away.

"You don't owe me anything," she continued.

Aeris lowered her eyes and pulled her brows into a frown. By the gods, could it be possible that she'd imagined those things she felt between them during the fight? *Hellfire, what's wrong with me?*

Before she could react, Kordrian closed the distance between them, placing his gloved hand beneath her chin. She offered no resistance as he lifted her face so that her gaze once more met his. His blue eyes were intense and she couldn't stop her heart from hammering in her chest. "You don't seem to understand," he replied in a husky voice. "I *want* to teach you the blade. You can consider it an apology, or if you want to remove any complication, you may simply believe it to be a part of your instruction. The choice is yours."

Aeris regarded him intently. She could feel the sincerity of his words, mirrored by his genuine expression. In spite of her desire to avoid Kordrian whenever possible, she didn't have the heart to refuse his gift. After all, she had always been such a patsy. Aeris merely nodded her reply and then brought her gaze to the floor, not wanting him to see her dismay. Her spirit sank, for she would be required to spend that much more time in his company. She couldn't really explain why she felt so strongly, only that she disliked the attraction she seemed to harbor towards him despite knowing that he didn't like her very much. It was a conundrum to say the least, one that she struggled to rectify.

One that she was *failing* to rectify.

Kord leaned into her, placing his face alongside hers. Once more she offered no resistance. He spoke into her ear. "Damaeris, you have not made a mistake. Quartermaster Falon is good, but I am the best that Lord Trebexal has to offer. In every way, you are receiving the training you deserve."

She felt her abdomen clench in response to his close proximity, yet kept her expression stolid. "So certain of yourself, aren't you?" she said impassively.

Aeris tensed when he lowered his head so that the side of his face rested against hers. By his demeanor, she could sense that he noticed her reaction. "Always," he said softly into her ear before slowly pulling away. Kord turned the corner of his mouth up into a slight grin as he unsheathed his blade from an ornate scabbard at his hip. Aeris swallowed heavily and raised her own weapon. Hells, she wasn't so sure she was up for this.

Noticing her pause of indecision, Kord chuckled. "Don't worry. I will go easy on you today."

Aeris pursed her lips, hating that she was so readable to him. Once more she couldn't help wondering why he cared so much now when he hadn't bothered to see her in the infirmary. He chuckled again just as he leaped towards her. Aeris raised her sword just in time to deflect Kord's attack. She grimaced with the power behind his swing, yet found herself able to recoup quickly. She was surprised with her ability to do so, chalking it up to the fact that she'd recently had more than her fair share of rest.

With a renewed sense of her abilities, Aeris spun away from Kord's next attack. She moved behind him, but he was quick to follow her and parried her swiftly executed lunge. And so it continued. Every so often, he would offer advice as to the placement of her feet, the angle of another thrust, or the timing of her next swing. It wasn't long before she began to sweat, the water dripping down the sides of her face, between her breasts, and down the small of her back.

By the end of the exercise, Aeris was breathing heavily, and she was gratified to see that Kord did the same. She parried yet another blow, and swung around to position herself for her own attack. But suddenly the wall torches were guttering and burning out; the chamber was bathed in darkness. She sensed someone behind her, and the hairs at the back of her neck rose in response. However, she remained still and waited for her opponent to make his move.

Feeling a shift in the air behind her, Aeris spun out of the way as Kordrian's sword swept past. She lunged out with her own blade and the two weapons sparked as they met. Kordrian pressed towards her and she fell back for a moment before offering resistance. Within the darkness they strained at one another. She briefly sensed his closeness, feeling his breath against her face as they both attempted to achieve the upper hand.

Abruptly he was gone. She stumbled forward, crying out as she landed on her knees. She cursed and was about to rise when he came barreling into her.

Aeris dropped her blade and fell onto her side, grunting with the impact. She then rolled onto her back, Kordrian moving with her to maintain his overhead position. She felt the unmistakable bite of his blade at her throat where it pressed into her vulnerable flesh. Both of his knees rested alongside her hips and her breasts pressed against the firm plane of his chest. Her breaths came in ragged gasps, and Kord's breathing stirred the wisps of her hair that always found a way to escape her attempts to keep it controlled.

"Do you yield?" His voice sounded deeper than usual.

"I thought you were going to be easy with me," she replied without answering his question.

Aeris suddenly felt the warmth of his lips alongside hers as he replied. "I changed my mind." She didn't dare move as he paused, her body beginning to respond to the intimate nature of their position. He paused and then asked the question again. "Do you yield?"

"Do I have a choice?" she whispered.

He was silent for a moment before his reply. "No."

Aeris felt bereft when his weight was suddenly lifted. The torches flared back to life, and she blinked to find Kordrian standing above her. He held her gaze intently as he held out a hand. She took it, pushing herself up from the floor to stand before him. She sensed a certain energy surrounding him, an energy that reminded her of Tallachienan. It was then she finally understood; *it was the attraction he felt for her.*

It was good to know she wasn't alone.

Aeris was about to say something when she noticed movement against the far wall. The figure leaning there pulled away and began to move towards them. She quickly recognized that it was Franchiera. The other woman's brows were drawn into a frown as she strode across the chamber, her gaze focused disdainfully on her. Aeris only raised an eyebrow and pursed her lips. Hells, she didn't need competition for Kordrian's favor. Franchie could have him for all she cared.

Kordrian turned to glance at the object of Aeris' distraction, sheathing his sword when he saw that it was Franchiera. He offered the other woman a tight smile, his gaze losing its intensity. "Demeter, we are waiting for you in the next chamber," she said.

Kordrian nodded. "I will be there in a moment."

Franchiera took the dismissal for what it was and swiftly turned and made her way back across the chamber. However, it wasn't before Aeris saw the hatred written on her pretty face. Perturbed, Aeris frowned and was about to turn away when she felt a hand on her arm. She turned back to Kordrian, and his gaze was solemn as he spoke. "I will plan to see you the day after next here in this chamber."

Aeris sensed his regret but gave only a mute nod before turning away once more. She felt a pang of it herself when she felt his hand drop away from her arm, yet she didn't hesitate to leave the chamber. Their moment together had fled when Franchiera made her presence known. Aeris made her way back to the barracks and once there, she lay down on her bedpallet. Truth be told, she was exhausted from her spar with Kordrian, and needed to rest for just a moment. Franchiera forgotten, she closed her eyes. She lay there for a while, her thoughts remaining nebulous until they shifted to Tallachienan. Where was he? How did he fare? Was it she whom he thought about, or her mother?

Aeris was abruptly thrust back into mental awareness from the anguish those thoughts caused and she cursed inwardly. She loved the man and hated him so much at the same time. She clenched her hands into fists, wondering why the Hells she persisted in tormenting herself.

Suddenly she thought of Kordrian, remembered the energy she felt between them after their spar and knew that he would be able to make her forget.

Aeris recoiled. No! It wasn't right, and not what she really wanted. She needed to learn to rely solely on herself for solace, not another person, especially a man. Besides, she would only be setting herself up for more confusion and heartache later on. A single tear escaped her closed eyelids. If only she had never been taken by Queen Tholana and ultimately presented to her chief mage, Aeris wouldn't have gotten pregnant with Ranaghar's cimmerean bastards.

If only she had never left Elvandahar with her brother and agreed to accompany him with the caravan he had been hired to protect, she would never have met Magnus.

If only she and her comrades had never gone to Celuna after their tests in Andahye, they never would have been attacked by the behiraz and everyone killed except for her.

If only her mother hadn't been so weak as to succumb to the temptation offered her master, Adrianna wouldn't have become Tallachienan's mistress.

If only . . .

✕ ✕ ✕ ✕ ✕

Aeris suddenly shot upright, her hands gripping the sides of her bedpallet. The klaxon rang stridently throughout the air, easily awakening her from the deepest sleep. Fumbling beside her, Aeris had the strength of mind to loosen the shutter of the lantern situated on top of a small stand alongside her pallet. The paltry flame immediately brightened, and upon the pallet nearby, Aeris saw that Faleema had been similarly awakened. Across the chamber she heard movement, and the brightening of another lantern. Franchiera had also risen and was making her way towards her riding leathers.

<Elirya, dress yourself appropriately and come to the ledge. Training begins early today.>

She frowned. <What time is it?>

<Early. The sun has barely begun its ascent.>

Her frown deepened, for she would have thought that the young rays would have already begun to shine upon the nearby ledge. <How come I can't tell?>

She felt the momentary pause in his speech-path before he replied. <Because there is a storm coming.>

Aeris was taken up short. However, she refrained from any more questioning until she had done as her bondmate requested. Swiftly clothing herself appropriately for riding, she made her way to the ledge with Faleema and Franchie. Sidranth awaited them there, and hovering in the airspace nearby were Jaxom and Mira. Once astride, the three pairs joined Falon, Saliel, Thulnar and their dragons. The twelve of them then made their way towards the four distant dragons hovering before a backdrop of ominously approaching storm clouds. Two of them belonged to Demeters Fo and Kord. The others were two helzethryn and their riders whom Aeris had never met before.

Jaxom heard her question in his mind and responded. <They are the two who have been instructing me and the others since arriving upon Haldorr. It must be something serious for the demeters to be here together. >

Aeris' concern strengthened, the winds buffeting them while the dragonriders hovered together in one place. Jaxon sent soothing thoughts through their link, hoping to set her at ease. After a few moments, Demeter Fo began to speak, his words transmitted through the mind link Seldonraxis shared with the other dragons. <The storms on Haldorr are the most awesome you will ever encounter. They are yet another reason why we have brought you here, for there are none upon Shandahar that can give the same experience. Not all battles are fought in the calmest of environments. As such, this upcoming exercise will determine the extent of the dragon's flight skills.>

Jaxom was stupefied. No one flew during a storm on Haldorr. The titanic twisters were almost impossible to maneuver, and the winds were unpredictable. The rains could be torrential and the hail damaging. This was idiocy at its greatest. Aeris sensed his distress and all his efforts to calm her were nullified.

<This will also be an evaluation of strength and endurance. Both are

needed to be the superior combatants we are training you to be.>

Jaxom could scarcely believe what was about to happen. All his life, he had been conditioned to avoid these storms at all costs. Not long from now he would be deliberately flying into one. Opening his mind-path, he could sense the disturbance of the other dragons. More intimately, he could feel Aeris' increasing apprehension as the storm approached. Unfortunately, he had no comfort to offer. Damn! What the Hells were they thinking?

The voices of Hobarthix and Garbinath were next to be heard. <All right. Let's move.>

Jaxom snorted his discontent. The dragons didn't even offer any words of advice. He felt Aeris take extra precaution by checking the harness straps, tightening them accordingly, and making sure that she was well-anchored. He then felt her press her body close to his back, resigning herself to the inevitable.

Jaxom closed his eyes and followed his bondmate's lead. He surged forward with the others, winging towards a danger he had never before encountered. The skies around them quickly darkened. He snorted again, this time to clear his nostrils so that he could maximize air intake whilst in battle. *Only they weren't going to battle in the traditional sense.*

<Everyone, open your speech-path wide. We will need to keep communication as easy as possible so that we can function as a team and offer aid where it is needed,> said Fo.

The winds suddenly intensified and Jaxom focused on the trial before him. He fought for stability as the gusts tossed him about, seeking to attain some semblance of control. The pressure against his wings was quickly becoming stronger and he struggled to minimize it. But the winds shifted direction so precipitously; he had very little chance to right himself before he was forced to make another adjustment.

Jaxom concentrated, focusing his mind inward. The winds continued to increase and the rains began. He felt Aeris' worry through their link and wished he could comfort her, but he wouldn't allow himself to waver. It wasn't long before visibility became limited, another detriment to his efforts. Yet he remained engrossed with his task. He surmised that the key was to keep his massive wings close to his body, unfurling them slightly every so often in order to navigate the powerful winds. He could feel the flexible bones within bending against the power unleashed against them. Yet they did not break, and he was awed by the discovery he made about a body he had used for many decades.

Jaxom rode the storm. He released his mind, allowing it to reach beyond the fetters within which he ordinarily bound it. The sound of the winds rushing past became only a vague nuance, and the feel of the rain against his hide a caress. He could hear the beating of his heart, the rush of the air in and out of his chest with each breath, and the mind of his bondmate joined so closely with his.

Suddenly something was changing. He could feel it in the air and his concentration broke. Free of his reverie, his eyes strained within the torrential rain. It took him a moment, but then he saw it. The twister was magnificent, more than he had ever imagined it would be. Through their link, he could feel Aeris' dread. He could sense the raw power of the thing barreling towards him and he wavered even more. In the end, he went with his instincts and he veered to the side.

Within moments Jaxom felt himself being caught up in the twisting motion of the storm. The sheer power of it nearly took his breath away and he felt himself losing control within the debris-laden field in which he found himself. Aeris' thoughts were strong in his mind, made that way by the strength of her fear. The sensations she experienced were beyond frightening and she clutched at him for dear life. The vortex sought to bring him in. Whilst at the periphery he still had a chance to escape; he had only to regain his focus.

As the twister pulled Jaxom within, he closed his eyes. He ignored the rock and other debris that struck him and allowed his other senses to take over, focusing his consciousness on his innermost self. Once more the external senses died away, and he was left with only the beating of his heart, the breaths he took, and the movements of his wings and body as he navigated the storm. And once he felt the opportunity to be free, Jaxom took it.

Pulling his wings close to his body, he spiraled. Down, down, down he fell. A large rock collided with the side of his head, and he grunted with the impact. Yet he continued. With escape paramount in his thoughts, Jaxom didn't consider the approaching ground.

<Jaxom, pull up! Pull up!>

Aeris' desperate voice rang stridently through his mind, and he obeyed her immediately. Only later would he realize how quickly he executed her command. He spread his wings and beat them wildly. Finally he caught an updraft, and opened his eyes to find the jungle canopy uncomfortably close. He could only imagine the extensive injury that could have been done to them had he crashed there.

As the twister moved farther away, Jaxom made his way through the continuing storm, gazing across the canopy in search of any place he might land. The rain and hail beat at him mercilessly. His head ached and the sight in his right eye had become blurred. Through their link, he could feel the pain Aeris suffered from the abrasions the ice made as they struck the most vulnerable parts of her uncovered by leather trousers and vest. His heart went out to her and he wished he could protect her beneath the sanctuary of an extended wing. *Why had the demeters done this to them? Why? Was it so much worth the risk to their lives and limbs?*

Jaxom gave a massive exhale. He knew the moment he was spent. There was only so much the body could endure before it finally gave out. He was buffeted about for another moment or two before he began to fall once more. Almost as though in a dream, he heard Aeris' voice in his mind, urging him back to her. Jaxom wondered how much of the vagueness had to do with the hit he took to his head. He tried rousing himself, attempting to shake himself free of the shadowy obscurity. But it clung to him like a sticky web.

But then they were there. It was his friends, those dragons whom he had begun to call his comrades. They circled him, extending their wings so that he could lean his weary body on them—much as he had done for the ailing Zestrimath not so long ago. As his mind shifted to unconsciousness, the dragons settled him onto solid ground. Only then did Jaxom know that Aeris was safe, and he could succumb to the oblivion that beckoned.

✖ ✖ ✖ ✖ ✖

Razlul stared into the purple flames. The heat felt divine, and made him want to step a little closer. Of course it was no ordinary fire, but shutaska. The *hellfire* was both balm and bane, a necessity that dictated every movement in his life. He loved and hated the fire at the same time, wishing that he could *choose* to bathe in its flames as opposed to being *forced* to do so. Such was the price he paid for the awesome being he became that fateful day when the Wildrunners had defeated Gaknar and sent the daemon Tharizdune of Malchur back into the Hells from which he had come. He used to believe that the price was worth the power he'd gained, but then he'd discovered the existence of Triath Solanar. Triath was much like himself, infused with daemon essence that made him a hybrid. There were a few differences that made each man unique, but only one that really mattered.

Triath didn't need to bathe in *hellfire* to keep himself strong. Armed with this knowledge, Razlul no longer felt he should pay such a high price.

Razlul clenched his hands into fists and hissed his displeasure. Damn Triath Solanar! He thought surely by now the man would have come for his addled wife! But no, Triath had yet to make an appearance, and he wondered if he should just kill Tianna and be done with her. Triath was the only reason he allowed her to live, convinced that the other hybrid was the key to discovering a way for him to escape the indignity of the shutaska.

Noticing movement at the other side of the chamber, Razlul looked away from the fire and to the place where his captive sat. For the most part she was quiet, speaking only to herself. He found this to be rather irritating, for he'd come to expect an answer to any dialogue he chose to visit on someone. No matter what he did, he could no longer get the woman to speak to him, mayhap a result of the merzillith's invasion of her mind over a fortnight or two ago. It was an unfortunate consequence, one that was unanticipated. He didn't care to admit it aloud, but the fact that she no longer seemed to be entirely cognizant of her surroundings bothered him. It was no longer a pleasure to force himself on her, so he'd almost entirely ceased the activity quite a while ago. But that wasn't all. She was the only link he had remaining that bound him to the boyhood he remembered so vividly. He supposed he must have been happy with his life in the Beorian temple in spite of the frailty of his human nature. Mayhap much of that had to do with the broken woman across the room.

Tianna Trigovise had once been his superior; it was strange how things had a way of changing so much over the years.

Razlul focused on her intently, narrowing his eyes. In spite of the passage of so much time, Tianna was beautiful. She had aged very little, a characteristic she had somehow acquired from her daemon pregnancy. She also had the capacity to heal swiftly, an attribute that had served to keep her alive thus far. However, Razlul knew there was more, knew that Tianna possessed many other abilities and qualities prior to her union with Triath. This knowledge was obtained by the merzillith when he infiltrated her mind. The daemon had searched diligently through her memories, finally recognizing the presence of certain thought patterns during the times when she experienced the most adversity.

Once this information was imparted to him, Razlul was intrigued so much that it came to the forefront of his mind when Chorlak mentioned certain aspects about the Mondemer girl he'd ordered the daemon to acquire for him. Since then he had found a different innocent to be the sacrifice he would use to bring a parent leviathan into Shandahar. He now intended for the Mondemer girl to be the mother of the child he wished to sire on her. Razlul was no fool. He had many enemies. One day he would be overcome, and his offspring would rule in his stead.

However, there was more. Razlul had learned even more about his dear Tianna when the merzillith revealed all he had learned. It had much to do with a mother's bond with her son, a bond that had formed before birth, before either one ever saw the face of the other. It was a bond made only of the love a mother feels for the unborn life growing inside her, a bond reinforced by a reciprocating sentiment. It was something that was not experienced by human, faelin, or halfen kind. Razlul had learned that it was something shared only by some daemon mothers and their offspring, a connection called rasartha. In spite of the fact that she was not daemon, Tianna had once shared this bond with her child.

Razlul imagined the bond was still there, merely hidden beneath the constraints opposed by human society, *and that it would ultimately lure the son to his mother.*

Razlul turned away from Tianna and left the chamber. He then took a staircase back up to the main level of the temple. It seemed that, at the moment, he had much to consider. Not only should he expect to see Triath at his doorstep, but mayhap his son as well. Meanwhile, Chorlak would deliver the Mondemer girl, and Queen Tholana had expressed a desire to pay him a visit. He'd received the correspondence very recently, and wondered why she was suddenly so interested in coming to him. This was much opposed to the fact that he'd always been the one to make such an effort in the past, and that he had been the one to go to her. He could only guess about this shift in behavior, but it was only one of many concerns dominating his thoughts. The last was his discovery of who had been the one to take control of the dragon-riders he had lost several fortnights ago. Quite interestingly it was a dragon—the dragon goddess known as Ma-tia. The knowledge made him feel both pleased and uneasy at the same time. It seemed that she had quite a dislike for humans, much as did he. In that regard, they were on the same side. However, their very natures were disparate, for traditionally they were on opposing sides of the Bakharas Pact. He was of daemon descent, and she was one of the oldest dragons to walk Shandahar. They were meant to hate one another and were sworn enemies.

Razlul had once liked to think he was the most powerful force upon all of Shandahar. Now there were Ma-tia and many others who had stepped forward since the *Fall*—other gods and goddesses who sought to gain a solid foothold on Shandahar. *Damn, he could hardly wait to witness the power play that would ensue.*

CHAPTER SEVENTEEN

*A*eris stared at the construct before her. It was beautiful, much more than she ever could have imagined. She'd spent as much time as she could with Nampaul at his forge, much to the exclusion of some of her training sessions with Demeter Kord and Demeter Bart. It was easy to see that the time was well spent, for the glove fit her perfectly. The intricate artistry on the metallic surface was magnificent to behold, something she'd seen only on the most costly of shields, bracers, and other protective accoutrements.

However, the exterior details weren't what made the glove so special. The real beauty lay in the way the glove was created. The smith had provided a rare opportunity to incant her spell into the molten braxen as it was being cast. It wasn't a well-known practice; the only reason he knew about it was because of his years spent in the company of magic-users. An arcane weapon forged in this way wasn't just more powerful, but it was almost impossible for it to be stripped of that power by another spellcaster.

Aeris looked up from the glove and took in the hopeful expression on Nampaul's face. She gently laid it down on the table beside her, struggling to keep her emotions in check. Nampaul's expression shifted to one of worry as she began walking towards him. He spoke as she approached. "Milady, is somethin' wrong? Jus' tell me an I'll try my bes' ta fix it."

Aeris swallowed heavily, feeling the first tears escape her eyes. Damn, she could never keep herself under control. She shook her head. "It's perfect. There is nothing to change."

Nampaul frowned and splayed his hands out before him beseechingly. "Den what is it milady Aeris? I thought ya wud be happy."

She swallowed again and then propelled herself between his outstretched arms. She wrapped her own arms around his neck, not caring that he was covered in his customary layer of soot. "By the gods, what you have done for me is so wonderful. I . . . I can never repay you."

Without looking at his face, Aeris could sense that he was taken aback. A few short moments passed before he reciprocated and enclosed her within his embrace. "But I ne'er aksed you for payment. You don' owe me nothin'!"

"I know that Nampaul. But I only wish I could repay you. What you have done is so above and beyond anything I could have imagined. Thank you so *much for helping me. I will never forget your generosity."*

Aeris felt him immediately relax. "Hells, woman! I'd do anathin' if ya aksed me." He then increased his grip, holding her tighter. "Damn, you shur are diff'rent den other folks."

She chuckled and sniffed back more tears that threatened. "Why do you say that?"

He shook his head. "I jus' never met anyone like you afore."

She sniffed again. "Should I take that as a compliment?"

Nampaul chuckled heartily and released her enough to take a step back. "Yes, milady. 'Tis a compliment."

Aeris abruptly looked up from her thoughts as Jaxom belched for the third time. She could sense his immense dissatisfaction, for he hated the taste of Zarefessia more than anything. He cringed every time he ingested the red-veined plant, and then again when he belched it. She couldn't wait until his torment was over, for he tended to be grouchier after these outings.

Of course Jaxom denied it.

Aeris turned back to the spellbook that rested in the circle of her legs. Unconsciously, she gingerly rubbed at one of the lacerations she had sustained during their last training exercise—an effort she later discovered had been a test. Of course, no one had anticipated Jaxom's flight *into* a twister. However, in Aeris' humble estimation it should have always been a possibility somewhere in the back of their minds when the demeters decided that a massive storm on the world of Haldorr was a good way to evaluate the aerial maneuverability of their fledgling dragonrider pairs.

Such foolishness.

Aeris' eyes skimmed over the text, but she wasn't really reading it. Her mind mulled over the fact that they could have so easily perished in the storm. Hells, no one would have been able to stop it. No magic or weapon could have saved them from those unbelievably strong winds. She'd been terrified the entire time, her eyes staring into the gale as her bondmate somehow made his way through. At first he struggled, but it wasn't long before she felt something sweep through their link. His mind had become so concentrated on moving through the storm, he could perceive little else.

To see a massive concentration of those winds emerging from out of the space before them was petrifying. Her heart had skipped a beat, and she found it even more difficult to breathe than before. Yet Jaxom was their savior once again, maneuvering through the twisting winds that would otherwise have sucked them within. Somehow he persevered, and when he made that dive, her heart stopped in her chest. She remembered screaming at him, and when he finally pulled out of the dive just in time, she could barely breathe a sigh of relief before she felt his mind begin to slip away.

She recalled Jaxom's thoughts before his consciousness began to waver.

And now here she was, sitting on a rocky cliff side, only a mere two days after the storm. She brought her fingertips to the long gash on her cheek, and then to the deep wound on her forearm where she had been struck by flying debris. Jaxom was much worse for wear, and his silvery hide was tattered by so much more. Fortunately he healed much more quickly than did she.

Aeris was instantly aware when Jaxom sensed the approach of another dragon. She sighed inwardly, for she had divulged to no one where she would be going that day, not even Faleema. She wanted to be alone to ruminate over her situation, to simmer over her anger before returning to normal training the next day. And she wanted to figure a way out of this insanity. Not only was she beginning to think she was ready to go home, *but she felt prepared to face the life she so easily left behind.*

Aeris didn't bother to turn when the other dragon landed nearby. She knew who it was, for Jaxom greeted Riloriandrix barely a moment after she was aware of their approach. Rilo had returned the greeting, but immediately sensed Aeris' perturbation through the mind-path Aeris had deliberately left open. Aeris was certain Rilo communicated the sentiment to her bondmate, but it didn't really matter. Kordrian would come to her no matter what Rilo communicated to him.

The man was stubborn that way.

Jaxom wisely said nothing.

Aeris was still as Kordrian walked up behind her, remaining that way even when he hunkered down behind her. She closed her eyes as the days leading up to the storm flitted through her mind: training sessions both arcane and physical, confusing feelings that tended to hover in the air between them, and thoughts that made her think much less often of Tallachienan. He was silent for a moment before he spoke. "Aeris, I have come as a messenger."

She drew her brows together. "A messenger from whom?"

"Jaxom knows. I am surprised he did not tell you," he replied gently.

Aeris shook her head. "Jaxom knows that I am currently unreasonable. Actually, through communication with Rilo, you should know the same. Jaxom is smart enough to leave me alone when I am like this. Pity it is not the same with you."

Aeris didn't even blink as she assailed the man with her caustic words. Hells, it wasn't as though he cared much for her in spite of his claim to want to teach her the sword. Kord had stood by with the other demeters as she, Jaxom, and their comrades were swept away by the storm. She was understandably irate.

He paused for barely a moment before making his reply. "The other demeters have sent me."

"In regards to what?" Aeris heard a brief sigh before silence reigned. Several moments passed before she became impatient. "Listen, I don't want you here. And actually, I don't care what anyone has to say right now. If indeed you are a messenger, tell the others that I don't care what they think anymore." Aeris shook her head and rose from her place. She finally turned to face him. "I'm done with you people."

Kordrian rose to stand with her. His expression was thoughtful as he regarded her, mayhap somewhat chagrined. It was then that she noticed the dragons were quiet, and through her link with Jaxom realized they were focused on the faelin drama playing out before them. Kordrian's gaze lowered for a moment and he cleared his throat to fill the silence. "I lied. No one sent me."

Aeris cocked her head, somewhat taken aback. *What the Hells was he doing?* Her expression must have shown the question for his reply was timely. "The other demeters and I talked about what happened, but no real decision was made. I took it upon myself to find you."

Aeris shook her head once more. "Why? Why not just let me go? Besides, you feel that my affiliation with Tallachienan Chroalthone earns me extra credit here. It would behoove you to be rid of me."

Kordrian pursed his lips. "You know I only spoke out of anger when I uttered those words. Why do you mention them now?"

Aeris felt her eyes flare with emotion and she flung her arms outward. "Because they weigh on me! Just because you have dismissed them doesn't mean that I have done the same. I am not a fool. There is some truth to everything a person says. A part of you truly believes that I feel privileged."

Kordrian nodded in agreement. "You are right; I did believe that once. But now I know the truth."

Aeris furrowed her brows and placed her hands at her hips. "What truth?"

"That you are just like the rest of us, hoping only to make yourself better than what anyone thought you would be."

Aeris gave an outward sigh and she allowed herself to deflate. Anger deserted her and she was left only with sorrow. "Demeter Kordrian, I ask you again. Why are you here?"

Once more he pursed his lips. "To convince you to stay."

Aeris became pensive. "What makes you think I would listen?"

Kordrian frowned. "Why wouldn't you? There are many who have sacrificed their time and effort to train you to accomplish something. Would you really deny them a bit of your time?"

Aeris returned the expression and narrowed her eyes. "I just might. With what you people have put me through, you deserve nothing from me."

She watched as Kordrian struggled to control himself. She angered him purposefully, wanting to see him rise to her bait. Her anger was fueled by the ache deep in her body, the sting of the healing lacerations over her flesh, and the memory of her bondmate's mind slipping away from hers and into the oblivion that beckoned. She couldn't speak for the others, but felt that both she and Jaxom had been wronged when they were bidden to enter the storm. This time, the risk had severely outweighed any benefit.

Kordrian shook his head. "Perhaps my initial assessment of you was correct after all—selfish to a fault. I don't know why I bothered to make an attempt to see you in a different light."

"I have wondered the same myself, *Demeter* Kordrian. Why the Hells would you do such a thing?" She grimaced as she stressed his title, remembering how he had once corrected her when she called him 'master'.

He suddenly stepped towards her almost menacingly. "I suppose I thought more from a daughter of Adrianna Darnesse."

Aeris stumbled back, momentarily unable to keep the fleeting reflection of fear from her eyes. She couldn't help it, for she still carried conditioning from her horrific days within the captivity of Tholana's citadel. She felt Jaxom in her mind, soothing her through their link, and then heard his warning to Rilo that she had better mind her recalcitrant bondmate.

Too late, Aeris reached out to tell Jaxom that no foul was done. Unfortunately her response alone had pulled Kordrian up short. His expression continued to be one of perturbation, but she could somehow sense that the reason for it had shifted. She could tell when he received the warning from Rilo, for his concentration turned inward for a moment before his gaze sharpened on her.

Silence reigned as Kordrian began to make some realizations. Aeris felt her cheeks burn as she became even more of an open book to him. She could see the conflicting emotions on his face: anger versus sympathy, agitation versus understanding. She felt herself reacting more adversely than she would have ever thought she might, and she lashed out.

"What? Aren't you going to continue berating me? Isn't that what you want? Please, don't stop on my account."

Kordrian simply stood there.

Tears sprang to her eyes and she found herself even angrier. She hated the reaction he had elicited, and of the things his small action had reminded her. She had almost begun to forget from where she had come, the atrocities she had endured, and the memories she had hoped to leave behind. She liked to think that she was ready to face all of that again. But she was wrong. She was not ready, still trapped within the unforgiving quagmire her mind had created.

Aeris turned away from him. "If you have nothing left to say, just go. I don't want you here."

Kordrian remained quiet for a moment before he replied in a low voice. "I will see you tomorrow for sword practice."

Aeris blinked away her tears as she heard his retreating footfalls. She hadn't long to wait before she felt the familiar *whoosh* of air as Rilo flew away. Once they were gone, Aeris turned to Jaxom. Her dragon was already there, standing right behind her, ready for her arms to wrap themselves around his curved neck.

He remained there as she cried onto his smooth silvery hide, stayed well into the evening as she lay within the curve of his forelegs, sleeping a healing sleep. He didn't move from his place until the first rays of a new dawn lit the distant Haldorrian horizon.

All the while, Jaxom's heart ached for the pain he could never take away.

Jonesy frowned as her eyes skimmed over the pieces scattered atop the table. She looked for the one that had the color she sought, the color of the lirylacs she had been reconstructing since early the evening before when Asgenar had first brought them to her. Atop the sizable conference table that dominated the outer dongo, he had spread the thin wooden pieces, each one cut into a different shape. Each piece happened to fit into another and that piece into yet another until an image was formed, an image that had been painted onto the wood before it was artfully cut into small pieces.

The faelin called it *jigsaw*, a type of puzzle that many people often liked to play whilst they had little else to do. Many times it was during a recovery period such as hers. Jonesy had never seen such a thing before, and she quickly became engrossed with reconstructing the image. She could only imagine the time it must have taken for the maker to so intricately cut each piece, making it so that when it was fit back into position with its neighbor, it was 'locked' into place with the connection of subsequent pieces.

Jonesy grinned to herself when she finally found the piece she was looking for lying hidden beneath another. She picked it up and fit it into the appropriate spot, smiling even more widely when it completed the part of the image upon which she had been working so diligently. According to the pieces she had already placed together, it appeared as though it might be the image of a house, or mayhap a series of houses. She couldn't be entirely certain.

Jonesy startled when she suddenly felt the presence of someone standing behind her. She put a hand to her chest in an attempt to quiet her wildly racing heart as Asgenar chuckled. "By the gods, man! Do you really wish to kill me?" she exclaimed.

Asgenar struggled to school his expression into one of seriousness. "Of course not, my lady. You wouldn't be half as entertaining to me if you were dead."

Jonesy pursed her lips. "You are such a scoundrel," she said. Then, before she could stop herself, she reached out a closed fist and struck the man on his upper arm.

Asgenar gripped his arm, his expression shifting into one of surprise. She had meant for the act to be one of playfulness. However, she did she not know him well enough to take such a liberty.

And she was also his prisoner.

Jonesy watched the myriad expressions pass over his face before he chuckled. "I suppose I have been called much worse." He cocked his head and rubbed his arm. "That was a bit weak; I am certain you can do better than that."

Jonesy smiled tremulously, realizing he was unaware of her impropriety. "I assure you that I cannot, my lord. I don't really know much about such physical things."

Asgenar's gaze became piercing. "Why do I not believe you?"

Jonesy shrugged. "Really, my lord; how many princesses do you know who are well versed in hand-to-hand combat?"

Asgenar gave a mocking frown and cupped his chin between his thumb and forefinger. "I don't know; my sister is one perhaps."

Jonesy finally relaxed enough to allow her smile to widen, realizing he had not taken her physical playfulness wrongly. Once, she never would have considered such an action, but since her experiences with the group, she had changed. She now had to remember that the same rules did not apply in upper class society.

"Your sister, eh?" Jonesy tried to recall if she had ever seen Aeris exhibit any forte with unarmed combat. Meanwhile, she turned away from Asgenar and placed her focus back onto the table before her, not wanting her expression to give anything away. She picked up a piece of the jigsaw and pondered its placement.

"I see you enjoy the puzzle I brought for you."

Once more Jonesy looked up. "Indeed. It is the perfect means to take my mind away from my infirmity."

"It seems you are rather good at it. In truth, there are few I know who have been able to work a jigsaw so well within such a short amount of time. Has anyone been here to help you?"

Jonesy shook her head, not knowing what to think. Then she grinned, feeling as though she had figured out the confusion. "Mayhap you have known few others who have had so much time at their disposal. I have been working at this much of the day."

Asgenar shook his head and shrugged. "I have known many who have been in your situation. None have shown such capability. Believe me, my lady, when I say you are quite adept. I brought you one of our most difficult so that it would keep your attention for a long time. There are over two hundred pieces to this jigsaw."

Jonesy said nothing as he snagged a nearby chair and seated himself at an adjacent side of the table. He offered her a grin before setting to work, and it wasn't long before he had placed several pieces. With growing irritation, she watched from lowered lids. It was difficult to concentrate, for he was very obviously someone who was very good at puzzle-working. What the Hells was he hoping to accomplish by sweeping in and upstaging her with his jigsaw working abilities? However, it wasn't but a moment later that she stopped to examine the situation. It wasn't *his* fault that she couldn't control her emotions. Most likely, it was not his purpose to make a show of dominance and that his intent was much more innocent.

Jonesy allowed herself to relax and tried to keep optimistic thoughts. Perhaps all he wanted was to spend a little bit of time in her company. Hells, she knew she could do with some intelligent interaction. However, she couldn't help but feel some measure of surprise when Asgenar broke the silence with a chuckle followed by a story about something funny that had happened earlier that morning. In spite of herself, Jonesy couldn't help but smile at the absurdity of the tale.

Asgenar continued to talk as they worked the puzzle, reminiscing about his childhood and of the struggle he tried to balance between the crown and his family. At first she was a little taken aback by his desire to offer her conversation, but it wasn't long before she was absorbed by his words. He spoke about his younger brother and how he wished that there was more between them. He yearned for the tie that connected other men he knew to their own brothers, wished that Alasdair could look beyond his own trials to see the ones that Asgenar endured alone. Of course, Asgenar had their grandfather, King Thalios, but it wasn't the same as having a brother there by his side. And Alasdair had their sister, Damaeris, with whom to commiserate.

Jonesy felt her interest pique when Asgenar mentioned her good friend for the second time. She was reminded of the ache she felt when remembering Aeris, but easily kept it hidden since Asgenar was so focused on his narrative.

He went on to say that his sister had always been the most difficult for him to reach, and, unfortunately, he had a history of being rather hard on her. Because of that, Aeris held a grudge against him, one he could not entirely disprove, although it wasn't from lack of trying.

The two of them remained there for quite some time, and afterward they shared the mid-day repast. In truth, Jonesy loved hearing about his life. Some aspects were so similar to hers, while others were starkly different. She didn't know why he cared enough to share this time with her, but she thrust the question from her mind. She would simply accept it at face value and appreciate the gesture no matter what the cause. After a while, she knew that he hoped to hear something about her in return, and she regretted that she could not reciprocate. The tales would be much too dark in contrast to his brighter narratives.

He stood there as the servants cleared away the remnants of their meal, regarding her intently. "Mayhap I shall return to visit you on the morrow. It appears that our jigsaw needs a bit more work."

Jonesy looked over at the table as he indicated the unfinished image. She replied in a teasing tone. "Perhaps more of it would have been completed if you had been more focused."

Asgenar's eyes narrowed. "What do you mean, my lady?"

She struggled to keep the smile from her lips and shrugged. "It is only that I have never heard a man talk so much before. Certainly it must consume much of your attention."

He intensified his gaze. "Mayhap you are right. I shall endeavor to speak less and listen more when next we meet."

Suddenly realizing the corner in which she found herself, she grimaced inwardly. Looking into his eyes, she saw that he also realized he had the upper hand. He smiled and gave a brief bow of respect. "Until next time then."

Jonesy watched as he left the dongo. She found herself looking forward to the morrow in spite of his expectations. The Prince of Elvandahar was much more interesting that she ever would have imagined. She still didn't know why he cared to offer her his company, but somehow it just didn't matter.

Aeris frowned as she donned the armored vest over her sleeveless tunic. Hells, what was happening this time that they were awakened so early? Certainly not a storm, for the skies outside looked clear from her vantage point within the cavern. What required everyone to attire themselves in their battle-gear? Aeris gave a heavy sigh and placed the belt around her waist, then donned the boots, fastening them tightly against her calves. She then began to work with her hair, combing it out and then attempting to plait it. Damn, she should have done her hair prior to placing the vest. It provided more bulk than what she was accustomed, making her task that much more difficult.

Aeris suddenly felt the thick hair being taken from her hands. Faleema proceeded to finish the braid, and then turned Aeris around to face her. "Calm down. It is only a silly exercise. Just take it all in stride and all will be fine."

Aeris nodded and pulled on the arm-guards. "You know how I dislike the mornings."

Faleema gave her a lopsided grin. "Oh yes, I know."

Aeris playfully chucked Faleema on the shoulder and grabbed her helm as they began to make their way out to the ledge. Once there, she asked Jaxom what he knew about the goings on, but he informed her that he knew nothing. The dragons and their riders dropped from the ledge towards the largest of the practice fields. Once there, they joined Thulnar and Sordra, Saliel and Borgestrix. Moments later, quartermasters Falon and Franchie also landed astride their own dragons.

It wasn't long after that Demeters Kordrian and Forigard approached in the company of several dragons they had never met. Just like the dragon elders living upon Shayamalan, these dragons were huge, and their colors no longer silver or gold, but a rather strange shade somewhere in between. Aeris could immediately feel the depth of their *talent*. These dragons were immensely powerful. Something was about to happen here, and she found herself suddenly on edge. It made her second guess her decision to remain with the others and stay on Haldorr despite the misgivings she'd been having since riding through the twister storm.

Through their link, Jaxom sent soothing vibes. It was useless for her to get worked up, especially if it were for nothing, although, both of them seriously doubted that. How often did one have the opportunity to see so many dragon arcanists in the same place at the same time?

Almost never.

The twelve dragons landed on the field. Silver and gold eyes watched them silently from the half circle they made. Demeters Fo and Kord approached the small group, their expressions ones of complete seriousness.

Demeter Fo was the first to speak. "Today you are about to be tested. Another group of dragons is soon to arrive, and for all intents and purposes in regards to this test only, they will be your enemy."

Aeris inhaled deeply. Oh gods, now she knew why they had been bid to arrive fully armored. However, unknowing of what she would be facing this day, she had foolishly left her newly constructed glove behind. *Damn!*

Aeris refocused her attention when Kord began to speak. "Before you is a group of the most powerful dragon magic users upon all of Haldorr. They will use their magic on each and every one of you that will create a special type of armor. It will protect you from the mortal wounds that any lethal attacks might bring. Meanwhile, it will also keep track of the number of hits it takes, where, and from whom. In the end, the numbers will be tabulated and the winning team announced." Kordrian paused before continuing. "We will also announce who would have died."

Saliel spoke up. "Then why are we bothering to wear all of our battlegear if we are already protected by the magic?"

"The magic will only protect you from the lethal blows. Your armor will protect you from the rest. It is entirely possible you could still be injured in the fight, so practice caution and remain alert," said Kordrian.

"Not to mention, you need to fight with the encumbrance of your armor so that you will experience something as close to the real thing as possible," said Fo.

Aeris glanced beside her to see that Faleema was just as surprised as was she. On her other side, Thulnar was the same. Then, from out of the skies before them emerged a small contingent of dragons, all equipped with their own riders. From whence they had come, Aeris had no idea, for it was her understanding that Trebexal's program was a relatively new one. As they flew closer and landed on the other side of the field, Aeris noticed that these dragons and their riders were a bit older than Aeris and her own teammates. They would have youthfulness on their side, but the opposing dragons were larger, and the riders most likely a bit wiser.

Kordrian held up his hands, palms outward. "You will feel a strange sensation when the dragon mages cast their spells, but there is nothing to fear. Keep in mind that the spells are for your ultimate protection."

"Your goal is to strike out at the enemy and acquire as many points as possible while keeping your own vulnerable areas protected," explained Fo. "Each team is endeavoring to protect their mountain keep. Ours is directly behind you."

Aeris turned to look at the ledge that characterized the entrance to their cavern. In the opposite direction across the field, she recalled that there was another cavern, one that was not used as often as this one. It would be the perfect residence for dragon-riders such as these, dragon-riders who had no formal training yet carried the wisdom of having been with their bondmates far longer than any of the ones standing around her.

Kordrian gestured to them. "Come, the dragon mages are awaiting you."

Aeris could feel Jaxom's hesitancy through their link. It was understandable, for he had never willfully allowed spells to be cast upon his person. She sent encouraging vibes to him in an attempt to alleviate his unease as they followed their comrades to the semi-circle of dragons. She knew the skill it would take for the mages to cast spells such as these, for the magic required some level of attention to detail. Hells, it would take Aeris decades to learn something of this caliber.

From the opposite side of the field, the other dragons and their riders also approached. In numbers, they matched their opponent six against six, three helzethryn and three rezwithrys against their five helzethryn and one rezwithrys. Only one of the opposing riders was a woman. Six of the dragon mages turned to position themselves behind their brethren. Before them, the opposition positioned themselves. Aeris couldn't help but wonder how they were being compensated for the inconvenience of posing as 'enemy' to Trebexal's students.

Aeris immediately focused her gaze on the dragon mage as he began to cast his complex spell. Within moments she felt it begin to wash over her, the magic causing her skin to prickle. She sent reassurances to Jaxom through their link and hoped he would find it within him to remain calm. Mentally, she continued to struggle with her lack of weapon, for she and Nampaul had worked so hard on the glove. Now, to be unable to use it was more than frustrating. It was cruel and unusual punishment.

Aeris relaxed once the spellcasting was complete. Much like Jaxom, she had little experience with magic being cast on her. It was quite disconcerting to say the least, but she had enough faith in her masters to believe they would never allow anyone or anything to harm her whilst she remained within their care, at least in this capacity, immune to any attacks that might kill her during mock battle.

Ah, Hells!

With naught but a slight inclination of their heads, the dragon mages turned away. Each vaulted into the air after his incantations were compete, and the only ones remaining on the field were Demeters Fo and Kord, the two opposing teams, and one other dragon. It was apparent the dragon spoke on behalf of the six 'enemy' dragons and their riders, and once conferring with the opposition, he also took to the air. The 'enemy' followed, most likely to position themselves for battle. It was then that Aeris heard the voice of Rilo within her mind as she spoke to all the dragons. <Prepare for assault.>

Aeris lay forward over Jaxom's back as he leaped into the air alongside their comrades. She felt her heartbeat increase as they winged higher, a wave of excitement sweeping through her. She began to prepare a mental list of the spells she had at her disposal, for since she had neither rod nor glove, she would be forced to rely on her ability to cast whilst in the midst of aerial melee. It was frustrating, but it would be the perfect test for her at this particular juncture in her training. Of course she didn't have to like it.

The six dragonriders spread out and took their places within the initial combat formation they had learned in practice exercises. Led by the spellcasters, the force proceeded towards the enemy stronghold. The strategy focused on the magic users' ability to begin long range assault. Then, once the initial spells were cast, the formation would shift. Quartermaster Falon at the lead, the fighters would make up the front of the wedge while the sorcerers dropped back to bring up the rear.

It wasn't long before the opposition was within sight. Aeris donned her helm and bid Jaxom communicate to Sidra and Borge the spell she wished to cast, not wanting their riders to cast something that would cause interference. However, it was most likely they had never heard of the spell, for it was a dimensionalist thing. She began to concentrate on the incantation as Jaxom increased his speed with the rest of the formation. She called it from out of one of the Hells, a storm born of wind and fire. The heat was distracting if not almost unbearable, and once within the cooler climate of Haldorr, the winds would condense to form a funnel reminiscent of a twister cloud. Only vaguely did she note that Saliel and Franchiera had resorted to *Magic Missile* spells as she directed the energy towards the approaching enemy. She was both gratified and relieved to see the *Firestorm* emerge from out of the empty airspace directly in the path of the oncoming opposition.

In spite of the hot winds spiraling in the near distance, Aeris, Saliel, and Franchiera continued their approach with the others following suit. They watched as the unwitting 'enemy' flew into the storm, unable to react with the sudden emergence of it before them. The other dragons were swept off course and before the opposition could think about opening communications to bring themselves back together, Aeris and the other spellcasters were commanded to drop back. Jaxom didn't hesitate to comply. With Thulnar and Faleema following behind on both sides, Falon took the forefront. Arrayed in their new positions, the entire force swept in for the close range attack.

Within moments the group found themselves flying into the remnants of the short-lived *Firestorm*. The area was hot, but nothing like it was when the winds were at their apex. For just a moment, Aeris was reminded of the *Maelstrom* she had somehow called when the group was beset by the daemon horde outside of the catacombs leading from Tholana's citadel. It seemed like a lifetime had passed since that day.

Aeris was suddenly brought back to her present as more *Magic Missiles* emerged from both sides of her, each striking their nearest targets. Franchiera and Saliel had once again taken the easy route, yet it was effective. The *Missiles* flew towards their opponents, and moments later the 'enemy' dragons screamed with the impact. As the fighters lowered their lances, Aeris began to concentrate on casting her next spell. Time was of the essence, for it wouldn't be long before the enemy would rally and begin to cast their own spells. Her *Firestorm* had succeeded, for it had given Falon, Thulnar, and Faleema the opportunity to strike first. Oftentimes in battle it made all the difference. The only drawback was that it was costly, as it stripped her of the energy she needed for the rest of the battle.

Aeris vaguely sensed a disturbance just before the *Flamespheres* erupted before her. Positioned in the middle behind Thulnar and Faleema, she saw both dragons knocked off course by the two searing balls of flame. Jaxom swerved abruptly, just narrowly missing them himself. Too distracted to complete her own incantation, Aeris shook her head in response to the brief, mild disorientation she always felt when interrupted in her spellcasting.

Jaxom veered around the foundering Miramanth as Aeris fought to compose herself. She had just witnessed the incapacitation of her two closest friends, and even though she knew they would not die in this fight, she couldn't help but worry about them. <Elirya, focus!> Jaxom shouted through their link. <We have to keep fighting!>

She struggled to calm herself enough to begin another incantation. Damn, this was too real, much too real for her to simply sit tight within her combat harness.

<Then don't just sit there!> said Jaxom. <Fight with all you have!>

Aeris breathed deeply and exhaled. Taking another deep breath, she found the calm she was searching for. She held onto it as she began to cast her next spell. On either side of her, Saliel and Franchie began to break out of formation as the two opposing forces interspersed together. However, Aeris kept her attention on the closest of the enemy spellcasters, her aim to incapacitate him the way he and his comrade had done Thulnar and Faleema.

Aeris cast her spell just as her fellow magic-users cast theirs. Their *Prismatic Spheres* struck two of the opposing fighters just as her *Lightning* spell smote her helzethryn target. She saw the golden dragon fall away, much as Thulnar and Faleema had just moments before. She happened to see Falon strike the closest of the blinded dragons with his lance just as Jaxom swept upward in order to achieve some altitude. She then watched another of the enemy come up to the quartermaster from behind, the enemy rezwithrys dragon reaching out to leave deep gouges on Jeriandrith's golden hindquarters. Aeris hissed to herself with the pain it must have caused. And when she turned away from the scene to suddenly find herself within close proximity to the other enemy spellcaster, she hissed again.

Hellfire!

Jaxom screamed his anger, and Aeris quickly drew her blade. Within the space of a single heartbeat, the other silver dragon was raking his talons across Jaxom's side. Aeris almost cried out with the pain, for she was so much more attuned to her bondmate than she ever had been before. She somehow kept her seat as Jaxom winged backward and she felt him begin to inhale.

<Jaxom, no! Descend below him . . . NOW!>

Jaxom obeyed the command just as the enemy's fiery breath rolled over the space he had just vacated. In her mind's eye, she had visualized the potential outcome of the fire-breathing duel, and it had ended only in disaster for all. *However, she didn't anticipate the course of events that would take place instead.*

Situated below their opponent, Jaxom and Aeris found themselves thrust into a vulnerable position. Aeris cursed herself for her mistake, and when she looked up and into the eyes of the rider of the opposing rezwithrys, she knew their time had come. The enemy swept towards them, claws extended. Aeris cowered close to Jaxom's back, forgetting about the spell that protected them. Should the wickedly sharp talons rake her, she could be maimed, mayhap even killed.

However, Jaxom was wily. She grappled to keep herself in place as he swiftly pulled his wings close to his body and flipped onto his back. Hanging upside down, she felt his wings unfurl in an effort to keep them from falling. She prayed that the battle harness would keep her astride long enough for Jaxom to finally right himself.

This time Aeris screamed when she felt the opposing dragon's talons sink into Jaxom's hide. The pain was excruciating, as though several daggers were being thrust into her all at once. In his rather vulnerable position, Jaxom was quick to retaliate. The other dragon wasn't fast enough to escape. Jaxom reached out to hook his talons into the sides of his opponent. The two dragons hovered for barely a moment before their wings became fouled.

As they fell, the dragons began to twine their bodies about one another.

Aeris struggled just to breathe. She knew she should do something, anything to disengage the two dragons. They grappled savagely at one another, their claws making deep gouges within one another's hides as they spiraled helplessly out of control. She wanted to find the focus she needed to concentrate on a spell she thought to cast, but it simply refused to come. Glancing at the other mage, she noticed she wasn't the only one. The opposing magic-user seemed similarly unable to cast her spells.

However, the revelation was assuaging for only a brief moment. There was a vast difference between Aeris and her 'enemy'.

Aeris was being trained to overcome her frailties, to find the focus she needed to cast her spells in spite of her fears. Aeris was being trained to become a part of the force that would be combating the darkness that currently imperiled Shandahar.

In this particular exercise, Aeris had obviously failed.

CHAPTER EIGHTEEN

Tianna hummed the song beneath her breath, one she remembered her mother singing when she was a young girl. It was a haunting melody, one that Soraya would sing most often when Tianna's father was away from the house on business. The sound of her mother's voice was so beautiful that it had brought tears to Tianna's eyes, and she had always wondered what made Soraya so sad.

Thunder rolls, and the embers grow
A fire to melt the heavens.
A mourning wail, the death toll hail
The arrival of its fallen warrior.

Walk slowly through the dusky vale
A place of dreams and shadows.
Lie down thy sword and remove thy boots
At the gates of Hiedor-thael.

Suddenly hearing a sound from the other side of the large chamber, Tianna stopped humming. She remained quiet for a moment, making certain that the place was empty save for herself and the *hellfire*. Ah! Razlul had finally left. The man hated to hear her humming, but she did it anyway just to spite him. Similarly, she ignored him when he spoke to her, and refused to respond when he laid his hands on her. The feel of them didn't bother her so much anymore—she had found a place deep in her mind to escape his hands when he beat her, and he had ceased raping her a few weeks ago when he could no longer make her cry.

Tianna went back about her business. She stepped on any stones on the floor that seemed strangely shaped or colored, went to the bookcase and caressed each spine with a light caress, sat before the desk and swept her fingertips across all the surfaces, walked around the periphery of the chamber with a hand to the wall and felt for any bumps or cracks. She hummed to herself all the while, wondering where her mother was. Where was her father? Were they wondering about their little girl, maybe looking for her? But finally Tianna stopped before the looking glass, and saw the fully grown woman staring back.

Only then did she remember that both her parents were dead, brutally murdered within the chamber beneath which Soraya had hidden her.

What she remembered most was the color red. Thick and wet, it had seeped between the floorboards to drip on her where she lay. She'd been terrified beyond belief, never leaving the place her mother bade her stay. Finally she must have made some sound, for the druids of Reshik-na had found her. By then she'd spent many days beneath the floorboards, her hair and clothes stiff with dried blood. She'd soiled herself many times over, but the smell that pervaded the most was of a different kind.

Tianna blinked to awareness and found she was sitting on the bed. Taking a deep breath, she looked around the dim chamber, certain that someone had called out to her. But it was the same as before, the *hellfire* casting eerie shadows on the walls.

But then she heard it again. Tianna narrowed her eyes, standing up and walking towards the shutaska. Before long she was standing at the edge of the firepit, looking at the purple flames contained within. The *hellfire* danced and wavered, the same as always. Razlul would often immerse himself in the fire. She'd learned to dread what came after. His thirst for cruelty was seemingly unquenchable, and it was during those times she'd suffered the most.

As such, she'd come to hate the *hellfire*.

But for some reason, she now felt drawn to it.

Tianna took a deep breath and moved closer, setting aside her dislike. Besides, the flames were pretty, all shades of purple, lavender and indigo. They twisted and curved about one another seductively, and reminded her of the times she'd spent in bed with her husband. *Oh gods, Triath. Where are you? Why haven't you come for me?*

Tianna slowly walked into the shutaska. The flames seemed to reach out to her, urging her towards their warm embrace. She remained wary enough to keep out of touch, but felt the intensity of the heat they emitted. Once again she heard someone calling out to her.

Tianna stopped. She stared into the flames, wondering why she was hearing a voice that sounded so familiar. The fire danced and wavered, showing her nothing until she looked closer. It was then she saw him, the flames coalescing to form the image of a young man. She could see that he was very tired, his head and shoulders slumped, somehow maintaining his balance astride the back of his faithful lloryk. She frowned, wondering who he was, and why his image could be seen within these flames.

Then she heard it again, the familiar voice. The image of the man stirred, and his face suddenly became visible.

Tianna felt her heart stutter in her chest as memories suddenly flooded her mind. It was her son! After years of thinking she couldn't bear children, her husband had given her a child! The pregnancy had been difficult, and she'd almost died giving birth to the boy. But somehow Triath had managed to save them from certain death.

Tianna began to tremble, and within moments it was uncontrollable. By the gods, her son was approaching Razlul's stronghold. Her mind struggled through the haze that shrouded it. Oh yes, his name was Tigerius! She had always loved that name and Triath had succumbed to her whimsy, just like he had done with so many other things in their life together. Gods, how she loved her husband! Certainly he'd made his mistakes, but he'd always made them up to her tenfold. She hated to think that something had befallen him.

Tianna breathed deeply. She had been greatly disturbed when Tigerius rebelled and left home all those moon cycles ago. She was glad that Triath had been there to offer the hope and support she needed to make it through his desertion. Triath had always said that Tiger would return to her, and that it would only be a matter of time.

Now, as Tianna stared forlornly into the flames, she knew that time had come. *And she wished Triath had been wrong.*

13 Finoren CY 634

Jonesy blinked open her eyes. Something had awakened her, a strange sound she had never heard before. Without the customary lethargy she felt when first waking in the morning, she rose from the bedpallet with alacrity. *What the Hells is that sound?* She grabbed her robe from off a nearby chest and pulled it over her shoulders before pushing aside the privacy flap and stepping into the dongo proper. With bare feet she padded across the empty space and paused at the heavier external flap. Pushing it aside, she stepped outside to find herself surrounded.

The creatures were twenty to thirty strong, each standing at least three times the height of the faelin archers interspersed among them. She looked out over the field in amazement, one that, heretofore, had been littered only with tent-like dongos. But those simple structures were now gone, only to be replaced by the vision before her. The animals were awesome to behold, their feather-like reptilian scales shining brightly with colors reminiscent of a newly risen sun. Their body color tended towards simple gold, but as the scales approached the legs and feet, they mimicked the more vibrant orange and red hues also seen on their feathered wings. Each finely chiseled head was similarly colored, and their pale yellow eyes shone with intelligence. Their hooked beaks opened and closed in quick succession to make a series of clacking sounds, simple testament to their level of agitation.

Jonesy turned when she suddenly found herself joined by Asgenar. "I suppose the secret is out now," he said with a grin.

"They are so magnificent! She exclaimed. I have never seen anything like them!"

Asgenar shook his head. "And you never will again. The chyvian are beings that remain elusive to everyone but the most determined, hailing from the northernmost reaches of the Sartingel Mountains. One of my strongest commanders was finally able to harness a hatchling. It didn't take long for Caedrus to realize that his captive was intelligent, more so than any lloryk or larian, and over time, he discovered how to communicate with his new friend. In the process, he realized that the beast liked to make him happy by doing things for him, things that a corubis might do for his or her companion. So Caedrus began teaching the chyvian, training it to accept him as a rider, and finally to carry him into aerial melee."

Jonesy was enthralled by the story, but even more so by the creatures standing so near. She so much wanted to reach out and touch one, wondered what the strangely scaled hide would feel like. The one standing closest eyed them askance, obviously wondering what they were about.

Somehow divining her thoughts, Asgenar took her hand. "Come over here. Mayhap you would like to touch one. I promise you they have been gentled by the calm hands of the rangers who ride them."

Jonesy felt a sensation of warmth course through her when his hand closed around hers, but she didn't have the time to contemplate it as he led her over to the nearest chyvian, the very one that had been watching them. She hesitated as they approached, nervously pulling back her hand. Damn, the beast was bigger than she thought it would be.

But it was too late. She had already wandered close enough so that the chyvian could reach her.

Jonesy squelched the urge to scream as the creature swiftly lowered its head to investigate her. Even Asgenar tensed a little, but he somehow maintained an aura of cool composure. A beautiful golden eye suddenly hovered in front of her, staring intently. Jonesy allowed herself to take one breath, and then another, as the eye continued to regard her. As the moments passed, the eye slowly moved closer, and finally she began to have the feeling that the creature was waiting for something.

Jonesy took a deep breath and hesitantly raised a hand from where it clutched at the length of her robe. She slowly brought it to rest along a place below the watching eye and gave a timid smile as she felt the smooth texture of the crimson scales. She then noticed something begin to rise from the top of the chyvian's head. The beautiful crest lifted high, elongated scales curling at the tips to make them look like feathers. She heard a low-pitched trill emanate from the creature's throat, and the eye moved ever closer, staring as though in hopes of divining what lay deep within her.

"Hells, I wouldn't have believed it if I hadn't seen it myself. She likes you."

The spell broken, Jonesy turned towards the man who approached. His skin tone was paler than many of the other hinterleans, mayhap as a result of the myriad of tiny scars that pitted his face. His dark brown hair curled down to his shoulders, and his build was lean and muscular. By the presence of the bronze bracers that circled his upper arms, she determined him to be someone of authority.

The man stopped before them and turned to Asgenar. "She's a bit difficult, this one, quite an enigma." The man shook his head. "She refuses to imprint. Poor beast doesn't even have a name."

"What is wrong with her?" asked Asgenar.

The man shrugged. "I'm not sure, but I know that she certainly seems to like the lady here."

Asgenar put a hand on Jonesy's shoulder, and once again she felt the sensation of warmth. "Lord Caedrus, this is the Princess Joneselia of Karlisle."

The pocked face shifted into an expression of pleasure. "Ah, it is so good to finally meet you, my lady." Jonesy allowed Caedrus to take her hand, and he bowed over it in a gesture of respect. She was taken aback, for he was the first of any of Asgenar's men to give her such honor, and it prompted her to consider him more fully. Whatever caused the facial scarring was such an injustice, giving him a harsh appearance that was disparate from his true nature. For him to be the first man to harness a creature such as this was very special. He must have a plethora of gentleness and patience, attributes that any woman would want in a husband and the father of her children. However, she imagined him to be without a family, for the way Asgenar described it, Lord Caedrus had spent much time away from home in order to build the force currently surrounding her.

"And you my lord," Jonesy finally replied.

Caedrus released her hand and turned back to the chyvian standing beside them. The beast had resumed her previous position, her golden gaze perusing the encampment. Jonesy had the distinct feeling that she attempted to ignore them. Caedrus continued to watch the chyvian speculatively for a moment. "If I didn't know any better, I would say this animal is finally showing a preference," he said.

Asgenar raised a pale eyebrow and regarded the man questioningly. "What are you talking about?"

Caedrus turned back to face them, his countenance indecipherable. "It is when a chyvian first breaks out of the shell that it is the most impressionable. It immediately looks for the thing that will care for it and nurture it through the vulnerable days to come. Traditionally this would only be the mother. However, if a man wishes to have the devotion of such a creature in the future, he must also be there. The animal will often show a preference for some of the men it will consider in its endeavor to form a bond. Most often, it the man who is usually in the hatchling's company with whom it will imprint. It is just as well, for a man who chooses to spend so much time with a single hatchling must certainly have that creature's best interests at heart.

"As it turns out, not all chyvian are made the same, much as any faelin, human, or halfen. Inasmuch, I have discovered that some are choosier than their siblings and will have a preference for only one of the rangers present at the hatching. There are even those who have had no preference at all. But even the most fastidious of beasts have eventually been able to bond with someone." Caedrus was quiet for a moment as he once more looked up at the animal standing alongside them. "Except for this one; she has gone well beyond the age for imprinting, but is gentle enough to still carry a rider. One of my most skilled rangers has been assigned to her, a woman who has yet to acquire the preference of her own chyvian."

Asgenar chuckled. "My friend, what are you trying to say?" he replied.

Caedrus shrugged. "The chyvian often have no care about a person's gender or race. Sometimes they simply gravitate towards whomever strikes their fancy. Although, I must say that most of my riders are women. Having a tendency to be smaller than men, they weigh less, and are much easier for the chyvian to carry. A chyvian with a lighter rider will have more endurance during battle."

Asgenar smiled and nodded. "I think I understand. You think that you have discovered the one whom this animal fancies."

Caedrus' expression remained the epitome of seriousness. "Maybe."

Asgenar resumed his air of solemnity, nodding and offering a brief bow while Caedrus did the same. "Give me a few moments with the lady and I will join you," he said.

The other man gave a brief nod, then took hold of the soft rope around the chyvian's neck and began to lead her away. The animal seemed somewhat hesitant and kept looking back at Jonesy until she was out of sight. Jonesy didn't understand the full implication of what the men had been speaking about, but she knew enough to feel sadness for the creature that seemed so drawn to her. There was a part of Jonesy that wanted to call Caedrus back and ask him to allow the chyvian to remain. But she knew the idea was a silly one, for every one of the animals would be needed for upcoming battle.

Jonesy gave a tremulous breath, the realization suddenly washing over her. Battle was imminent, for the chyvian would not be there otherwise.

Jonesy became still. Oh gods, she needed to reach Karlisle's army, to tell those in command to cease their endeavors against Elvandahar. Asgenar silently took her by the elbow and urged her back to the dongo. The air between them had become thick, telling her that the Prince of Elvandahar was remembering all that lay between them. Of course, it made her remember the same thing, and a wave of apprehension swept through her.

Asgenar pulled aside the tent flap. "It seems you have made quite an impression on my senior advisor."

Jonesy didn't really know what to think of those words, too caught up in the reality of what would be happening. Her mind sped through the plethora of statements she could make, none of them what she really wanted to articulate. "It seems that everyone will soon be leaving," she finally said.

Asgenar kept his expression impassive as he nodded. "By mid-day we will be well on our way."

She frowned. Before now she hadn't even known that the fu-ulcrym was preparing for battle, much less with their future king at the forefront. "My lord, you are planning to accompany your forces?"

Asgenar turned to regard her intently where they stood in the middle of the dongo. "Of course, I would have it no other way."

Jonesy shook her head and brought her eyes up to meet his. "But you can't just leave me here. I . . .."

Asgenar placed a forefinger before her lips. "Shhh. Don't worry; I have someone who will see to your well-being whilst I am gone. Heath will be sure that you aren't neglected and that you are in good health by the time I return."

"But you could be gone for days, or even weeks," she retorted.

Asgenar nodded. "It is indeed possible. Yet, you have nothing about which you should worry."

Once more she was shaking her head. "But you don't understand—I can't stay here for so long. I need to return to Karlisle."

Asgenar regarded her incredulously. "You must surely be joshing me. My lady, you will be going nowhere anytime soon. First of all, you have been sick and need ample time to recover. Secondly, you are my prisoner, and I shall be making any decisions concerning you. Thirdly, I wouldn't allow you to return to Karlisle anyway, even if you were the paradigm of fitness."

Jonesy frowned petulantly. "Why the Hells not?"

His gaze became intense and his tone deepened. "You and I have unfinished business to which we must attend upon my return."

Jonesy exhaled sharply, immediately knowing what he was speaking about. He wanted answers to the questions he had asked her that first night she spent in his detainment. Thoughts of the other times they had spent together since then suddenly swept through her mind. She couldn't help but wonder if it was only his interest in the information she might divulge to him that had continued to bring him to her.

Jonesy tore her gaze away from him and felt her throat begin to ache with suppressed emotion. She couldn't help but feel hurt, and she hated that he held so much power over her. Obviously he didn't have the decency to simply let her be on her way, especially now that he knew she meant no one any harm. Well, at least she thought he knew.

Jonesy shook her head. "Please, you can't do this to me. I need to return to Karlisle. My people depend on it." She uttered the very same words he had spoken to her that first evening in his dongo. Her voice was pleading and she was certain her expression was just as pathetic.

Asgenar's expression was perplexed as he put his hands at his hips. For once she could see what he was thinking. *Why is she so adamant about returning now when she had been more than willing to wipe her hands clean of Karlisle not so very long ago?* Then he did something unexpected. He swept an arm around her back, pulling her close so that her body was pressed against his. He pressed his face along hers and spoke in a monotone voice. "You will be going nowhere, my lady. You had best accept that now." He then pulled away, but his lips were still close enough that she could smell the chag he'd imbibed earlier that morning. "I simply can't have you on my conscience whilst I am gone."

He then released her. Without looking back, Asgenar left her standing there in the middle of the dongo. With tears in her eyes she watched him go. She was angry that he had disregarded her so easily, and even more so that he had made not only a mental impression on her, but a physical one as well. Even now she could feel his arm around her.

Sitting at the dongo entry, Jonesy unhappily spent the remainder of the morning watching the preparations. The chyvian were carefully loaded with the most basic of supplies so as to not overtax them during combat flight. They were offered plenty of water, and some of them were given a burbana or two, mayhap those who hadn't eaten prior to their arrival. By mid-day, they were finally led by their riders towards the southern periphery of the encampment. Eventually Jonesy realized she was alone, for everyone had gone to see the fuulcrym off to battle. A part of her really wanted to go, but she was sulky and stubborn. For a brief moment she considered making an escape, but she was no fool. She was still recovering from her ill treatment at the hands of Asgenar's rangers before making it there, and without a lloryk her chances of success were small.

For what seemed like the hundredth time since she had parted company with the rest of the group, Jonesy wept. She couldn't seem to help herself, and she wondered how much of it had to do with her circumstances versus her gravid condition. Regardless, she disliked feeling so weak. Her vulnerability made her an easy target, and she could ill afford any additional hardship.

It didn't take her long to find control. She stood and entered the dongo, taking herself to the very back where her bed-pallet resided. She lay down and closed her eyes, her mind ruminating over the situation. Right now Jonesy was being detained against her will. However, she took solace in the knowledge that Asgenar wouldn't be able to keep her there forever, and that one day she would be freed. Deep within, she somehow knew that it would be the Prince of Elvandahar himself who would be the one to let her go. She had only to remain patient.

Unfortunately, patience was not one of her strengths.

EPILOGUE

Chorlak feasted his eyes on the scene surrounding him. He took a deep breath, inhaling the tantalizing scent of fresh blood. The small caravan didn't have a chance against his minions. Agonized screams rent the air as the gremlins and devils satiated their sexual cravings while slowly feeding on the soft flesh of their victims. Chorlak stopped to watch the baalor beside him. Blood from a previous victim dripped from his maw onto the milky white breasts of the woman beneath his massive form. Her screams had weakened into a mewling sound she made with each hard thrust, the activity slowly tearing her apart.

He could scarcely wait to take advantage of his own meal. But he would wait until everyone else had their fill first.

Chorlak finally turned away, closed his eyes and took another breath. Ah! He sensed his objective more with each passing day and could hardly believe his good fortune. He was glad he had taken Tarian's advice and attempted to find a connection with the half breed, Tigerius. He knew that he'd succeeded only because of the boy's inexperience and lack of awareness in regards to his burgeoning abilities. It had taken some time and an even greater output of energy, but Chorlak had secured a tenuous connection. Through it, he was able to determine the approximate location of the group of people with whom the boy had chosen to share his company.

And over the past couple of moon cycles, Chorlak had come to realize that all good things come to those who wait.

Having made his connection with the half breed, Chorlak and his retinue were doing just that. He knew he was taking a chance by just waiting, but he really had no other alternative. Even if he wanted it, neither could he take the portal system back from where he'd come from, nor could he go to the druid stronghold where his target resided. Somehow, the mirror that should have been enveloped by the strong metallic brackets was broken. Without it, the system was unusable except by a magic-user that specialized in such things. Of course, Chorlak hadn't any spellcasters in his company, much less one who specialized in teleportation.

The daemons made themselves at home in the Selmist Forest and the neighboring Bryton Hills, making certain to keep their distance from scouts from both the Karlislian army and the Elvandaharian fu-ulcrym. Their main food sources were leschera and the occasional alothere, but when those began to vacate the surrounding area, the more predatory wemic and kyerrean became a mainstay. Meanwhile, Chorlak assiduously maintained the connection he'd managed to establish with the half breed. After a while, he realized that Tigerius and the girl had bifurcated from the rest of their group. While he wondered what caused the separation, he was pleased it had taken place. It meant that, once catching up with Joneselia, he would have only one man to contend with as opposed to him and several others who had proven their worth in battle many times already.

Besides, it was only these two in whom he had any interest.

At first it seemed that Tigerius and Jonesy were moving *away* from Chorlak and his followers. He was tempted to make a radical decision that may have been the end, but he stayed himself. Barely a couple of fortnights had passed when one day he realized that the two comrades had parted ways; the half breed had altered his course entirely and was moving towards the Sheraxi Forest. At first Chorlak was quite disturbed. Hells, how would he keep track of the girl if her daemon-spawned companion no longer traveled by her side? However, as the days went by, he realized he could still sense her. From the time when she escaped from Seth and the other vampyr, she had begun to grow into her own attributes, whatever they might be. Those energy signals had somehow served to keep him abreast of her location.

Then suddenly one day she was close, traveling north of them from the portal. Joneselia's energy pattern was strong; just like his daemon brethren, Chorlak was very attuned to it. Much to his benefit, he was much stronger of will. Chorlak had no doubt as to his ability to keep himself from her in spite of the temptation she exuded.

Chorlak had spurred everyone into motion. They had wandered a bit further south than he'd intended, following their primary food sources as they sought to escape the danger of a daemon cohort. However, as they swiftly moved towards his target, Chorlak had sensed the distance between them closing with each passing moment.

All of a sudden, Joneselia's location became stationary.

It didn't take Chorlak long to figure out what might have happened; the Karlislian princess had been taken by Elvandaharian forces. To be certain, he sent two of his most trustworthy minions ahead of them towards the Denegal River. He knew the endeavor was fraught with risk, for the river was a place that had yet to be claimed entirely by one side or the other. However, he felt the knowledge was worth it. He hadn't long to wait, for his minions were fleet.

The news was not unexpected, yet derailing. He had been hoping for an unobstructed chance to cross the girl and take her without anyone's knowledge.

Instead, he was now forced to strategize and use whatever means possible to get her away from the protection offered by the Prince of Elvandahar. He knew that Asgenar's mentality was a bit skewed; they were in the midst of war after all, and Prince Asgenar's captive was quite the gem. But Chorlak happened to know that Asgenar was a good man; he would never hurt the princess if he could avoid it. Quite honestly, the girl was much safer with her enemy than she was with her own brother.

Chorlak refocused his attention to the present. The area was silent, his minions having moved to the place they had designated for rest. Meanwhile, the dead lay littered about on the ground in varying stages of disembowelment. His belly rumbled and he was uncomfortably aware of his hunger. Unwilling to wait to see if anything had been left for him, Chorlak picked up the closest body and tore away a leg. He was pleased to note that it was still warm as he brought the thigh to his mouth and bit deeply into the flesh. His long black tongue licked at the blood that dribbled down his chin, but some escaped to trickle down his neck to his hairy chest. Meanwhile, Chorlak thought about his next course of action.

Then it came to him. It was the perfect plan; he wondered why he hadn't thought of it sooner.

Prince Rigel of Karlisle would be pleased to know that the object of his greatest desire was so near.

Glossary of Terms

Alcrostat (al-kro-stat) The largest city within the realm of Elvandahar. Residence of the Sherkari Fortress, home to the King.

Aldehirra (al-de-here-uh) A small savanlean realm nestled deep in the western Sartingel Mountains.

Alothere (al-o-thayr) Large porcines that are cousins to the wild boar. They live in the forests and steppes of the temperate regions of Shandahar.

Andahye (an-duh-high) Mystical city located at the northern edge of the Sheldomar Forest. It is the place where many mages receive their arcane training.

Ansalar (an-sal-ar) One of the three main continents of Shandahar. It is the most inhabited.

Astralon (as-tra-lon) One of the worlds comprised of Tharmagellan's Gate.

Azmatharcana (az-math-ar-kana) A mystical tome that delivers many necromantic secrets, including those contained within the Azmathion.

Azmathion (az-math-ee-on) The arcane artifact that gives Aasarak much of his power. It is a geometrical work of art, and one must work the puzzles contained within it in order to divine its secrets.

Azmathous (az-math-us) The most powerful of Aasarak's undead creations. With the power of the Azmathion, they are reborn and are able to retain the skills and abilities they possessed in life.

Baalor (bay-loor) The largest of the greater daemons, their skin is colored deep red, and large black horns arise from the sides of their skulls. They are the most powerful in the Nine Hells.

Behiraz (be-heer-az) A worm of gargantuan proportions. It lives beneath the ground finding its prey by the vibrations they make upon the surface. Swift and deadly, very few survive an encounter.

Braxen (brak-sen) The strongest metal on Shandahar. Only halfen miners have access to the secret places where it can be found.

Buffelshmut (buffel-shmut) A slang term for buttocks.

Burbana (bur-ban-uh) A small ermine-like animal with exquisitely soft fur.

Calotebas (kal-o-tee-bas) A large foul-tempered herbivore that lives near swamps. The taste of their flesh is equally as repugnant as their personality.

Cansandia (kan-san-dee-uh) One of the worlds comprising Tharmagellan's gate.

Cenloryan (sen-lor-yan) A creature made of the twisted magic of the Kronshue, it has the lower body of a lloryk and the upper torso, arms, and head of a human.

Chag (chag) A drink made from the large seeds of the chagatha plant, which grows in the more southern regions of Ansalar.

Chamdaroc (sham-dar-ok) A shrub that grows within Elvandahar and other forested regions of northwestern Ansalar. It has small white flowers that are said to have intoxicating qualities.

Cimmerean (sim-ur-ee-an) One of the faelin sub-races, also known as 'dark' faelin. They live in vast labyrinths below the surface of the world.

Common (com-mun) The universal language across most of the main continent of Ansalar.

Cortubro (cor-too-bro) A realm situated north of Elvandahar.

Corubis (kor-oo-bis) Large canines that have tawny fur with dark dappling. They live in packs headed by an alpha male, but many of them find companionship with faelin, especially hinterlean rangers.

Croxis (krok-sis) A plant that has hallucinogenic properties, often making the person feel a false sense of well-being. The extract is called croxian.

Curse of Odion (o-die-on) The arcane influence that causes time on Shandahar to repeat itself after certain events have taken place. Only the most knowledgeable of sages are aware of the phenomenon.

Cycle (sye-kel) The word used to describe the period of time that elapses before it starts over again. Shandahar goes through five *cycles* before the Curse of Odion is broken.

Daemundai (day-mun-die) An organization of those who strive to give daemon-kind influence and power in Shandahar.

Daladin (dal-a-din) A hinterlean house in the trees.

Darban (dar-ban) A major port city located at the western tip of the Tanze Peninsula.

Degethozak (deg-eth-o-zak) The smallest and most numerous of the dragon sub-races. At maturity their color ranges from black to varying shades of green with darker backs and feet. Their alignment tends towards evil and chaos.

Denedrian (den-ed-ree-an) One of the human sub-races. They are largely nomadic, originating from the western plains and deserts.

Dimensionalist (dim-en-shen-al-ist) A sorcerer who specializes in otherworldly knowledge and travel.

Doppleganger (dop-pel-gang-er) A bipedal being once thought to be made of magic, it is a daemon that has the ability to shift its shape into any humanoid between four and eight feet tall. It is a master of trickery and disguise that works for the most powerful of sorcerers.

Eldranza (el-dran-za) The savanlean term for someone with the gift of foresight.

Elvandahar (el-van-da-har) Large forested region in the vee of the Terrestra and Denegal Rivers. It is ruled by hinterlean faelin, and gives residence to the largest population of these people.

Ezekul (ez-e-kul) A star-shaped projectile weapon developed by the Kronshue.

Farlo (far-low) The equivalent of several feet.

Filopar (fil-o-par) One of the five domains of Elvandahar.

Fistantillus bush (fist-an-til-lus) A plant bearing poisonous thorns that can make a person violently ill for several days.

Garbatezu (gar-bat-eh-zoo) A greater daemon that appears to be a large oroc with the hind legs of a lloryk. They tend to be the most treacherous and intelligent, rallying other daemons to their nefarious causes.

Golem (goh-lem) A magically created automaton—usually used as a guardian or sentinel for something of great value.

Grang (grang) Slightly shorter than halfen, these small, bony humanoids live primarily on the steppes. They are primitive and voracious, but not very smart, their greed often getting in the way of thieving strategies.

Gremlin (grem-lin) An intermediate daemon that has the ability to scale walls and manipulate metals with supernatural ease. They are often the staunch followers of the baalor and garbatezu.

Griffon (grif-fon) Large animals that have both feline and avian features. They are friendly and intelligent, and can often be found in the company of druids.

Haldorr (hal-door) One of the worlds comprising the Seven Heavens, it has the highest population of dragon-kind.

Hamzin/Hamza (ham-zin/ham-zuh) The title given by the King to the one who rules within one of the five domains in Elvandahar.

Helzethryn (hel-zeth-rin) One of the dragon sub-races. At maturity their color ranges from pale gold, to deep bronze, to fiery red. They have the highest propensity towards *bonding* with other species.

Hestim (hes-tim) One of the three moons of Shandahar.

Himrony (him-ron-ee) A type of grass that grows abundantly throughout the central Ansalar – the preferred vegetation of larian.

Hinterlean (hin-ter-lee-an) One of the faelin subraces. They live in treetop villages within temperate forests.

Hralen (her-ay-len) The name used for the household staff within the Sherkari Fortress.

Humanoid (hue-man-oyd) Any creature that walks upright on two legs (bipedal).

Hybanthis (hie-ban-this) A vine that has poisonous blue thorns. The poison has brain-based affects that heighten a person's emotional state, making emotions difficult to handle.

Imp (imp) The least of the lesser daemons, these small creatures are the pests of the Nine Hells. They make themselves present whenever there is any type of activity.

Isterian (iz-ter-ee-un) The name used for the guards that keep patrol throughout the Sherkari Fortress.

Karlisle (kar-lyle) The human realm neighboring Elvandahar on the other side of the Denegal River.

Kleyshes (klie-shays) One of the five domains of Elvandahar.

Krathil-lon (kruh-thil-lon) A forested glen located within the southern reaches of the Sartingel Mountains.

Kronshue, Brotherhood of the (kron-shoo) A 'technological' society that dominates eastern Ansalar.

Kyrrean (kie-reen) Large blond felines with dark brown dappling and oversized paws. They make their existence on the warm temperate plains and borderlands.

Larian (layr-ee-an) With only minor differences, these are smaller cousins to the lloryk. They are able to carry faelin and most humans.

Leschera (le-sher-uh) Very gentle, larian-sized, deer-like creatures that grace the temperate woodlands.

Lloryk (loor-ik) Large muscular equine-like creatures that are able to carry humans and small orocs. They are omnivorous and beneath the top coat of silky fur, have modified hair shafts that appear similar to scales one would see on a reptile.

Lycanthrope (lie-kan-thrope) One afflicted with the disease of lycanthropy. They are humans, faelin, or halfen that can transform into animals (beginning with the prefix *shir*-wemic, alothere, or kyrrean). The disease is spread through the bite.

Lytham powder (lye-tham) A component used in a spell that creates a noxious vapor.

Mane (main) A lesser daemon that stands about two and a half feet tall and has vulture-like features. Tend to go wherever there is an opportunity to cause trouble.

Mehta (may-tuh) The title given to the leader of the daemundai.

Meriliam (mer-il-lee-am) One of the three moons of Shandahar.

Merzillith (mir-zil-lith) Otherwise known as a mind flayer, this intermediate daemon is from one of the Nine Hells. It has psionic power, the ability to use the energy of the world in a way that is different from the *talent* possessed by mages.

Migallon Mechanism (mi-gal-on) A large ship-board device created by the mage bearing the same name, it is used as a weapon against seascrags.

Mirpur (mir-poor) One of the five domains of Elvandahar.

Mistygia (mist-i-gee-uh) One of the worlds comprising Tharmagellan's Gate.

Monaf (mon-af) The human realm neighboring Torimir on the other side of the Ratik Mountains.

Mordelayan Rift (mor-del-ay-an) A stationary portal that exists between Shandahar and one of the worlds comprising the Nine Hells.

Morden (mor-den) One of the halfen sub-races. They live in deep caverns within the mountains.

Murg (murg) An alcoholic beverage distilled from fermented cane sugar.

Necromancer (nek-ro-man-ser) A sorcerer who focuses on the darker aspects of spellcasting.

Nivorlan (ni-voor-lan) A hinterlean medicine man/woman.

Oorg (oorg) One of the humanoid races of Shandahar, they are even larger than orocs and are often called giants. They often fight with brute strength alone, but aren't good with any type of real strategy.

Oroc (or-ok) One of the native races of Shandahar, they are muscular and broad, standing at least six to seven feet tall. Faelin are their greatest enemies, and the two races find any excuse to maim and kill one another.

Pact of Bakharas (bak-hair-us) An agreement between daemon and dragon kind that does not allow one or the other too much influence over Shandahar.

Papas fruit (pay-pas) A small pink orb about the size of a nectarine. It grows on the papas tree, which is prevalent throughout the temperate borderlands of Ansalar.

Pedora (pe-dor-ah) A hinterlean signal tower with a firepit at the top that is lit in the event of trouble.

Peruven (per-oo-ven) Hinterlean ceremonial priests.

Pfelzipat (felt-zee-pat) The thick bluish colored grass that grows abundantly throughout central Ansalar. It is the preferred vegetation of lloryk.

Portal (por-tal) An arcane bridge that connects two places. It appears as a circle of swirling color.

Ptarmigan (tar-mig-an) A squat, grouse-like bird that is often hunted for its flavorful meat.

Rasartha (ras-ar-thuh) The mental connection a daemon mother has with her unborn offspring.

Rathis (rath-is) The leaves of this plant are known for their pain-relieving capabilities.

Recondian (re-con-dee-an) One of the human sub-races. They mostly live in the central regions of Ansalar.

Reshik-na (resh-ik-na) An order of druids that lives within the Elvandaharian domain of Filopar.

Rezwithrys (rez-with-ris) The largest of the dragon sub-races. At maturity their color ranges from silver to steel blue to metallic violet. They have a propensity for magic.

Roxalayas Rift (rox-uh-lie-us) A stationary portal that exists between Shandahar and Haldorr.

Samshin/Samshae (sam-shin/sam-shay) The son/daughter of the hamzin or hamza.

Sangrilak (sang-ri-lak) A very diverse city located in the northwestern quadrant of the realm of Torimir.

Savanlean (sav-an-lee-an) One of the faelin sub-races. They live in majestic cities built into mountainsides located in the more northern regions of the Ansalar.

Seascrag (see-scrag) A four-armed, marine bipeds that stand about two feet tall—they inhabit the southern seas and are notorious for attacking and overwhelming ships with their large numbers

Serenitee (sir-en-i-tee) One of the worlds comprising the Seven Heavens.

Shagendra (shuh-gen-dra) The root from this plant can be used to make a person's mind vulnerable to suggestions. It also causes general lethargy, dulls the senses, and slows reflexes.

Shayamalan (shy-ah-mal-an) One of the three main continents of Shandahar.

Shockwave (shok-wave) A game that is popular throughout Ansalar. It involves cards, bones, and no small amount of strategy and luck.

Shutaska (shu-tas-kuh) A highly volatile flame that comes from the Nine Hells. It must be nurtured in order to survive on Shandahar, and it is a requirement for many daemonic ceremonies.

Steralion (stir-a-lee-an) One of the three moons of Shandahar.

Suresh (sue-resh) The subconscious pull a dragon feels for the one who is meant to be his/her bondmate.

Tabanakh drink (ta-ban-ak) A drink prepared by the druid elders as a right of initiation for their tyros. It has properties that exaggerate the visions of those who are so *gifted.*

Talent (tal-ent) (adj) The ability that some people possess to harness the energy of the world and use it. (n) Someone who uses magic.

Talsam (tal-sam) The root from this plant is ground into a powder from which a pain-relieving tea is made.

Tambour (tam-boor) A major port city located in southeastern Karlisle.

Tankard (tank-erd) A vessel for holding liquid. It is the equivalent of approximately two mugs and is usually used in taverns.

Terralean (ter-a-lee-an) One of the faelin sub-races. They inhabit many of the borderlands between the forests and steppes and are the most widespread.

Thalden (thal-den) One of the halfen sub-races. They live within the temperate hills.

Tharmagellan's (thar-ma-jel-an) **Gate** The universe that encompasses Shandahar, Astralon, Cansandia, and Mistygia.

Thritean (thrye-teen) Very large silver felines with black striping and six legs. They live in cold northern forests.

Tobey (toe-bee) A small, goat-like creature. Many nomadic peoples breed them for the creamy textured milk they produce.

Torimir (tor-eh-meer) The realm neighboring Elvandahar on the other side of the Terrestra River.

Tremidian (tre-mid-ee-an) One of the human sub-races. They live on the eastern side of the continent.

Trolag (trol-ag) One of the humanoid races of Shandahar. They are tall and stooped, their long, gangly bodies covered with dark brown wiry hair. They have the ability to heal quickly.

Umberhulk (um-ber-hulk) Large, stout burden beasts with thick, umber colored skin virtually devoid of hair. They are used to pull carts in cities, towns, and many times even in the caravan trains.

Varanghelie Vault (vair-an-gay-lee) A highly protected storage facility located within Andahye. It is where many people keep their most valuable possessions.

Wemic (wee-mik) In some places better known as wolves, these animals appear to be distant cousins to the corubis. They run in temperate to sub-arctic forests and have never been tamed.

Wraith (rayth) A corpse that has been re-animated. They are mindless, following the commands of their necromantic masters. Their bodies are ravaged by the effects of decay and they wield only the simplest of weapons.

Wyvern (why-vern) A large snake-like creature with four stubby legs and a poisonous barbed tip on its long sinuous tail. It lives in shallow caverns in temperate climes.

Xordrel (zor-drel) A major port city located in southeast Torimir.

Zacrol (zak-rol) The equivalent of about a mile.

Zivet (ziv-et) The bolt from a specialized crossbow developed by the Kronshue.

Tracy R. Chowdhury was born in the small town of Tunkhannock Pennsylvania in 1975 and moved to Cincinnati Ohio when she was twelve years old. Growing up, she was an avid reader, especially of fantasy and science fiction, and she loved to write. She attended college at Miami University in Oxford, Ohio and studied her other passion, Biology. She graduated in 2002 and worked in cancer research for several years. During that time she picked up her love for writing again, and in 2005, her first book, Shadow Over Shandahar- Child of Prophecy, was put into print. With the help of her co-author, Ted Crim, the sequel was published two years later.

Tracy currently lives in Montgomery, Ohio. She is married with four children, a huge dog, two hairless cats, and three ferrets. She runs a thriving real estate business with her husband, and in her 'spare' time she continues to write and promote her books. In 2011 the novels were picked up by a small press and her original duology was re-mastered and separated into smaller volumes to make a series. More books have followed, as well as several short stories. More information about the books can be found on her website at www.worldofshandahar.com, and she can be found on Facebook and Twitter.

TED M. CRIM was born and raised in Cincinnati Ohio. As a youth, he was always interested in fantasy role-play, and enjoyed playing Dungeons & Dragons with his friends. When he was a junior in high school he went into a vocational program called Animal Conservation and Care located at the Cincinnati Zoo & Botanical Garden. He received his certificate in 1989 and worked in animal care for several years.

In his early twenties, Ted met his good friend, Tracy Chowdhury, and they shared an interest in Dungeons & Dragons. She was a writer, and it was upon the first campaign they played together that her first book, Shadow Over Shandahar- Child of Prophecy, was based. Together, they brought the world and the characters to life into a novelized format. He attends many of the conventions and festivals at which the books are sold, and goes by the moniker, Pirate Ted!

Ted currently still lives in Cincinnati with his sister, brother-in-law, and nieces and nephew. More information about the books can be found on his website at www.worldofshandahar.com, and he can also be found on Facebook.

www.ingramcontent.com/pod-product-compliance
Lightning Source LLC
Chambersburg PA
CBHW020414260626
47156CB00007B/2374